BACKTRACK 1

AN ONI PRESS PUBLICATION

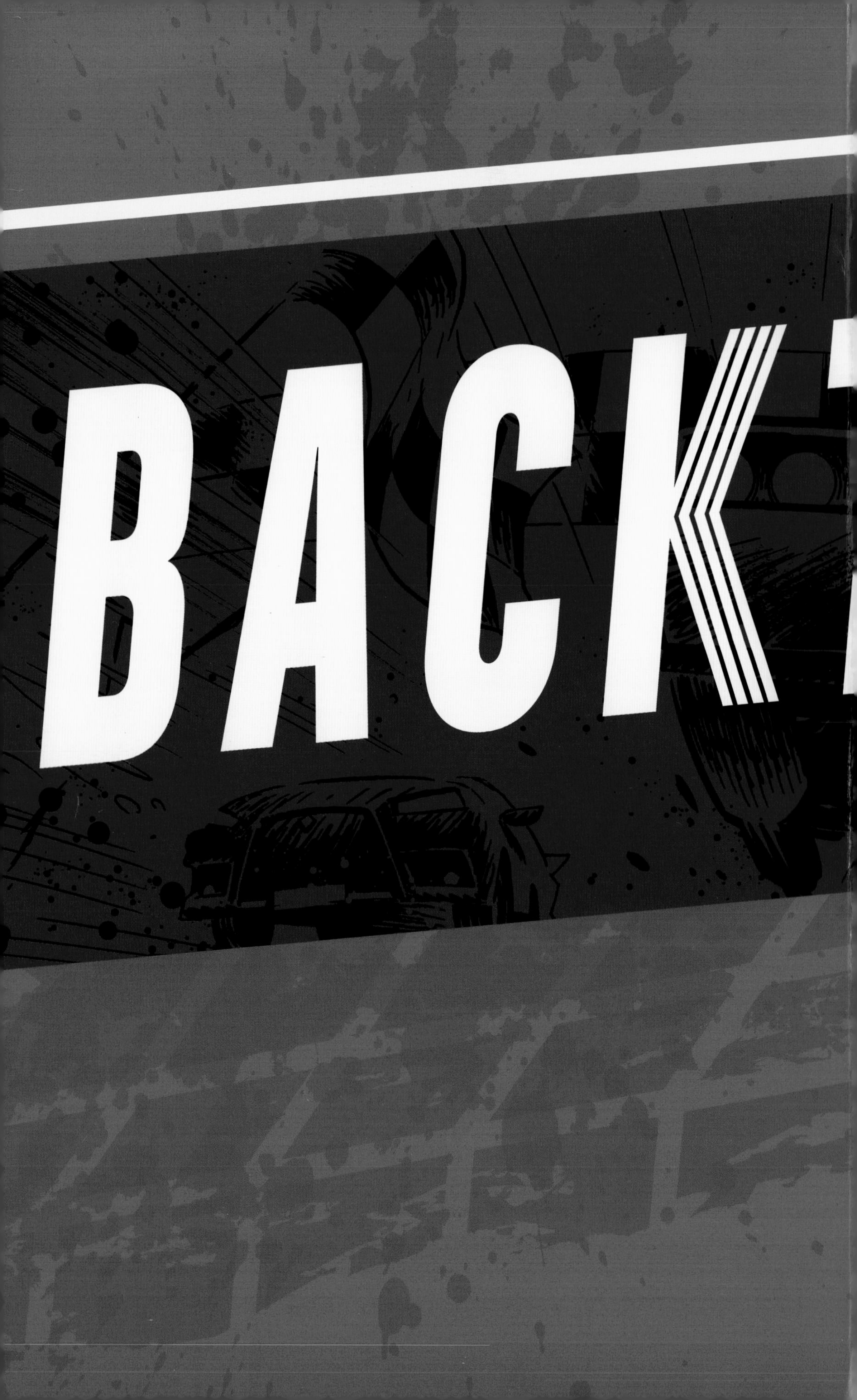
BACK

TRACK

1

WRITTEN AND CREATED BY:
BRIAN JOINES

ILLUSTRATED BY:
JAKE ELPHICK

COLORED BY:
DOUG GARBARK

LETTERED BY:
JIM CAMPBELL

COVERS BY:
MARCO D'ALFONSO

DESIGNED BY: **MIKE REDDY**

COLLECTION DESIGN BY: **SONJA SYNAK**

EDITED BY: **JASMINE AMIRI**

PUBLISHED BY ONI-LION FORGE PUBLISHING GROUP, LLC

James Lucas Jones, PRESIDENT & PUBLISHER • Sarah Gaydos, EDITOR IN CHIEF • Charlie Chu, E.V.P. OF CREATIVE & BUSINESS DEVELOPMENT • Brad Rooks, DIRECTOR OF OPERATIONS • Amber O'Neill, SPECIAL PROJECTS MANAGER • Harris Fish, EVENTS MANAGER • Margot Wood, DIRECTOR OF MARKETING & SALES • Devin Funches, SALES & MARKETING MANAGER • Katie Sainz, MARKETING MANAGER • Tara Lehmann, PUBLICIST • Troy Look, DIRECTOR OF DESIGN & PRODUCTION • Kate Z. Stone, SENIOR GRAPHIC DESIGNER • Sonja Synak, GRAPHIC DESIGNER • Hilary Thompson, GRAPHIC DESIGNER • Sarah Rockwell, JUNIOR GRAPHIC DESIGNER • Angie Knowles, DIGITAL PREPRESS LEAD • Vincent Kukua, DIGITAL PREPRESS TECHNICIAN • Jasmine Amiri, SENIOR EDITOR • Shawna Gore, SENIOR EDITOR • Amanda Meadows, SENIOR EDITOR • Robert Meyers, SENIOR EDITOR, LICENSING • Grace Bornhoft, EDITOR • Zack Soto, EDITOR • Chris Cerasi, EDITORIAL COORDINATOR • Steve Ellis, VICE PRESIDENT OF GAMES • Ben Eisner, GAME DEVELOPER • Michelle Nguyen, EXECUTIVE ASSISTANT • Jung Lee, LOGISTICS COORDINATOR

Joe Nozemack, PUBLISHER EMERITUS

First Edition: NOVEMBER 2020   ISBN 978-1-62010-786-7   eISBN 978-1-62010-807-9

Printed in China.
Library of Congress Control Number: 2020936283

10 9 8 7 6 5 4 3 2 1

ONIPRESS.COM   f · ✔ · ◎   LIONFORGE.COM

CHAPTER
1

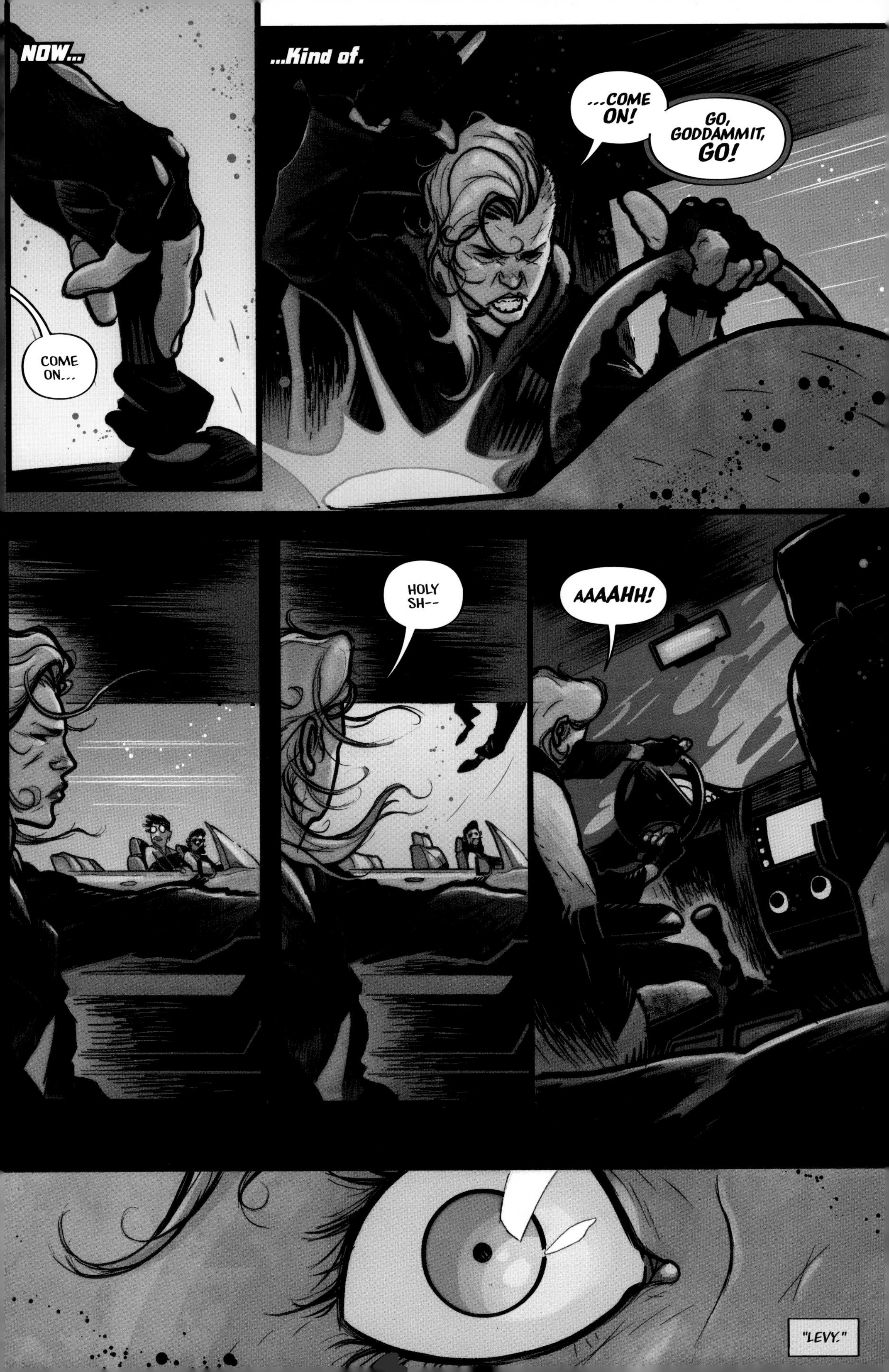
NOW...
COME ON...
...Kind of.
...COME ON!
GO, GODDAMMIT, GO!
HOLY SH--
AAAAHH!
"LEVY."

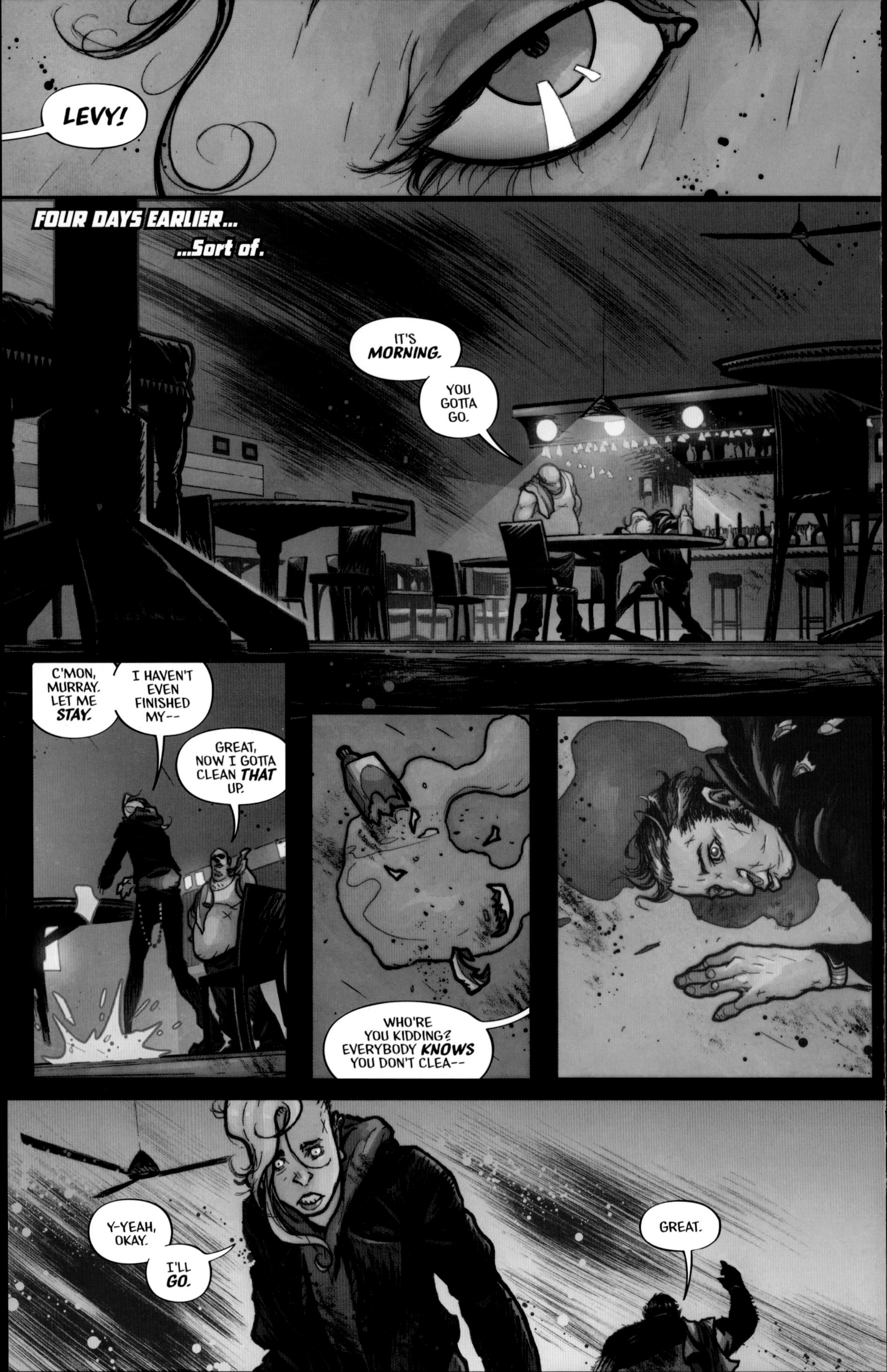
LEVY!
FOUR DAYS EARLIER...
...Sort of.
IT'S MORNING.
YOU GOTTA GO.
C'MON, MURRAY. LET ME STAY.
I HAVEN'T EVEN FINISHED MY--
GREAT, NOW I GOTTA CLEAN THAT UP.
WHO'RE YOU KIDDING? EVERYBODY KNOWS YOU DON'T CLEA--
Y-YEAH, OKAY.
I'LL GO.
GREAT.

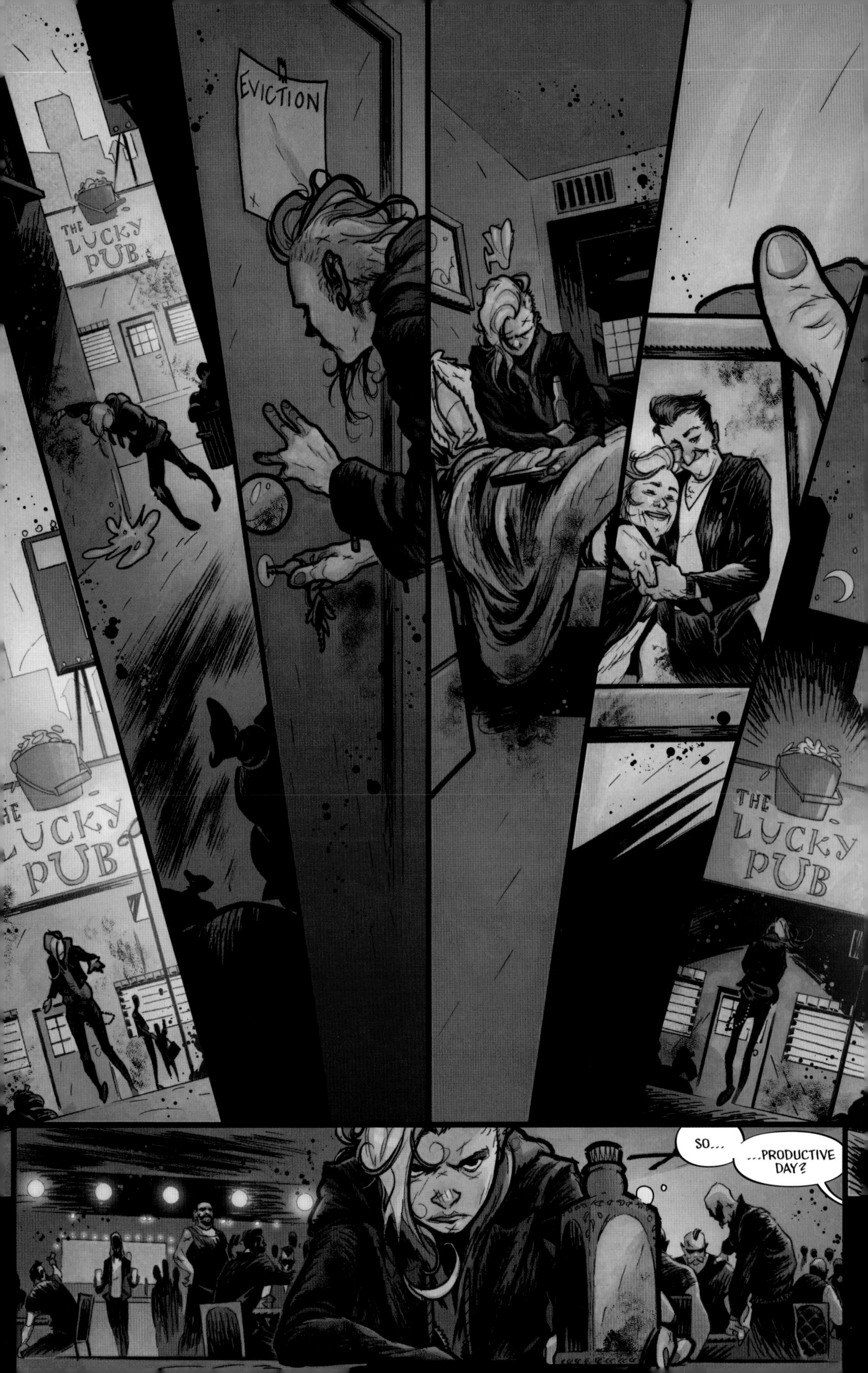

THE LUCKY PUB
EVICTION
THE LUCKY PUB
THE LUCKY PUB
SO...
...PRODUCTIVE DAY?

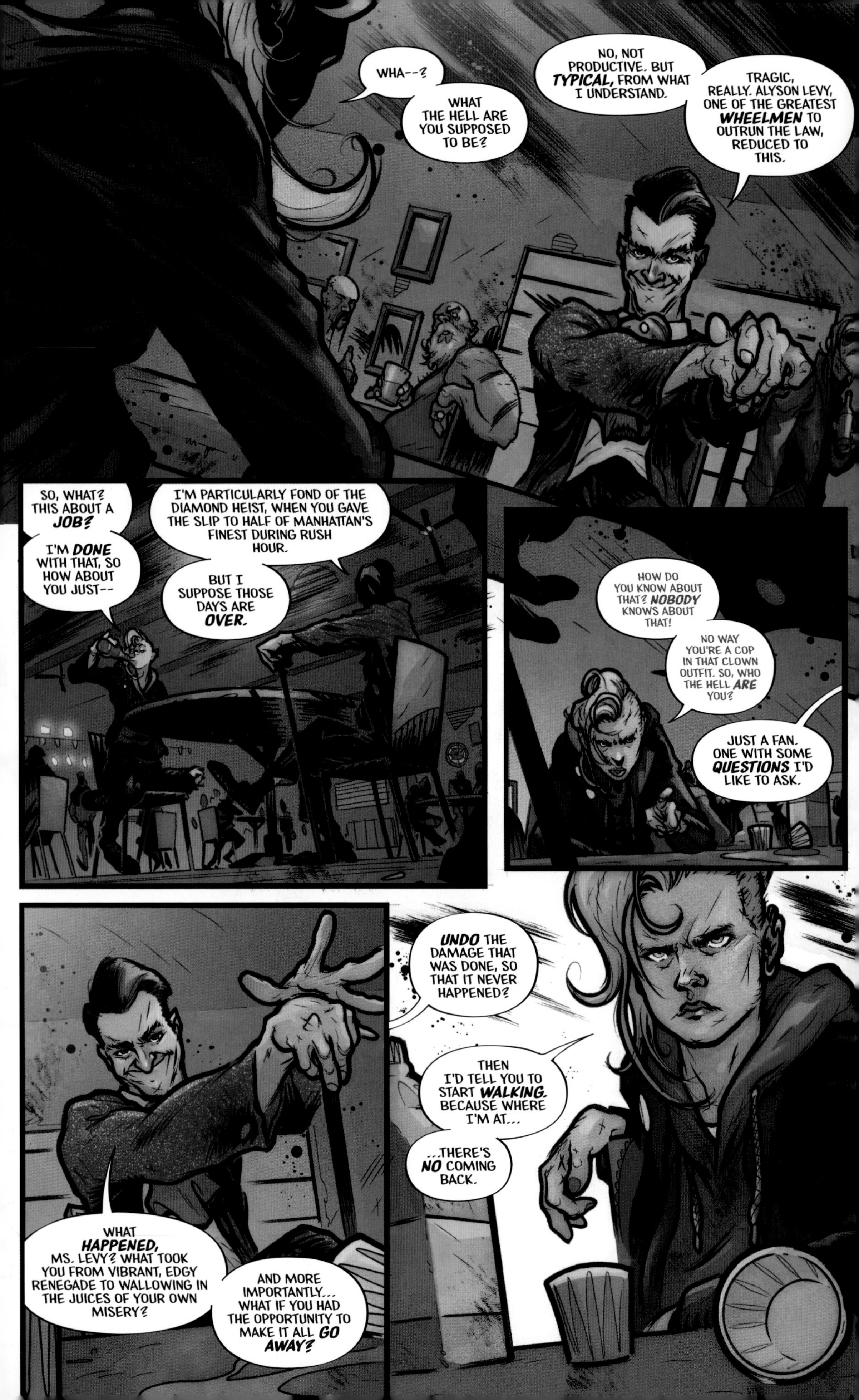

WHA--?
WHAT THE HELL ARE YOU SUPPOSED TO BE?
NO, NOT PRODUCTIVE. BUT TYPICAL, FROM WHAT I UNDERSTAND.
TRAGIC, REALLY. ALYSON LEVY, ONE OF THE GREATEST WHEELMEN TO OUTRUN THE LAW, REDUCED TO THIS.
SO, WHAT? THIS ABOUT A JOB?
I'M DONE WITH THAT, SO HOW ABOUT YOU JUST--
I'M PARTICULARLY FOND OF THE DIAMOND HEIST, WHEN YOU GAVE THE SLIP TO HALF OF MANHATTAN'S FINEST DURING RUSH HOUR.
BUT I SUPPOSE THOSE DAYS ARE OVER.
HOW DO YOU KNOW ABOUT THAT? NOBODY KNOWS ABOUT THAT!
NO WAY YOU'RE A COP IN THAT CLOWN OUTFIT. SO, WHO THE HELL ARE YOU?
JUST A FAN. ONE WITH SOME QUESTIONS I'D LIKE TO ASK.
WHAT HAPPENED, MS. LEVY? WHAT TOOK YOU FROM VIBRANT, EDGY RENEGADE TO WALLOWING IN THE JUICES OF YOUR OWN MISERY?
AND MORE IMPORTANTLY... WHAT IF YOU HAD THE OPPORTUNITY TO MAKE IT ALL GO AWAY?
UNDO THE DAMAGE THAT WAS DONE, SO THAT IT NEVER HAPPENED?
THEN I'D TELL YOU TO START WALKING. BECAUSE WHERE I'M AT...
...THERE'S NO COMING BACK.

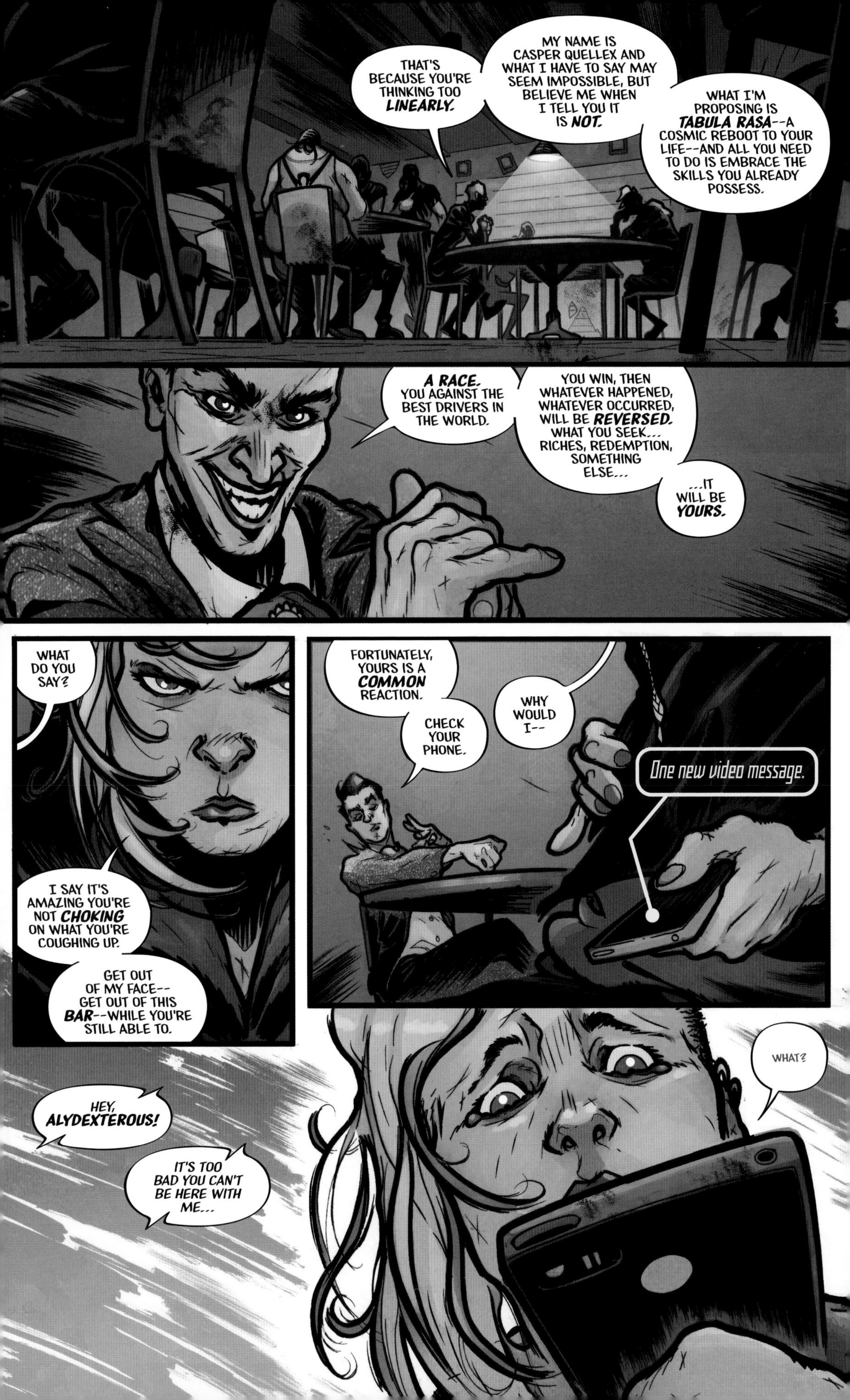
THAT'S BECAUSE YOU'RE THINKING TOO LINEARLY.
MY NAME IS CASPER QUELLEX AND WHAT I HAVE TO SAY MAY SEEM IMPOSSIBLE, BUT BELIEVE ME WHEN I TELL YOU IT IS NOT.
WHAT I'M PROPOSING IS TABULA RASA--A COSMIC REBOOT TO YOUR LIFE--AND ALL YOU NEED TO DO IS EMBRACE THE SKILLS YOU ALREADY POSSESS.
A RACE. YOU AGAINST THE BEST DRIVERS IN THE WORLD.
YOU WIN, THEN WHATEVER HAPPENED, WHATEVER OCCURRED, WILL BE REVERSED. WHAT YOU SEEK... RICHES, REDEMPTION, SOMETHING ELSE...
...IT WILL BE YOURS.
WHAT DO YOU SAY?
I SAY IT'S AMAZING YOU'RE NOT CHOKING ON WHAT YOU'RE COUGHING UP.
GET OUT OF MY FACE--GET OUT OF THIS BAR--WHILE YOU'RE STILL ABLE TO.
FORTUNATELY, YOURS IS A COMMON REACTION.
CHECK YOUR PHONE.
WHY WOULD I--
One new video message.
HEY, ALYDEXTEROUS!
IT'S TOO BAD YOU CAN'T BE HERE WITH ME...
WHAT?

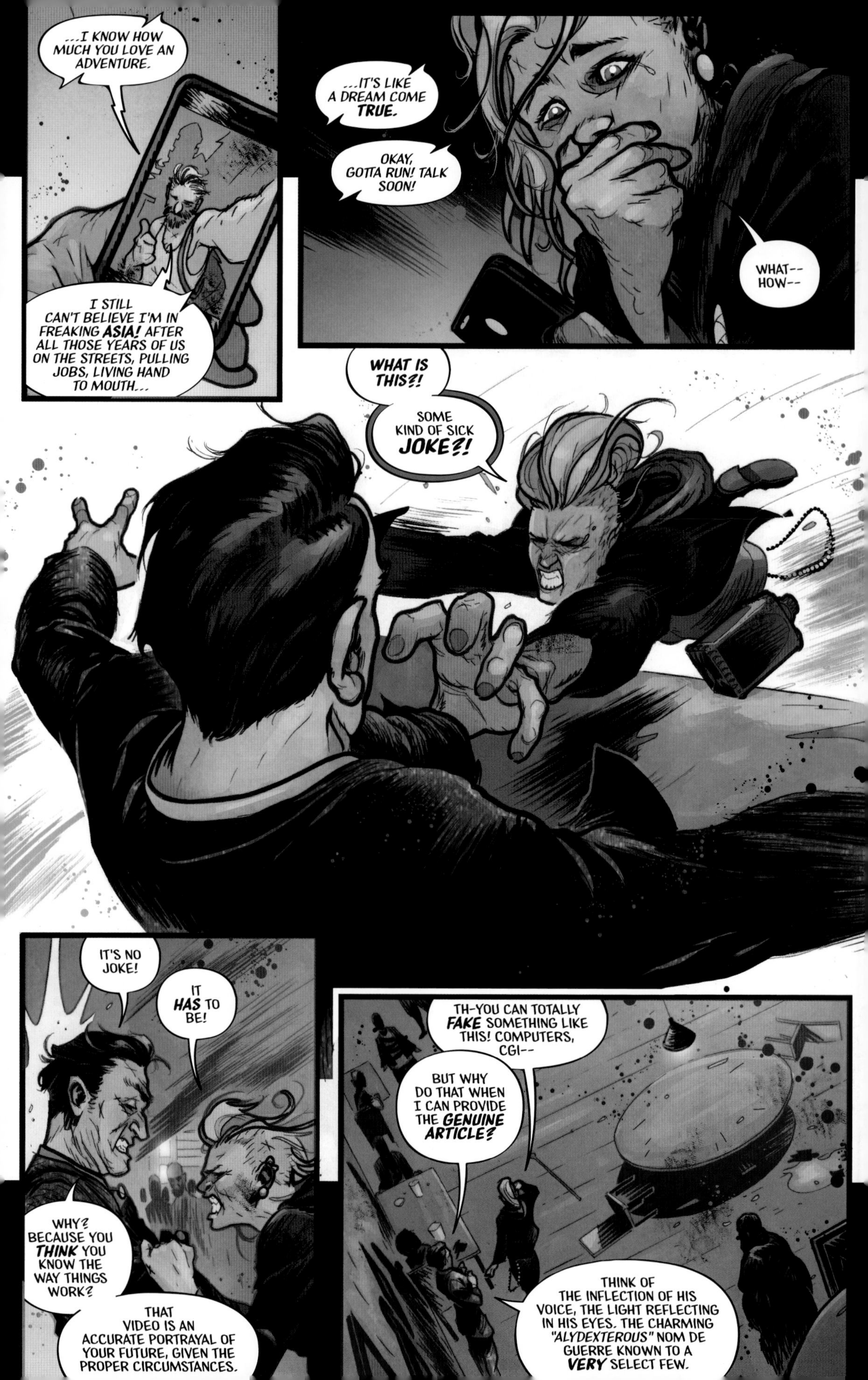
...I KNOW HOW MUCH YOU LOVE AN ADVENTURE.
I STILL CAN'T BELIEVE I'M IN FREAKING ASIA! AFTER ALL THOSE YEARS OF US ON THE STREETS, PULLING JOBS, LIVING HAND TO MOUTH...
...IT'S LIKE A DREAM COME TRUE.
OKAY, GOTTA RUN! TALK SOON!
WHAT-- HOW--
WHAT IS THIS?!
SOME KIND OF SICK JOKE?!
IT'S NO JOKE!
IT HAS TO BE!
WHY? BECAUSE YOU THINK YOU KNOW THE WAY THINGS WORK?
THAT VIDEO IS AN ACCURATE PORTRAYAL OF YOUR FUTURE, GIVEN THE PROPER CIRCUMSTANCES.
TH-YOU CAN TOTALLY FAKE SOMETHING LIKE THIS! COMPUTERS, CGI--
BUT WHY DO THAT WHEN I CAN PROVIDE THE GENUINE ARTICLE?
THINK OF THE INFLECTION OF HIS VOICE, THE LIGHT REFLECTING IN HIS EYES. THE CHARMING "ALYDEXTEROUS" NOM DE GUERRE KNOWN TO A VERY SELECT FEW.

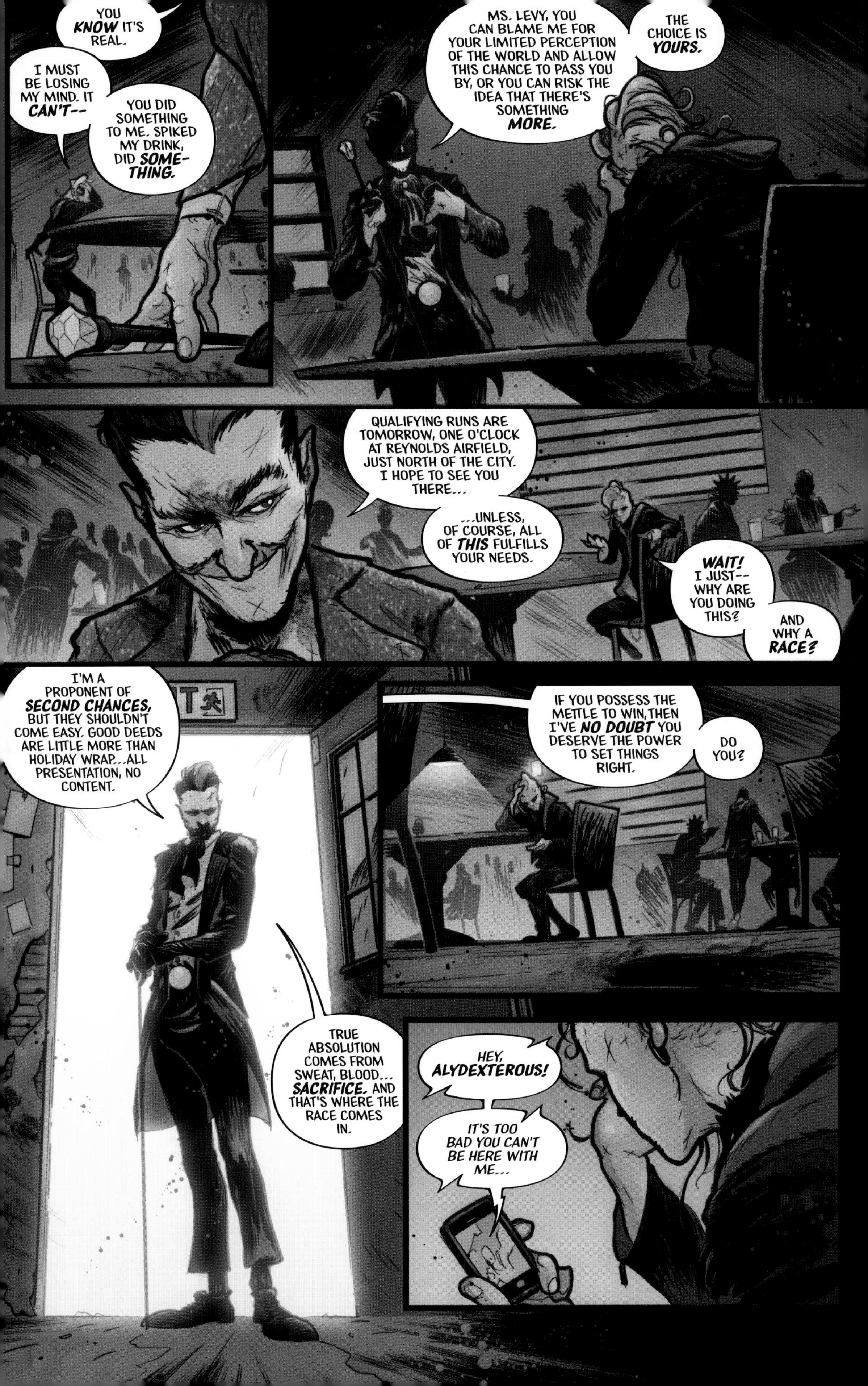
YOU KNOW IT'S REAL.
I MUST BE LOSING MY MIND. IT CAN'T--
YOU DID SOMETHING TO ME. SPIKED MY DRINK, DID SOME-THING.
MS. LEVY, YOU CAN BLAME ME FOR YOUR LIMITED PERCEPTION OF THE WORLD AND ALLOW THIS CHANCE TO PASS YOU BY, OR YOU CAN RISK THE IDEA THAT THERE'S SOMETHING MORE.
THE CHOICE IS YOURS.
QUALIFYING RUNS ARE TOMORROW, ONE O'CLOCK AT REYNOLDS AIRFIELD, JUST NORTH OF THE CITY. I HOPE TO SEE YOU THERE...
...UNLESS, OF COURSE, ALL OF THIS FULFILLS YOUR NEEDS.
WAIT! I JUST-- WHY ARE YOU DOING THIS?
AND WHY A RACE?
I'M A PROPONENT OF SECOND CHANCES, BUT THEY SHOULDN'T COME EASY. GOOD DEEDS ARE LITTLE MORE THAN HOLIDAY WRAP...ALL PRESENTATION, NO CONTENT.
TRUE ABSOLUTION COMES FROM SWEAT, BLOOD... SACRIFICE. AND THAT'S WHERE THE RACE COMES IN.
IF YOU POSSESS THE METTLE TO WIN, THEN I'VE NO DOUBT YOU DESERVE THE POWER TO SET THINGS RIGHT.
DO YOU?
HEY, ALYDEXTEROUS!
IT'S TOO BAD YOU CAN'T BE HERE WITH ME...

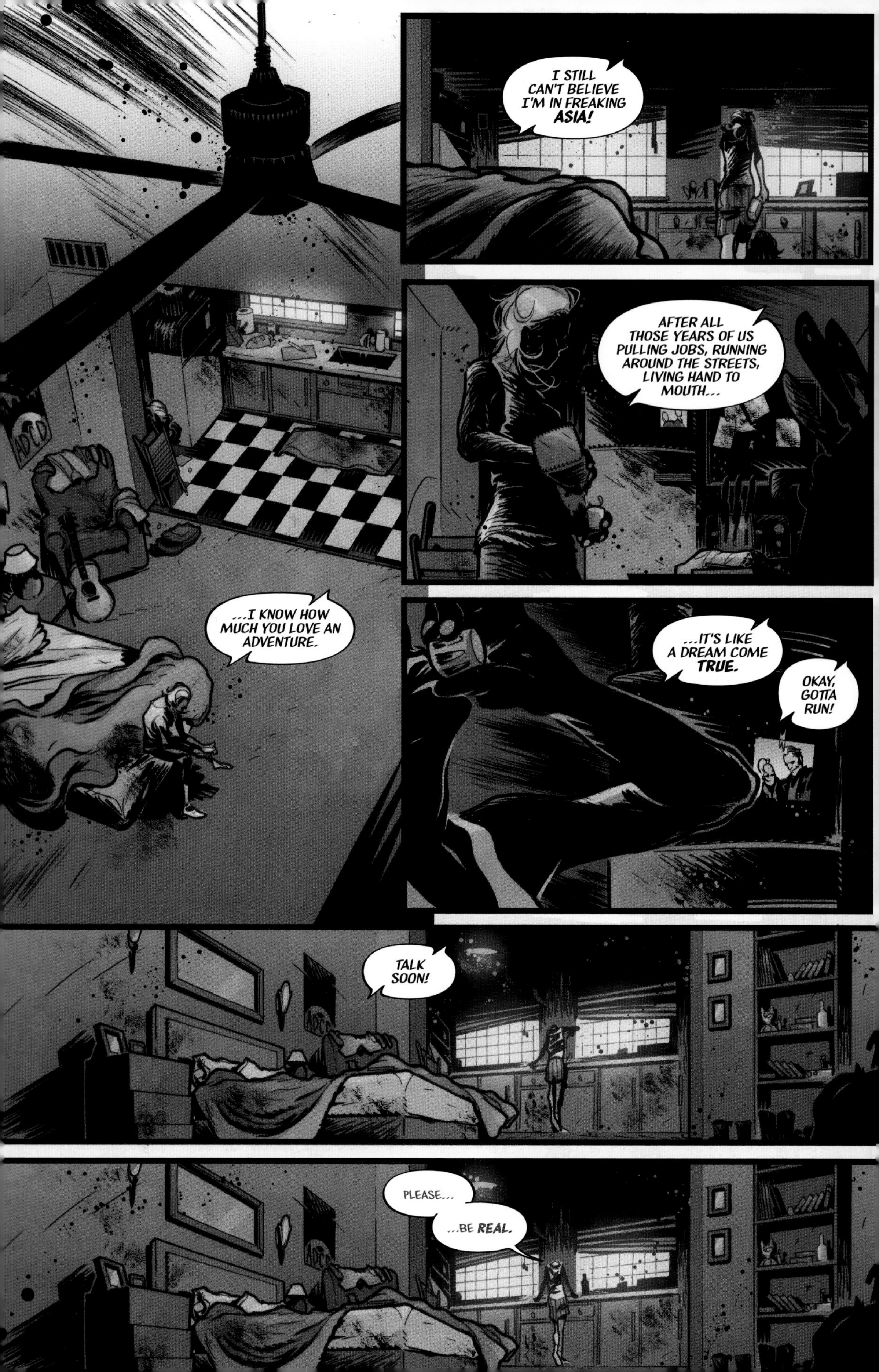
I STILL CAN'T BELIEVE I'M IN FREAKING ASIA!
AFTER ALL THOSE YEARS OF US PULLING JOBS, RUNNING AROUND THE STREETS, LIVING HAND TO MOUTH...
...I KNOW HOW MUCH YOU LOVE AN ADVENTURE.
...IT'S LIKE A DREAM COME TRUE.
OKAY, GOTTA RUN!
TALK SOON!
PLEASE...
...BE REAL.

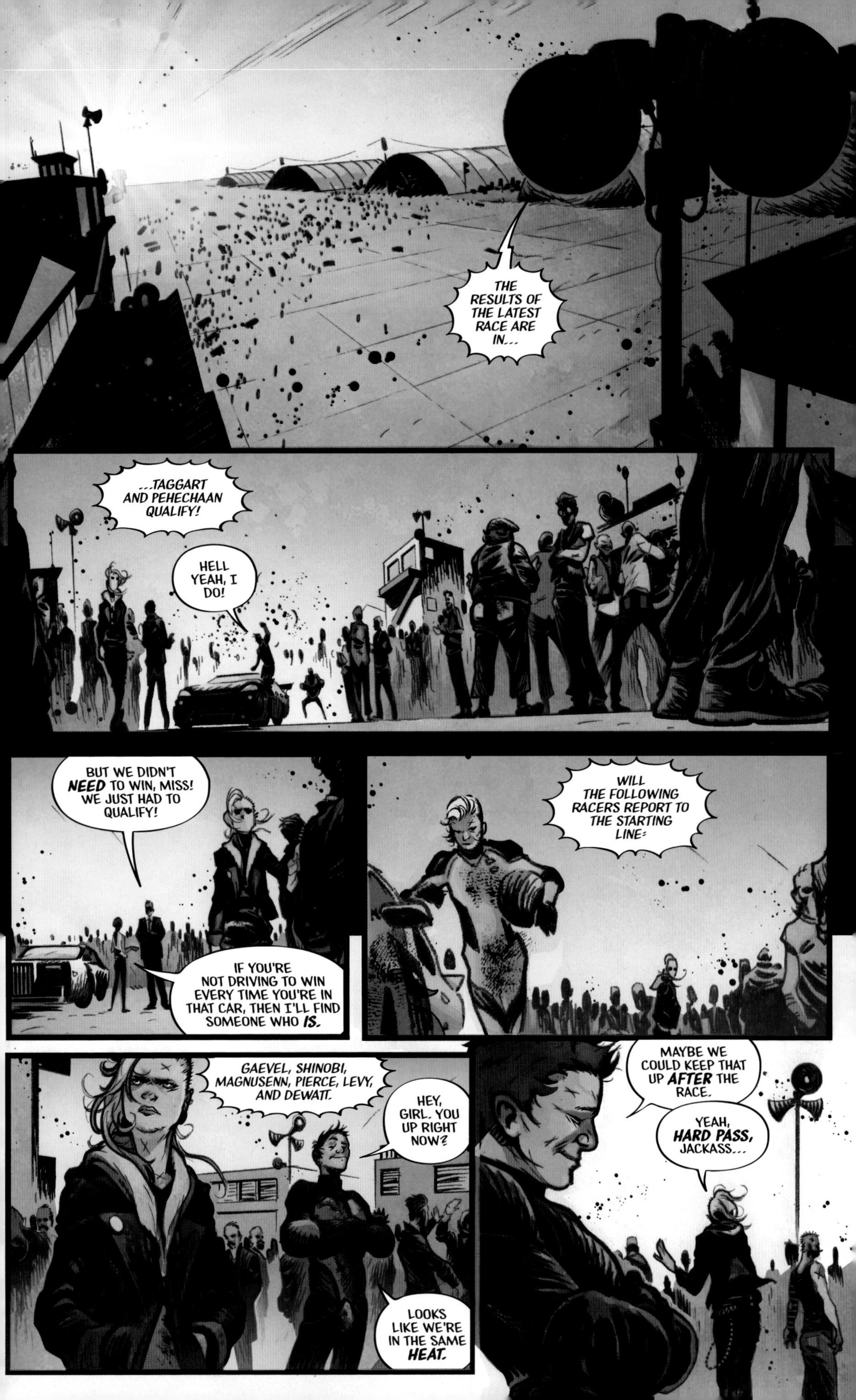
THE RESULTS OF THE LATEST RACE ARE IN...
...TAGGART AND PEHECHAAN QUALIFY!
HELL YEAH, I DO!
BUT WE DIDN'T **NEED** TO WIN, MISS! WE JUST HAD TO QUALIFY!
IF YOU'RE NOT DRIVING TO WIN EVERY TIME YOU'RE IN THAT CAR, THEN I'LL FIND SOMEONE WHO ***IS.***
WILL THE FOLLOWING RACERS REPORT TO THE STARTING LINE:
GAEVEL, SHINOBI, MAGNUSENN, PIERCE, LEVY, AND DEWATT.
HEY, GIRL. YOU UP RIGHT NOW?
LOOKS LIKE WE'RE IN THE SAME **HEAT.**
MAYBE WE COULD KEEP THAT UP **AFTER** THE RACE.
YEAH, **HARD PASS,** JACKASS...

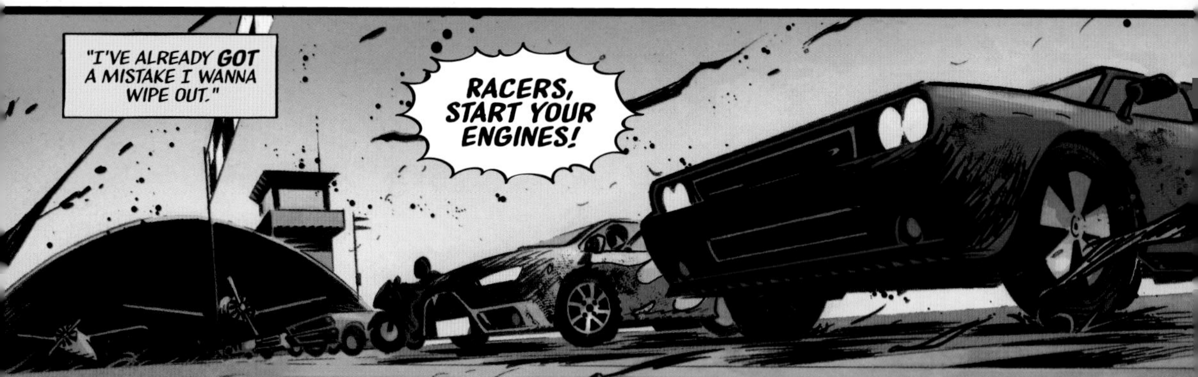
"I'VE ALREADY GOT A MISTAKE I WANNA WIPE OUT."
RACERS, START YOUR ENGINES!

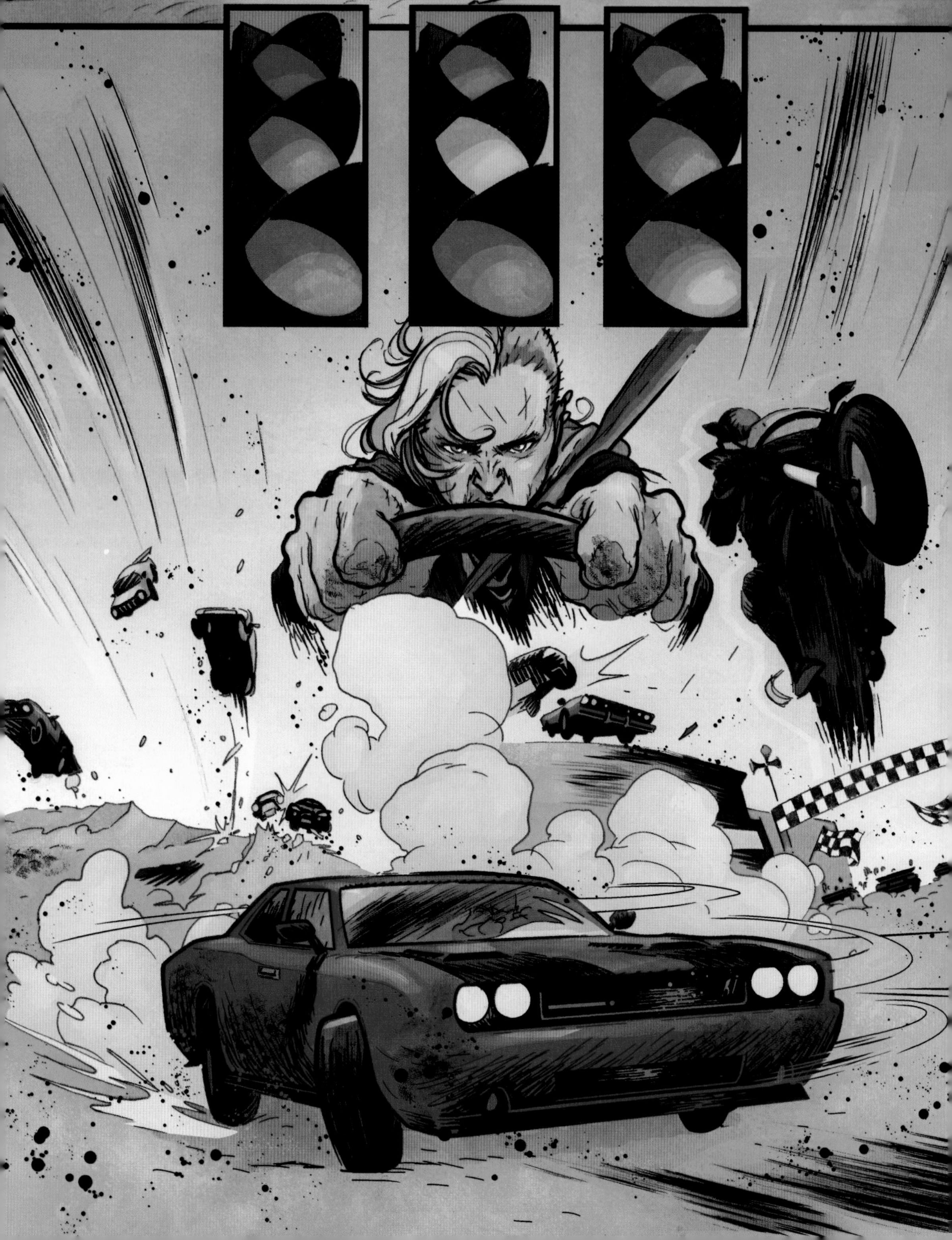

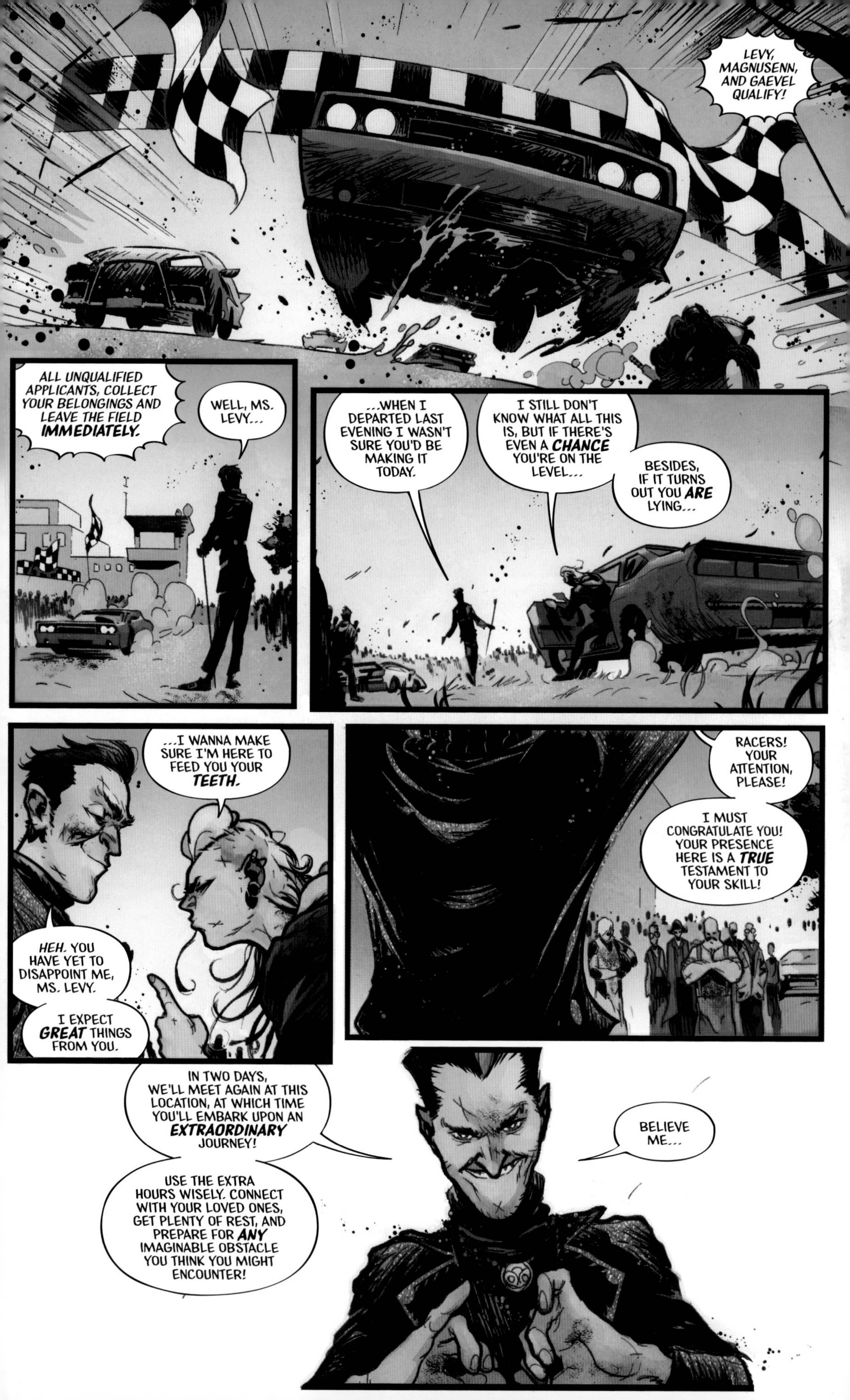
LEVY, MAGNUSENN, AND GAEVEL QUALIFY!
ALL UNQUALIFIED APPLICANTS, COLLECT YOUR BELONGINGS AND LEAVE THE FIELD IMMEDIATELY.
WELL, MS. LEVY...
...WHEN I DEPARTED LAST EVENING I WASN'T SURE YOU'D BE MAKING IT TODAY.
I STILL DON'T KNOW WHAT ALL THIS IS, BUT IF THERE'S EVEN A CHANCE YOU'RE ON THE LEVEL...
BESIDES, IF IT TURNS OUT YOU ARE LYING...
...I WANNA MAKE SURE I'M HERE TO FEED YOU YOUR TEETH.
HEH. YOU HAVE YET TO DISAPPOINT ME, MS. LEVY.
I EXPECT GREAT THINGS FROM YOU.
RACERS! YOUR ATTENTION, PLEASE!
I MUST CONGRATULATE YOU! YOUR PRESENCE HERE IS A TRUE TESTAMENT TO YOUR SKILL!
IN TWO DAYS, WE'LL MEET AGAIN AT THIS LOCATION, AT WHICH TIME YOU'LL EMBARK UPON AN EXTRAORDINARY JOURNEY!
USE THE EXTRA HOURS WISELY. CONNECT WITH YOUR LOVED ONES, GET PLENTY OF REST, AND PREPARE FOR ANY IMAGINABLE OBSTACLE YOU THINK YOU MIGHT ENCOUNTER!
BELIEVE ME...

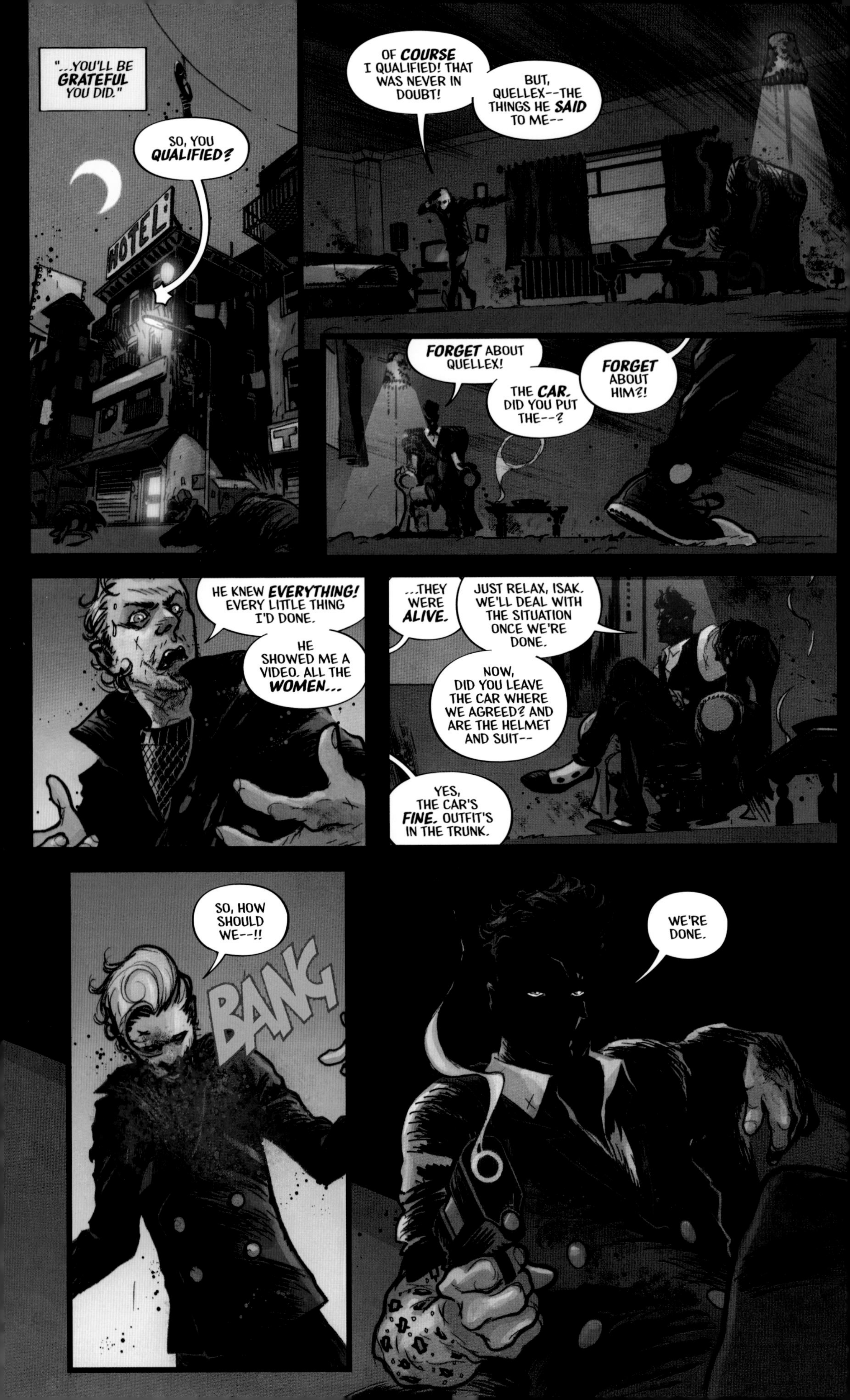
"...YOU'LL BE GRATEFUL YOU DID."
SO, YOU QUALIFIED?
HOTEL
OF COURSE I QUALIFIED! THAT WAS NEVER IN DOUBT!
BUT, QUELLEX--THE THINGS HE SAID TO ME--
FORGET ABOUT QUELLEX!
THE CAR. DID YOU PUT THE--?
FORGET ABOUT HIM?!
HE KNEW EVERYTHING! EVERY LITTLE THING I'D DONE.
HE SHOWED ME A VIDEO. ALL THE WOMEN...
...THEY WERE ALIVE.
JUST RELAX, ISAK. WE'LL DEAL WITH THE SITUATION ONCE WE'RE DONE.
NOW, DID YOU LEAVE THE CAR WHERE WE AGREED? AND ARE THE HELMET AND SUIT--
YES, THE CAR'S FINE. OUTFIT'S IN THE TRUNK.
SO, HOW SHOULD WE--!!
BANG
WE'RE DONE.

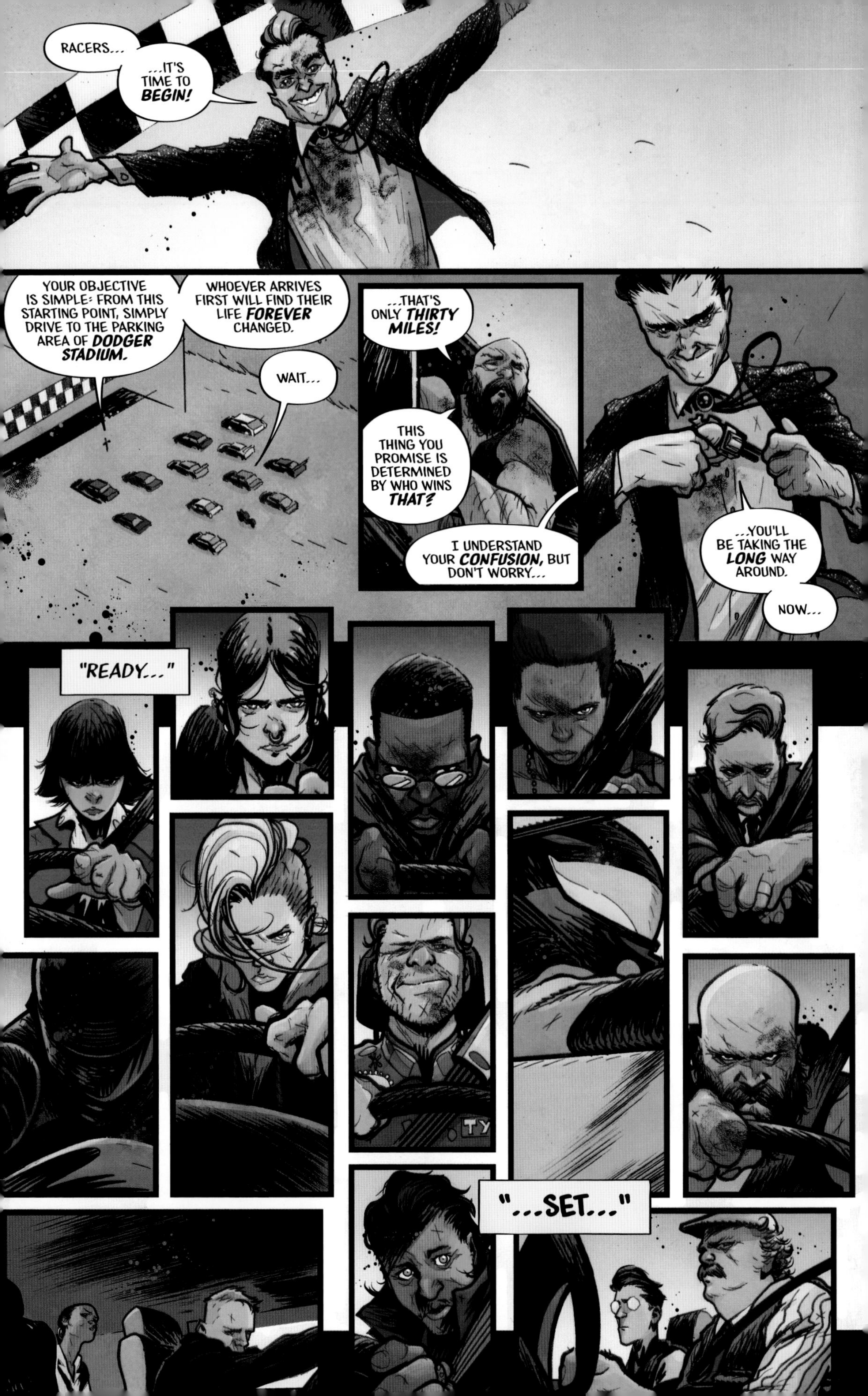
RACERS...
...IT'S TIME TO BEGIN!
YOUR OBJECTIVE IS SIMPLE: FROM THIS STARTING POINT, SIMPLY DRIVE TO THE PARKING AREA OF DODGER STADIUM.
WHOEVER ARRIVES FIRST WILL FIND THEIR LIFE FOREVER CHANGED.
WAIT...
...THAT'S ONLY THIRTY MILES!
THIS THING YOU PROMISE IS DETERMINED BY WHO WINS THAT?
I UNDERSTAND YOUR CONFUSION, BUT DON'T WORRY...
...YOU'LL BE TAKING THE LONG WAY AROUND.
NOW...
"READY..."
"...SET..."

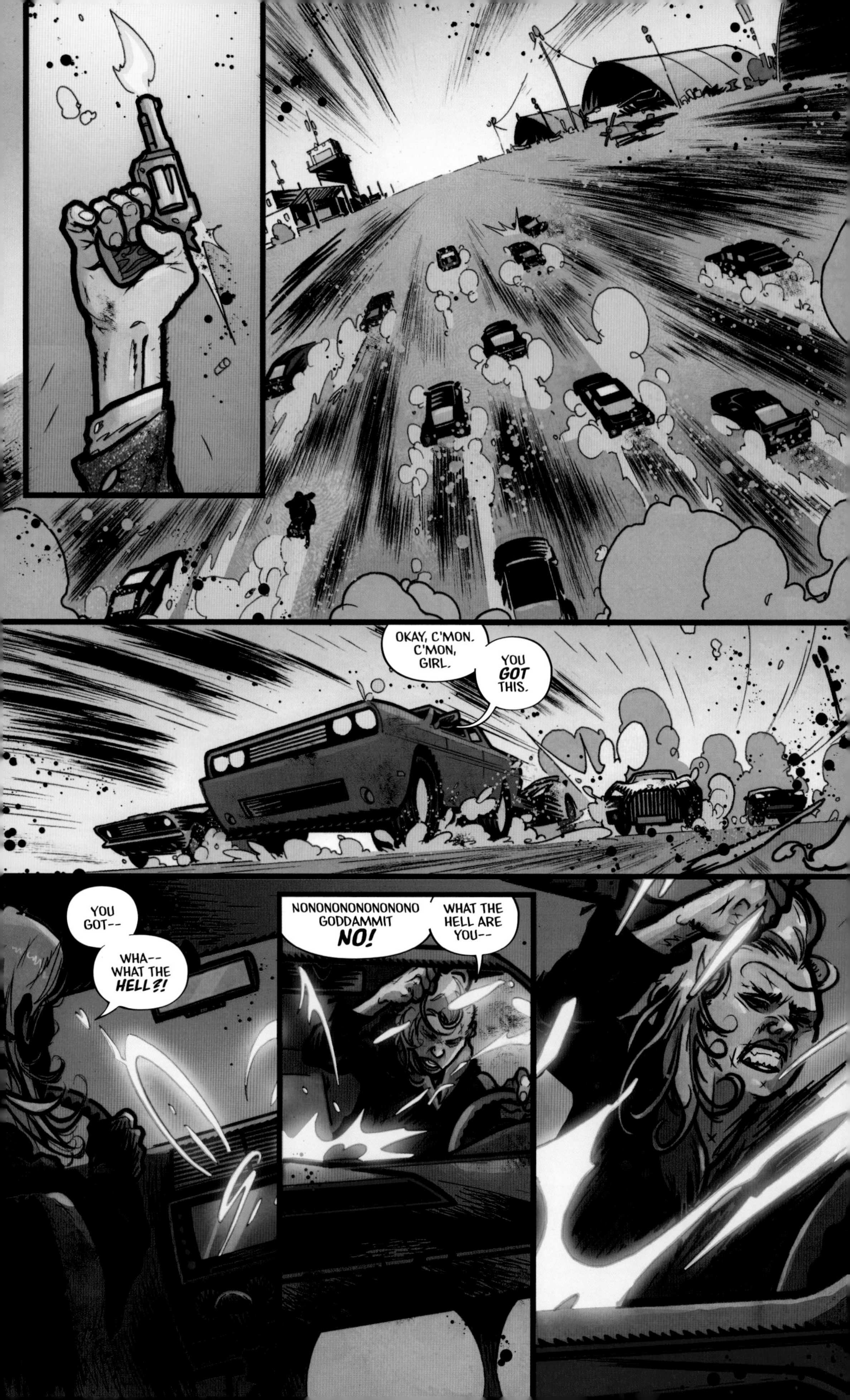

OKAY, C'MON. C'MON, GIRL.
YOU **GOT** THIS.
YOU GOT--
WHA-- WHAT THE **HELL?!**
NONONONONONONONO GODDAMMIT **NO!**
WHAT THE HELL ARE YOU--

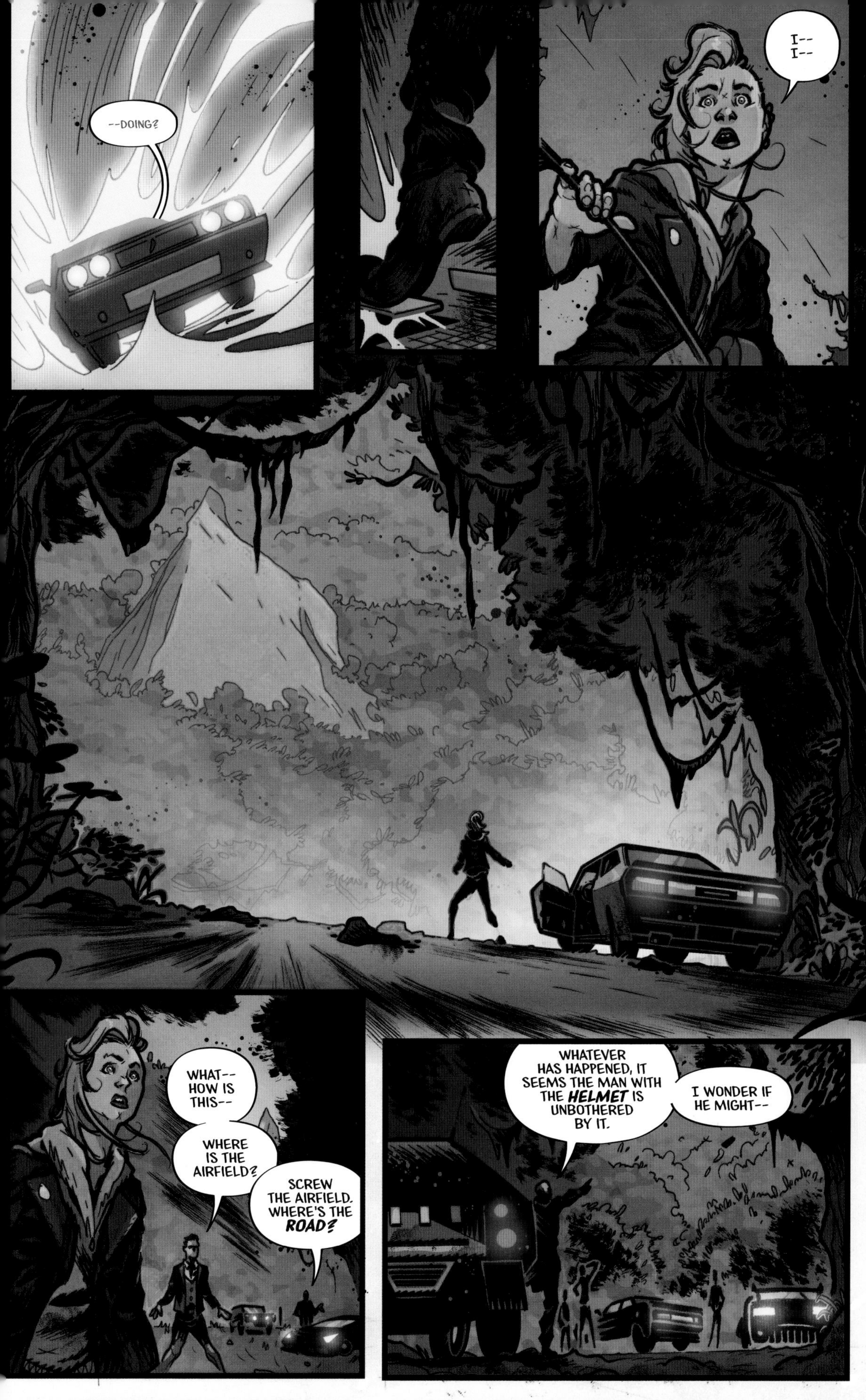
--DOING?
I--
I--
WHAT--
HOW IS
THIS--
WHERE
IS THE
AIRFIELD?
SCREW
THE AIRFIELD.
WHERE'S THE
ROAD?
WHATEVER
HAS HAPPENED, IT
SEEMS THE MAN WITH
THE HELMET IS
UNBOTHERED
BY IT.
I WONDER IF
HE MIGHT--

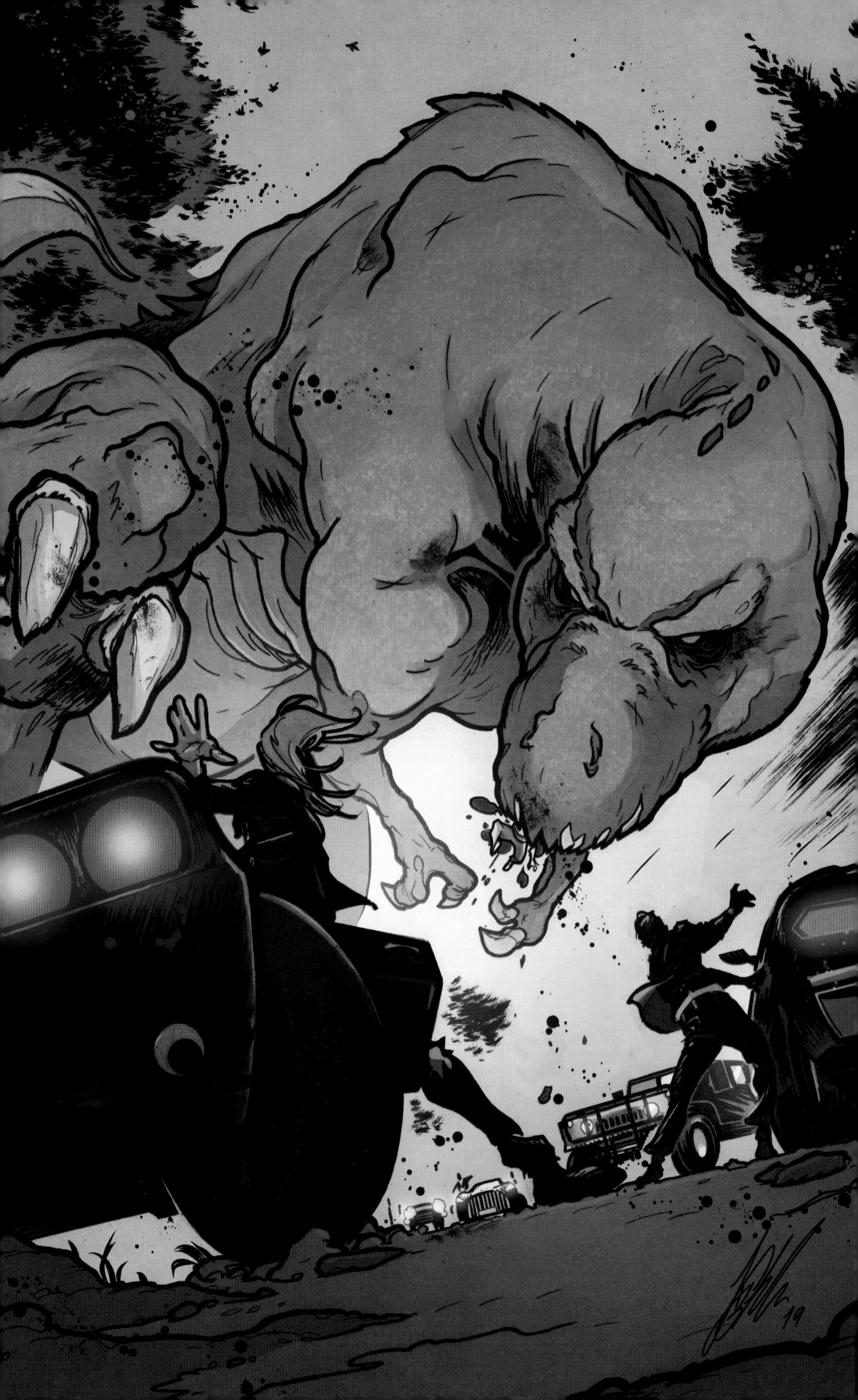

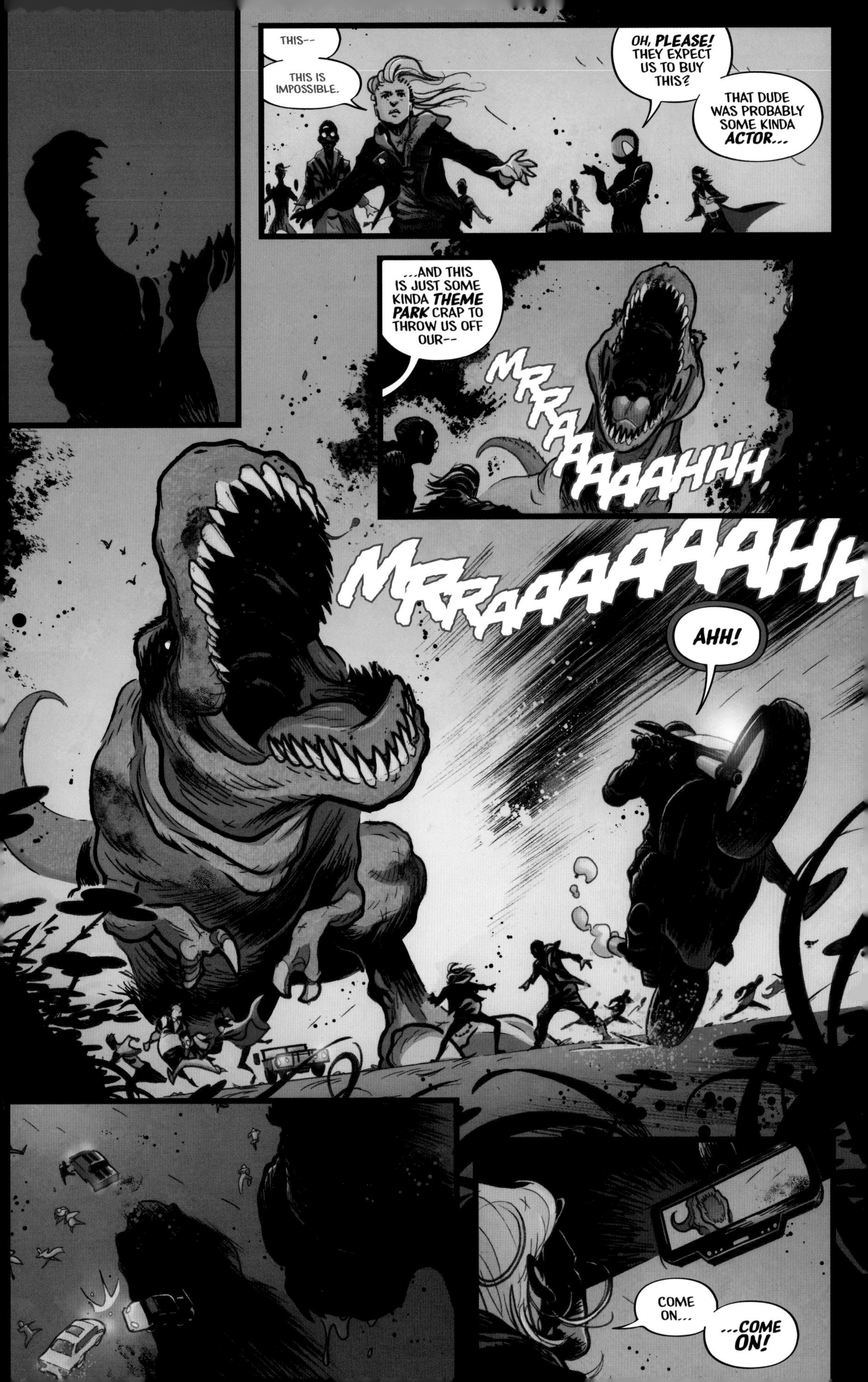
THIS--
THIS IS IMPOSSIBLE.
OH, PLEASE! THEY EXPECT US TO BUY THIS?
THAT DUDE WAS PROBABLY SOME KINDA ACTOR...
...AND THIS IS JUST SOME KINDA THEME PARK CRAP TO THROW US OFF OUR--
MRRAAAAAHHH
MRRAAAAAAAAHH
AHH!
COME ON...
...COME ON!

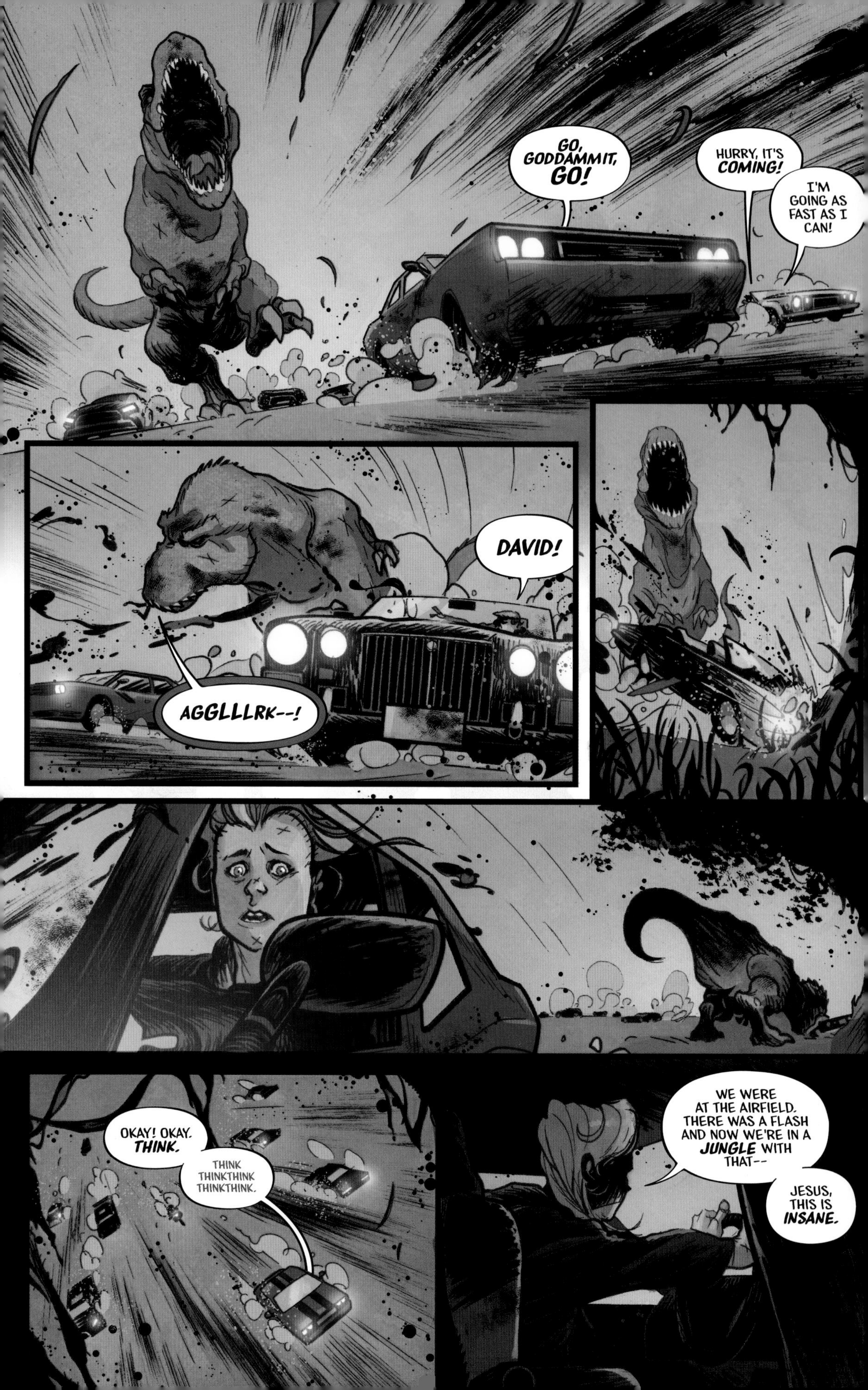
GO, GODDAMMIT, GO!
HURRY, IT'S COMING!
I'M GOING AS FAST AS I CAN!
DAVID!
AGGLLLRK--!
OKAY! OKAY. THINK.
THINK THINKTHINK THINKTHINK.
WE WERE AT THE AIRFIELD. THERE WAS A FLASH AND NOW WE'RE IN A JUNGLE WITH THAT--
JESUS, THIS IS INSANE.

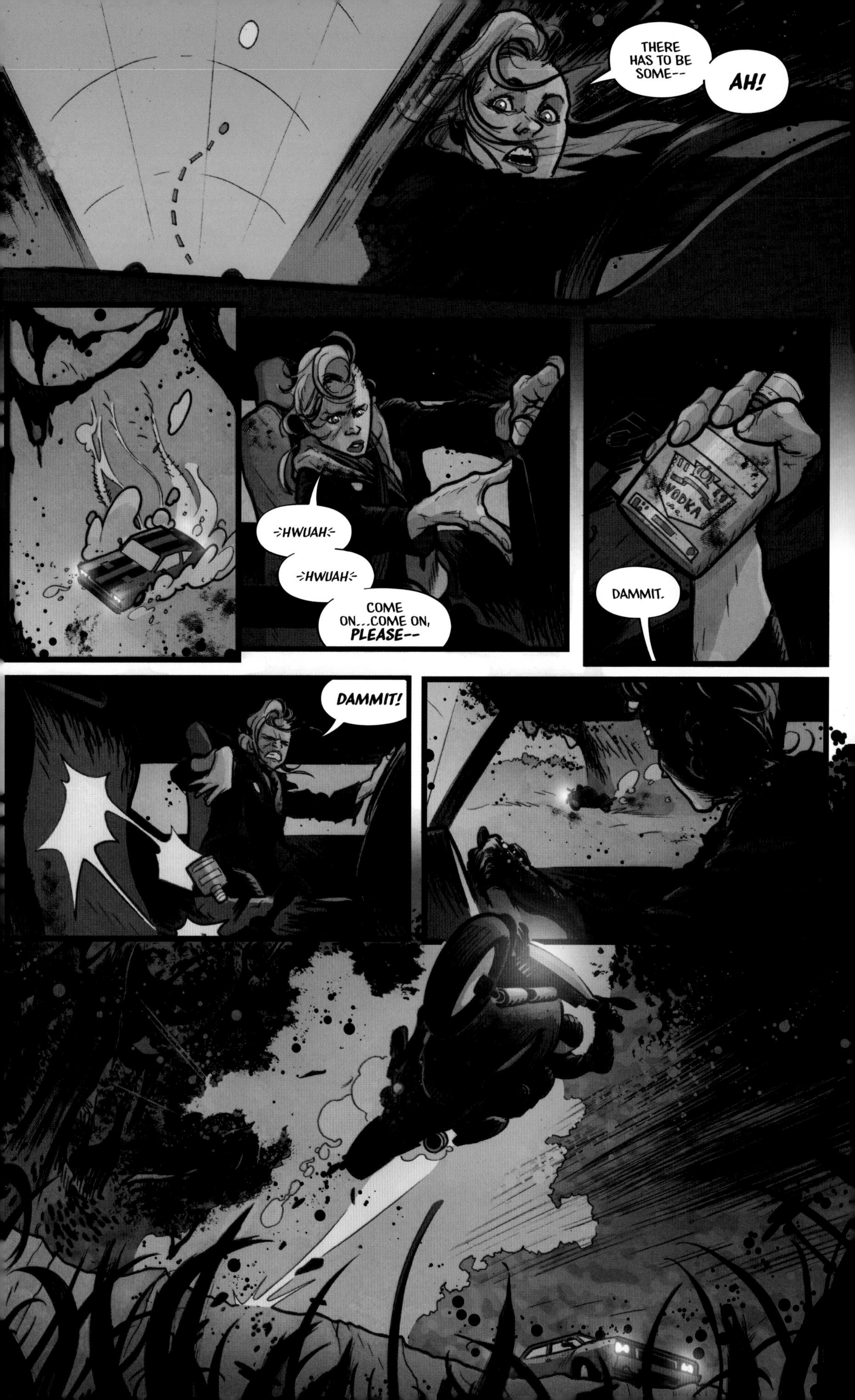
THERE HAS TO BE SOME--
AH!
HWUAH
HWUAH
COME ON...COME ON, PLEASE--
VODKA
DAMMIT.
DAMMIT!

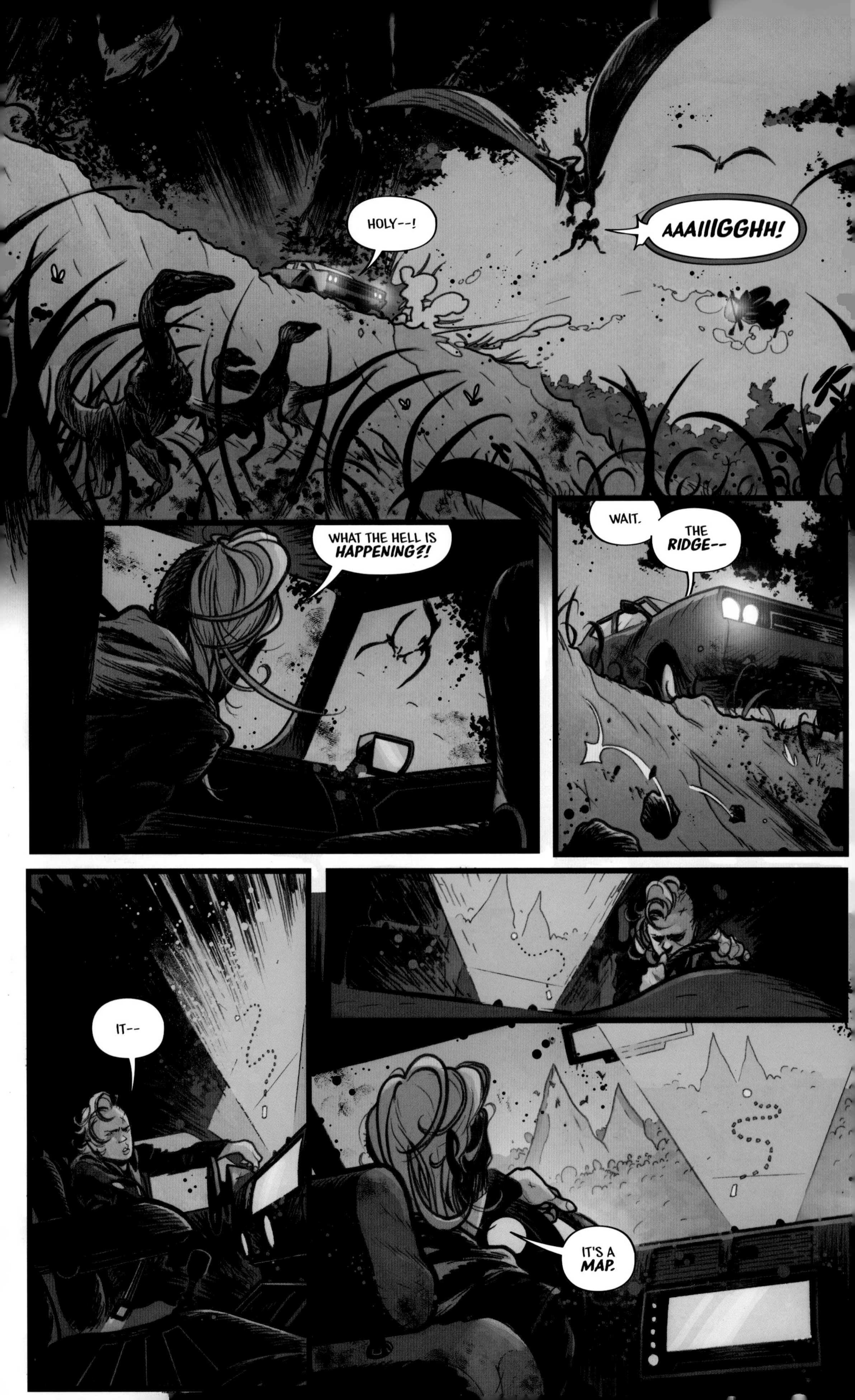
HOLY--!
AAAIIIGGHH!
WHAT THE HELL IS HAPPENING?!
WAIT.
THE RIDGE--
IT--
IT'S A MAP.

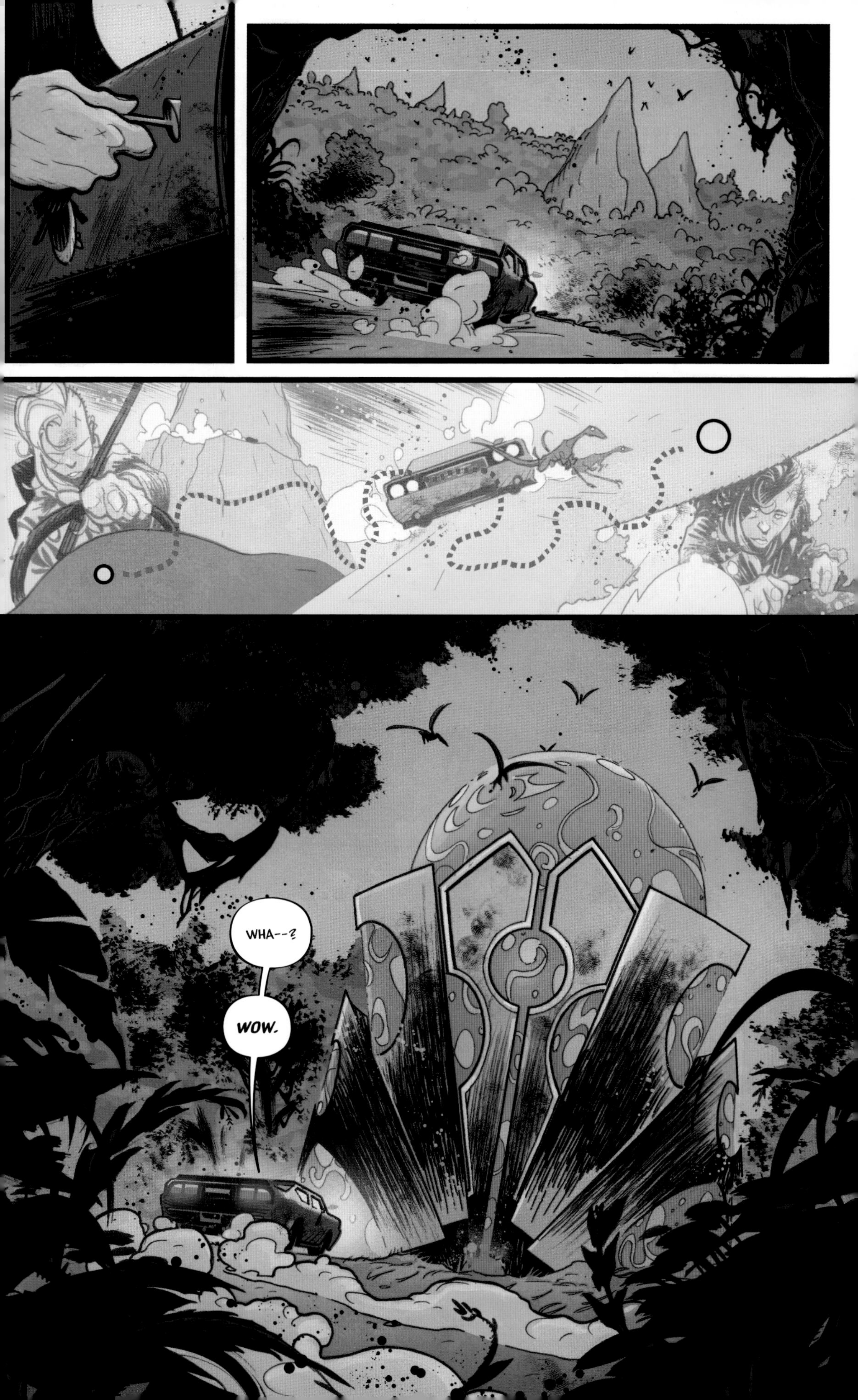

WHA--?
WOW.

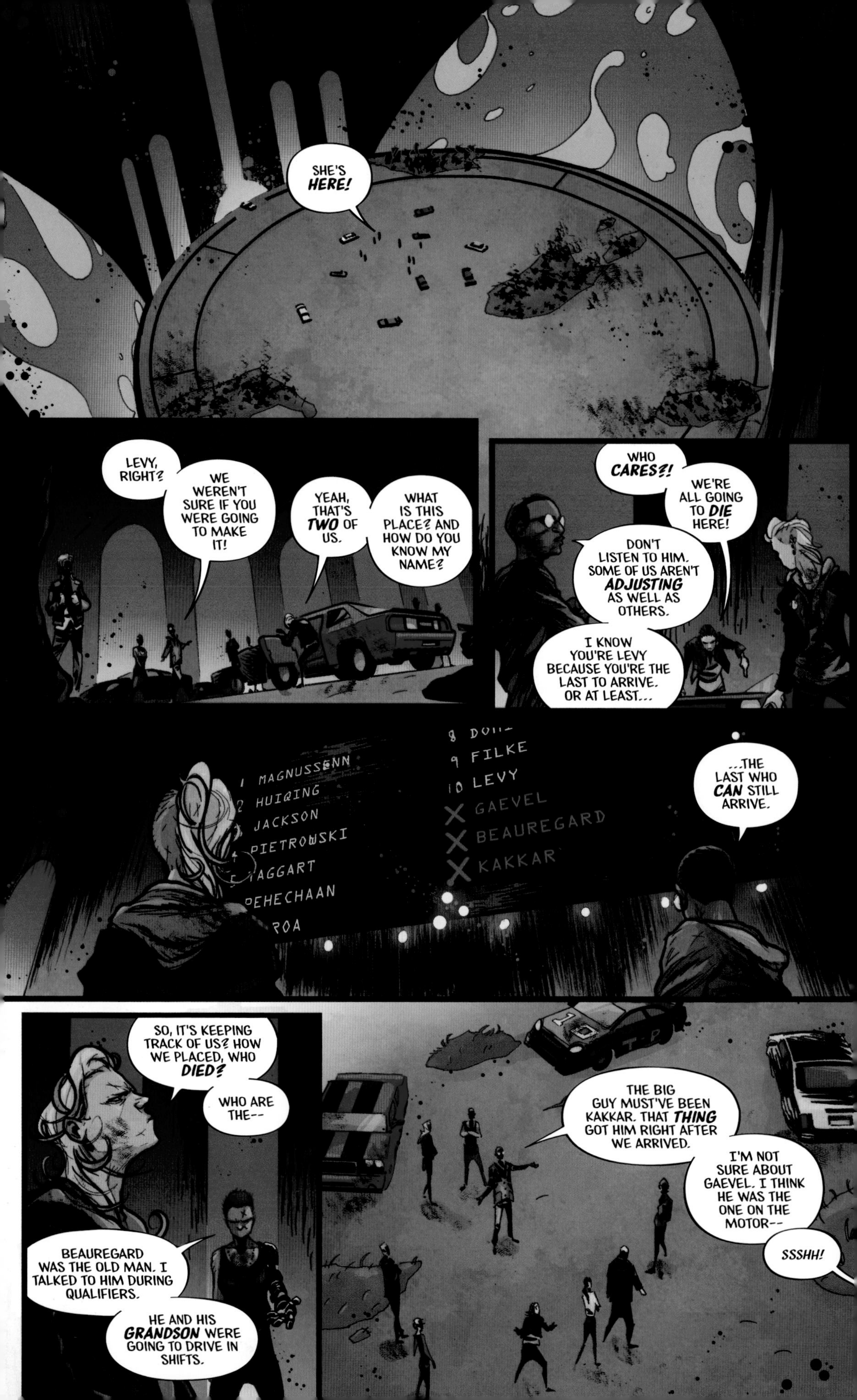
SHE'S HERE!
LEVY, RIGHT?
WE WEREN'T SURE IF YOU WERE GOING TO MAKE IT!
YEAH, THAT'S TWO OF US.
WHAT IS THIS PLACE? AND HOW DO YOU KNOW MY NAME?
WHO CARES?!
WE'RE ALL GOING TO DIE HERE!
DON'T LISTEN TO HIM. SOME OF US AREN'T ADJUSTING AS WELL AS OTHERS.
I KNOW YOU'RE LEVY BECAUSE YOU'RE THE LAST TO ARRIVE. OR AT LEAST...
1 MAGNUSSENN
2 HUIQING
JACKSON
PIETROWSKI
TAGGART
PEHECHAAN
ROA
9 FILKE
10 LEVY
GAEVEL
BEAUREGARD
KAKKAR
...THE LAST WHO CAN STILL ARRIVE.
SO, IT'S KEEPING TRACK OF US? HOW WE PLACED, WHO DIED?
WHO ARE THE--
BEAUREGARD WAS THE OLD MAN. I TALKED TO HIM DURING QUALIFIERS.
HE AND HIS GRANDSON WERE GOING TO DRIVE IN SHIFTS.
THE BIG GUY MUST'VE BEEN KAKKAR. THAT THING GOT HIM RIGHT AFTER WE ARRIVED.
I'M NOT SURE ABOUT GAEVEL. I THINK HE WAS THE ONE ON THE MOTOR--
SSSHH!

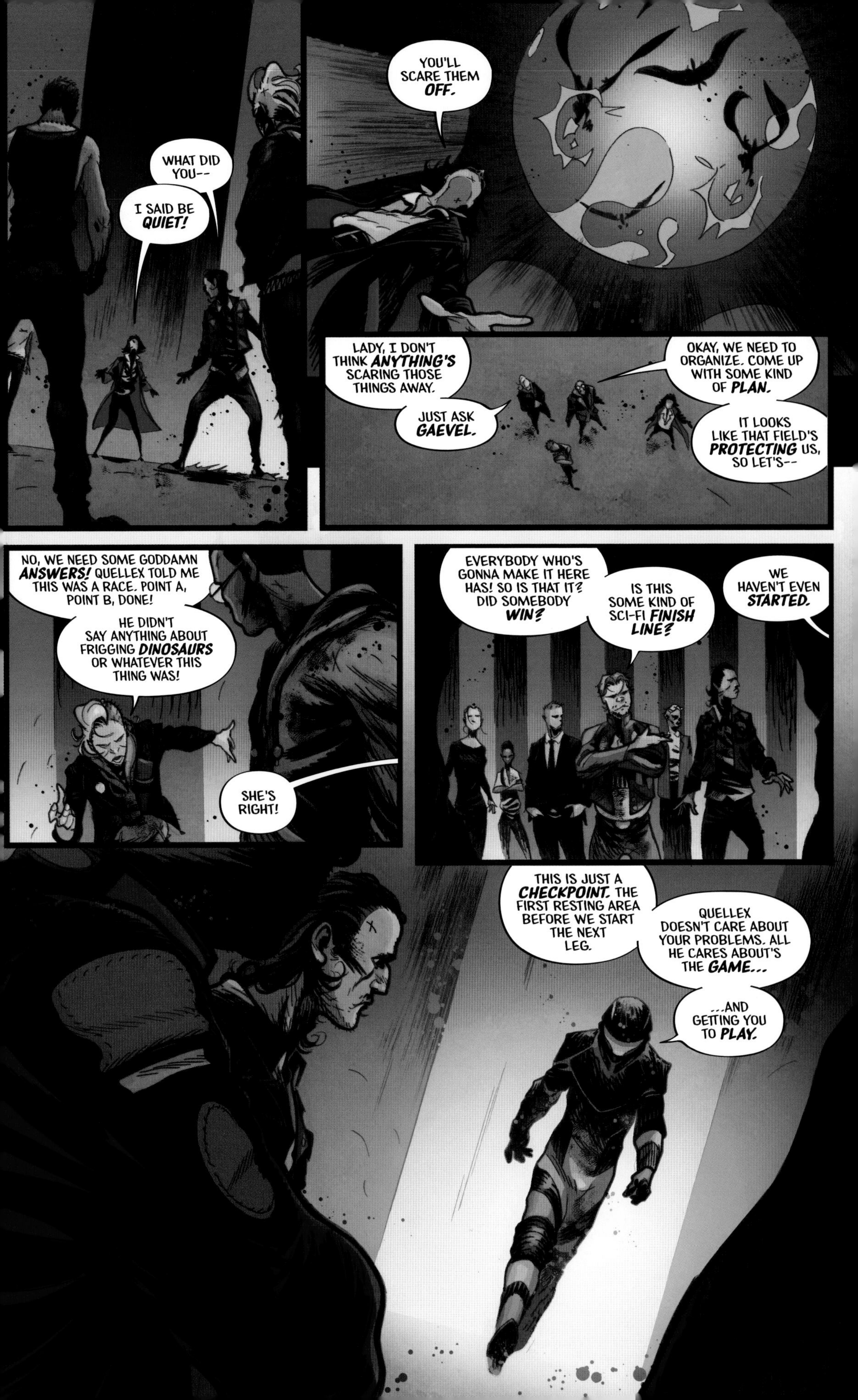
WHAT DID YOU--
I SAID BE QUIET!
YOU'LL SCARE THEM OFF.
LADY, I DON'T THINK ANYTHING'S SCARING THOSE THINGS AWAY.
JUST ASK GAEVEL.
OKAY, WE NEED TO ORGANIZE. COME UP WITH SOME KIND OF PLAN.
IT LOOKS LIKE THAT FIELD'S PROTECTING US, SO LET'S--
NO, WE NEED SOME GODDAMN ANSWERS! QUELLEX TOLD ME THIS WAS A RACE. POINT A, POINT B, DONE!
HE DIDN'T SAY ANYTHING ABOUT FRIGGING DINOSAURS OR WHATEVER THIS THING WAS!
SHE'S RIGHT!
EVERYBODY WHO'S GONNA MAKE IT HERE HAS! SO IS THAT IT? DID SOMEBODY WIN?
IS THIS SOME KIND OF SCI-FI FINISH LINE?
WE HAVEN'T EVEN STARTED.
THIS IS JUST A CHECKPOINT. THE FIRST RESTING AREA BEFORE WE START THE NEXT LEG.
QUELLEX DOESN'T CARE ABOUT YOUR PROBLEMS. ALL HE CARES ABOUT'S THE GAME...
...AND GETTING YOU TO PLAY.

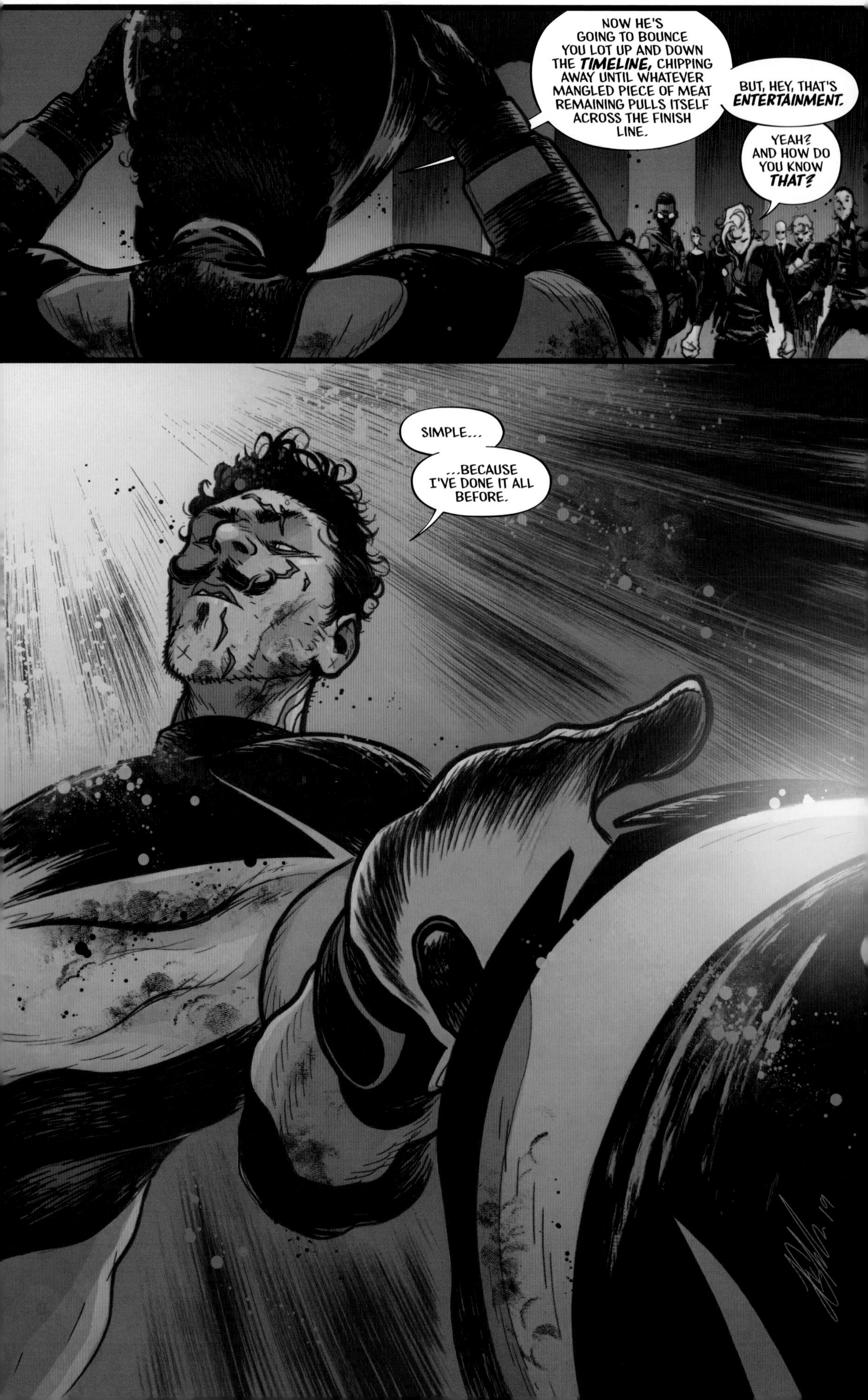
NOW HE'S GOING TO BOUNCE YOU LOT UP AND DOWN THE *TIMELINE,* CHIPPING AWAY UNTIL WHATEVER MANGLED PIECE OF MEAT REMAINING PULLS ITSELF ACROSS THE FINISH LINE.
BUT, HEY, THAT'S *ENTERTAINMENT.*
YEAH? AND HOW DO YOU KNOW *THAT?*
SIMPLE...
...BECAUSE I'VE DONE IT ALL BEFORE.

CHAPTER 2

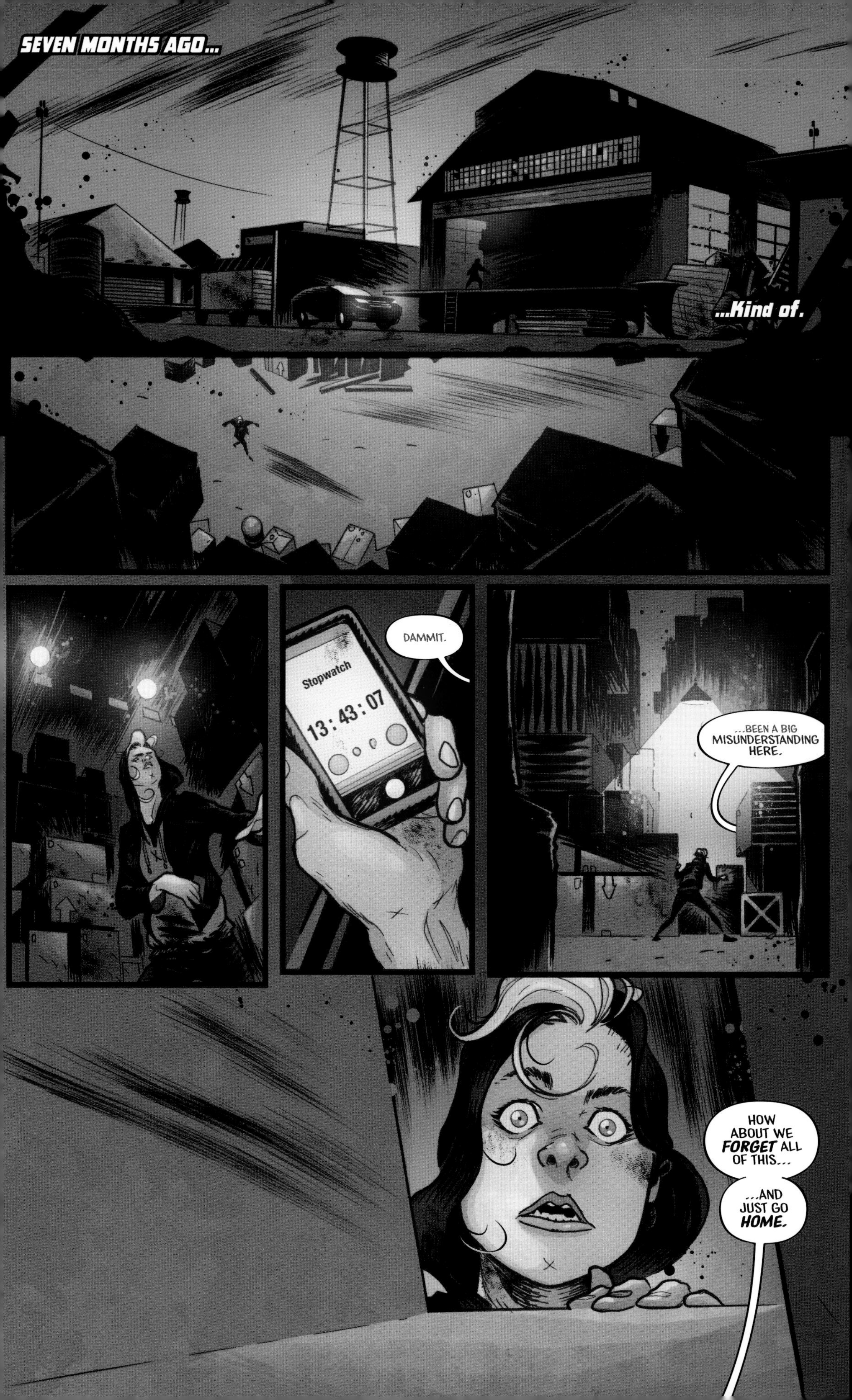

SEVEN MONTHS AGO...
...Kind of.
Stopwatch
13:43:07
DAMMIT.
...BEEN A BIG MISUNDERSTANDING HERE.
HOW ABOUT WE FORGET ALL OF THIS...
...AND JUST GO HOME.

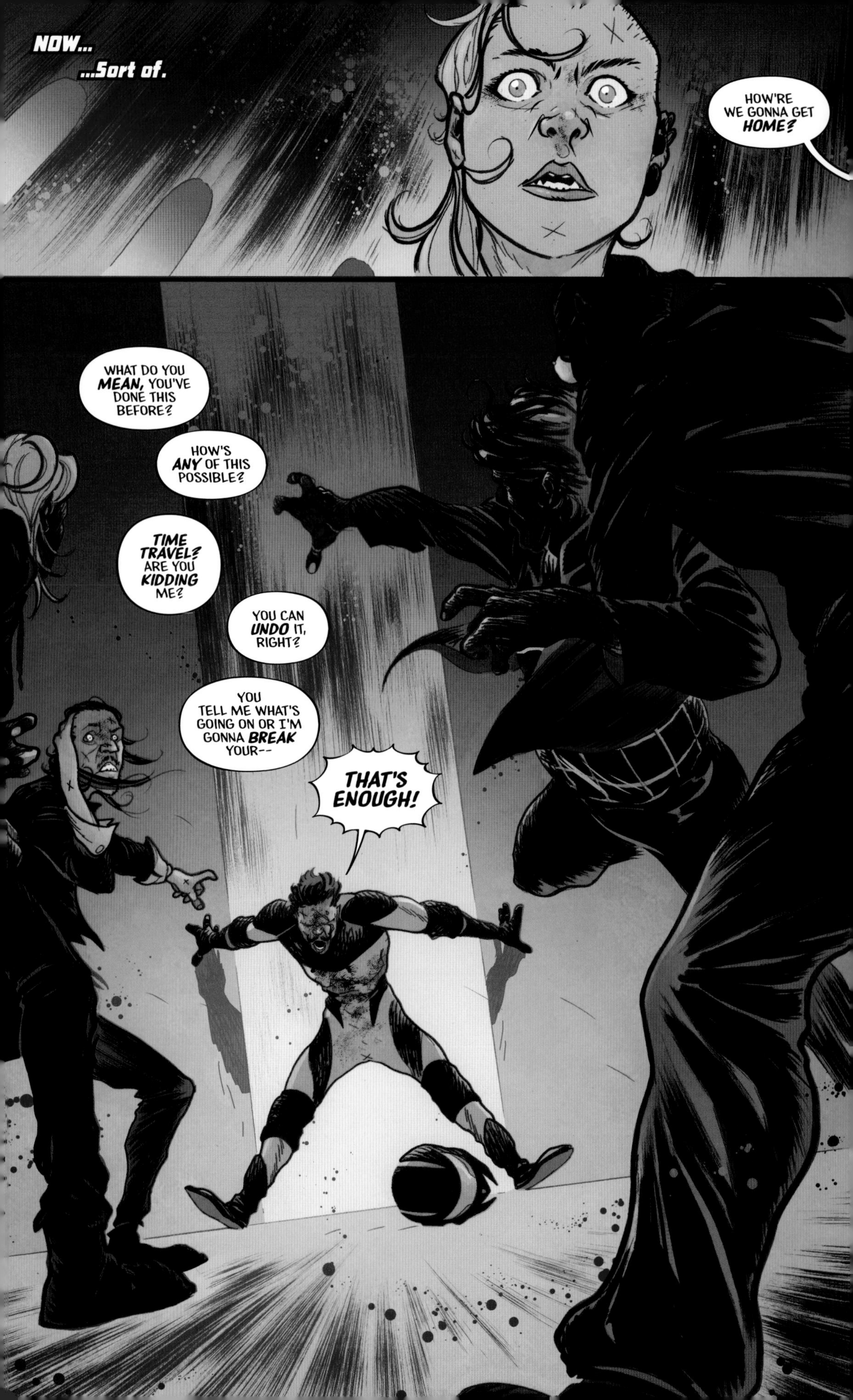
NOW...
...Sort of.
HOW'RE WE GONNA GET HOME?
WHAT DO YOU MEAN, YOU'VE DONE THIS BEFORE?
HOW'S ANY OF THIS POSSIBLE?
TIME TRAVEL? ARE YOU KIDDING ME?
YOU CAN UNDO IT, RIGHT?
YOU TELL ME WHAT'S GOING ON OR I'M GONNA BREAK YOUR--
THAT'S ENOUGH!

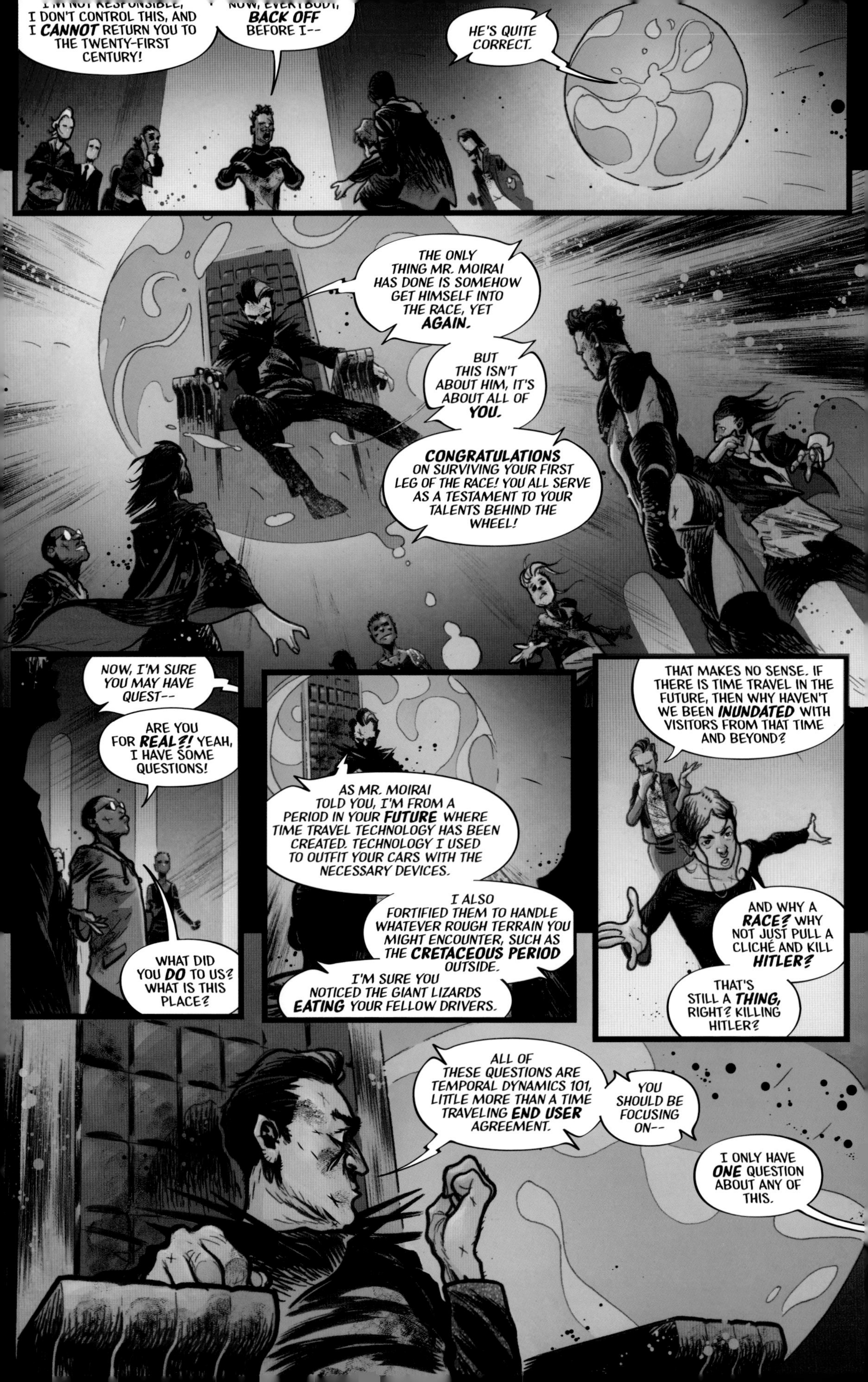
I DON'T CONTROL THIS, AND I CANNOT RETURN YOU TO THE TWENTY-FIRST CENTURY!
BACK OFF BEFORE I--
HE'S QUITE CORRECT.
THE ONLY THING MR. MOIRAI HAS DONE IS SOMEHOW GET HIMSELF INTO THE RACE, YET AGAIN.
BUT THIS ISN'T ABOUT HIM, IT'S ABOUT ALL OF YOU.
CONGRATULATIONS ON SURVIVING YOUR FIRST LEG OF THE RACE! YOU ALL SERVE AS A TESTAMENT TO YOUR TALENTS BEHIND THE WHEEL!
NOW, I'M SURE YOU MAY HAVE QUEST--
ARE YOU FOR REAL?! YEAH, I HAVE SOME QUESTIONS!
WHAT DID YOU DO TO US? WHAT IS THIS PLACE?
AS MR. MOIRAI TOLD YOU, I'M FROM A PERIOD IN YOUR FUTURE WHERE TIME TRAVEL TECHNOLOGY HAS BEEN CREATED. TECHNOLOGY I USED TO OUTFIT YOUR CARS WITH THE NECESSARY DEVICES.
I ALSO FORTIFIED THEM TO HANDLE WHATEVER ROUGH TERRAIN YOU MIGHT ENCOUNTER, SUCH AS THE CRETACEOUS PERIOD OUTSIDE.
I'M SURE YOU NOTICED THE GIANT LIZARDS EATING YOUR FELLOW DRIVERS.
THAT MAKES NO SENSE. IF THERE IS TIME TRAVEL IN THE FUTURE, THEN WHY HAVEN'T WE BEEN INUNDATED WITH VISITORS FROM THAT TIME AND BEYOND?
AND WHY A RACE? WHY NOT JUST PULL A CLICHÉ AND KILL HITLER?
THAT'S STILL A THING, RIGHT? KILLING HITLER?
ALL OF THESE QUESTIONS ARE TEMPORAL DYNAMICS 101, LITTLE MORE THAN A TIME TRAVELING END USER AGREEMENT.
YOU SHOULD BE FOCUSING ON--
I ONLY HAVE ONE QUESTION ABOUT ANY OF THIS.

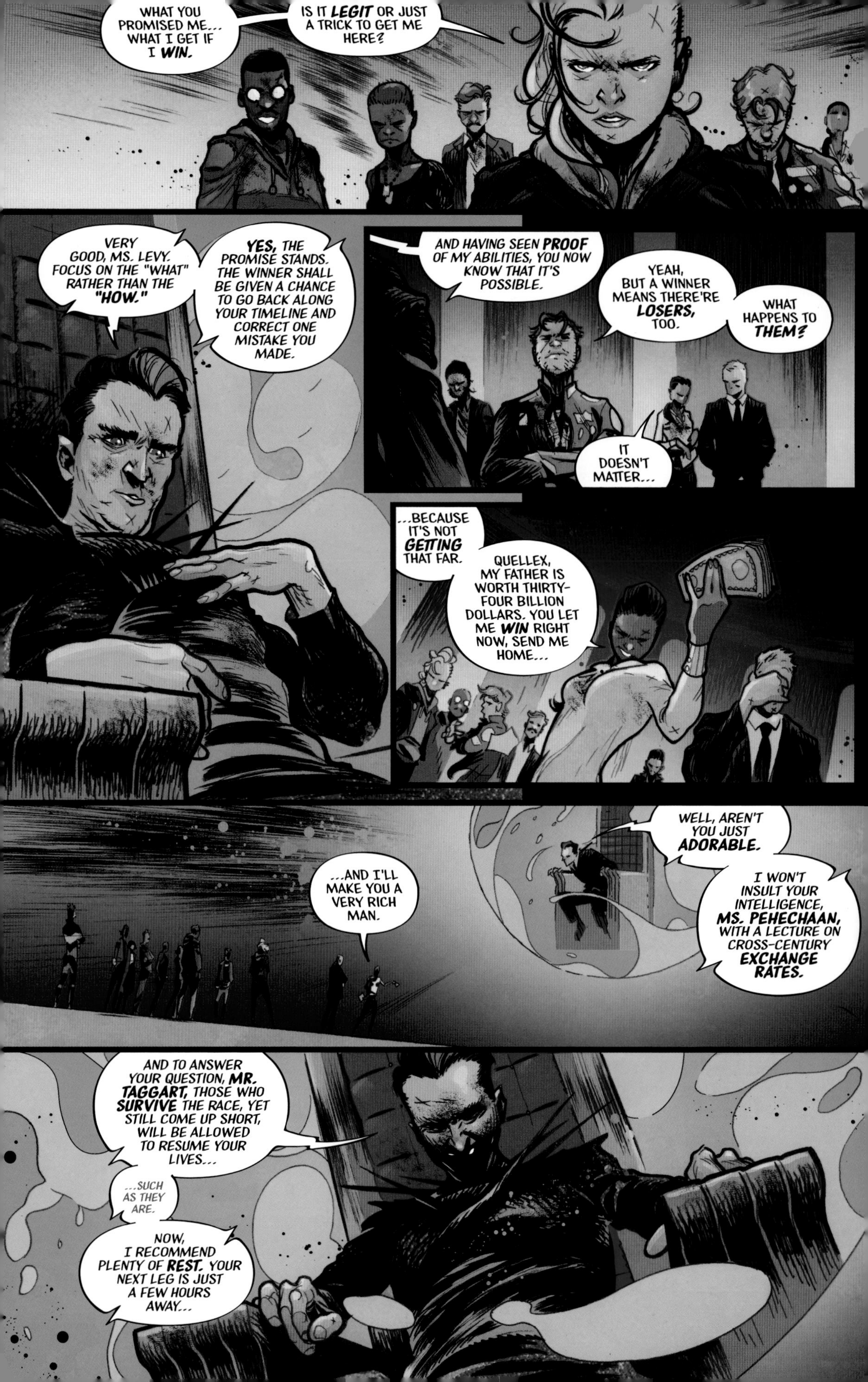
WHAT YOU PROMISED ME... WHAT I GET IF I WIN.
IS IT LEGIT OR JUST A TRICK TO GET ME HERE?
VERY GOOD, MS. LEVY. FOCUS ON THE "WHAT" RATHER THAN THE "HOW."
YES, THE PROMISE STANDS. THE WINNER SHALL BE GIVEN A CHANCE TO GO BACK ALONG YOUR TIMELINE AND CORRECT ONE MISTAKE YOU MADE.
AND HAVING SEEN PROOF OF MY ABILITIES, YOU NOW KNOW THAT IT'S POSSIBLE.
YEAH, BUT A WINNER MEANS THERE'RE LOSERS, TOO.
WHAT HAPPENS TO THEM?
IT DOESN'T MATTER...
...BECAUSE IT'S NOT GETTING THAT FAR.
QUELLEX, MY FATHER IS WORTH THIRTY-FOUR BILLION DOLLARS. YOU LET ME WIN RIGHT NOW, SEND ME HOME...
...AND I'LL MAKE YOU A VERY RICH MAN.
WELL, AREN'T YOU JUST ADORABLE.
I WON'T INSULT YOUR INTELLIGENCE, MS. PEHECHAAN, WITH A LECTURE ON CROSS-CENTURY EXCHANGE RATES.
AND TO ANSWER YOUR QUESTION, MR. TAGGART, THOSE WHO SURVIVE THE RACE, YET STILL COME UP SHORT, WILL BE ALLOWED TO RESUME YOUR LIVES...
...SUCH AS THEY ARE.
NOW, I RECOMMEND PLENTY OF REST. YOUR NEXT LEG IS JUST A FEW HOURS AWAY...

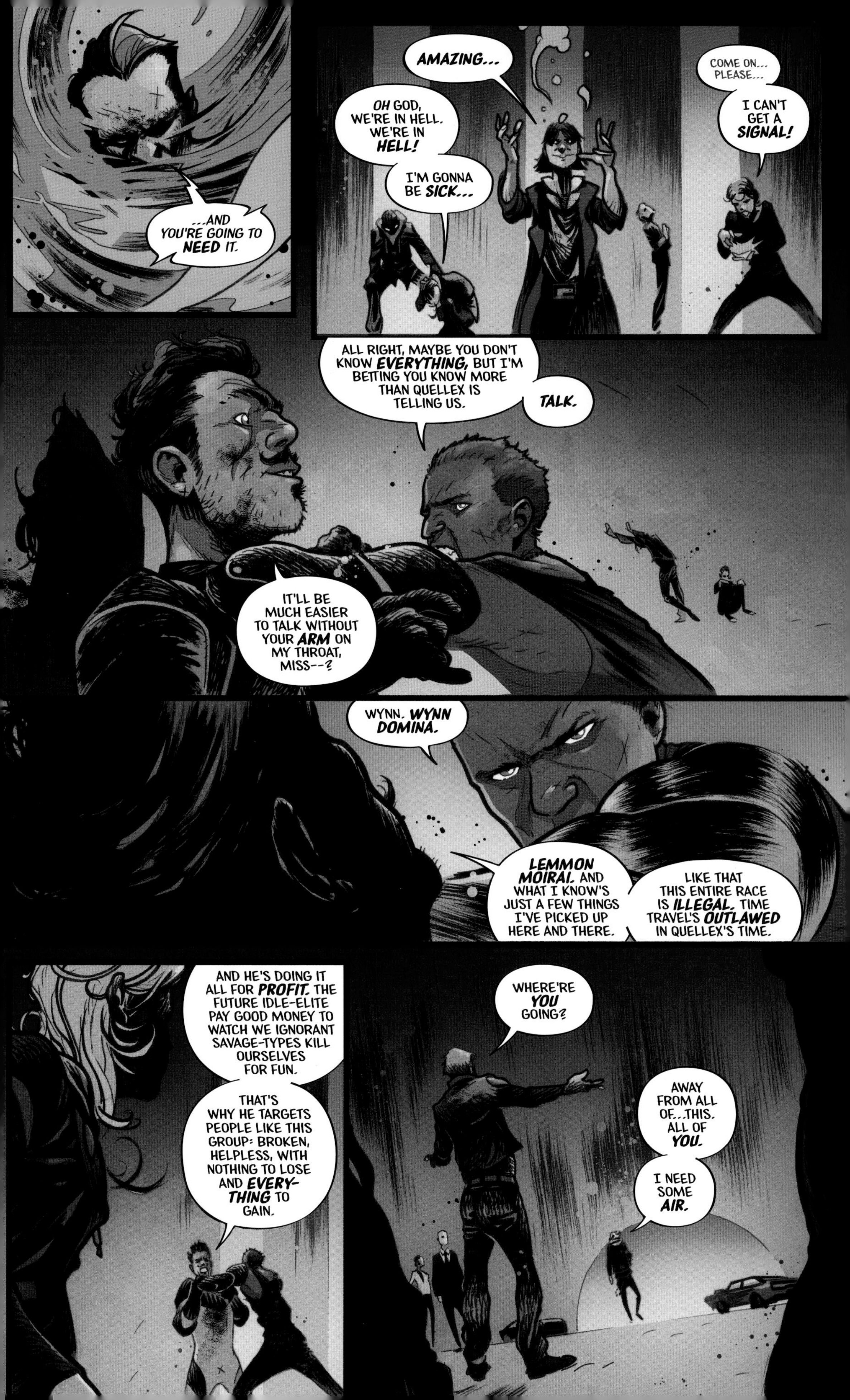
...AND YOU'RE GOING TO NEED IT.
AMAZING...
OH GOD, WE'RE IN HELL. WE'RE IN HELL!
I'M GONNA BE SICK...
COME ON... PLEASE...
I CAN'T GET A SIGNAL!
ALL RIGHT, MAYBE YOU DON'T KNOW EVERYTHING, BUT I'M BETTING YOU KNOW MORE THAN QUELLEX IS TELLING US.
TALK.
IT'LL BE MUCH EASIER TO TALK WITHOUT YOUR ARM ON MY THROAT, MISS--?
WYNN. WYNN DOMINA.
LEMMON MOIRAI. AND WHAT I KNOW'S JUST A FEW THINGS I'VE PICKED UP HERE AND THERE.
LIKE THAT THIS ENTIRE RACE IS ILLEGAL. TIME TRAVEL'S OUTLAWED IN QUELLEX'S TIME.
AND HE'S DOING IT ALL FOR PROFIT. THE FUTURE IDLE-ELITE PAY GOOD MONEY TO WATCH WE IGNORANT SAVAGE-TYPES KILL OURSELVES FOR FUN.
THAT'S WHY HE TARGETS PEOPLE LIKE THIS GROUP: BROKEN, HELPLESS, WITH NOTHING TO LOSE AND EVERYTHING TO GAIN.
WHERE'RE YOU GOING?
AWAY FROM ALL OF...THIS. ALL OF YOU.
I NEED SOME AIR.

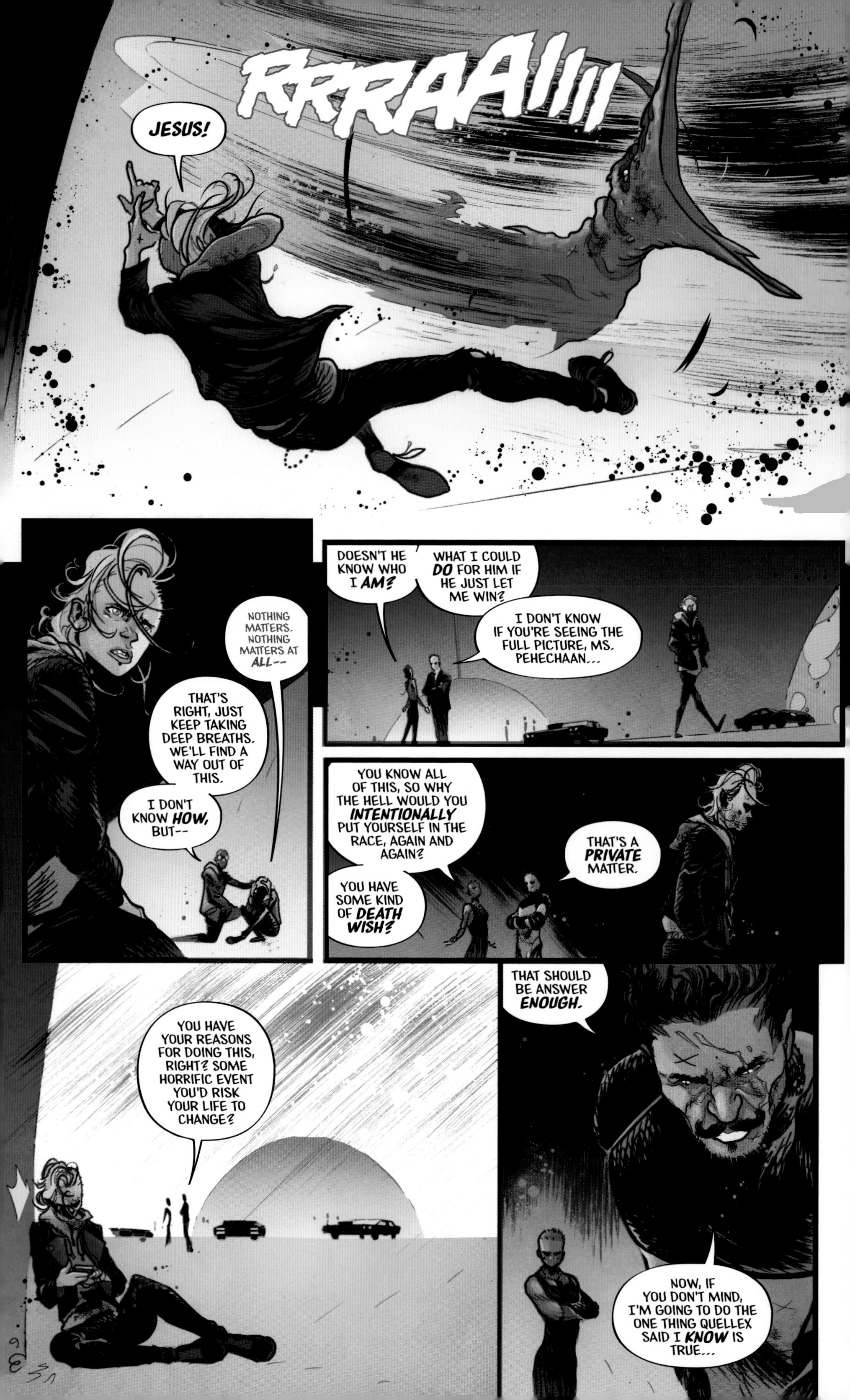
RRRAA!!!!
JESUS!
NOTHING MATTERS. NOTHING MATTERS AT ALL--
THAT'S RIGHT, JUST KEEP TAKING DEEP BREATHS. WE'LL FIND A WAY OUT OF THIS.
I DON'T KNOW HOW, BUT--
DOESN'T HE KNOW WHO I AM?
WHAT I COULD DO FOR HIM IF HE JUST LET ME WIN?
I DON'T KNOW IF YOU'RE SEEING THE FULL PICTURE, MS. PEHECHAAN...
YOU KNOW ALL OF THIS, SO WHY THE HELL WOULD YOU INTENTIONALLY PUT YOURSELF IN THE RACE, AGAIN AND AGAIN?
YOU HAVE SOME KIND OF DEATH WISH?
THAT'S A PRIVATE MATTER.
YOU HAVE YOUR REASONS FOR DOING THIS, RIGHT? SOME HORRIFIC EVENT YOU'D RISK YOUR LIFE TO CHANGE?
THAT SHOULD BE ANSWER ENOUGH.
NOW, IF YOU DON'T MIND, I'M GOING TO DO THE ONE THING QUELLEX SAID I KNOW IS TRUE...

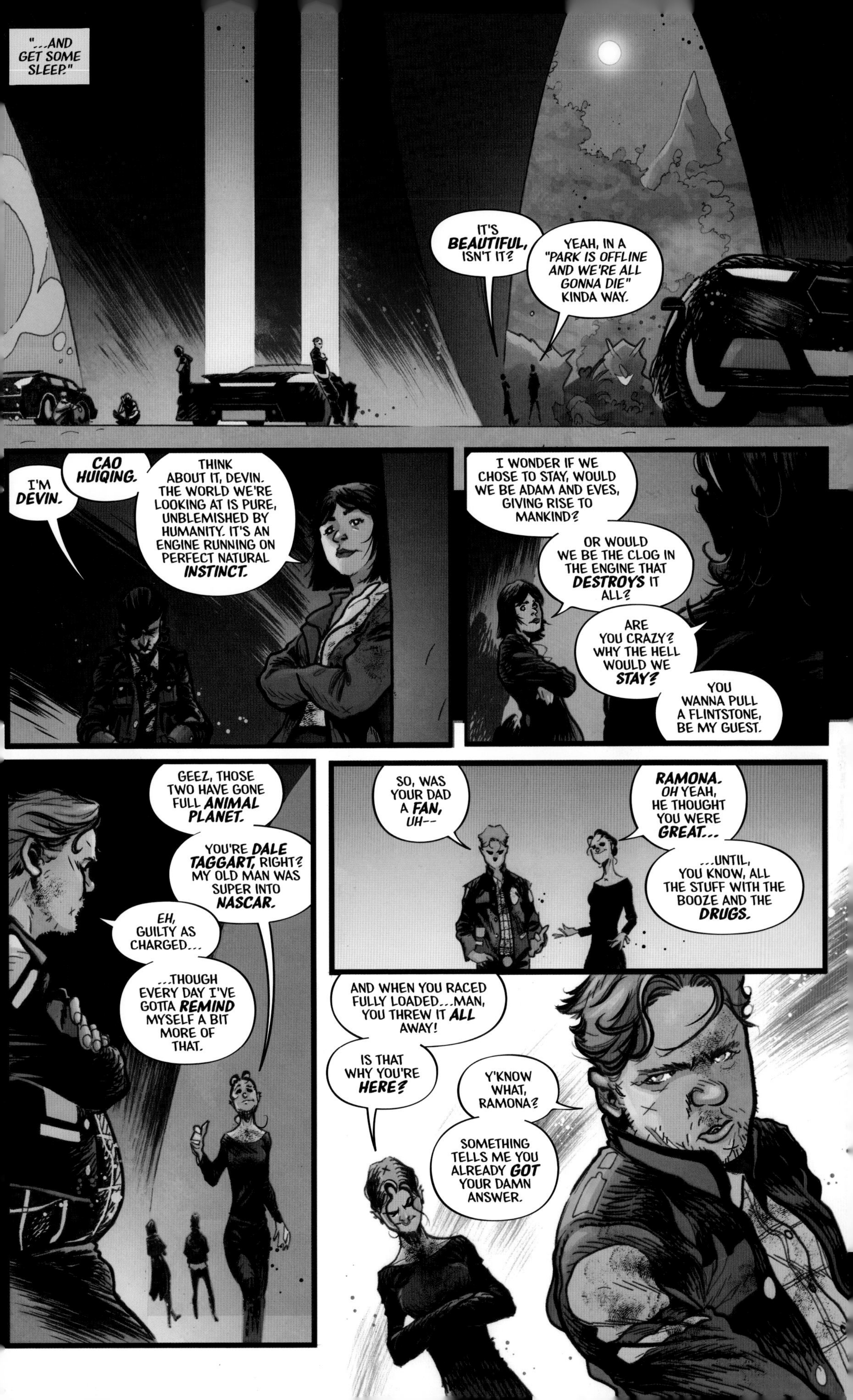
"...AND GET SOME SLEEP."
IT'S BEAUTIFUL, ISN'T IT?
YEAH, IN A "PARK IS OFFLINE AND WE'RE ALL GONNA DIE" KINDA WAY.
I'M DEVIN.
CAO HUIQING.
THINK ABOUT IT, DEVIN. THE WORLD WE'RE LOOKING AT IS PURE, UNBLEMISHED BY HUMANITY. IT'S AN ENGINE RUNNING ON PERFECT NATURAL INSTINCT.
I WONDER IF WE CHOSE TO STAY, WOULD WE BE ADAM AND EVES, GIVING RISE TO MANKIND?
OR WOULD WE BE THE CLOG IN THE ENGINE THAT DESTROYS IT ALL?
ARE YOU CRAZY? WHY THE HELL WOULD WE STAY?
YOU WANNA PULL A FLINTSTONE, BE MY GUEST.
GEEZ, THOSE TWO HAVE GONE FULL ANIMAL PLANET.
YOU'RE DALE TAGGART, RIGHT? MY OLD MAN WAS SUPER INTO NASCAR.
EH, GUILTY AS CHARGED...
...THOUGH EVERY DAY I'VE GOTTA REMIND MYSELF A BIT MORE OF THAT.
SO, WAS YOUR DAD A FAN, UH--
RAMONA. OH YEAH, HE THOUGHT YOU WERE GREAT...
...UNTIL, YOU KNOW, ALL THE STUFF WITH THE BOOZE AND THE DRUGS.
AND WHEN YOU RACED FULLY LOADED...MAN, YOU THREW IT ALL AWAY!
IS THAT WHY YOU'RE HERE?
Y'KNOW WHAT, RAMONA?
SOMETHING TELLS ME YOU ALREADY GOT YOUR DAMN ANSWER.

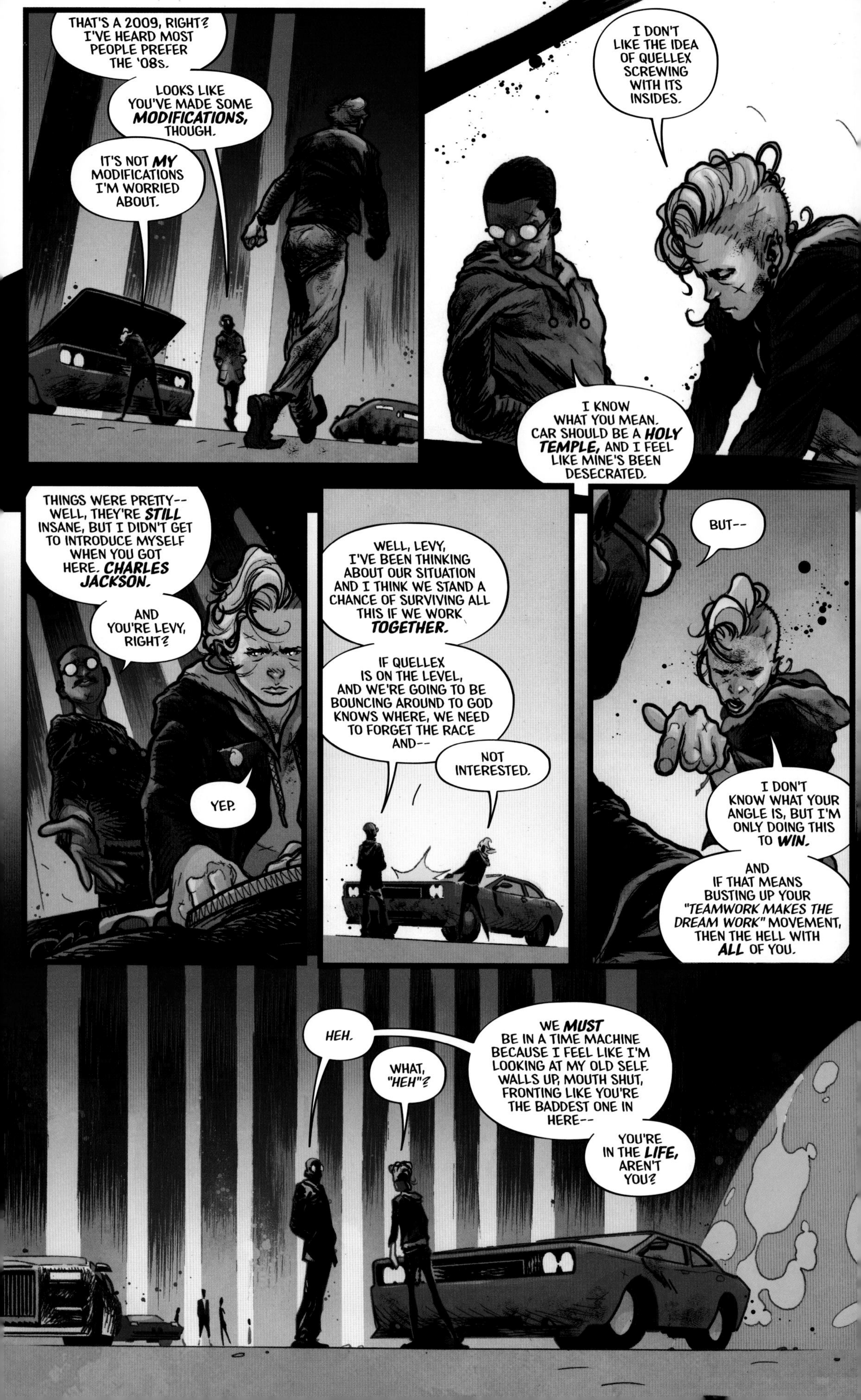
THAT'S A 2009, RIGHT? I'VE HEARD MOST PEOPLE PREFER THE '08s.
LOOKS LIKE YOU'VE MADE SOME MODIFICATIONS, THOUGH.
IT'S NOT MY MODIFICATIONS I'M WORRIED ABOUT.
I DON'T LIKE THE IDEA OF QUELLEX SCREWING WITH ITS INSIDES.
I KNOW WHAT YOU MEAN. CAR SHOULD BE A HOLY TEMPLE, AND I FEEL LIKE MINE'S BEEN DESECRATED.
THINGS WERE PRETTY-- WELL, THEY'RE STILL INSANE, BUT I DIDN'T GET TO INTRODUCE MYSELF WHEN YOU GOT HERE. CHARLES JACKSON.
AND YOU'RE LEVY, RIGHT?
YEP.
WELL, LEVY, I'VE BEEN THINKING ABOUT OUR SITUATION AND I THINK WE STAND A CHANCE OF SURVIVING ALL THIS IF WE WORK TOGETHER.
IF QUELLEX IS ON THE LEVEL, AND WE'RE GOING TO BE BOUNCING AROUND TO GOD KNOWS WHERE, WE NEED TO FORGET THE RACE AND--
NOT INTERESTED.
BUT--
I DON'T KNOW WHAT YOUR ANGLE IS, BUT I'M ONLY DOING THIS TO WIN.
AND IF THAT MEANS BUSTING UP YOUR "TEAMWORK MAKES THE DREAM WORK" MOVEMENT, THEN THE HELL WITH ALL OF YOU.
HEH.
WHAT, "HEH"?
WE MUST BE IN A TIME MACHINE BECAUSE I FEEL LIKE I'M LOOKING AT MY OLD SELF. WALLS UP, MOUTH SHUT, FRONTING LIKE YOU'RE THE BADDEST ONE IN HERE--
YOU'RE IN THE LIFE, AREN'T YOU?

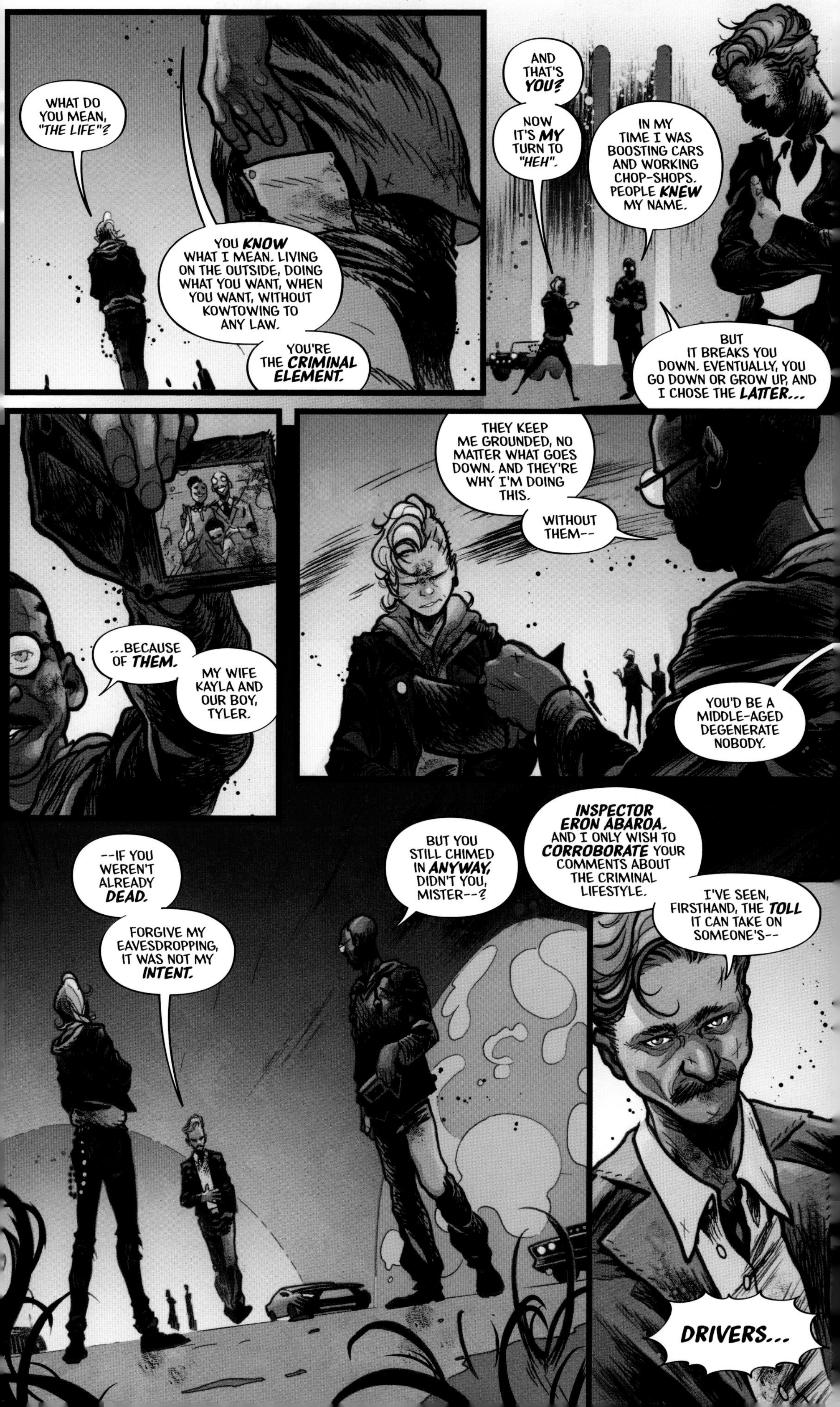

WHAT DO YOU MEAN, "THE LIFE"?
YOU KNOW WHAT I MEAN. LIVING ON THE OUTSIDE, DOING WHAT YOU WANT, WHEN YOU WANT, WITHOUT KOWTOWING TO ANY LAW.
YOU'RE THE CRIMINAL ELEMENT.
AND THAT'S YOU?
NOW IT'S MY TURN TO "HEH".
IN MY TIME I WAS BOOSTING CARS AND WORKING CHOP-SHOPS. PEOPLE KNEW MY NAME.
BUT IT BREAKS YOU DOWN. EVENTUALLY, YOU GO DOWN OR GROW UP, AND I CHOSE THE LATTER...
...BECAUSE OF THEM.
MY WIFE KAYLA AND OUR BOY, TYLER.
THEY KEEP ME GROUNDED, NO MATTER WHAT GOES DOWN. AND THEY'RE WHY I'M DOING THIS.
WITHOUT THEM--
YOU'D BE A MIDDLE-AGED DEGENERATE NOBODY.
--IF YOU WEREN'T ALREADY DEAD.
FORGIVE MY EAVESDROPPING, IT WAS NOT MY INTENT.
BUT YOU STILL CHIMED IN ANYWAY, DIDN'T YOU, MISTER--?
INSPECTOR ERON ABAROA. AND I ONLY WISH TO CORROBORATE YOUR COMMENTS ABOUT THE CRIMINAL LIFESTYLE.
I'VE SEEN, FIRSTHAND, THE TOLL IT CAN TAKE ON SOMEONE'S--
DRIVERS...

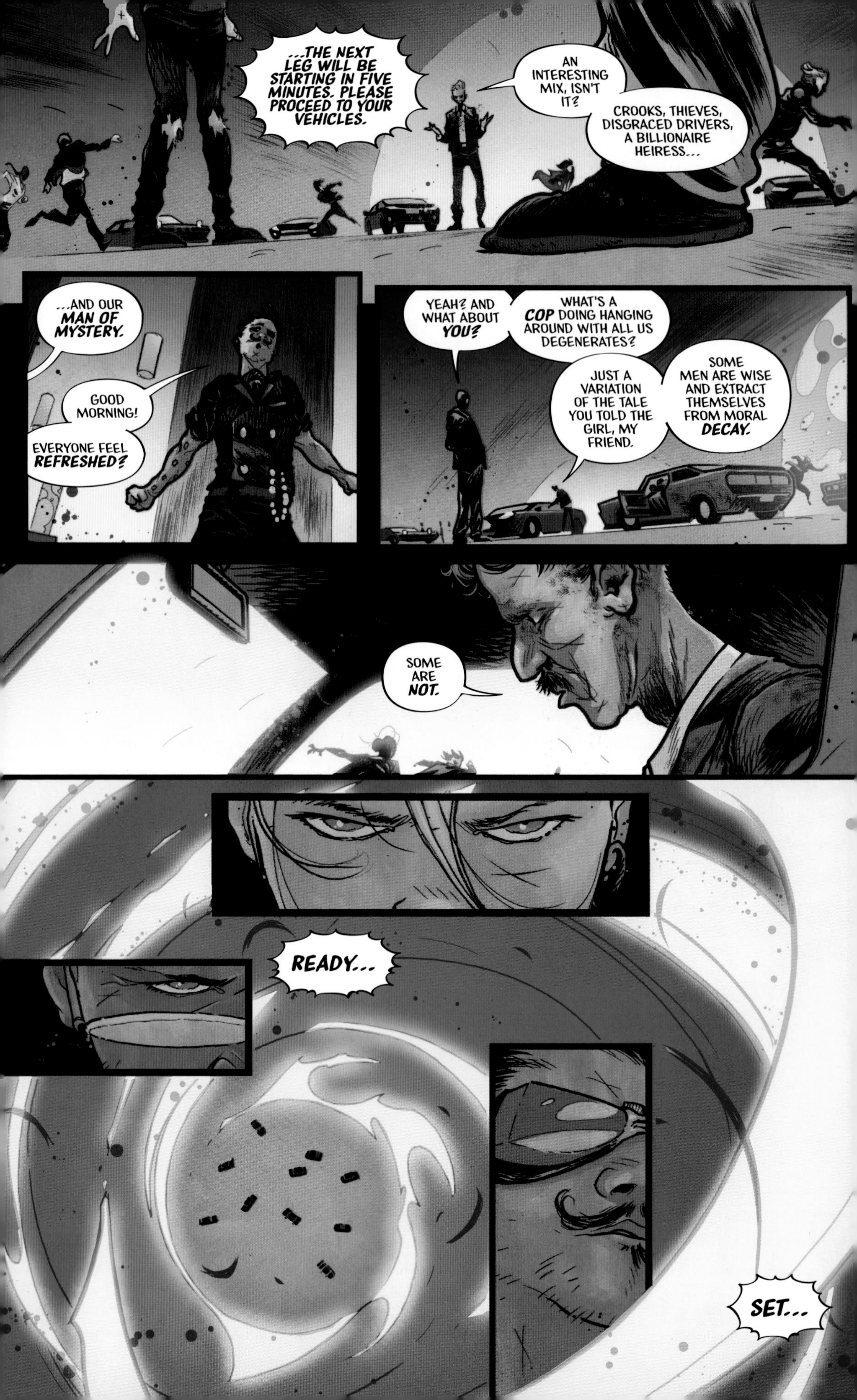
...THE NEXT LEG WILL BE STARTING IN FIVE MINUTES. PLEASE PROCEED TO YOUR VEHICLES.
AN INTERESTING MIX, ISN'T IT?
CROOKS, THIEVES, DISGRACED DRIVERS, A BILLIONAIRE HEIRESS...
...AND OUR MAN OF MYSTERY.
GOOD MORNING!
EVERYONE FEEL REFRESHED?
YEAH? AND WHAT ABOUT YOU?
WHAT'S A COP DOING HANGING AROUND WITH ALL US DEGENERATES?
SOME MEN ARE WISE AND EXTRACT THEMSELVES FROM MORAL DECAY.
JUST A VARIATION OF THE TALE YOU TOLD THE GIRL, MY FRIEND.
SOME ARE NOT.
READY...
SET...

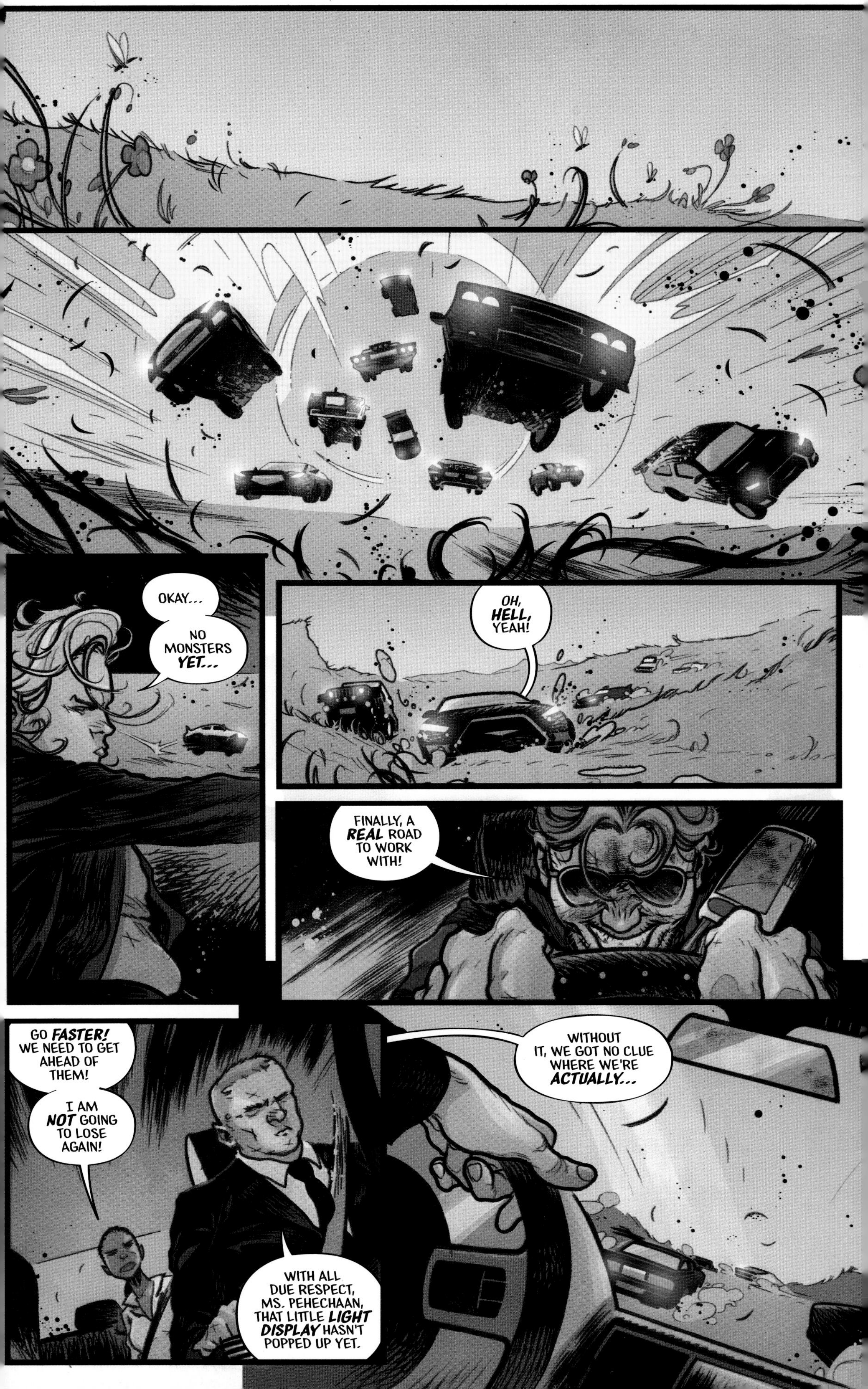
OKAY...
NO MONSTERS YET...
OH, HELL, YEAH!
FINALLY, A REAL ROAD TO WORK WITH!
GO FASTER! WE NEED TO GET AHEAD OF THEM!
I AM NOT GOING TO LOSE AGAIN!
WITH ALL DUE RESPECT, MS. PEHECHAAN, THAT LITTLE LIGHT DISPLAY HASN'T POPPED UP YET.
WITHOUT IT, WE GOT NO CLUE WHERE WE'RE ACTUALLY...

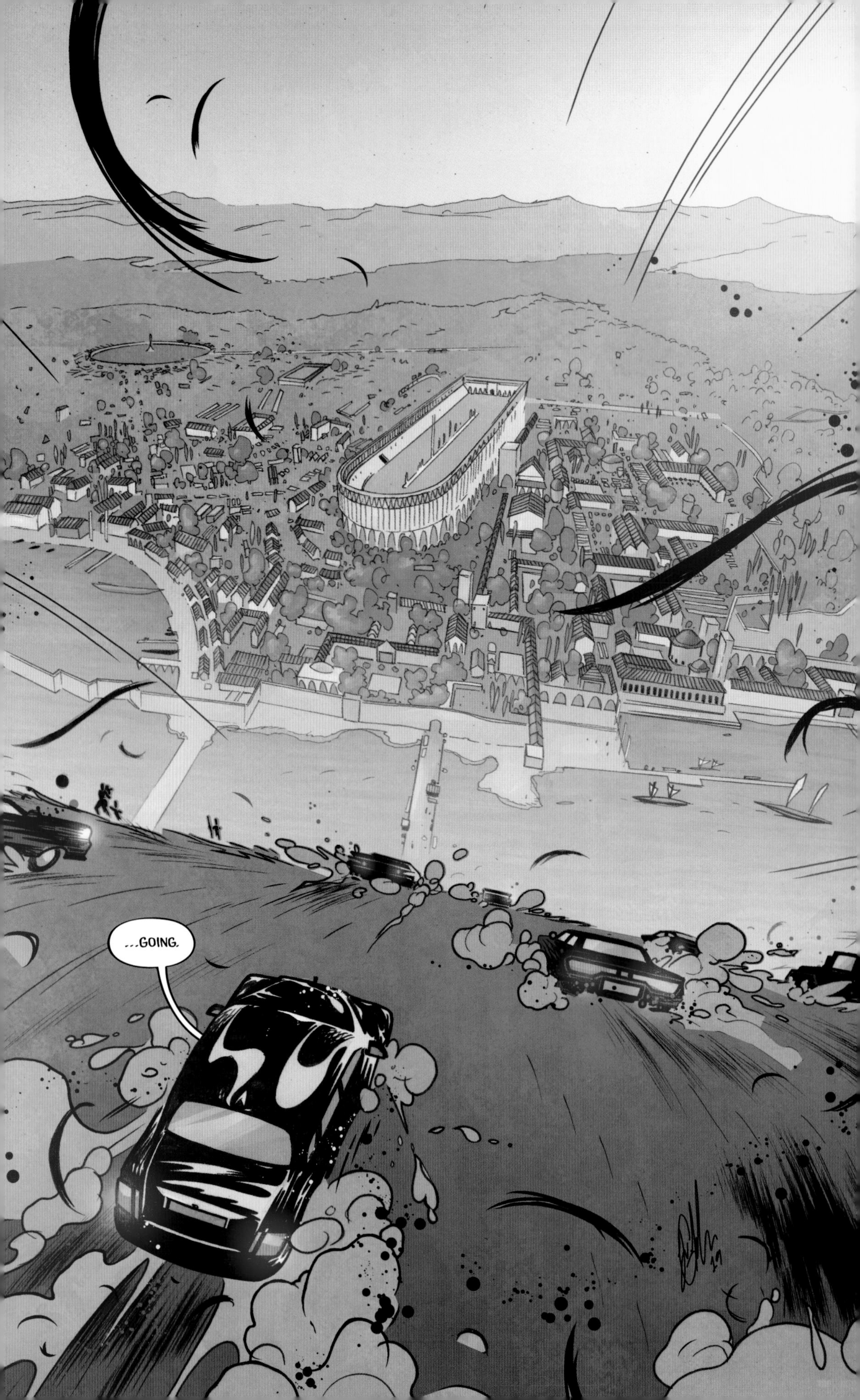
...GOING.

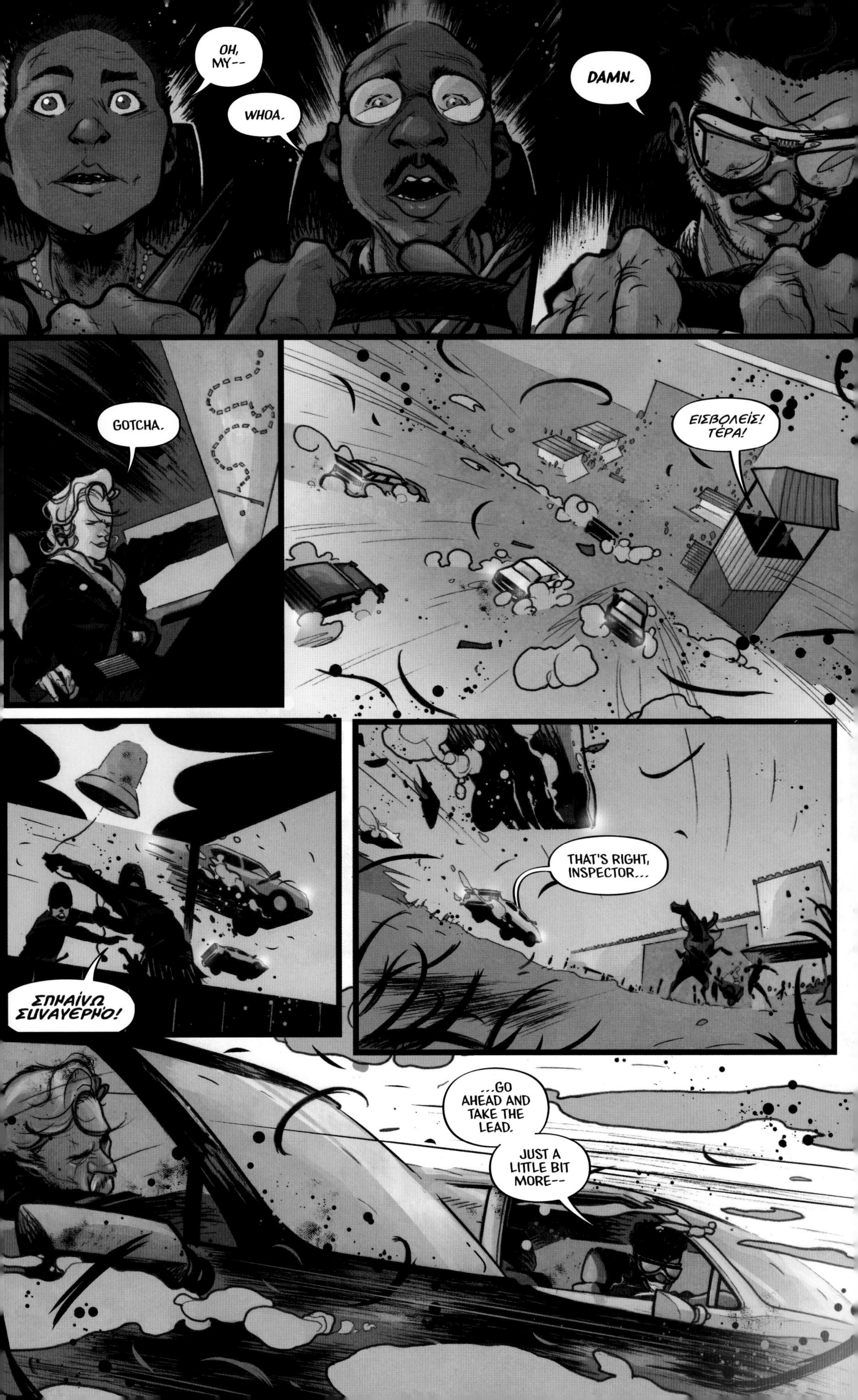

OH, MY--
WHOA.
DAMN.
GOTCHA.
ΕΙΣΒΟΛΕΙΣ! ΤΕΡΑ!
ΣΗΜΑΙΝΩ ΣΥΝΑΓΕΡΜΟ!
THAT'S RIGHT, INSPECTOR...
...GO AHEAD AND TAKE THE LEAD.
JUST A LITTLE BIT MORE--

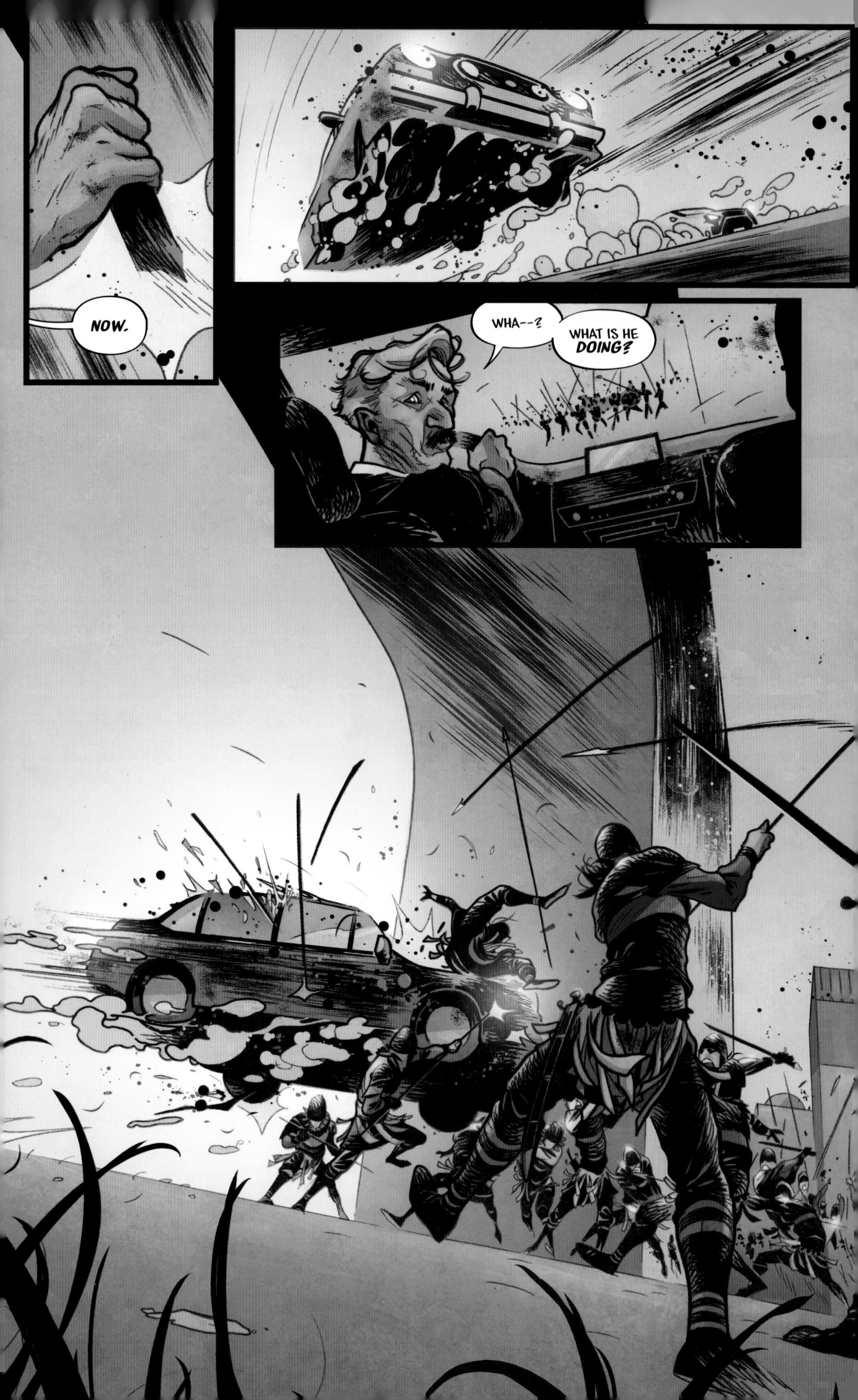
NOW.
WHA--?
WHAT IS HE DOING?

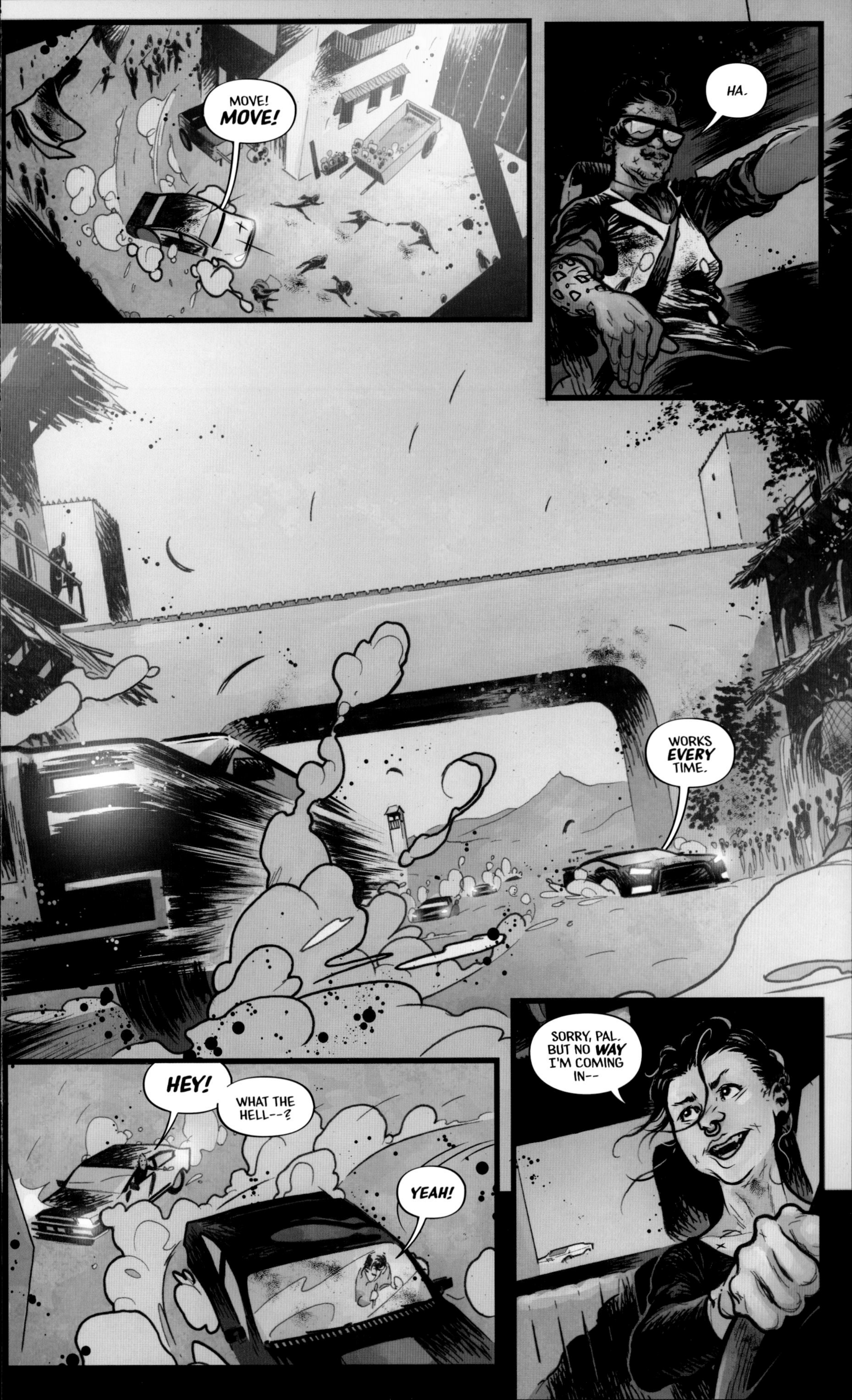
MOVE! MOVE!
HA.
WORKS EVERY TIME.
SORRY, PAL, BUT NO WAY I'M COMING IN--
HEY!
WHAT THE HELL--?
YEAH!

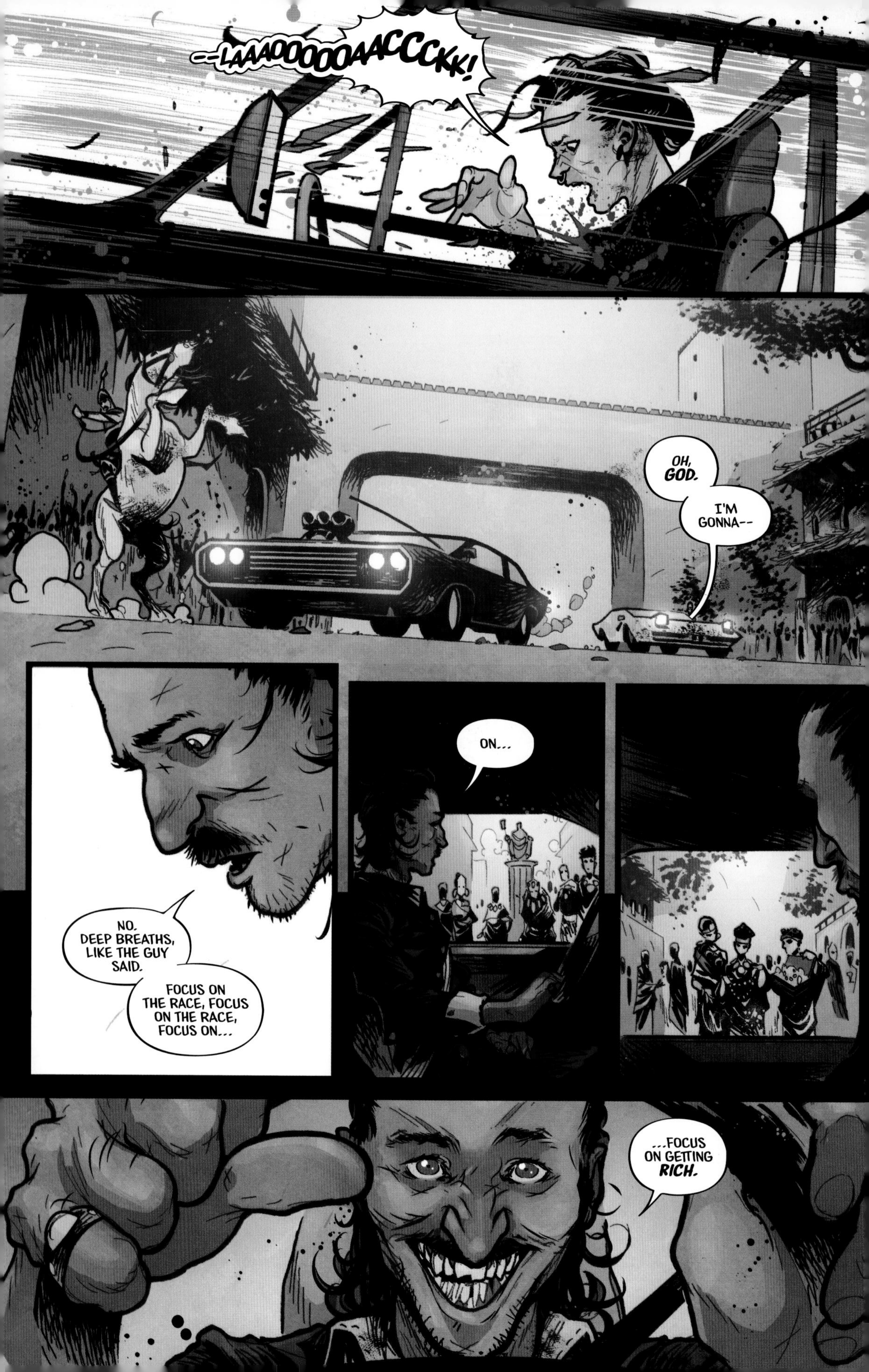
--LAAAOOOOOAACCCCKK!
OH, GOD.
I'M GONNA--
NO. DEEP BREATHS, LIKE THE GUY SAID.
FOCUS ON THE RACE, FOCUS ON THE RACE, FOCUS ON...
ON...
...FOCUS ON GETTING RICH.

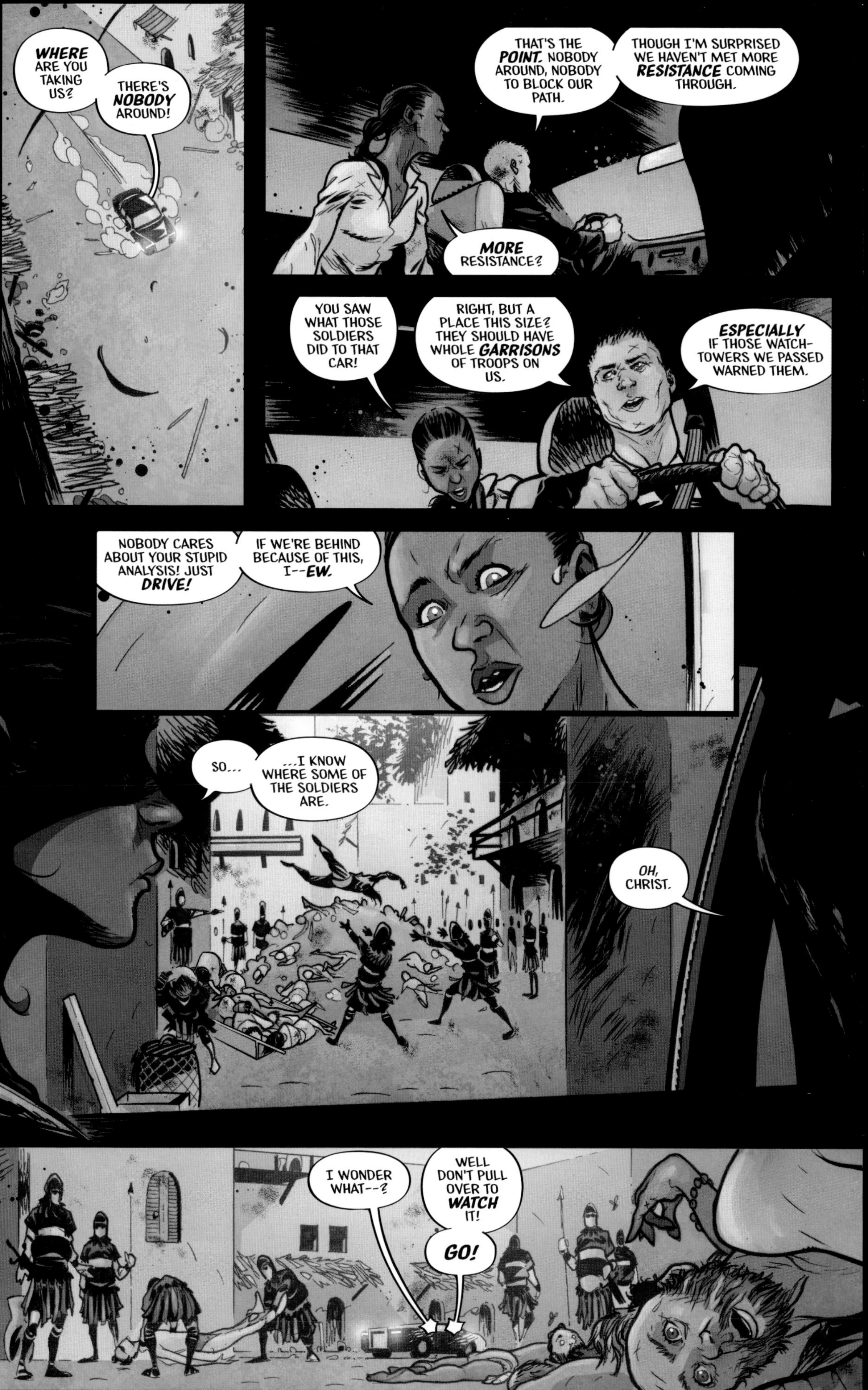
WHERE ARE YOU TAKING US?
THERE'S NOBODY AROUND!
THAT'S THE POINT. NOBODY AROUND, NOBODY TO BLOCK OUR PATH.
THOUGH I'M SURPRISED WE HAVEN'T MET MORE RESISTANCE COMING THROUGH.
MORE RESISTANCE?
YOU SAW WHAT THOSE SOLDIERS DID TO THAT CAR!
RIGHT, BUT A PLACE THIS SIZE? THEY SHOULD HAVE WHOLE GARRISONS OF TROOPS ON US.
ESPECIALLY IF THOSE WATCH-TOWERS WE PASSED WARNED THEM.
NOBODY CARES ABOUT YOUR STUPID ANALYSIS! JUST DRIVE!
IF WE'RE BEHIND BECAUSE OF THIS, I--EW.
SO...
...I KNOW WHERE SOME OF THE SOLDIERS ARE.
OH, CHRIST.
I WONDER WHAT--?
WELL DON'T PULL OVER TO WATCH IT!
GO!

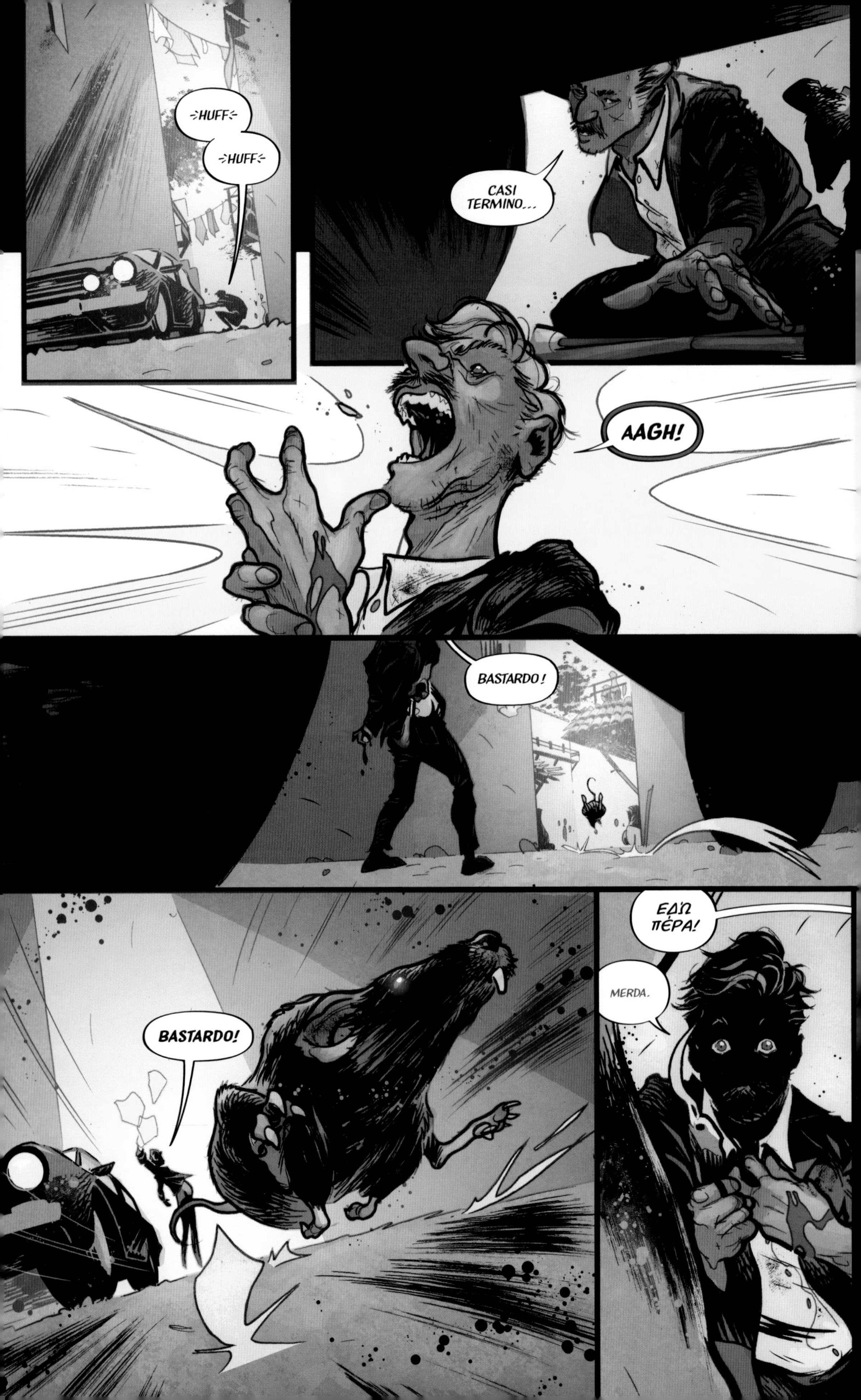

HUFF
HUFF
CASI TERMINO...
AAGH!
BASTARDO!
BASTARDO!
ΕΔΏ ΠΈΡΑ!
MERDA.

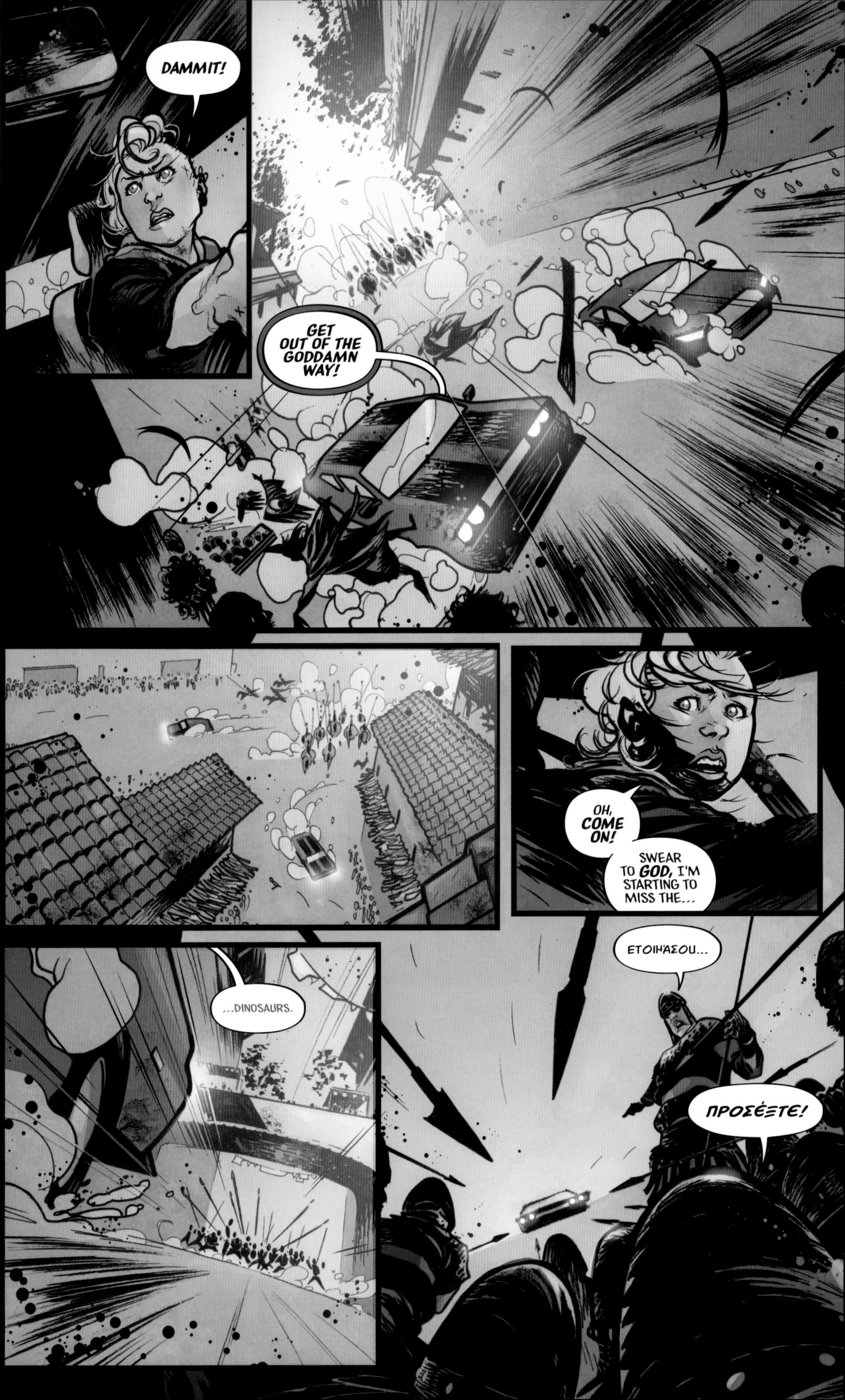
DAMMIT!
GET OUT OF THE GODDAMN WAY!
OH, COME ON!
SWEAR TO GOD, I'M STARTING TO MISS THE...
...DINOSAURS.
ΕΤΟΙΜΆΣΟΥ...
ΠΡΟΣΈΞΤΕ!

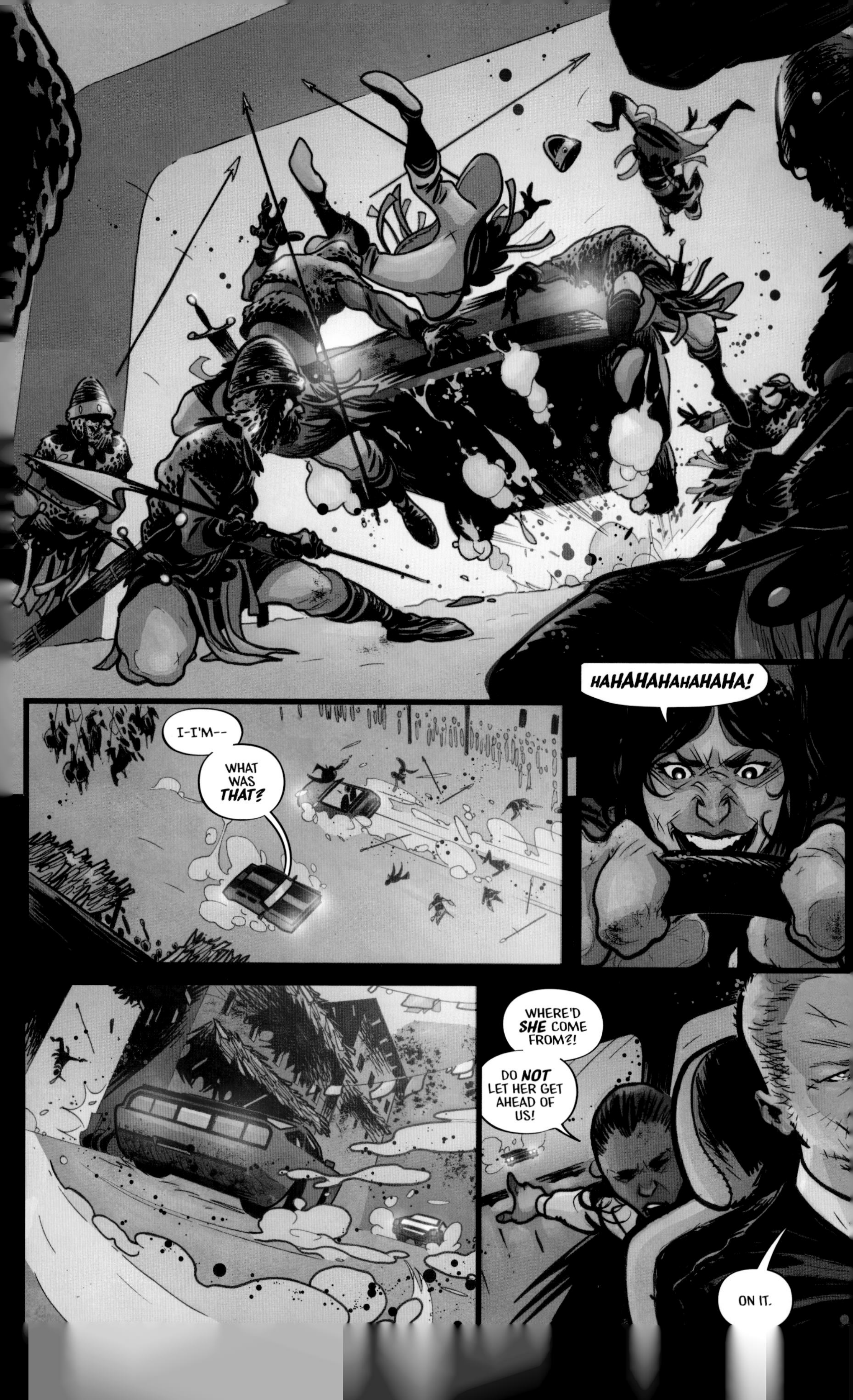
HAHAHAHAHAHAHA!
I-I'M--
WHAT WAS THAT?
WHERE'D SHE COME FROM?!
DO NOT LET HER GET AHEAD OF US!
ON IT.

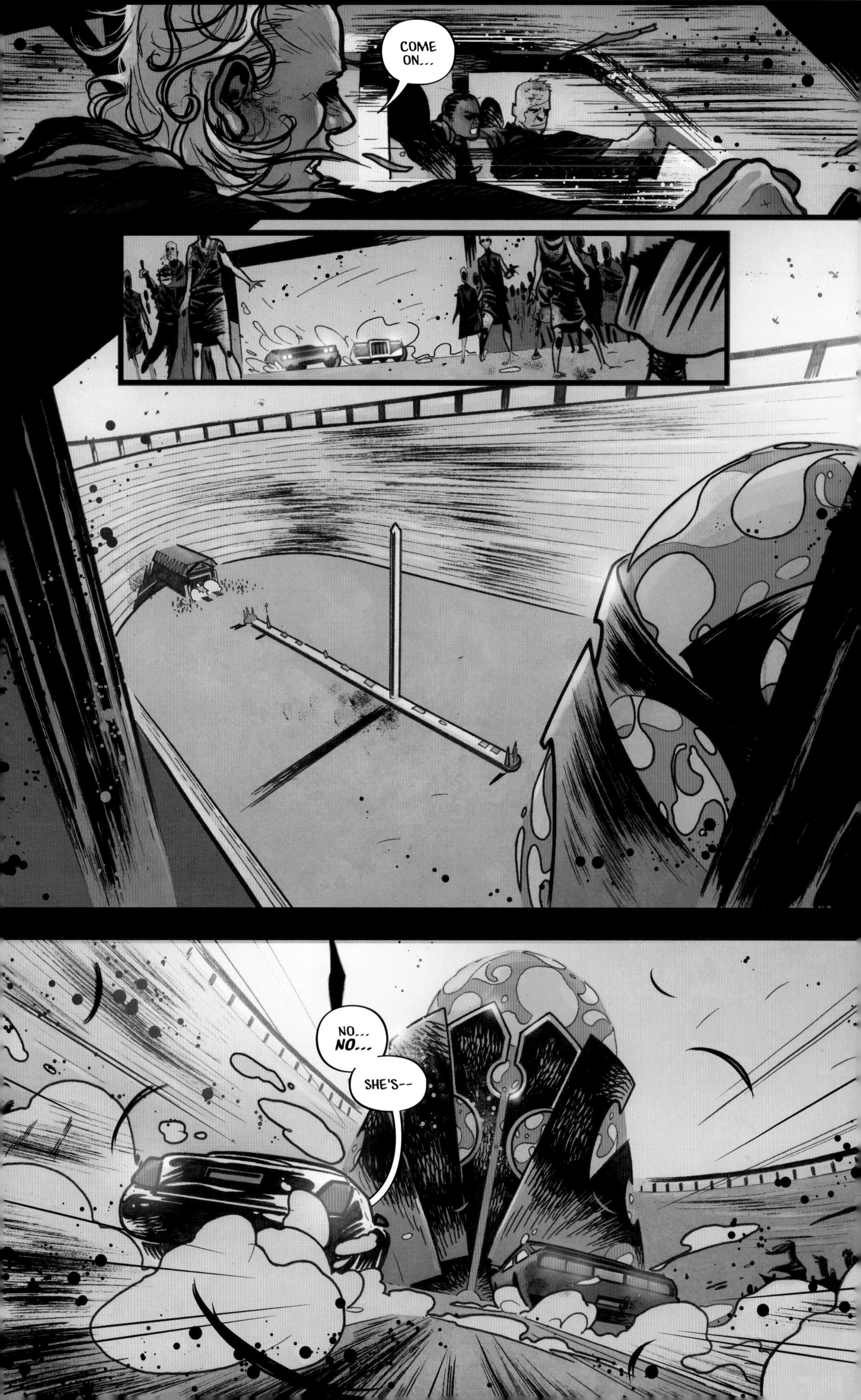
COME ON...
NO... NO...
SHE'S--

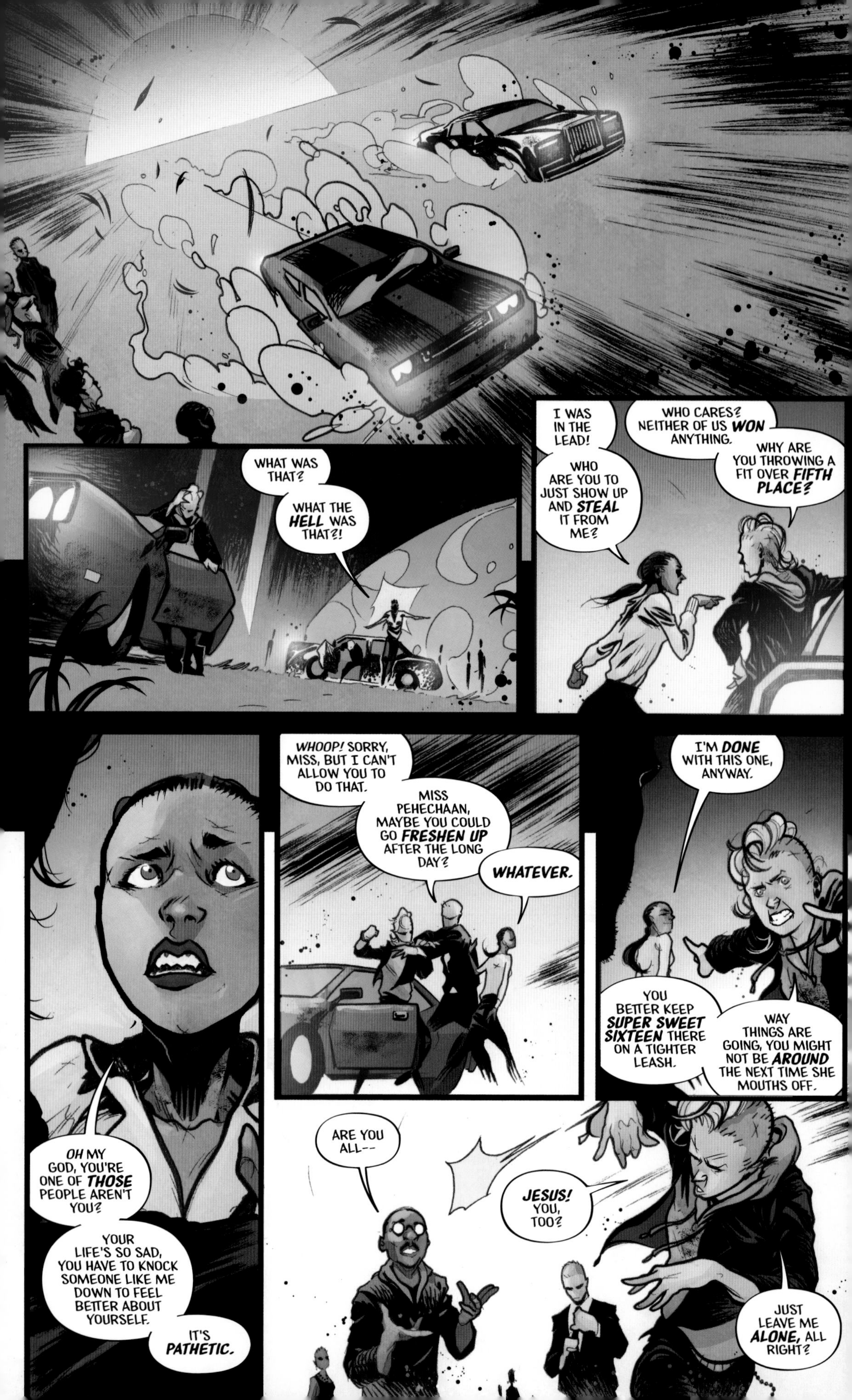
WHAT WAS THAT?
WHAT THE HELL WAS THAT?!
I WAS IN THE LEAD!
WHO ARE YOU TO JUST SHOW UP AND STEAL IT FROM ME?
WHO CARES? NEITHER OF US WON ANYTHING.
WHY ARE YOU THROWING A FIT OVER FIFTH PLACE?
OH MY GOD, YOU'RE ONE OF THOSE PEOPLE AREN'T YOU?
YOUR LIFE'S SO SAD, YOU HAVE TO KNOCK SOMEONE LIKE ME DOWN TO FEEL BETTER ABOUT YOURSELF.
IT'S PATHETIC.
WHOOP! SORRY, MISS, BUT I CAN'T ALLOW YOU TO DO THAT.
MISS PEHECHAAN, MAYBE YOU COULD GO FRESHEN UP AFTER THE LONG DAY?
WHATEVER.
I'M DONE WITH THIS ONE, ANYWAY.
YOU BETTER KEEP SUPER SWEET SIXTEEN THERE ON A TIGHTER LEASH.
WAY THINGS ARE GOING, YOU MIGHT NOT BE AROUND THE NEXT TIME SHE MOUTHS OFF.
ARE YOU ALL--
JESUS! YOU, TOO?
JUST LEAVE ME ALONE, ALL RIGHT?

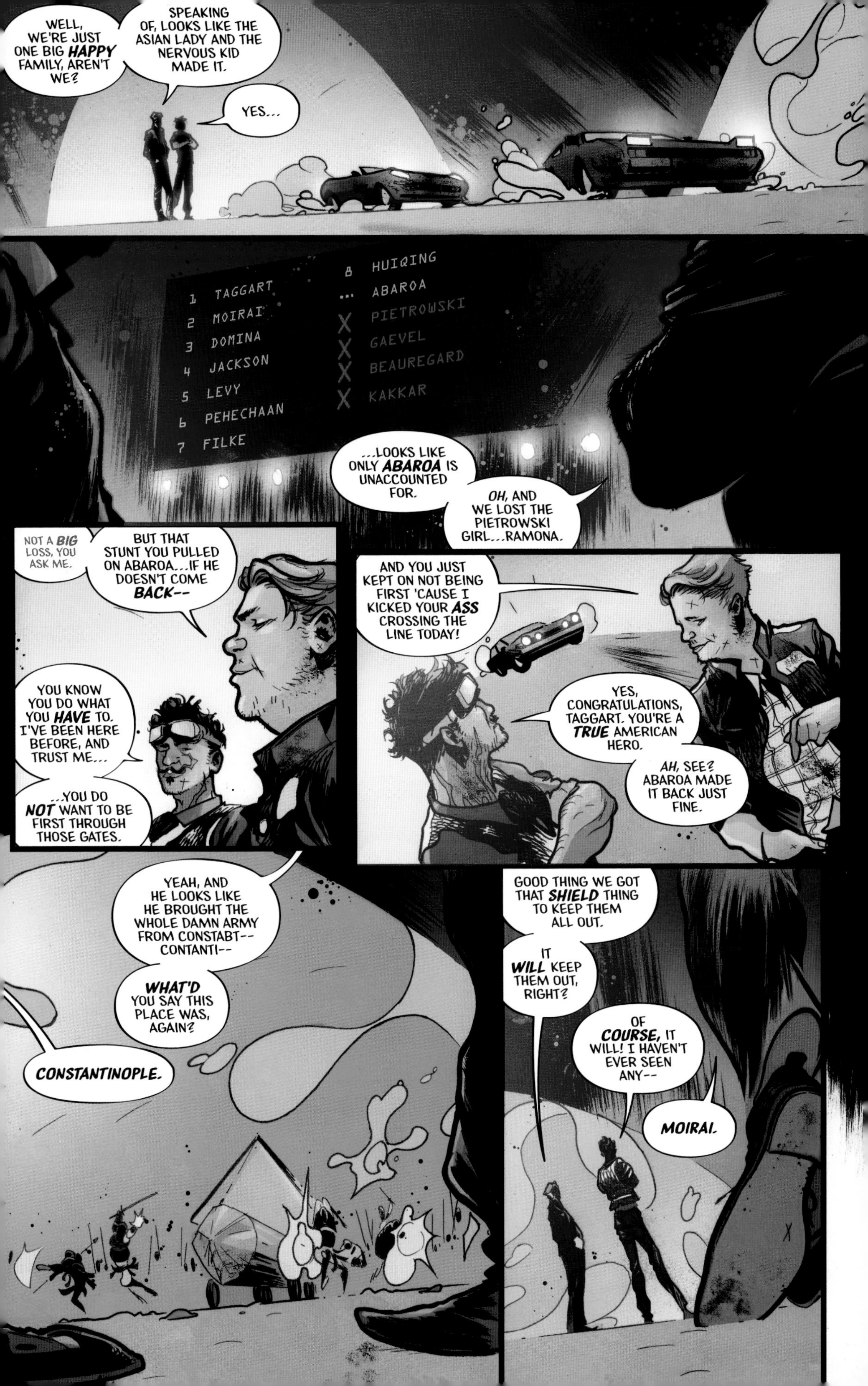

WELL, WE'RE JUST ONE BIG HAPPY FAMILY, AREN'T WE?
SPEAKING OF, LOOKS LIKE THE ASIAN LADY AND THE NERVOUS KID MADE IT.
YES...
1 TAGGART
2 MOIRAI
3 DOMINA
4 JACKSON
5 LEVY
6 PEHECHAAN
7 FILKE
8 HUIQING
... ABAROA
X PIETROWSKI
X GAEVEL
X BEAUREGARD
X KAKKAR
...LOOKS LIKE ONLY ABAROA IS UNACCOUNTED FOR.
OH, AND WE LOST THE PIETROWSKI GIRL...RAMONA.
NOT A BIG LOSS, YOU ASK ME.
BUT THAT STUNT YOU PULLED ON ABAROA...IF HE DOESN'T COME BACK--
YOU KNOW YOU DO WHAT YOU HAVE TO. I'VE BEEN HERE BEFORE, AND TRUST ME...
...YOU DO NOT WANT TO BE FIRST THROUGH THOSE GATES.
AND YOU JUST KEPT ON NOT BEING FIRST 'CAUSE I KICKED YOUR ASS CROSSING THE LINE TODAY!
YES, CONGRATULATIONS, TAGGART. YOU'RE A TRUE AMERICAN HERO.
AH, SEE? ABAROA MADE IT BACK JUST FINE.
YEAH, AND HE LOOKS LIKE HE BROUGHT THE WHOLE DAMN ARMY FROM CONSTABT--CONTANTI--
WHAT'D YOU SAY THIS PLACE WAS, AGAIN?
CONSTANTINOPLE.
GOOD THING WE GOT THAT SHIELD THING TO KEEP THEM ALL OUT.
IT WILL KEEP THEM OUT, RIGHT?
OF COURSE, IT WILL! I HAVEN'T EVER SEEN ANY--
MOIRAI.

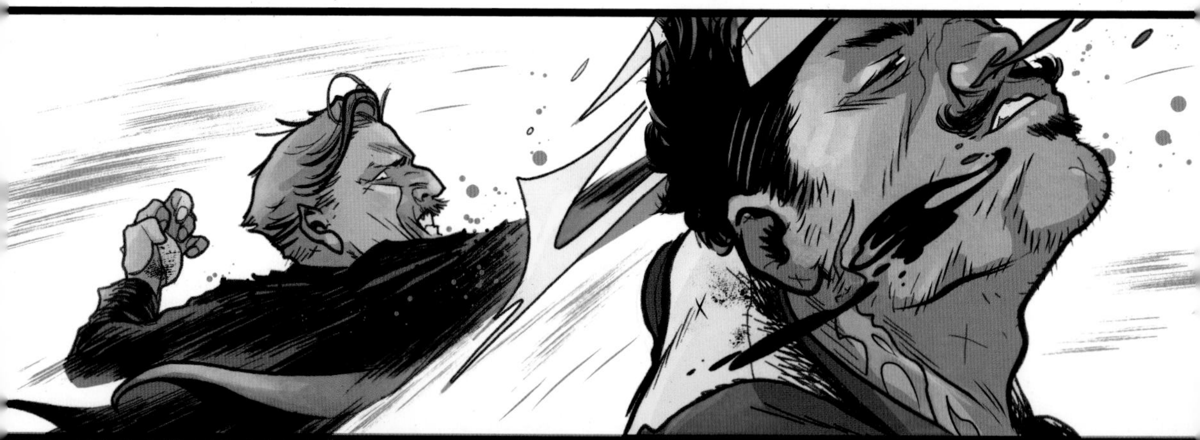

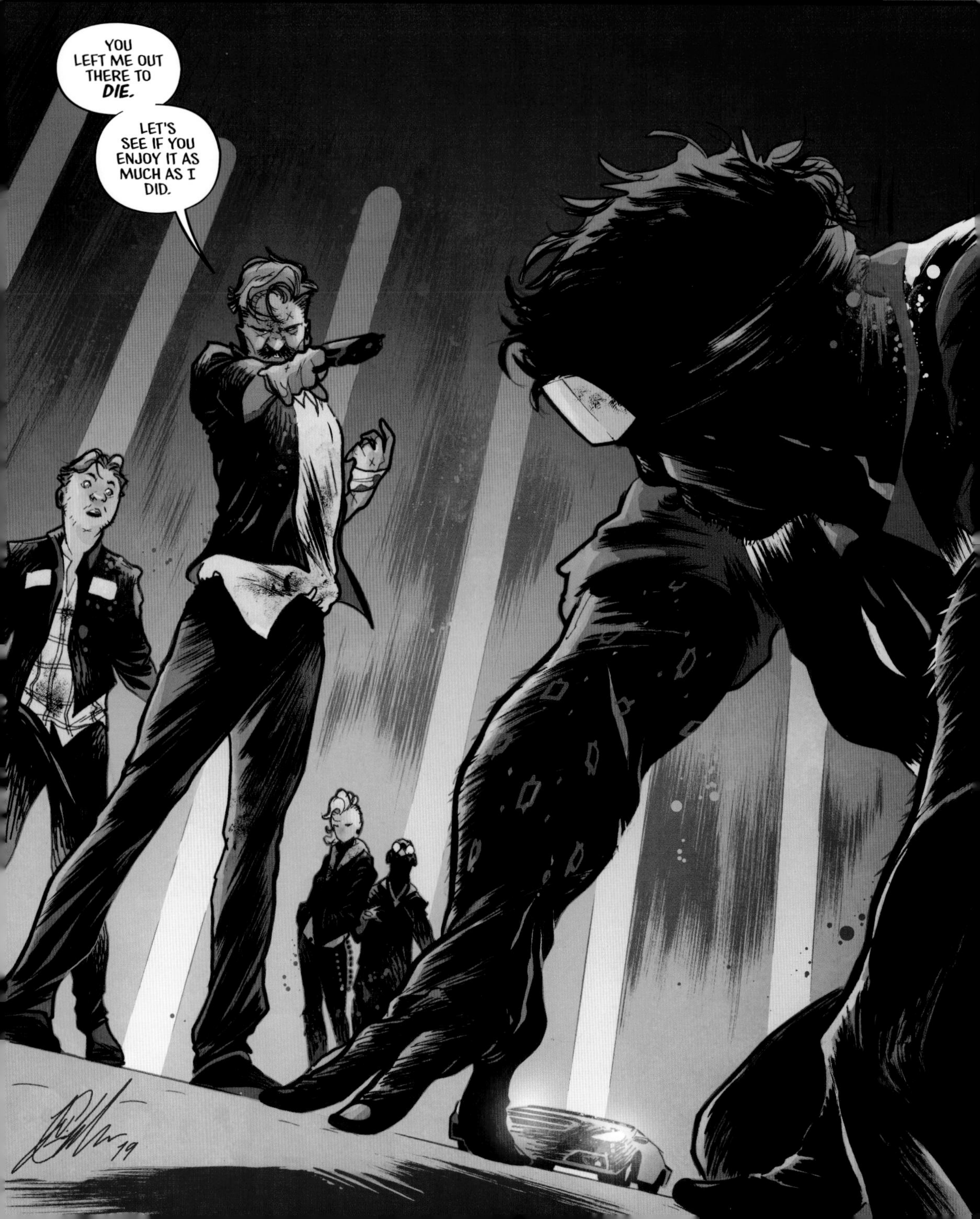
YOU LEFT ME OUT THERE TO DIE.
LET'S SEE IF YOU ENJOY IT AS MUCH AS I DID.

CHAPTER

3

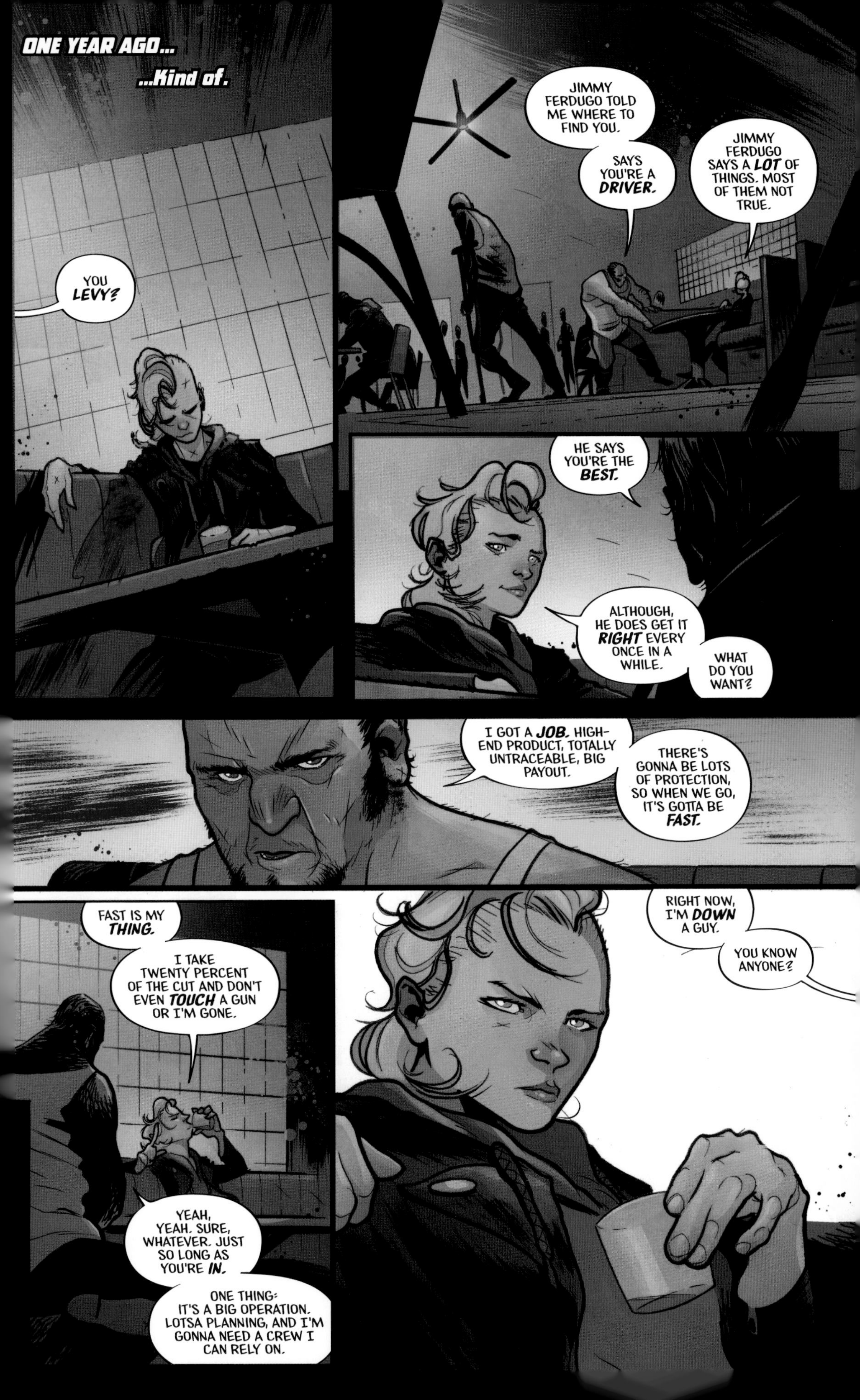
ONE YEAR AGO...
...Kind of.
YOU LEVY?
JIMMY FERDUGO TOLD ME WHERE TO FIND YOU.
SAYS YOU'RE A DRIVER.
JIMMY FERDUGO SAYS A LOT OF THINGS. MOST OF THEM NOT TRUE.
HE SAYS YOU'RE THE BEST.
ALTHOUGH, HE DOES GET IT RIGHT EVERY ONCE IN A WHILE.
WHAT DO YOU WANT?
I GOT A JOB. HIGH-END PRODUCT, TOTALLY UNTRACEABLE, BIG PAYOUT.
THERE'S GONNA BE LOTS OF PROTECTION, SO WHEN WE GO, IT'S GOTTA BE FAST.
FAST IS MY THING.
I TAKE TWENTY PERCENT OF THE CUT AND DON'T EVEN TOUCH A GUN OR I'M GONE.
YEAH, YEAH. SURE, WHATEVER. JUST SO LONG AS YOU'RE IN.
ONE THING: IT'S A BIG OPERATION. LOTSA PLANNING, AND I'M GONNA NEED A CREW I CAN RELY ON.
RIGHT NOW, I'M DOWN A GUY.
YOU KNOW ANYONE?

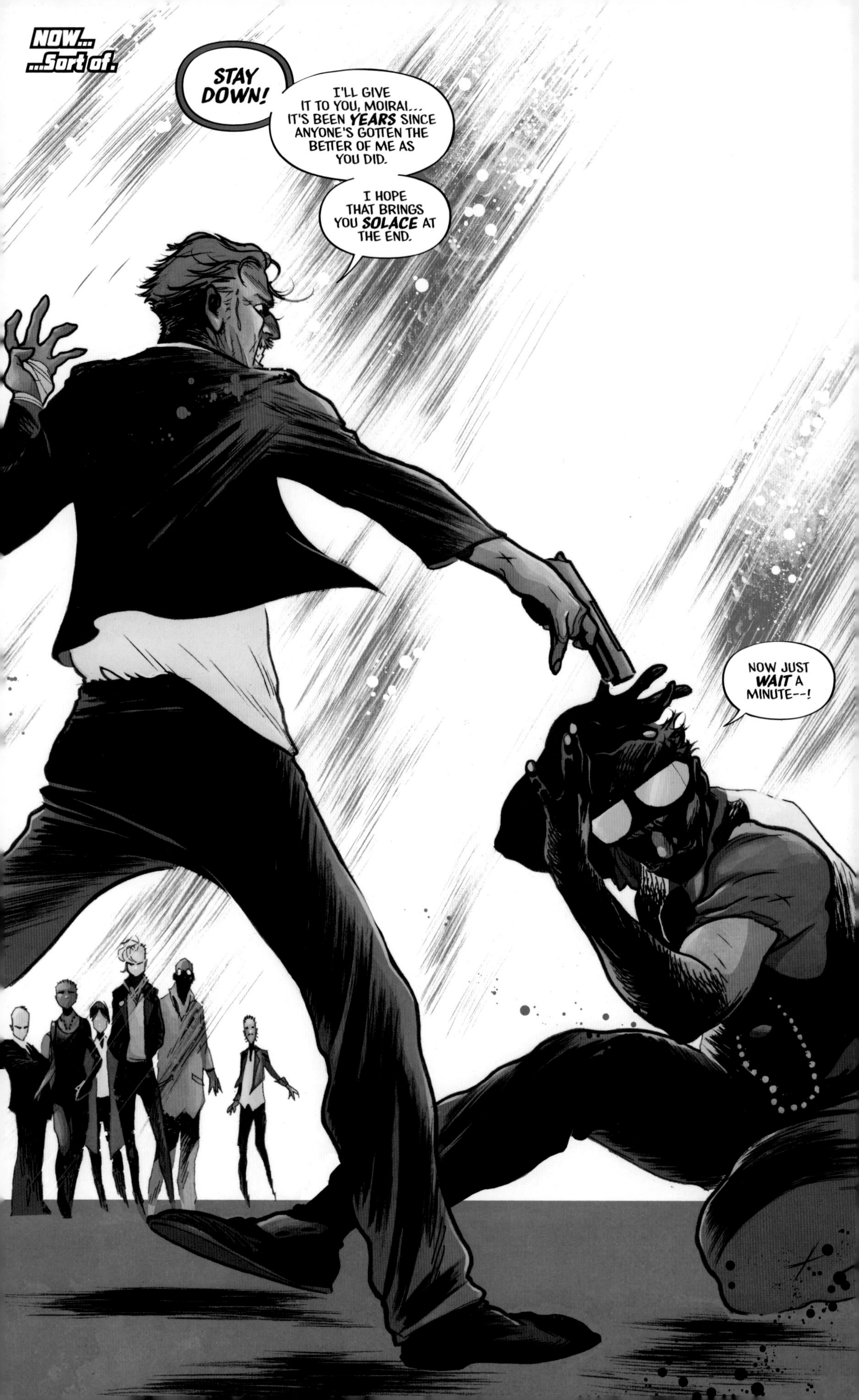
NOW...
...Sort of.
STAY DOWN!
I'LL GIVE IT TO YOU, MOIRAI... IT'S BEEN YEARS SINCE ANYONE'S GOTTEN THE BETTER OF ME AS YOU DID.
I HOPE THAT BRINGS YOU SOLACE AT THE END.
NOW JUST WAIT A MINUTE--!

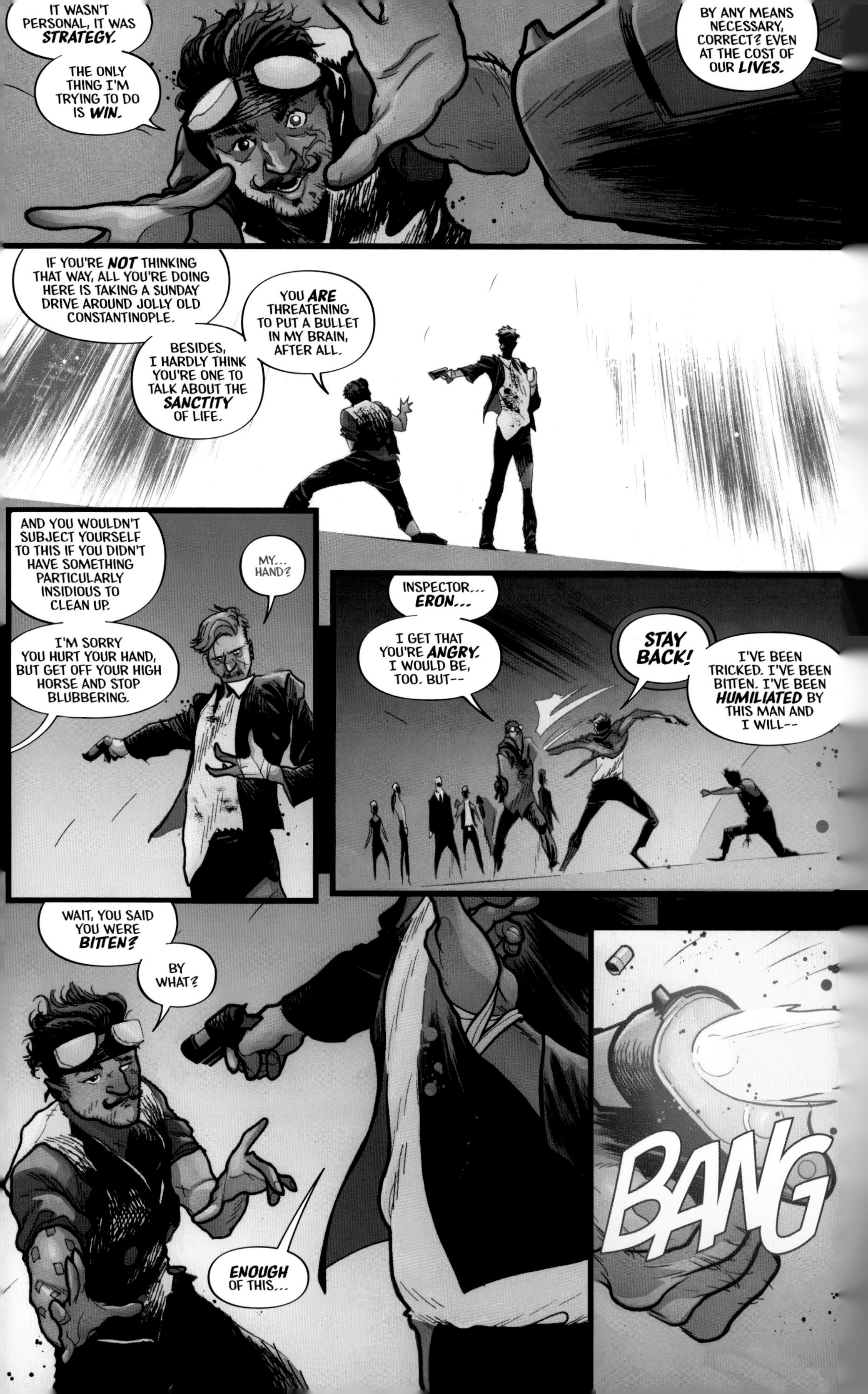
IT WASN'T PERSONAL, IT WAS STRATEGY.
THE ONLY THING I'M TRYING TO DO IS WIN.
BY ANY MEANS NECESSARY, CORRECT? EVEN AT THE COST OF OUR LIVES.
IF YOU'RE NOT THINKING THAT WAY, ALL YOU'RE DOING HERE IS TAKING A SUNDAY DRIVE AROUND JOLLY OLD CONSTANTINOPLE.
BESIDES, I HARDLY THINK YOU'RE ONE TO TALK ABOUT THE SANCTITY OF LIFE.
YOU ARE THREATENING TO PUT A BULLET IN MY BRAIN, AFTER ALL.
AND YOU WOULDN'T SUBJECT YOURSELF TO THIS IF YOU DIDN'T HAVE SOMETHING PARTICULARLY INSIDIOUS TO CLEAN UP.
MY... HAND?
I'M SORRY YOU HURT YOUR HAND, BUT GET OFF YOUR HIGH HORSE AND STOP BLUBBERING.
INSPECTOR... ERON...
I GET THAT YOU'RE ANGRY. I WOULD BE, TOO. BUT--
STAY BACK!
I'VE BEEN TRICKED. I'VE BEEN BITTEN. I'VE BEEN HUMILIATED BY THIS MAN AND I WILL--
WAIT, YOU SAID YOU WERE BITTEN?
BY WHAT?
ENOUGH OF THIS...
BANG

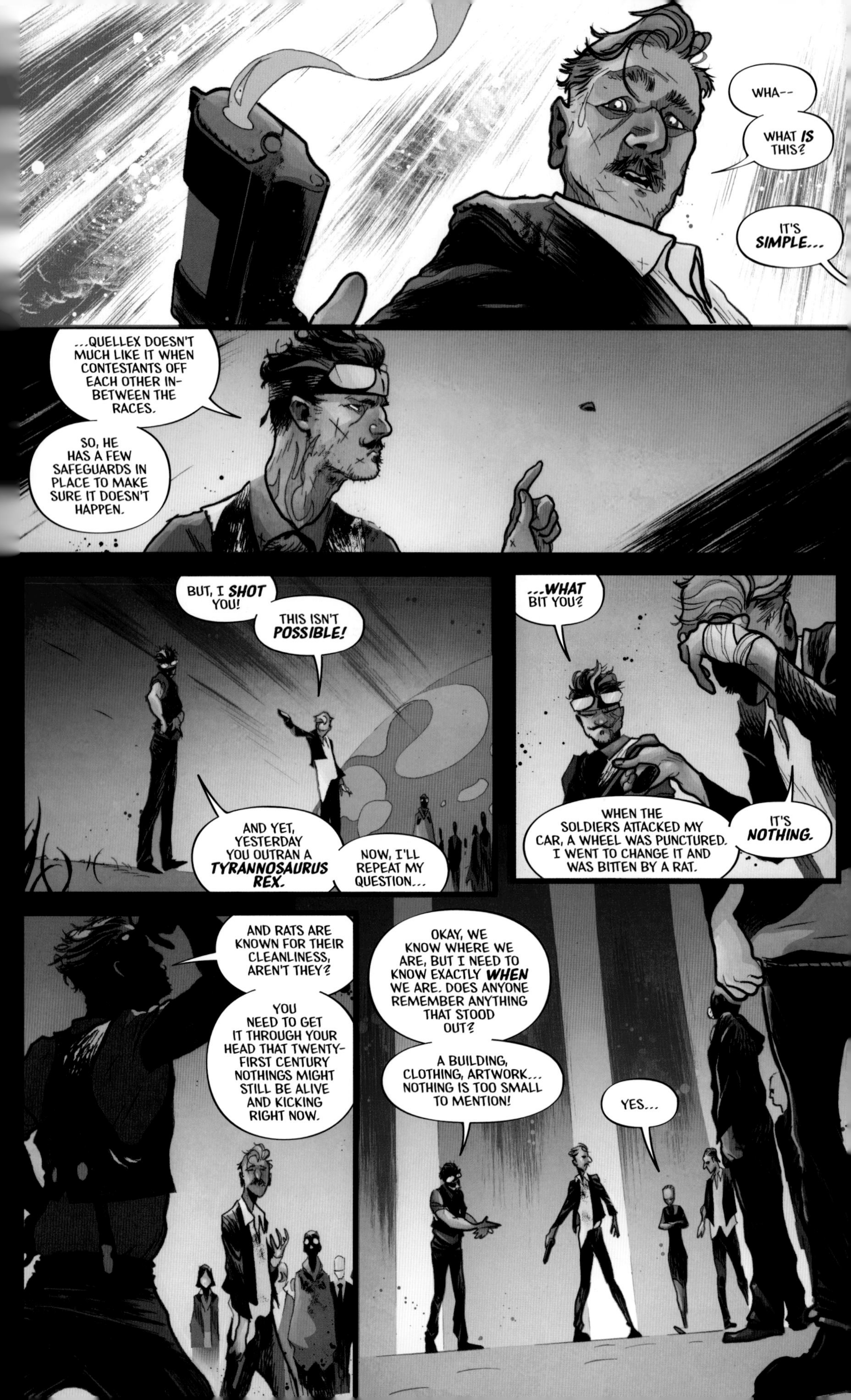
WHA--
WHAT IS THIS?
IT'S SIMPLE...
...QUELLEX DOESN'T MUCH LIKE IT WHEN CONTESTANTS OFF EACH OTHER IN-BETWEEN THE RACES.
SO, HE HAS A FEW SAFEGUARDS IN PLACE TO MAKE SURE IT DOESN'T HAPPEN.
BUT, I SHOT YOU!
THIS ISN'T POSSIBLE!
AND YET, YESTERDAY YOU OUTRAN A TYRANNOSAURUS REX.
NOW, I'LL REPEAT MY QUESTION...
...WHAT BIT YOU?
IT'S NOTHING.
WHEN THE SOLDIERS ATTACKED MY CAR, A WHEEL WAS PUNCTURED. I WENT TO CHANGE IT AND WAS BITTEN BY A RAT.
AND RATS ARE KNOWN FOR THEIR CLEANLINESS, AREN'T THEY?
YOU NEED TO GET IT THROUGH YOUR HEAD THAT TWENTY-FIRST CENTURY NOTHINGS MIGHT STILL BE ALIVE AND KICKING RIGHT NOW.
OKAY, WE KNOW WHERE WE ARE, BUT I NEED TO KNOW EXACTLY WHEN WE ARE. DOES ANYONE REMEMBER ANYTHING THAT STOOD OUT?
A BUILDING, CLOTHING, ARTWORK... NOTHING IS TOO SMALL TO MENTION!
YES...

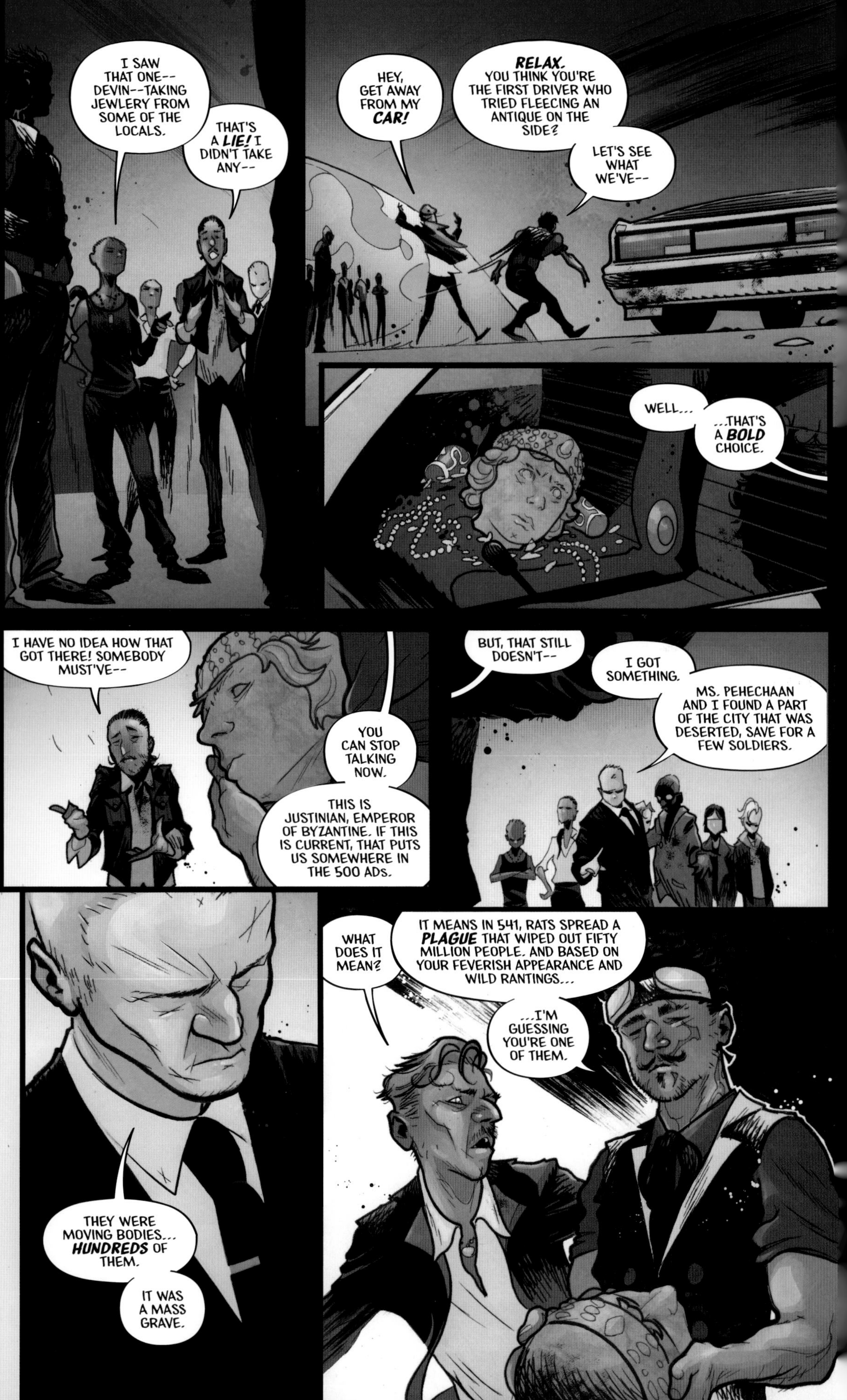
I SAW THAT ONE--DEVIN--TAKING JEWLERY FROM SOME OF THE LOCALS.
THAT'S A LIE! I DIDN'T TAKE ANY--
HEY, GET AWAY FROM MY CAR!
RELAX. YOU THINK YOU'RE THE FIRST DRIVER WHO TRIED FLEECING AN ANTIQUE ON THE SIDE?
LET'S SEE WHAT WE'VE--
WELL...
...THAT'S A BOLD CHOICE.
I HAVE NO IDEA HOW THAT GOT THERE! SOMEBODY MUST'VE--
YOU CAN STOP TALKING NOW.
THIS IS JUSTINIAN, EMPEROR OF BYZANTINE. IF THIS IS CURRENT, THAT PUTS US SOMEWHERE IN THE 500 ADs.
BUT, THAT STILL DOESN'T--
I GOT SOMETHING.
MS. PEHECHAAN AND I FOUND A PART OF THE CITY THAT WAS DESERTED, SAVE FOR A FEW SOLDIERS.
THEY WERE MOVING BODIES... HUNDREDS OF THEM.
IT WAS A MASS GRAVE.
WHAT DOES IT MEAN?
IT MEANS IN 541, RATS SPREAD A PLAGUE THAT WIPED OUT FIFTY MILLION PEOPLE. AND BASED ON YOUR FEVERISH APPEARANCE AND WILD RANTINGS...
...I'M GUESSING YOU'RE ONE OF THEM.

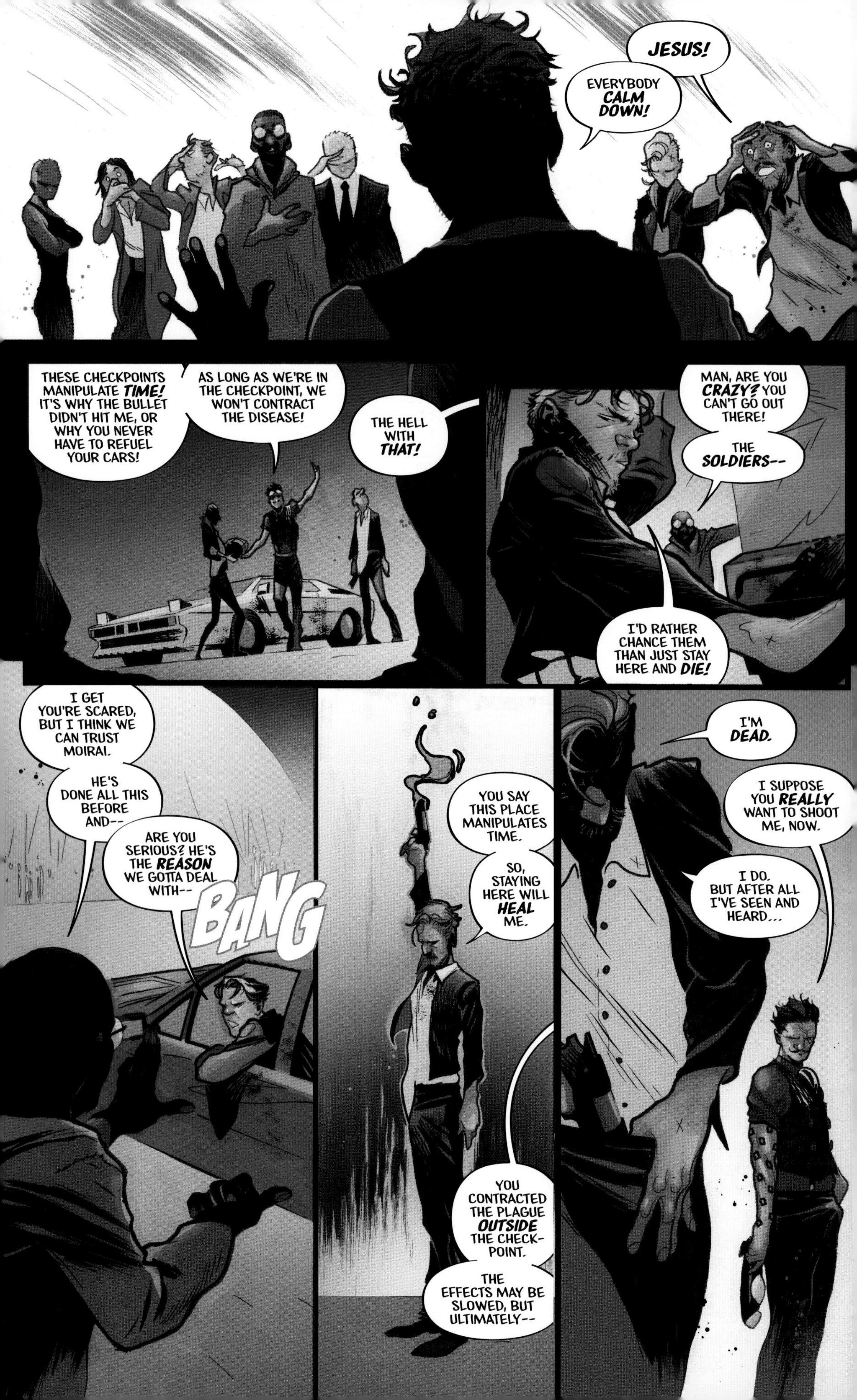

JESUS!
EVERYBODY CALM DOWN!
THESE CHECKPOINTS MANIPULATE TIME! IT'S WHY THE BULLET DIDN'T HIT ME, OR WHY YOU NEVER HAVE TO REFUEL YOUR CARS!
AS LONG AS WE'RE IN THE CHECKPOINT, WE WON'T CONTRACT THE DISEASE!
THE HELL WITH THAT!
MAN, ARE YOU CRAZY? YOU CAN'T GO OUT THERE!
THE SOLDIERS--
I'D RATHER CHANCE THEM THAN JUST STAY HERE AND DIE!
I GET YOU'RE SCARED, BUT I THINK WE CAN TRUST MOIRAI.
HE'S DONE ALL THIS BEFORE AND--
ARE YOU SERIOUS? HE'S THE REASON WE GOTTA DEAL WITH--
BANG
YOU SAY THIS PLACE MANIPULATES TIME.
SO, STAYING HERE WILL HEAL ME.
YOU CONTRACTED THE PLAGUE OUTSIDE THE CHECK-POINT.
THE EFFECTS MAY BE SLOWED, BUT ULTIMATELY--
I'M DEAD.
I SUPPOSE YOU REALLY WANT TO SHOOT ME, NOW.
I DO. BUT AFTER ALL I'VE SEEN AND HEARD...

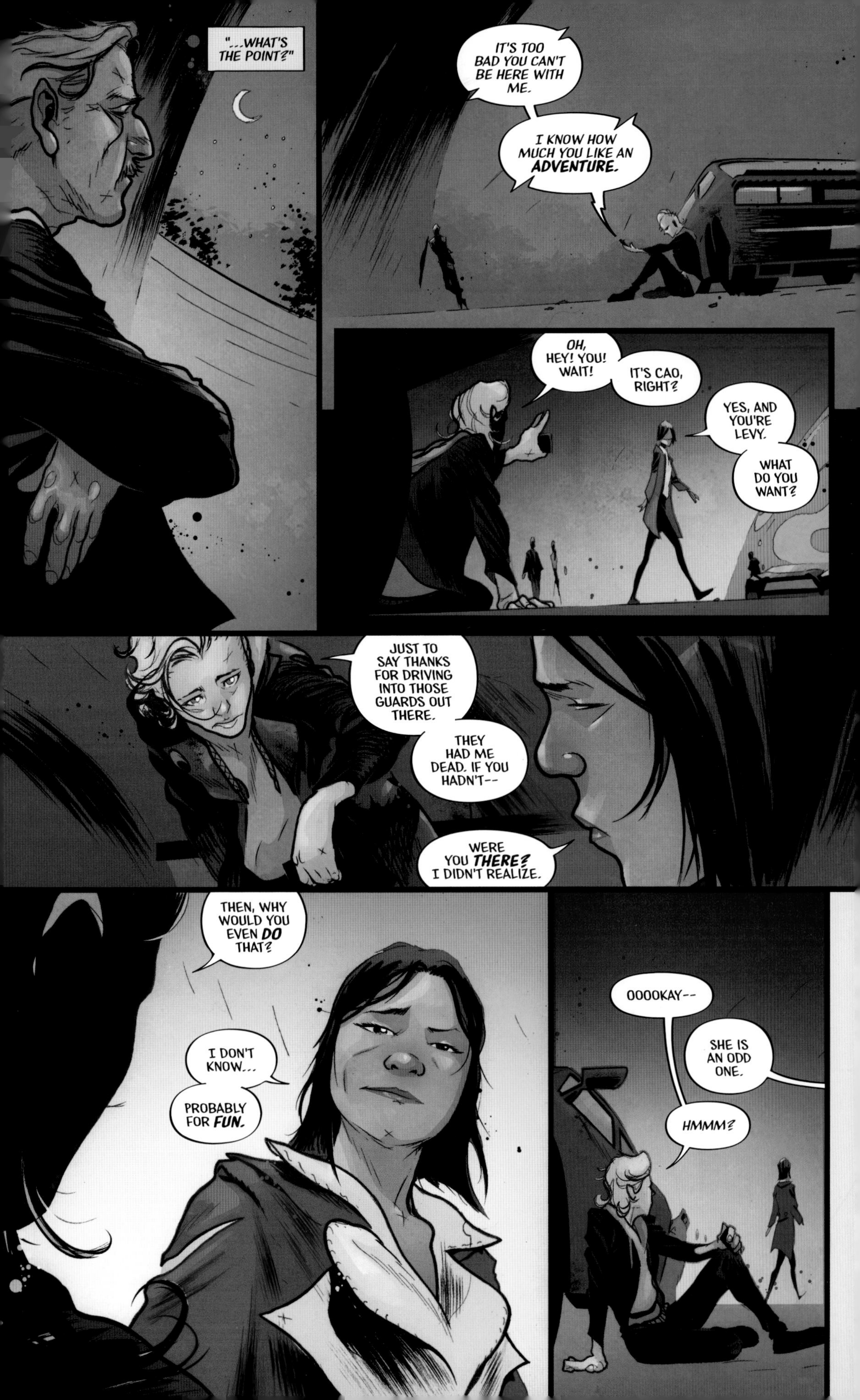
"...WHAT'S THE POINT?"
IT'S TOO BAD YOU CAN'T BE HERE WITH ME.
I KNOW HOW MUCH YOU LIKE AN **ADVENTURE.**
OH, HEY! YOU! WAIT!
IT'S CAO, RIGHT?
YES, AND YOU'RE LEVY.
WHAT DO YOU WANT?
JUST TO SAY THANKS FOR DRIVING INTO THOSE GUARDS OUT THERE.
THEY HAD ME DEAD. IF YOU HADN'T--
WERE YOU ***THERE?*** I DIDN'T REALIZE.
THEN, WHY WOULD YOU EVEN ***DO*** THAT?
I DON'T KNOW...
PROBABLY FOR ***FUN.***
OOOOKAY--
SHE IS AN ODD ONE.
HMMM?

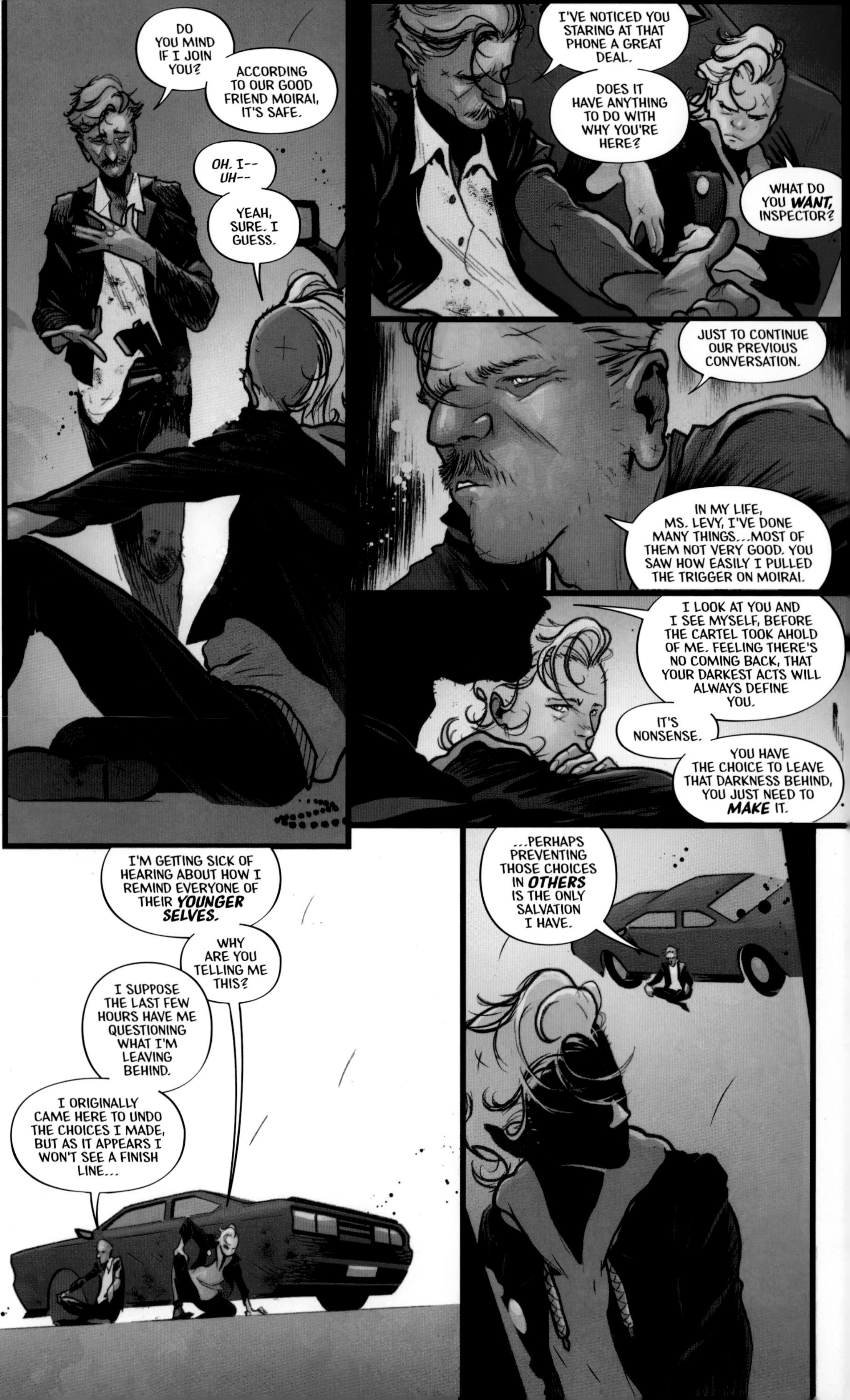
DO YOU MIND IF I JOIN YOU?
ACCORDING TO OUR GOOD FRIEND MOIRAI, IT'S SAFE.
OH. I-- UH--
YEAH, SURE. I GUESS.
I'VE NOTICED YOU STARING AT THAT PHONE A GREAT DEAL.
DOES IT HAVE ANYTHING TO DO WITH WHY YOU'RE HERE?
WHAT DO YOU WANT, INSPECTOR?
JUST TO CONTINUE OUR PREVIOUS CONVERSATION.
IN MY LIFE, MS. LEVY, I'VE DONE MANY THINGS...MOST OF THEM NOT VERY GOOD. YOU SAW HOW EASILY I PULLED THE TRIGGER ON MOIRAI.
I LOOK AT YOU AND I SEE MYSELF, BEFORE THE CARTEL TOOK AHOLD OF ME. FEELING THERE'S NO COMING BACK, THAT YOUR DARKEST ACTS WILL ALWAYS DEFINE YOU.
IT'S NONSENSE.
YOU HAVE THE CHOICE TO LEAVE THAT DARKNESS BEHIND, YOU JUST NEED TO MAKE IT.
I'M GETTING SICK OF HEARING ABOUT HOW I REMIND EVERYONE OF THEIR YOUNGER SELVES.
WHY ARE YOU TELLING ME THIS?
I SUPPOSE THE LAST FEW HOURS HAVE ME QUESTIONING WHAT I'M LEAVING BEHIND.
I ORIGINALLY CAME HERE TO UNDO THE CHOICES I MADE, BUT AS IT APPEARS I WON'T SEE A FINISH LINE...
...PERHAPS PREVENTING THOSE CHOICES IN OTHERS IS THE ONLY SALVATION I HAVE.

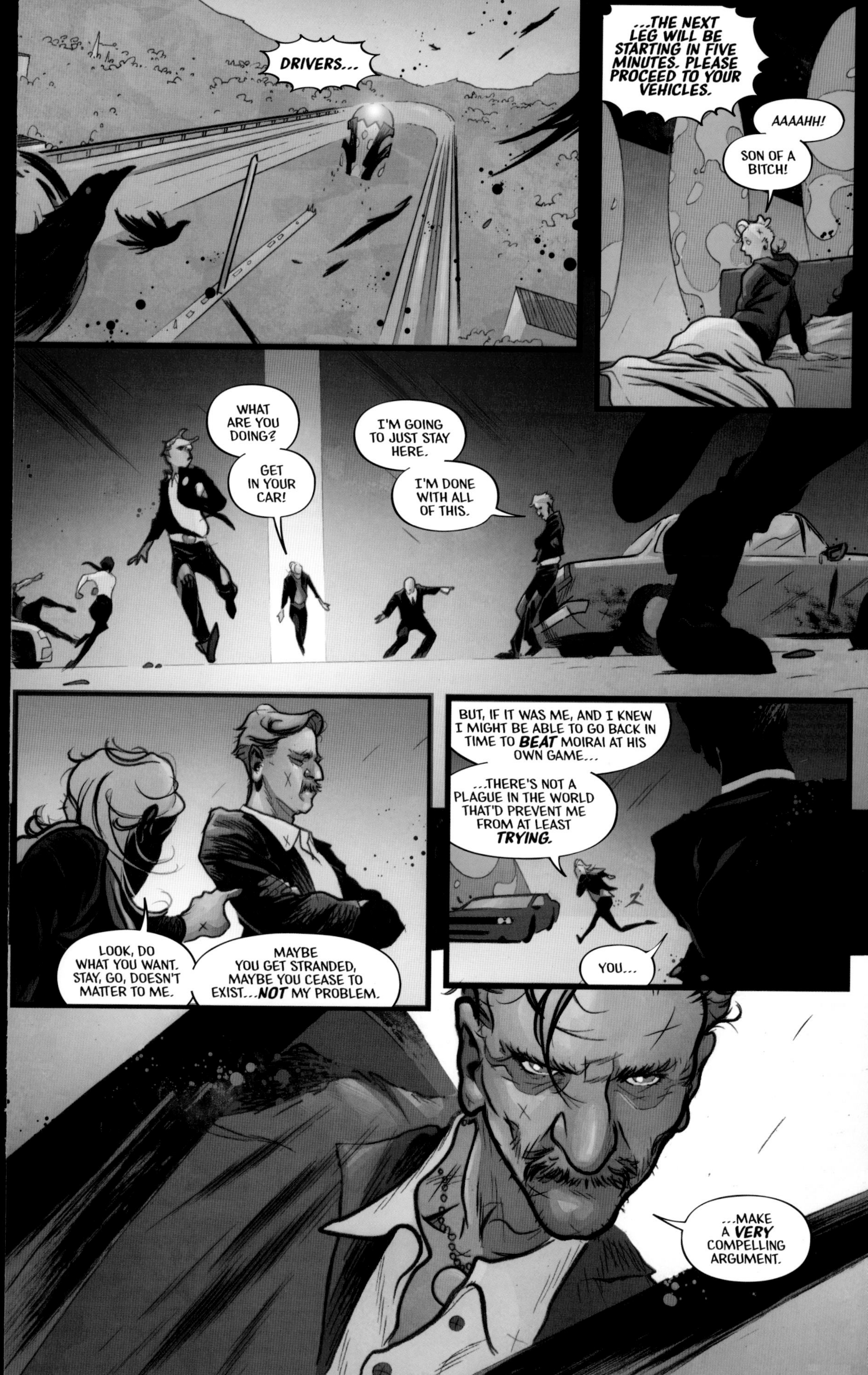
DRIVERS...
...THE NEXT LEG WILL BE STARTING IN FIVE MINUTES. PLEASE PROCEED TO YOUR VEHICLES.
AAAAHH!
SON OF A BITCH!
WHAT ARE YOU DOING?
GET IN YOUR CAR!
I'M GOING TO JUST STAY HERE.
I'M DONE WITH ALL OF THIS.
LOOK, DO WHAT YOU WANT. STAY, GO, DOESN'T MATTER TO ME.
MAYBE YOU GET STRANDED, MAYBE YOU CEASE TO EXIST...NOT MY PROBLEM.
BUT, IF IT WAS ME, AND I KNEW I MIGHT BE ABLE TO GO BACK IN TIME TO BEAT MOIRAI AT HIS OWN GAME...
...THERE'S NOT A PLAGUE IN THE WORLD THAT'D PREVENT ME FROM AT LEAST TRYING.
YOU...
...MAKE A VERY COMPELLING ARGUMENT.

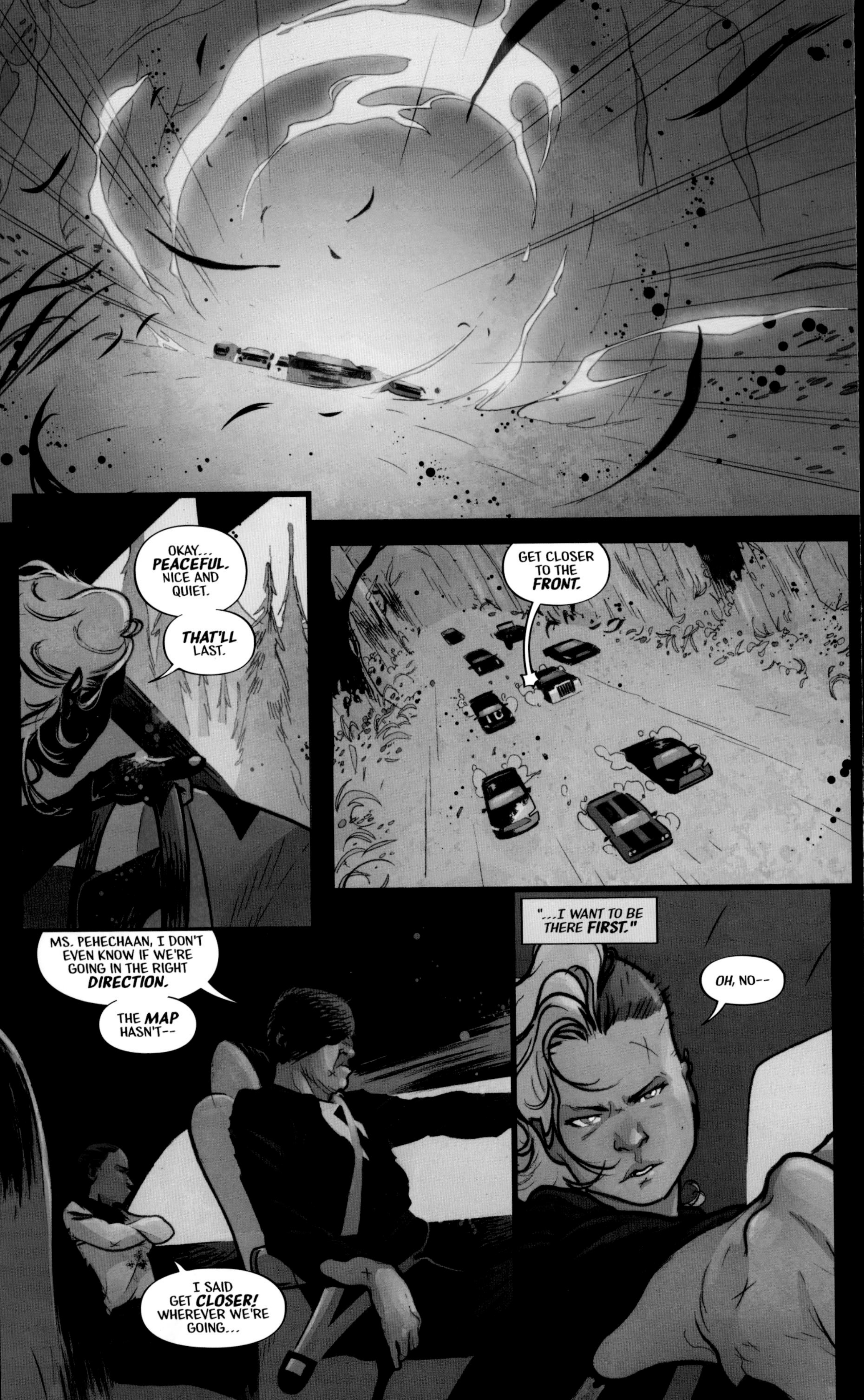

OKAY... PEACEFUL. NICE AND QUIET.
THAT'LL LAST.
GET CLOSER TO THE FRONT.
MS. PEHECHAAN, I DON'T EVEN KNOW IF WE'RE GOING IN THE RIGHT DIRECTION.
THE MAP HASN'T--
I SAID GET CLOSER! WHEREVER WE'RE GOING...
"...I WANT TO BE THERE FIRST."
OH, NO--

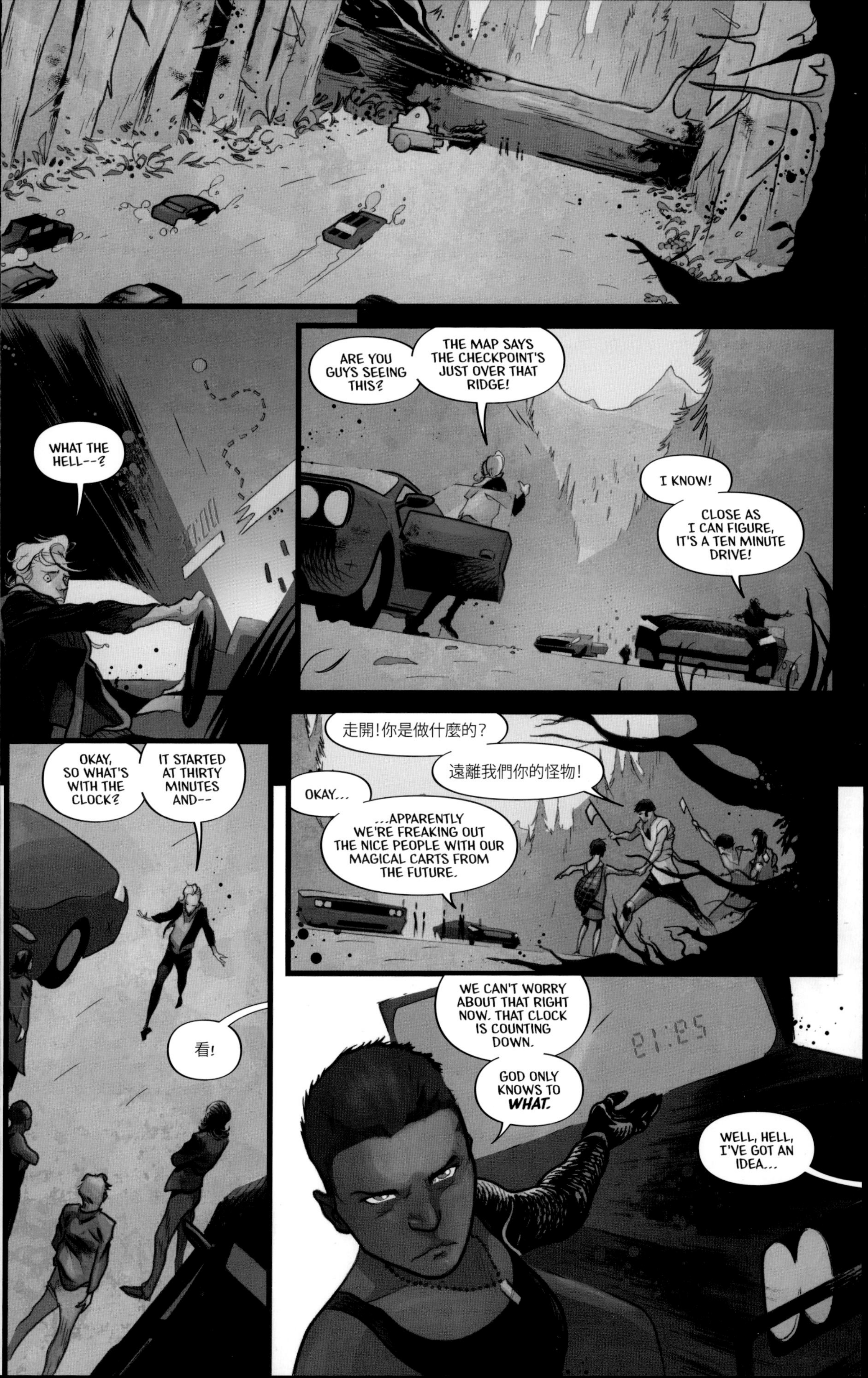
WHAT THE HELL--?
ARE YOU GUYS SEEING THIS?
THE MAP SAYS THE CHECKPOINT'S JUST OVER THAT RIDGE!
I KNOW!
CLOSE AS I CAN FIGURE, IT'S A TEN MINUTE DRIVE!
OKAY, SO WHAT'S WITH THE CLOCK?
IT STARTED AT THIRTY MINUTES AND--
走開!你是做什麼的?
遠離我們你的怪物!
OKAY...
...APPARENTLY WE'RE FREAKING OUT THE NICE PEOPLE WITH OUR MAGICAL CARTS FROM THE FUTURE.
看!
WE CAN'T WORRY ABOUT THAT RIGHT NOW. THAT CLOCK IS COUNTING DOWN.
GOD ONLY KNOWS TO ***WHAT.***
21:25
WELL, HELL, I'VE GOT AN IDEA...

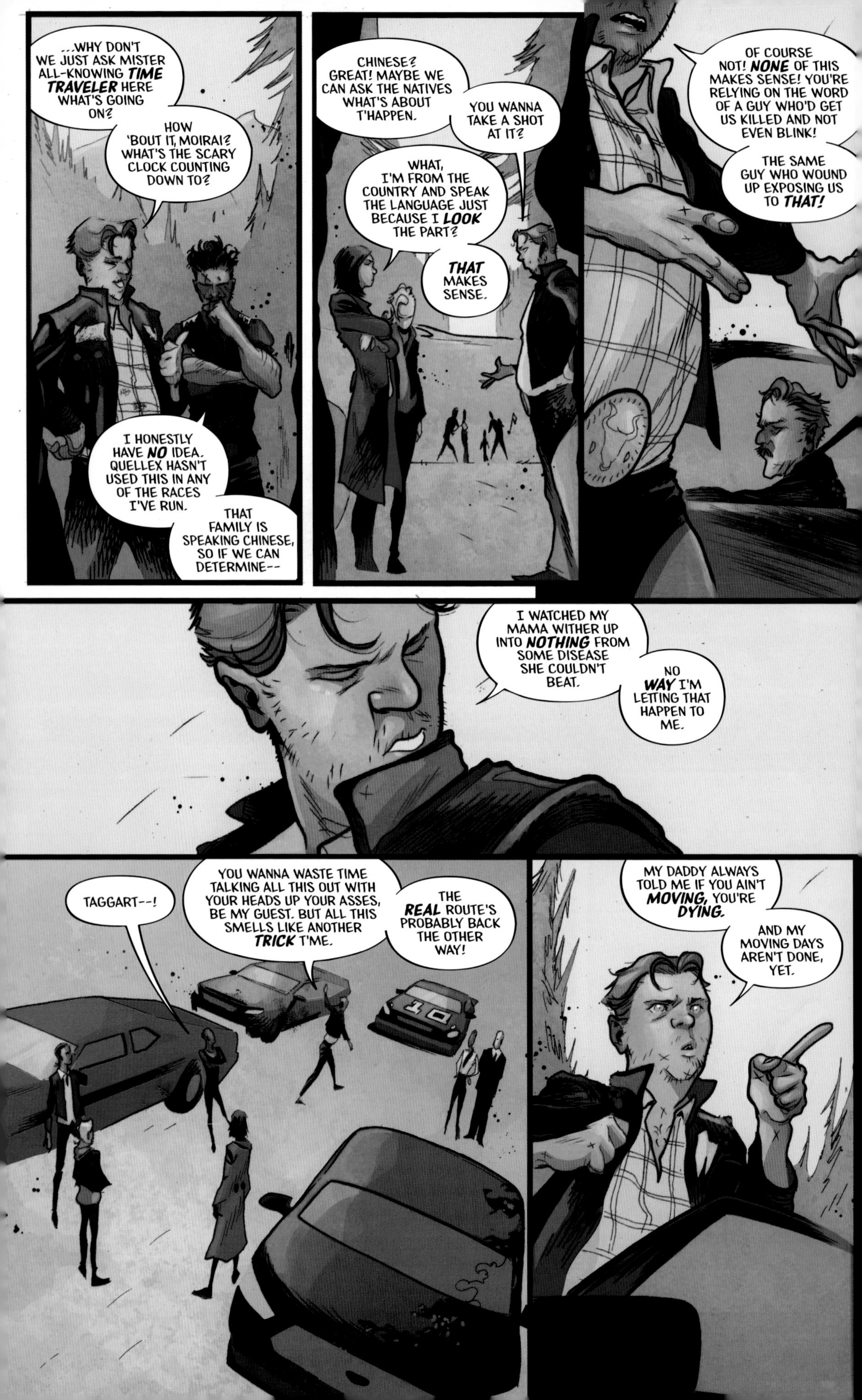
...WHY DON'T WE JUST ASK MISTER ALL-KNOWING TIME TRAVELER HERE WHAT'S GOING ON?
HOW 'BOUT IT, MOIRAI? WHAT'S THE SCARY CLOCK COUNTING DOWN TO?
I HONESTLY HAVE NO IDEA. QUELLEX HASN'T USED THIS IN ANY OF THE RACES I'VE RUN.
THAT FAMILY IS SPEAKING CHINESE, SO IF WE CAN DETERMINE--
CHINESE? GREAT! MAYBE WE CAN ASK THE NATIVES WHAT'S ABOUT T'HAPPEN.
YOU WANNA TAKE A SHOT AT IT?
WHAT, I'M FROM THE COUNTRY AND SPEAK THE LANGUAGE JUST BECAUSE I LOOK THE PART?
THAT MAKES SENSE.
OF COURSE NOT! NONE OF THIS MAKES SENSE! YOU'RE RELYING ON THE WORD OF A GUY WHO'D GET US KILLED AND NOT EVEN BLINK!
THE SAME GUY WHO WOUND UP EXPOSING US TO THAT!
I WATCHED MY MAMA WITHER UP INTO NOTHING FROM SOME DISEASE SHE COULDN'T BEAT.
NO WAY I'M LETTING THAT HAPPEN TO ME.
TAGGART--!
YOU WANNA WASTE TIME TALKING ALL THIS OUT WITH YOUR HEADS UP YOUR ASSES, BE MY GUEST. BUT ALL THIS SMELLS LIKE ANOTHER TRICK T'ME.
THE REAL ROUTE'S PROBABLY BACK THE OTHER WAY!
MY DADDY ALWAYS TOLD ME IF YOU AIN'T MOVING, YOU'RE DYING.
AND MY MOVING DAYS AREN'T DONE, YET.

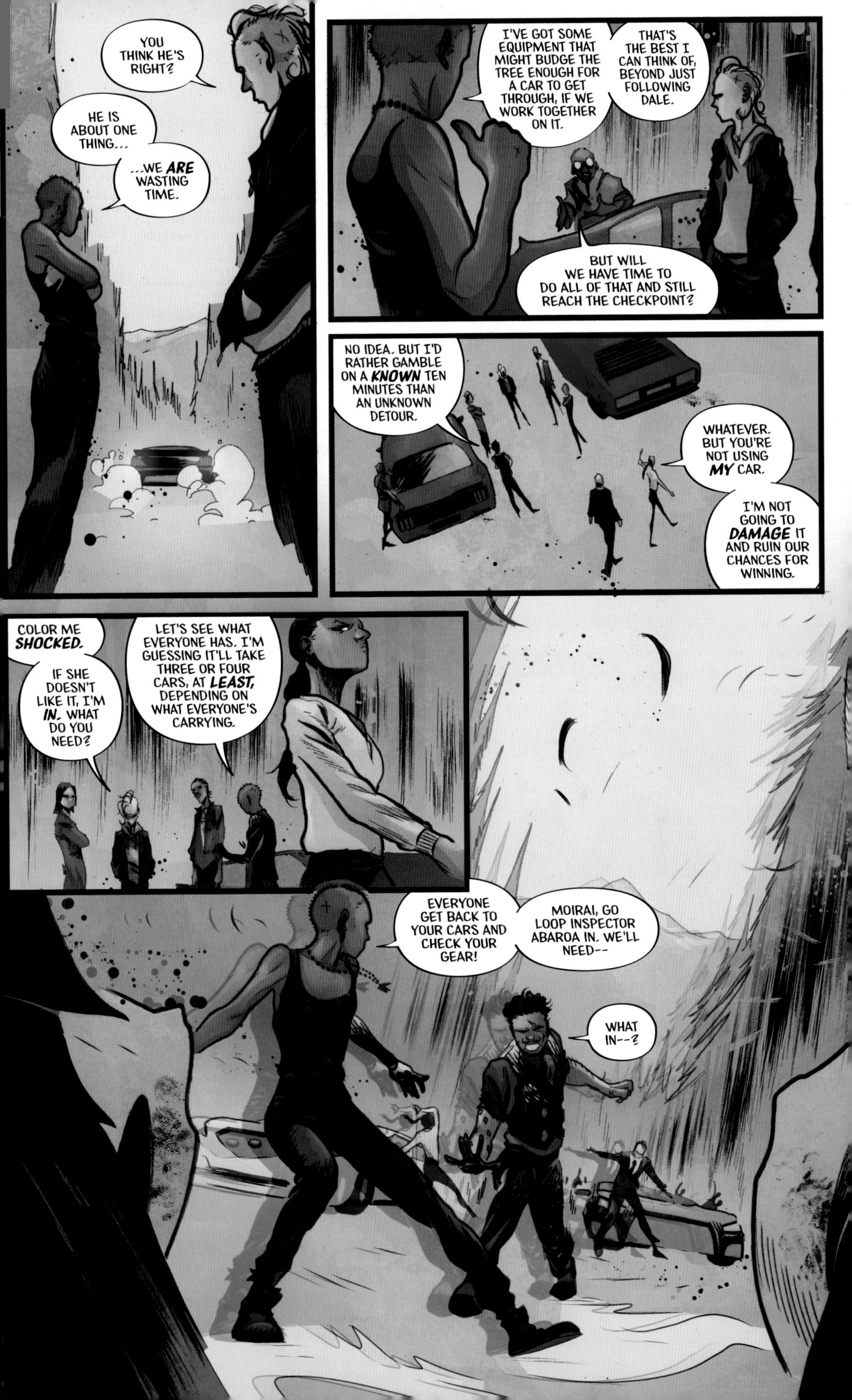
YOU THINK HE'S RIGHT?
HE IS ABOUT ONE THING...
...WE ARE WASTING TIME.
I'VE GOT SOME EQUIPMENT THAT MIGHT BUDGE THE TREE ENOUGH FOR A CAR TO GET THROUGH, IF WE WORK TOGETHER ON IT.
THAT'S THE BEST I CAN THINK OF, BEYOND JUST FOLLOWING DALE.
BUT WILL WE HAVE TIME TO DO ALL OF THAT AND STILL REACH THE CHECKPOINT?
NO IDEA. BUT I'D RATHER GAMBLE ON A KNOWN TEN MINUTES THAN AN UNKNOWN DETOUR.
WHATEVER. BUT YOU'RE NOT USING MY CAR.
I'M NOT GOING TO DAMAGE IT AND RUIN OUR CHANCES FOR WINNING.
COLOR ME SHOCKED.
IF SHE DOESN'T LIKE IT, I'M IN. WHAT DO YOU NEED?
LET'S SEE WHAT EVERYONE HAS. I'M GUESSING IT'LL TAKE THREE OR FOUR CARS, AT LEAST, DEPENDING ON WHAT EVERYONE'S CARRYING.
EVERYONE GET BACK TO YOUR CARS AND CHECK YOUR GEAR!
MOIRAI, GO LOOP INSPECTOR ABAROA IN. WE'LL NEED--
WHAT IN--?

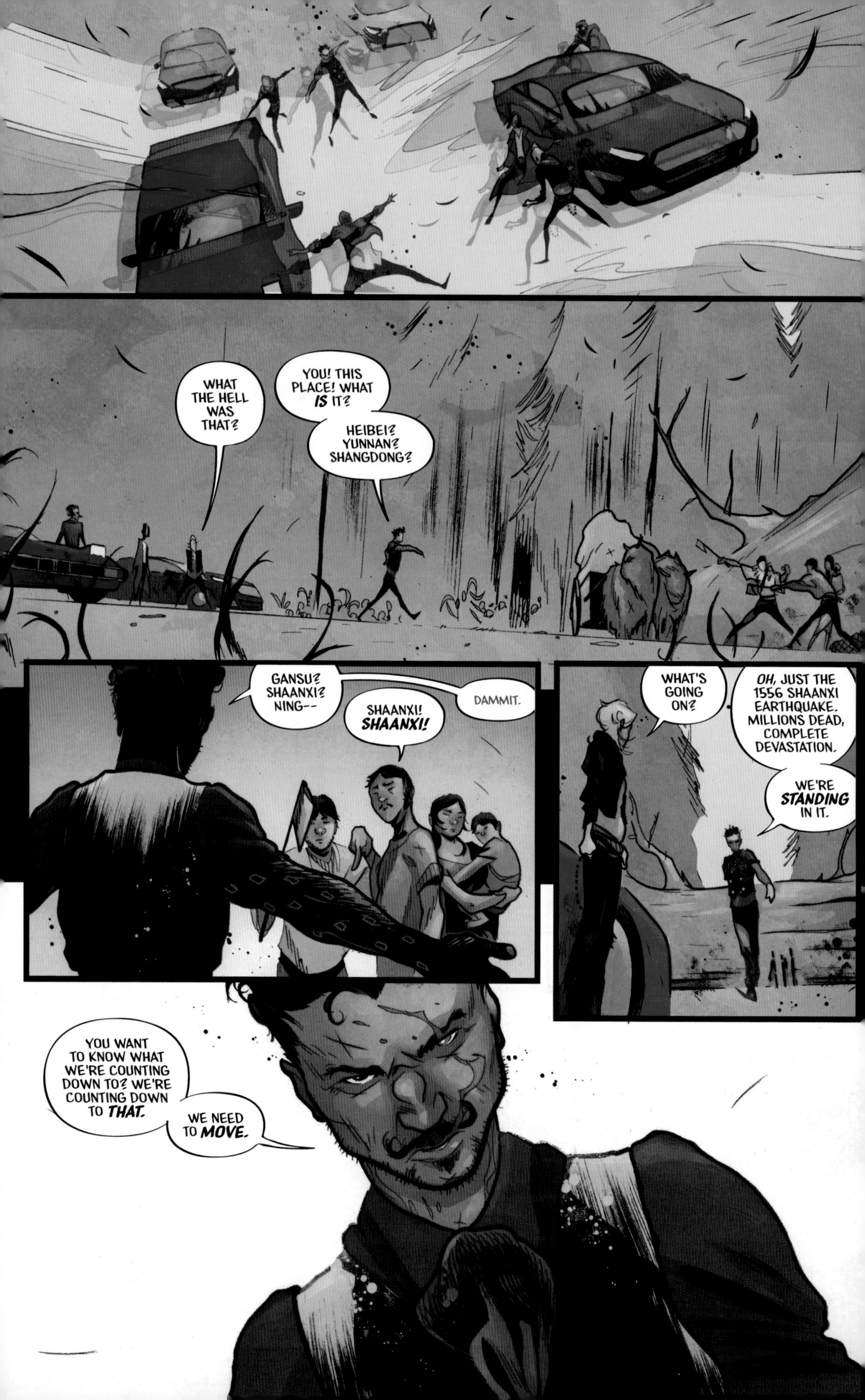
WHAT THE HELL WAS THAT?
YOU! THIS PLACE! WHAT IS IT?
HEIBEI? YUNNAN? SHANGDONG?
GANSU? SHAANXI? NING--
DAMMIT.
SHAANXI! SHAANXI!
WHAT'S GOING ON?
OH, JUST THE 1556 SHAANXI EARTHQUAKE. MILLIONS DEAD, COMPLETE DEVASTATION.
WE'RE STANDING IN IT.
YOU WANT TO KNOW WHAT WE'RE COUNTING DOWN TO? WE'RE COUNTING DOWN TO THAT.
WE NEED TO MOVE.

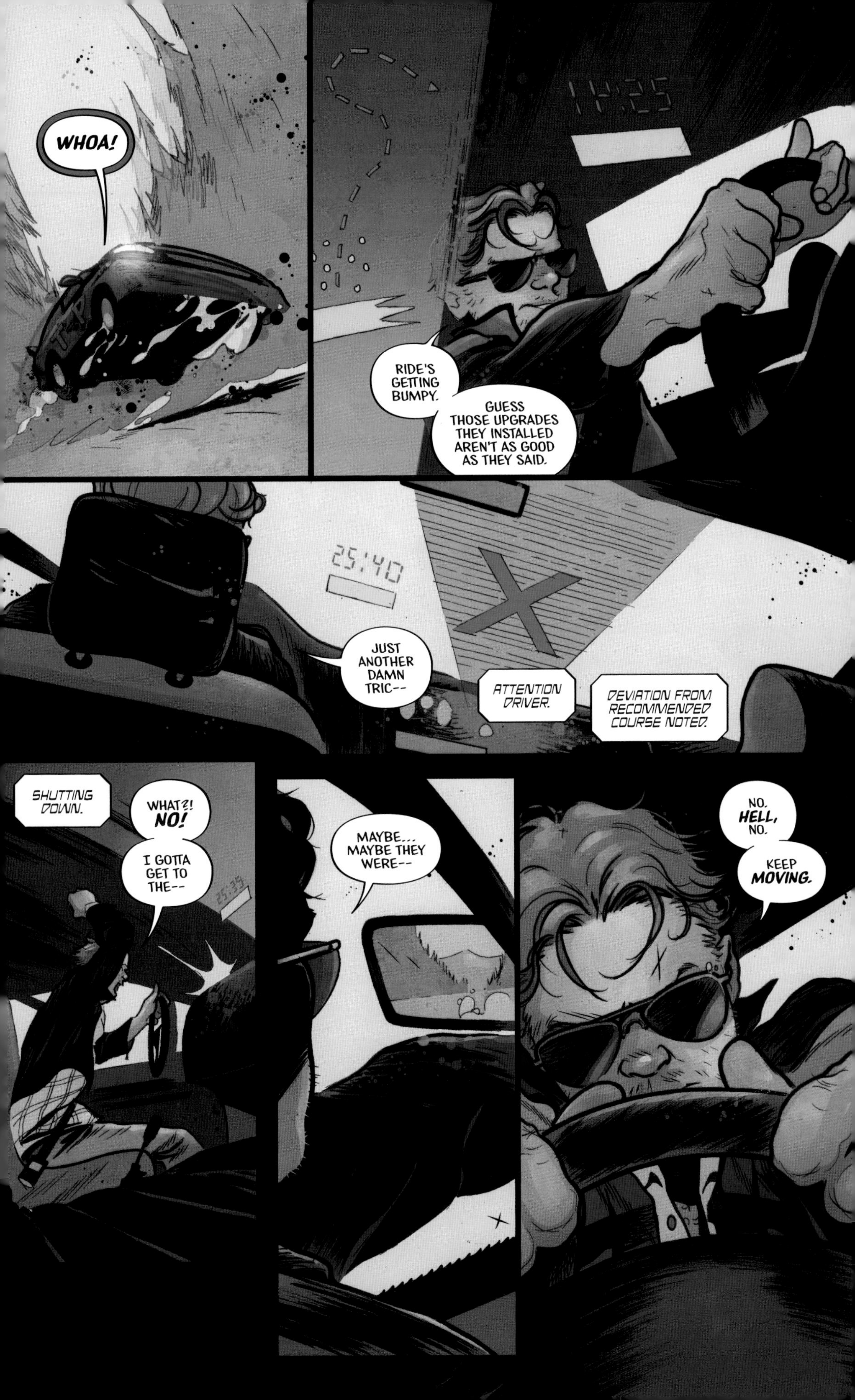
WHOA!
11:25
RIDE'S GETTING BUMPY.
GUESS THOSE UPGRADES THEY INSTALLED AREN'T AS GOOD AS THEY SAID.
25:40
JUST ANOTHER DAMN TRIC--
ATTENTION DRIVER.
DEVIATION FROM RECOMMENDED COURSE NOTED.
SHUTTING DOWN.
WHAT?! NO!
I GOTTA GET TO THE--
25:39
MAYBE... MAYBE THEY WERE--
NO. HELL, NO.
KEEP MOVING.

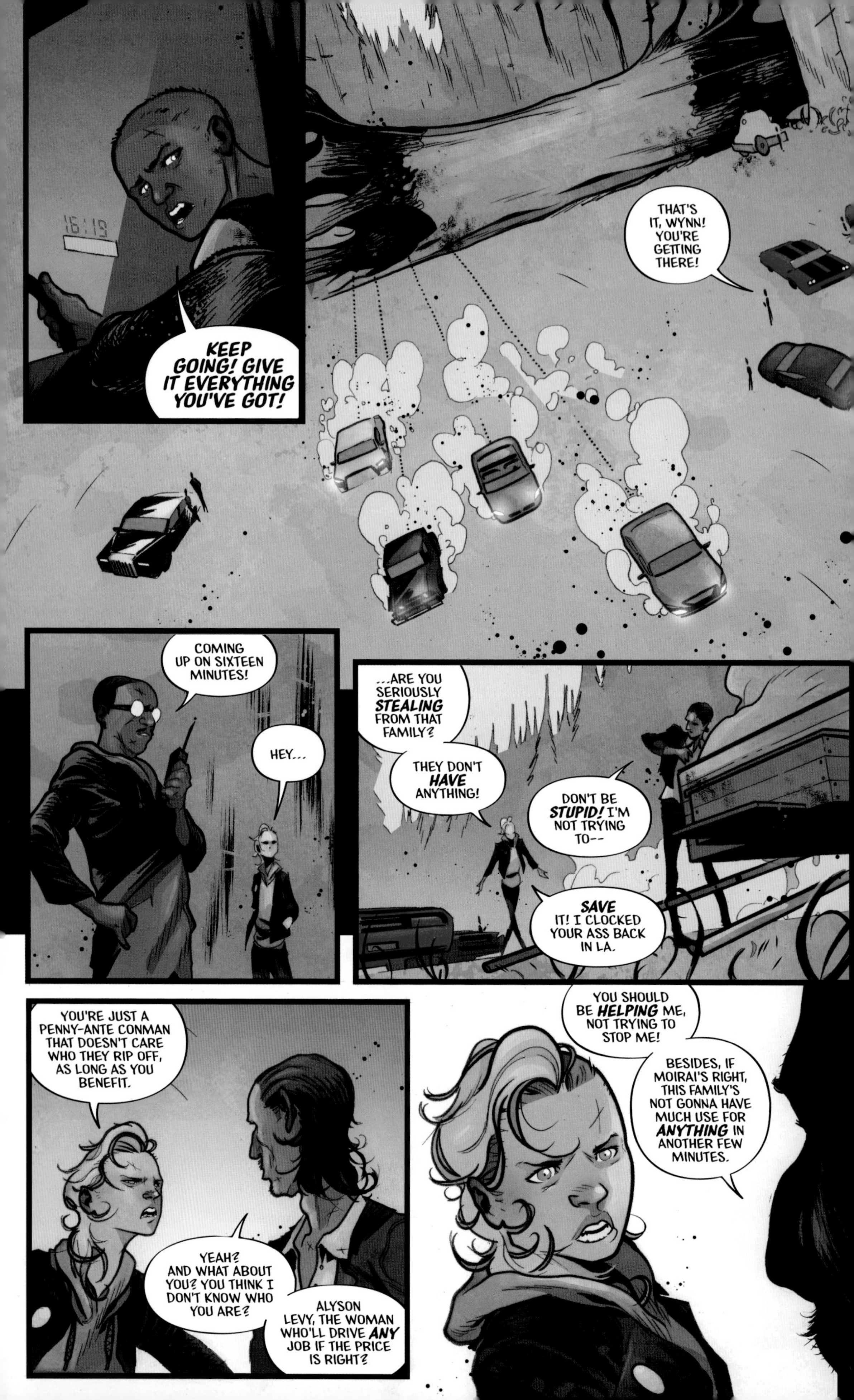
16:19
KEEP GOING! GIVE IT EVERYTHING YOU'VE GOT!
THAT'S IT, WYNN! YOU'RE GETTING THERE!
COMING UP ON SIXTEEN MINUTES!
HEY...
...ARE YOU SERIOUSLY STEALING FROM THAT FAMILY?
THEY DON'T HAVE ANYTHING!
DON'T BE STUPID! I'M NOT TRYING TO--
SAVE IT! I CLOCKED YOUR ASS BACK IN LA.
YOU'RE JUST A PENNY-ANTE CONMAN THAT DOESN'T CARE WHO THEY RIP OFF, AS LONG AS YOU BENEFIT.
YEAH? AND WHAT ABOUT YOU? YOU THINK I DON'T KNOW WHO YOU ARE?
ALYSON LEVY, THE WOMAN WHO'LL DRIVE ANY JOB IF THE PRICE IS RIGHT?
YOU SHOULD BE HELPING ME, NOT TRYING TO STOP ME!
BESIDES, IF MOIRAI'S RIGHT, THIS FAMILY'S NOT GONNA HAVE MUCH USE FOR ANYTHING IN ANOTHER FEW MINUTES.

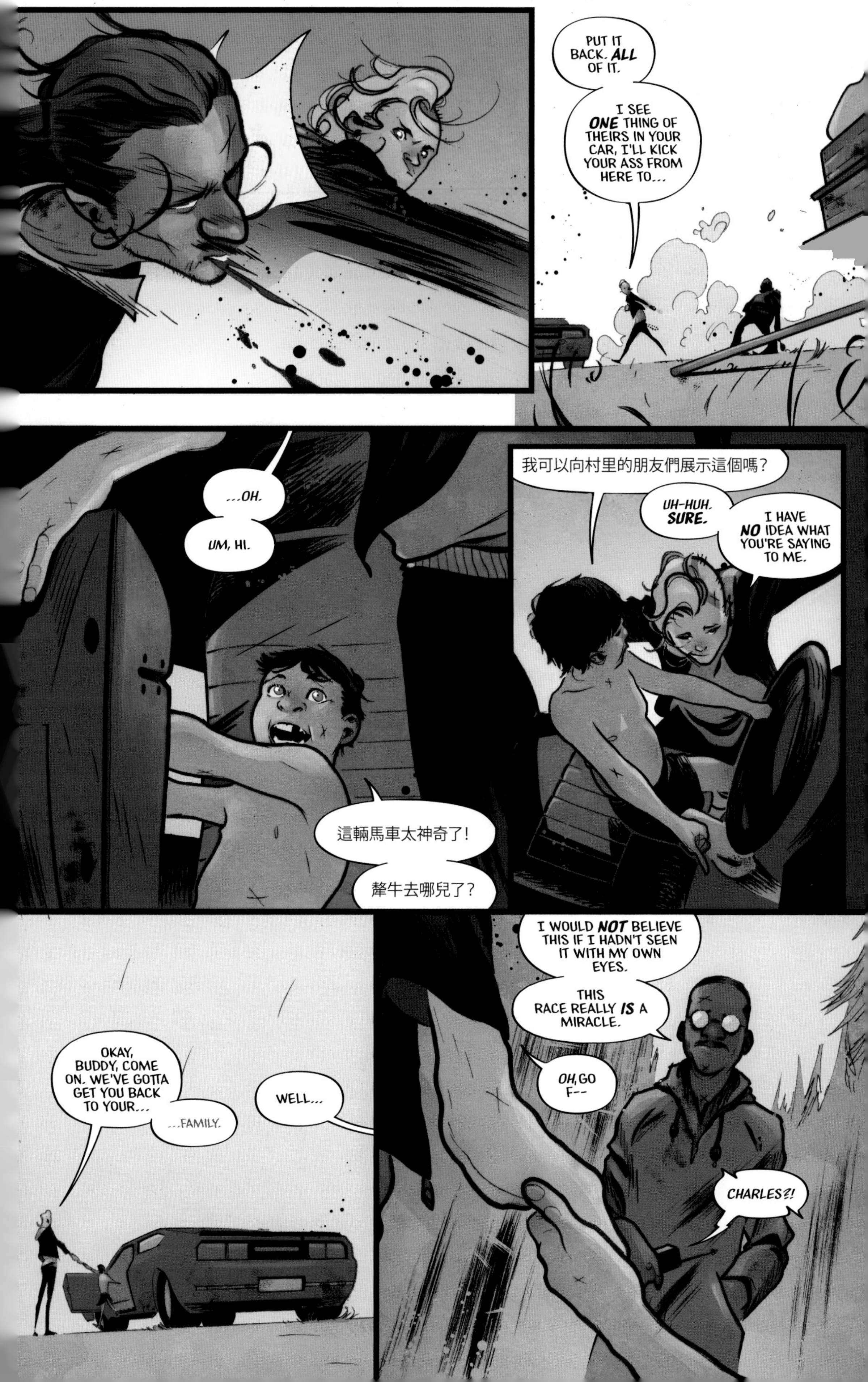
PUT IT BACK. ALL OF IT.
I SEE ONE THING OF THEIRS IN YOUR CAR, I'LL KICK YOUR ASS FROM HERE TO...
...OH.
UM, HI.
這輛馬車太神奇了!
犛牛去哪兒了?
我可以向村里的朋友們展示這個嗎?
UH-HUH. SURE.
I HAVE NO IDEA WHAT YOU'RE SAYING TO ME.
OKAY, BUDDY, COME ON. WE'VE GOTTA GET YOU BACK TO YOUR...
...FAMILY.
WELL...
I WOULD NOT BELIEVE THIS IF I HADN'T SEEN IT WITH MY OWN EYES.
THIS RACE REALLY IS A MIRACLE.
OH, GO F--
CHARLES?!

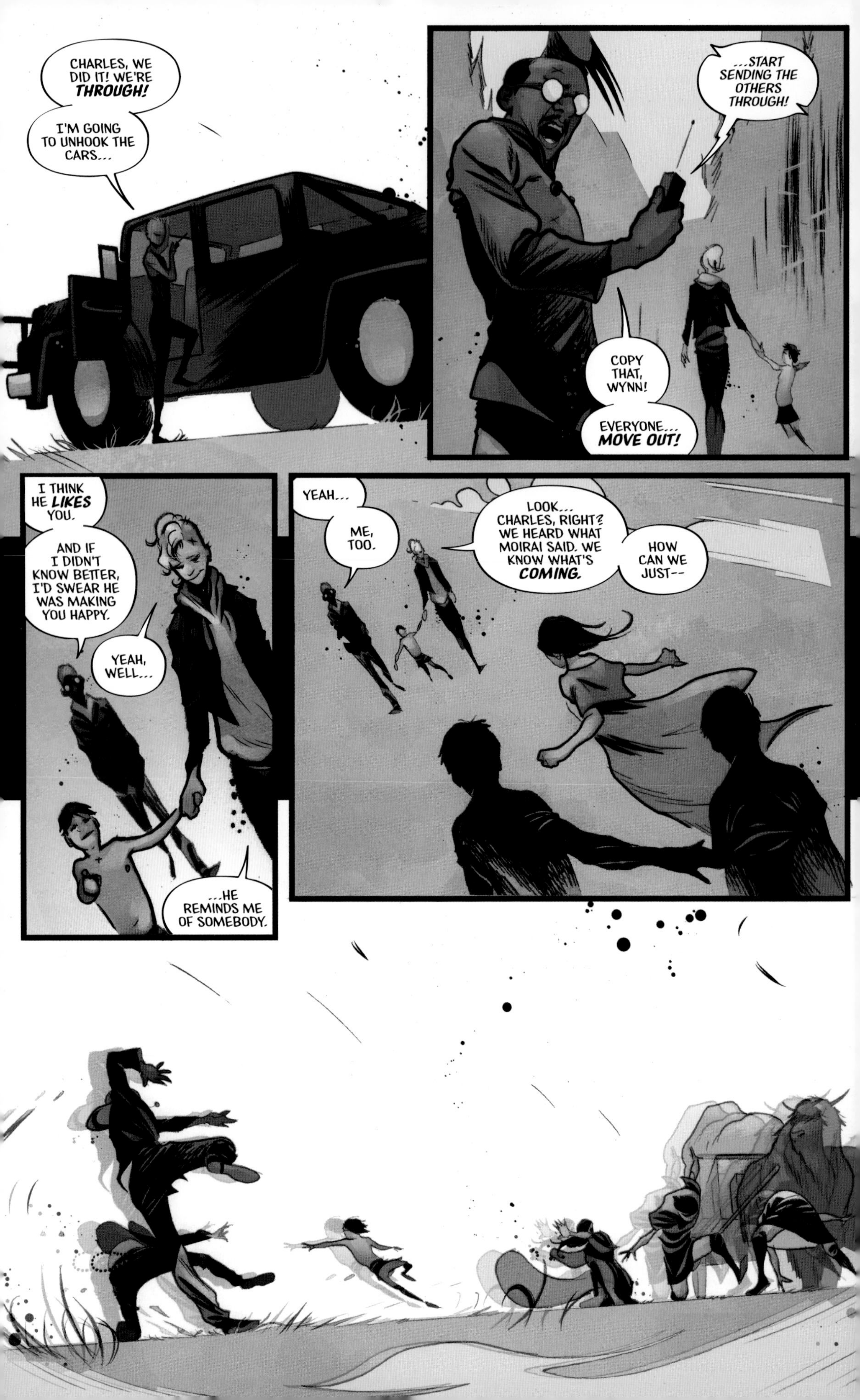
CHARLES, WE DID IT! WE'RE THROUGH!
I'M GOING TO UNHOOK THE CARS...
...START SENDING THE OTHERS THROUGH!
COPY THAT, WYNN!
EVERYONE... MOVE OUT!
I THINK HE LIKES YOU.
AND IF I DIDN'T KNOW BETTER, I'D SWEAR HE WAS MAKING YOU HAPPY.
YEAH, WELL...
...HE REMINDS ME OF SOMEBODY.
YEAH...
ME, TOO.
LOOK... CHARLES, RIGHT? WE HEARD WHAT MOIRAI SAID. WE KNOW WHAT'S COMING.
HOW CAN WE JUST--

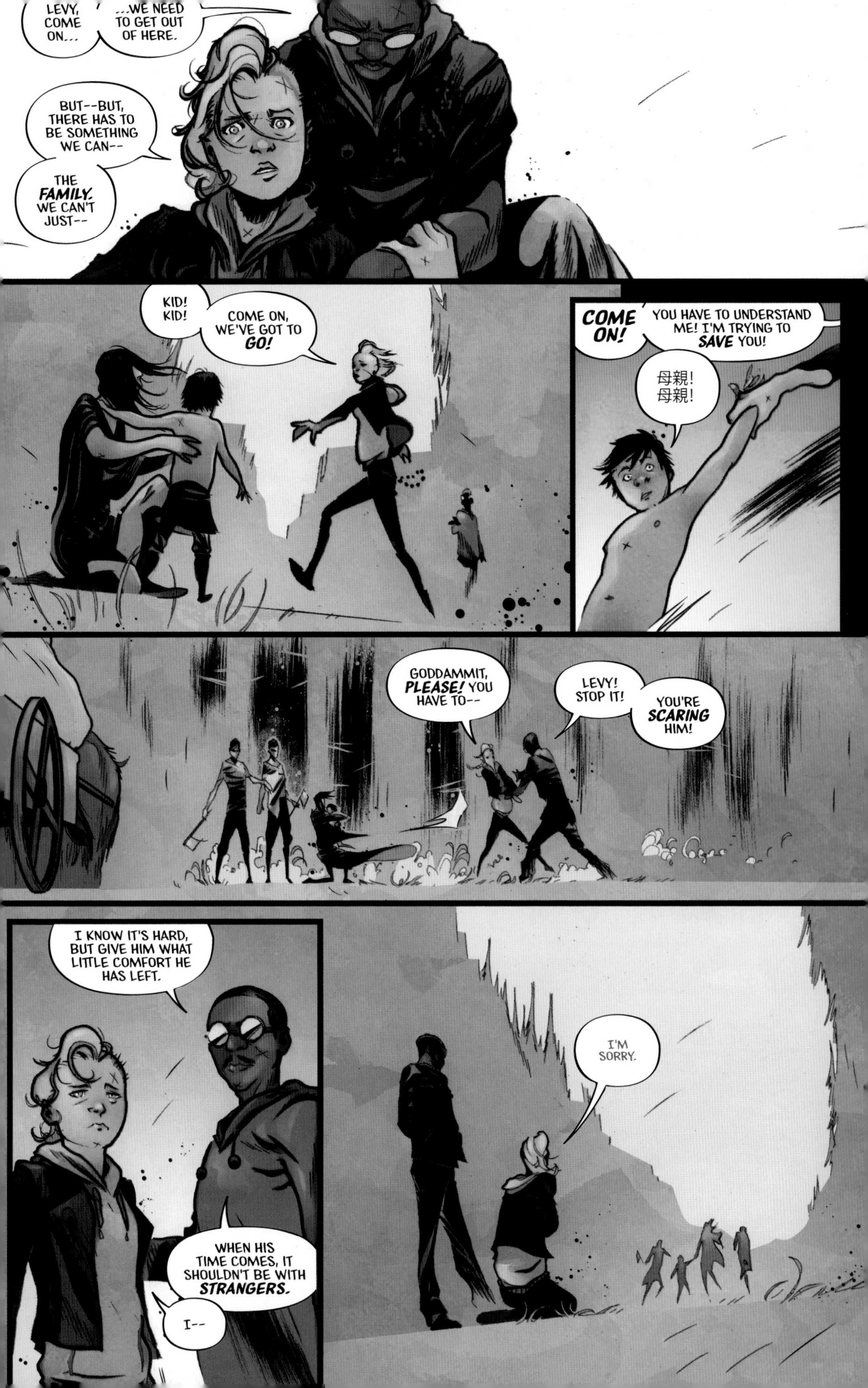
LEVY, COME ON...
...WE NEED TO GET OUT OF HERE.
BUT--BUT, THERE HAS TO BE SOMETHING WE CAN--
THE FAMILY. WE CAN'T JUST--
KID! KID!
COME ON, WE'VE GOT TO GO!
COME ON!
YOU HAVE TO UNDERSTAND ME! I'M TRYING TO SAVE YOU!
母親! 母親!
GODDAMMIT, PLEASE! YOU HAVE TO--
LEVY! STOP IT!
YOU'RE SCARING HIM!
I KNOW IT'S HARD, BUT GIVE HIM WHAT LITTLE COMFORT HE HAS LEFT.
WHEN HIS TIME COMES, IT SHOULDN'T BE WITH STRANGERS.
I--
I'M SORRY.

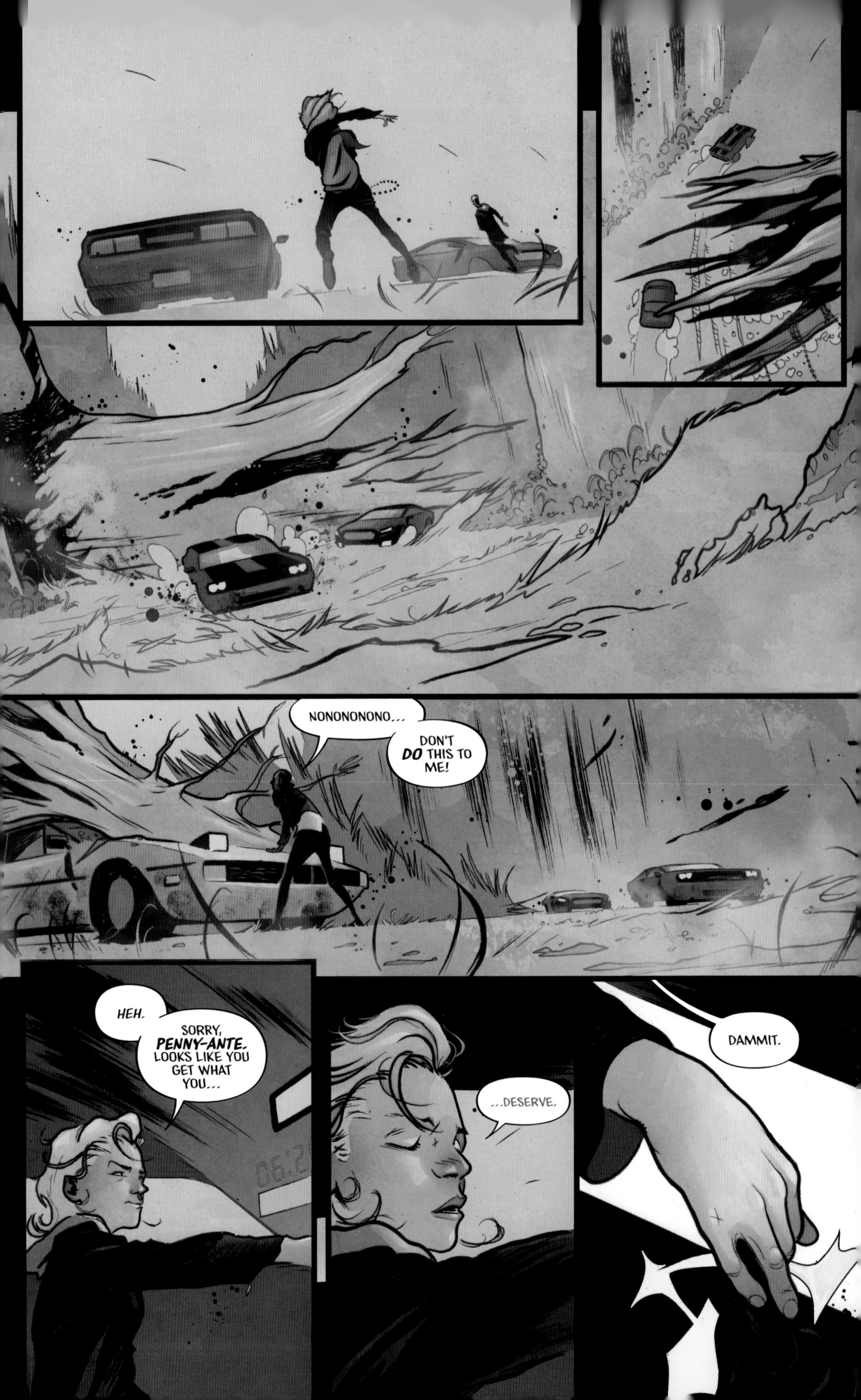
NONONONONO...
DON'T DO THIS TO ME!
HEH.
SORRY, PENNY-ANTE. LOOKS LIKE YOU GET WHAT YOU...
...DESERVE.
DAMMIT.

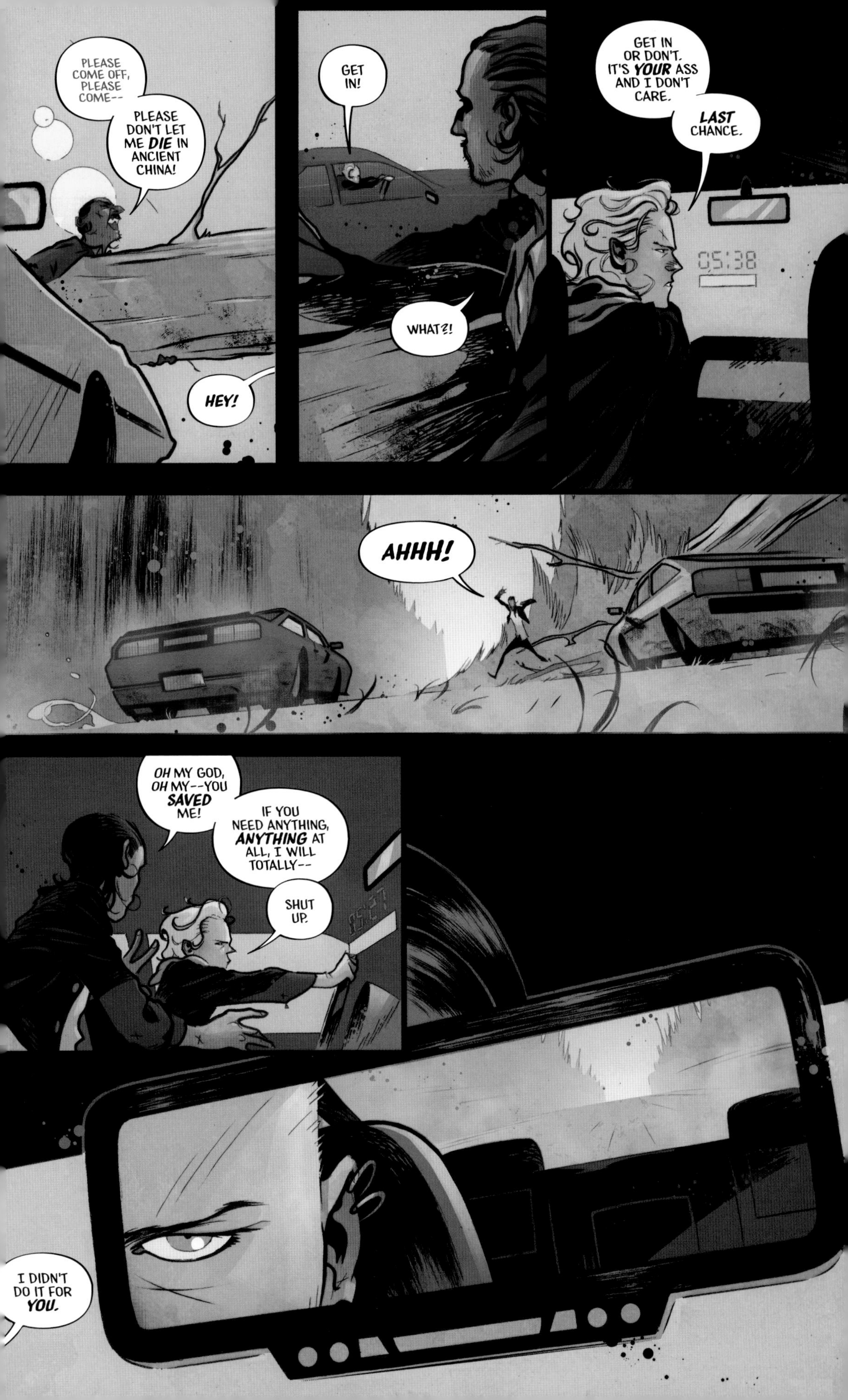
PLEASE COME OFF, PLEASE COME--
PLEASE DON'T LET ME DIE IN ANCIENT CHINA!
HEY!
GET IN!
WHAT?!
GET IN OR DON'T. IT'S YOUR ASS AND I DON'T CARE.
LAST CHANCE.
05:38
AHHH!
OH MY GOD, OH MY--YOU SAVED ME!
IF YOU NEED ANYTHING, ANYTHING AT ALL, I WILL TOTALLY--
SHUT UP.
I DIDN'T DO IT FOR YOU.

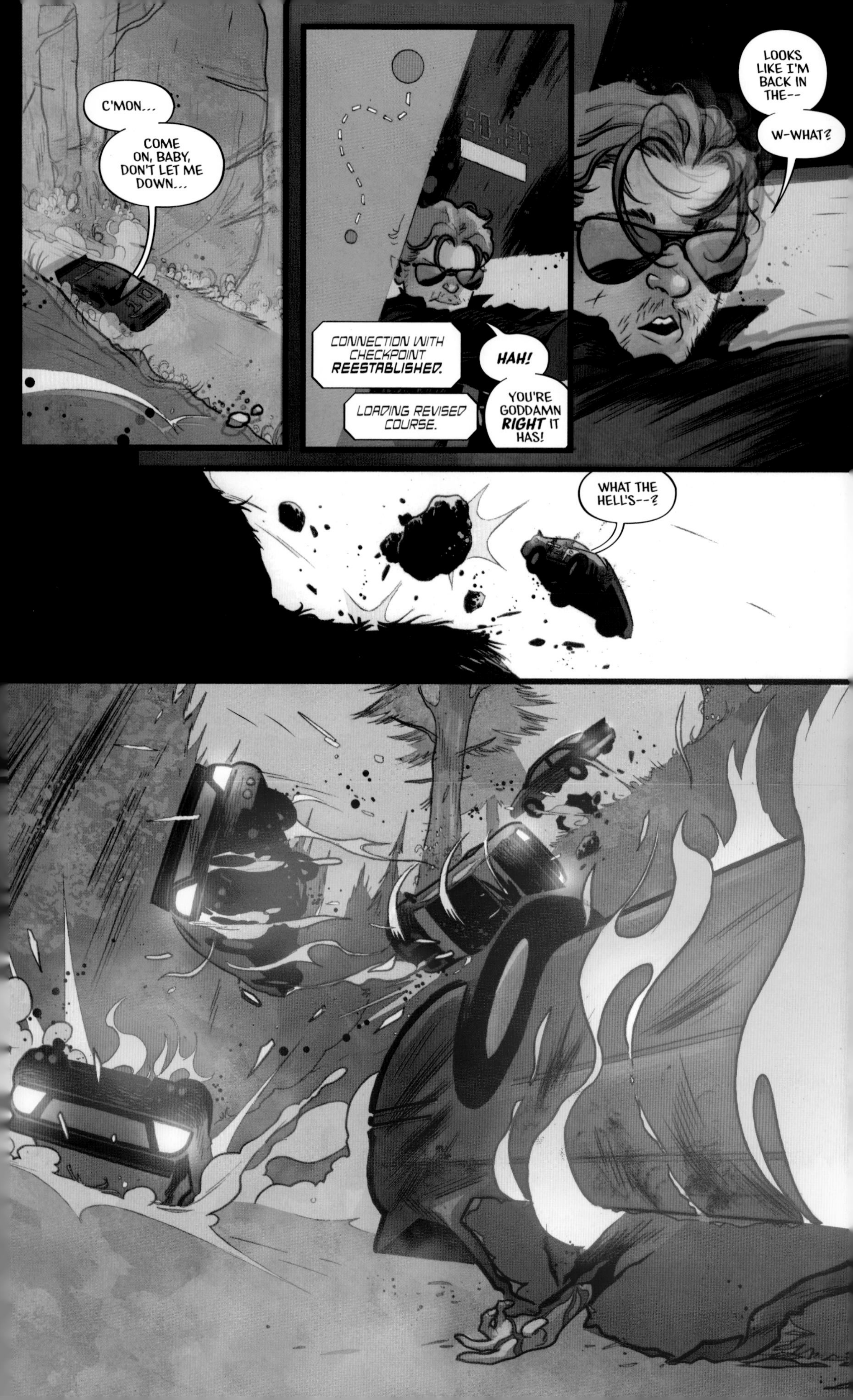
C'MON...
COME ON, BABY, DON'T LET ME DOWN...
CONNECTION WITH CHECKPOINT **REESTABLISHED.**
LOADING REVISED COURSE.
HAH!
YOU'RE GODDAMN **RIGHT** IT HAS!
LOOKS LIKE I'M BACK IN THE--
W-WHAT?
WHAT THE HELL'S--?

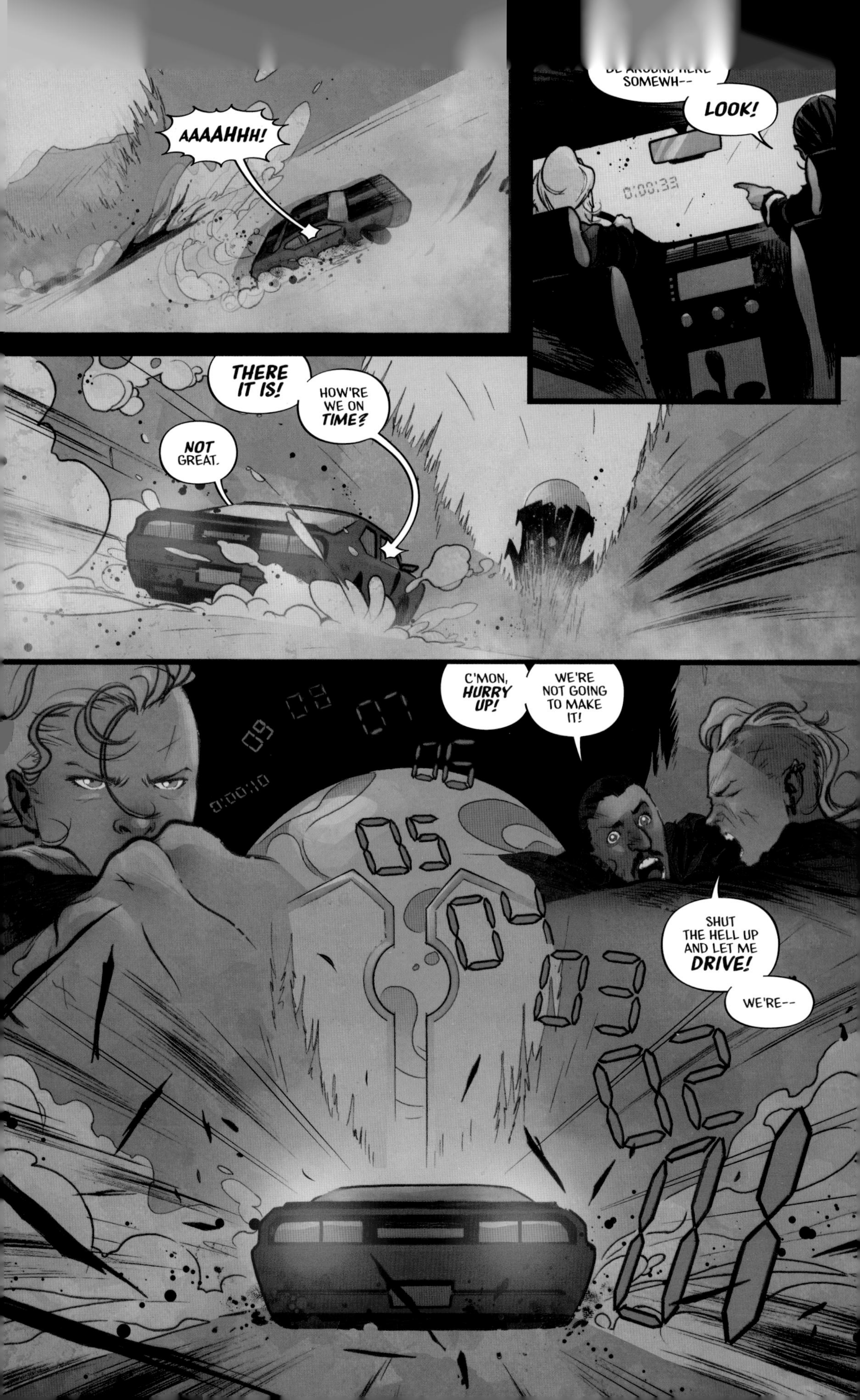
AAAAHHH!
SOMEWH--
LOOK!
THERE IT IS!
HOW'RE WE ON TIME?
NOT GREAT.
C'MON, HURRY UP!
WE'RE NOT GOING TO MAKE IT!
SHUT THE HELL UP AND LET ME DRIVE!
WE'RE--

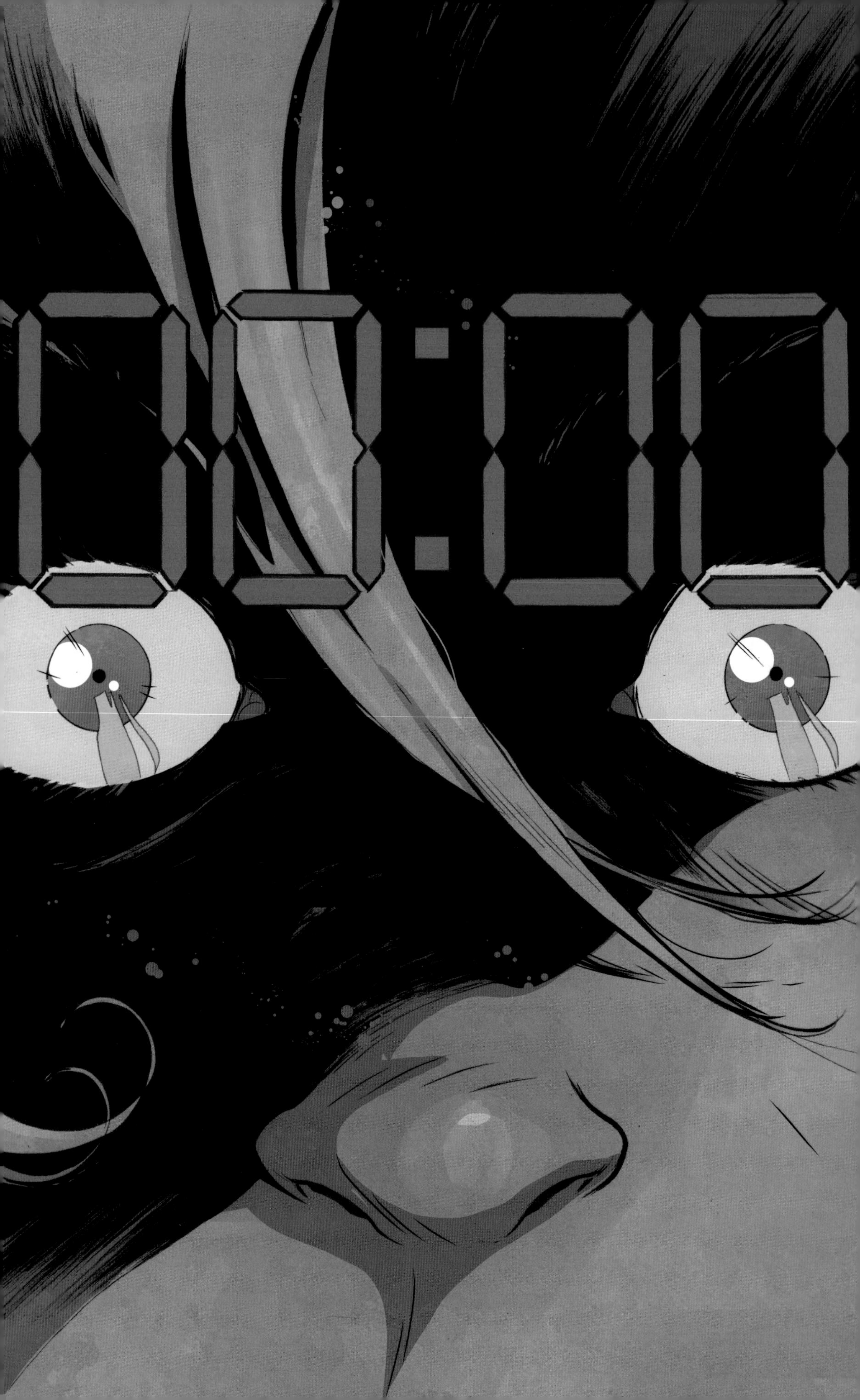
00:00

CHAPTER
4

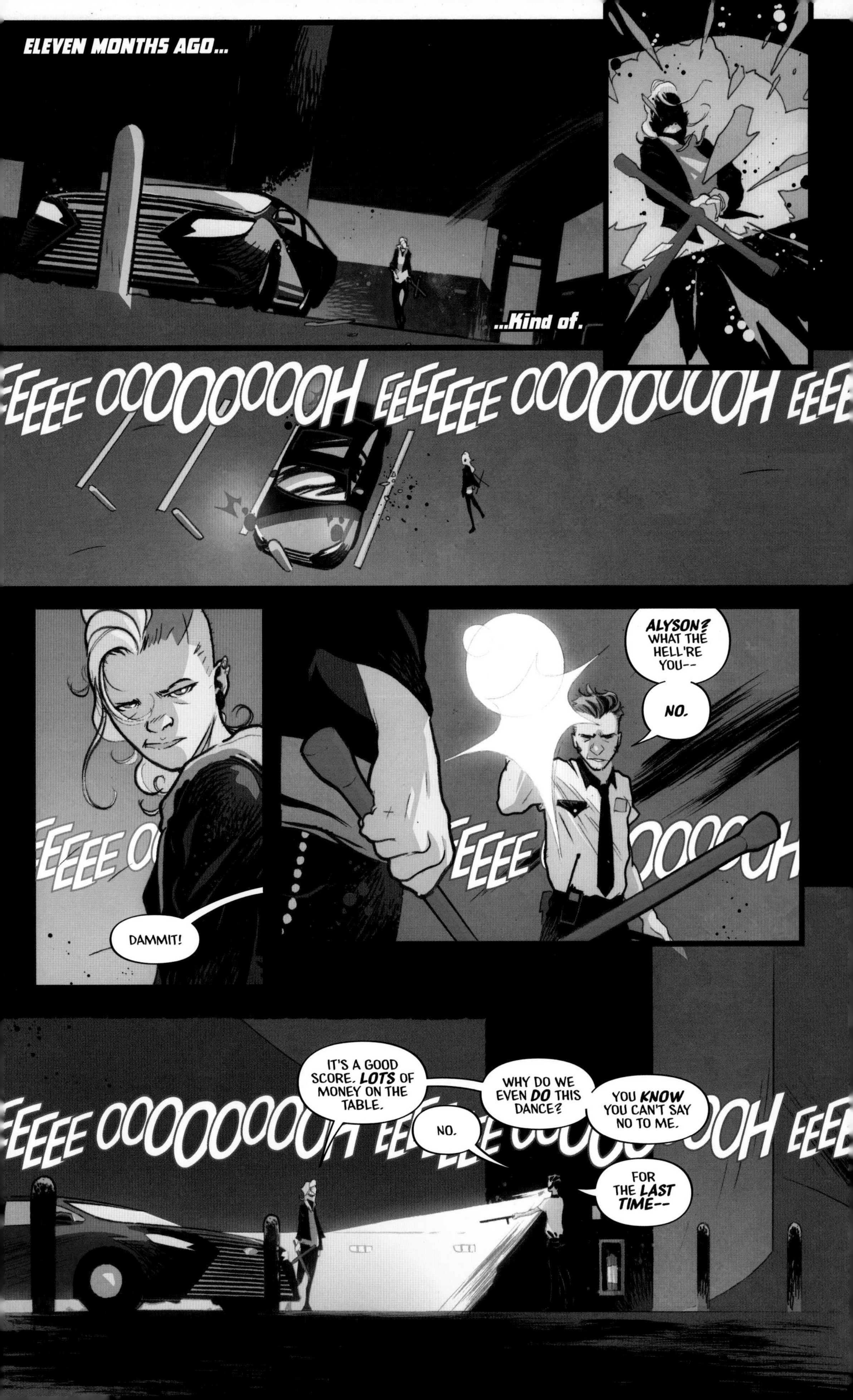
ELEVEN MONTHS AGO...
...Kind of.
EEEEE OOOOOOOOH EEEEEEE OOOOOUUUOH EEEE
EEEEE OO
DAMMIT!
ALYSON? WHAT THE HELL'RE YOU--
NO.
EEEE OOOOOOH
IT'S A GOOD SCORE. LOTS OF MONEY ON THE TABLE.
NO.
WHY DO WE EVEN DO THIS DANCE?
YOU KNOW YOU CAN'T SAY NO TO ME.
FOR THE LAST TIME--

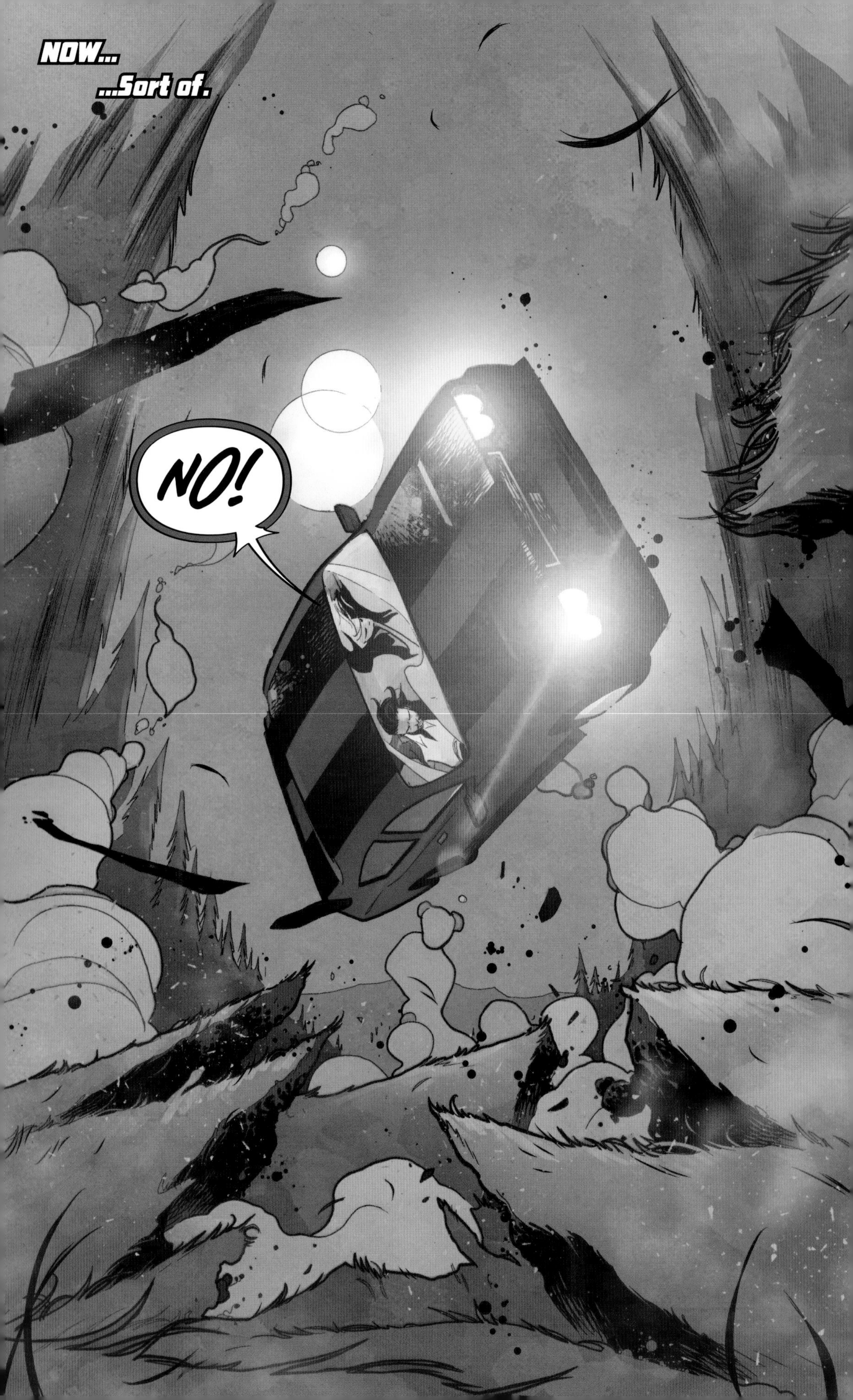
NOW...
...Sort of.
NO!

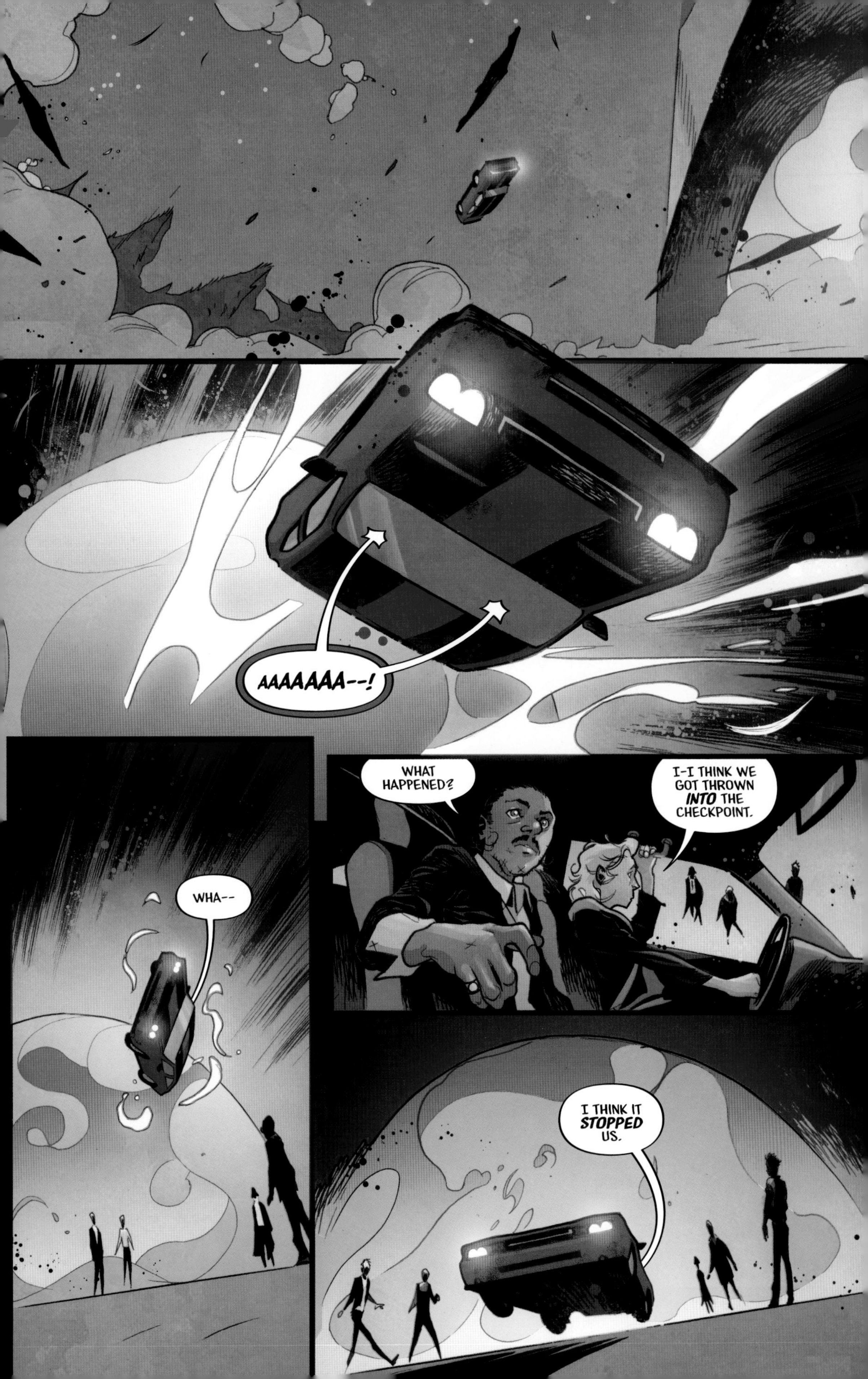
AAAAAAA--!
WHA--
WHAT HAPPENED?
I-I THINK WE GOT THROWN INTO THE CHECKPOINT.
I THINK IT STOPPED US.

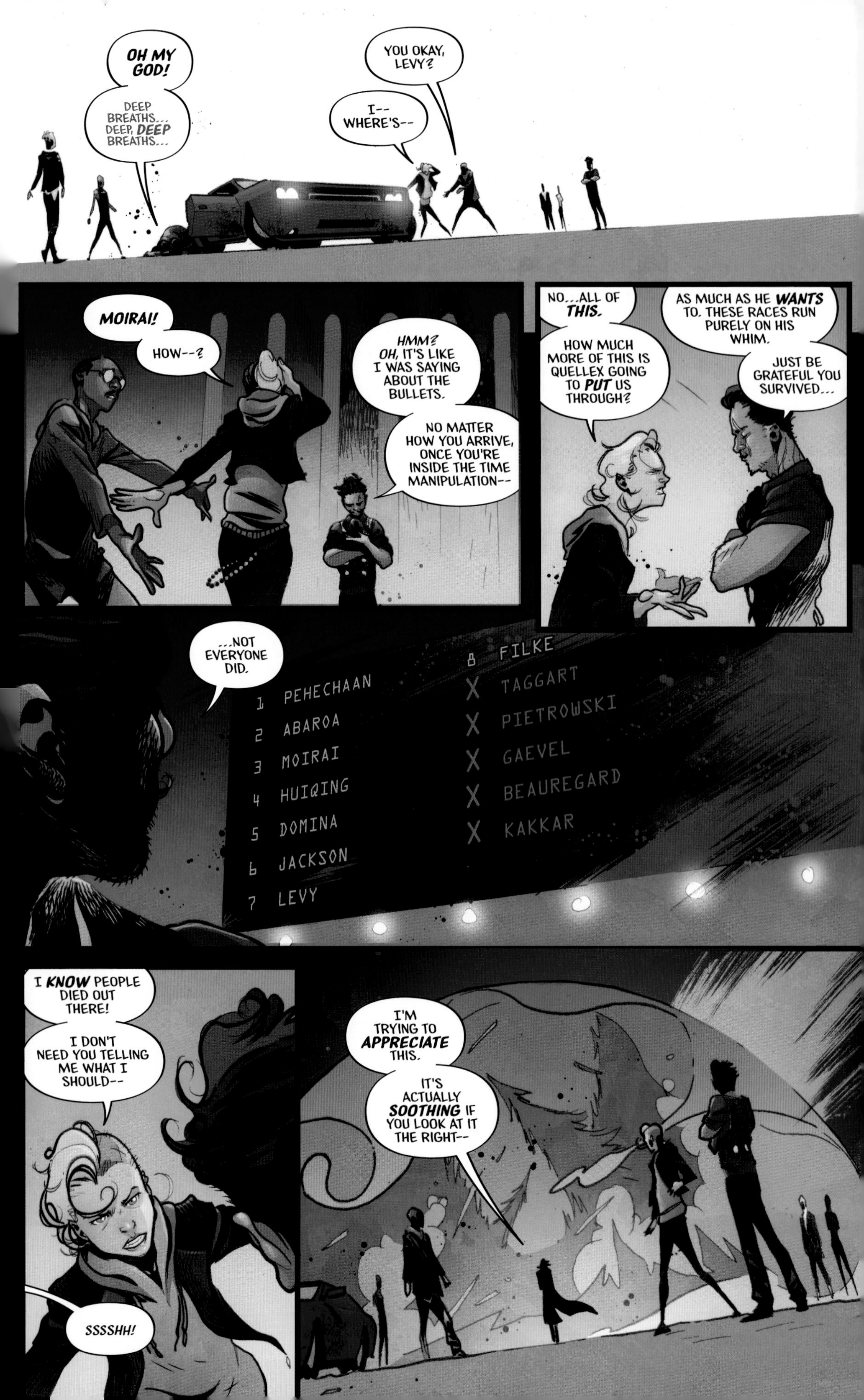
OH MY GOD!
DEEP BREATHS... DEEP, DEEP BREATHS...
YOU OKAY, LEVY?
I-- WHERE'S--
MOIRAI!
HOW--?
HMM? OH, IT'S LIKE I WAS SAYING ABOUT THE BULLETS.
NO MATTER HOW YOU ARRIVE, ONCE YOU'RE INSIDE THE TIME MANIPULATION--
NO...ALL OF THIS.
HOW MUCH MORE OF THIS IS QUELLEX GOING TO PUT US THROUGH?
AS MUCH AS HE WANTS TO. THESE RACES RUN PURELY ON HIS WHIM.
JUST BE GRATEFUL YOU SURVIVED...
...NOT EVERYONE DID.
1 PEHECHAAN
2 ABAROA
3 MOIRAI
4 HUIQING
5 DOMINA
6 JACKSON
7 LEVY
8 FILKE
X TAGGART
X PIETROWSKI
X GAEVEL
X BEAUREGARD
X KAKKAR
I KNOW PEOPLE DIED OUT THERE!
I DON'T NEED YOU TELLING ME WHAT I SHOULD--
SSSSHH!
I'M TRYING TO APPRECIATE THIS.
IT'S ACTUALLY SOOTHING IF YOU LOOK AT IT THE RIGHT--

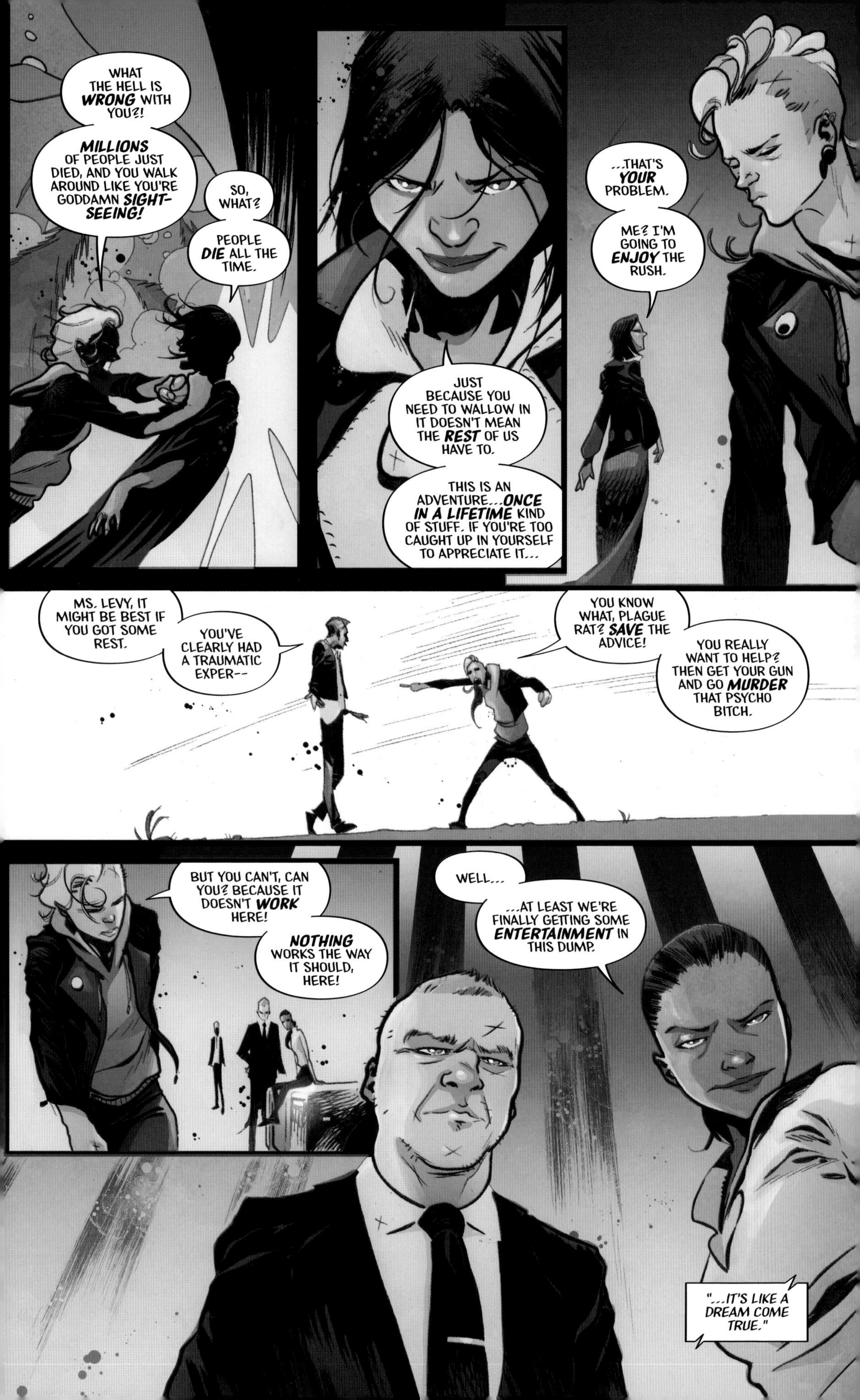
WHAT THE HELL IS WRONG WITH YOU?!
MILLIONS OF PEOPLE JUST DIED, AND YOU WALK AROUND LIKE YOU'RE GODDAMN SIGHT-SEEING!
SO, WHAT?
PEOPLE DIE ALL THE TIME.
JUST BECAUSE YOU NEED TO WALLOW IN IT DOESN'T MEAN THE REST OF US HAVE TO.
THIS IS AN ADVENTURE...ONCE IN A LIFETIME KIND OF STUFF. IF YOU'RE TOO CAUGHT UP IN YOURSELF TO APPRECIATE IT...
...THAT'S YOUR PROBLEM.
ME? I'M GOING TO ENJOY THE RUSH.
MS. LEVY, IT MIGHT BE BEST IF YOU GOT SOME REST.
YOU'VE CLEARLY HAD A TRAUMATIC EXPER--
YOU KNOW WHAT, PLAGUE RAT? SAVE THE ADVICE!
YOU REALLY WANT TO HELP? THEN GET YOUR GUN AND GO MURDER THAT PSYCHO BITCH.
BUT YOU CAN'T, CAN YOU? BECAUSE IT DOESN'T WORK HERE!
NOTHING WORKS THE WAY IT SHOULD, HERE!
WELL...
...AT LEAST WE'RE FINALLY GETTING SOME ENTERTAINMENT IN THIS DUMP.
"...IT'S LIKE A DREAM COME TRUE."

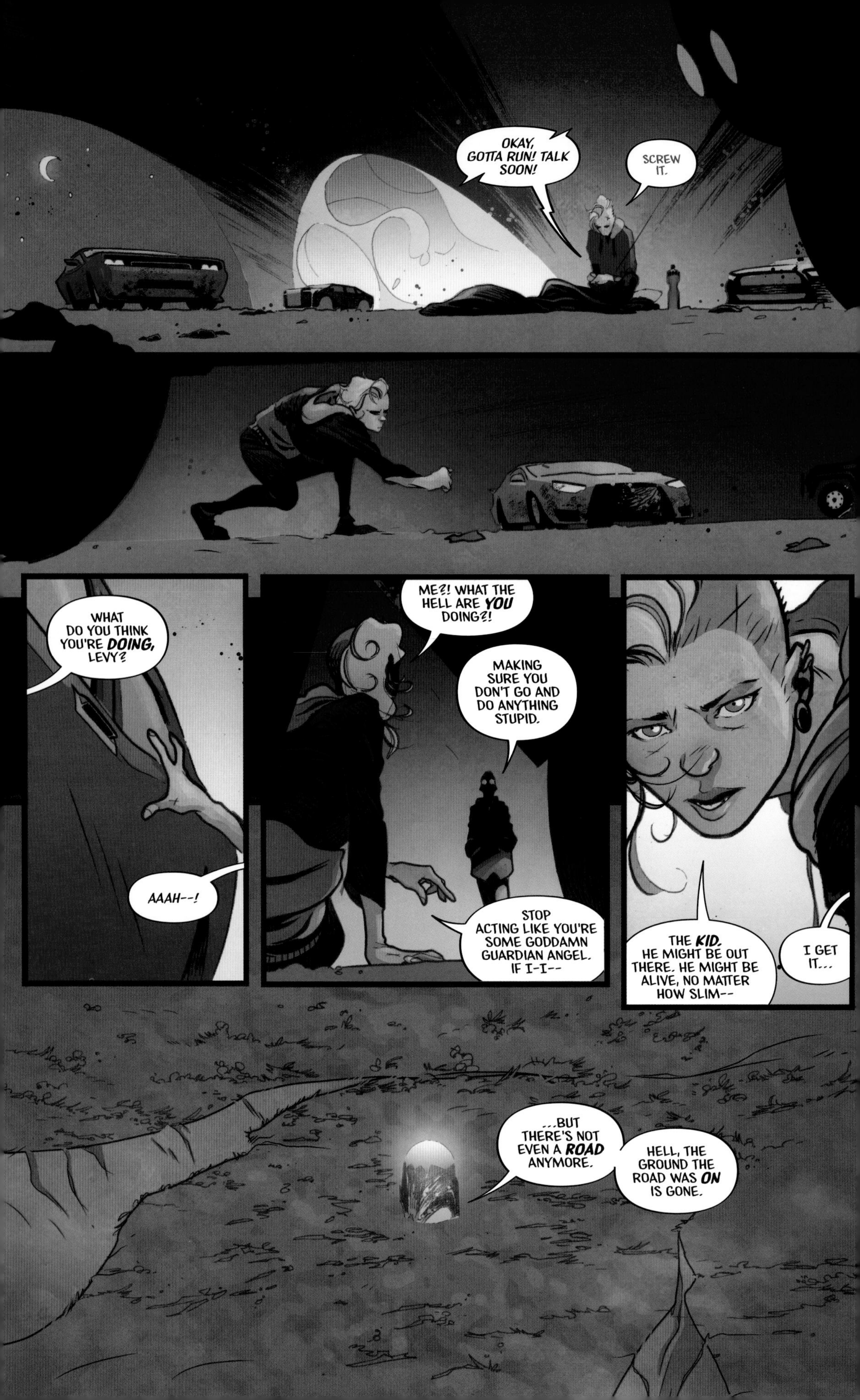
OKAY, GOTTA RUN! TALK SOON!
SCREW IT.
WHAT DO YOU THINK YOU'RE ***DOING,*** LEVY?
AAAH--!
ME?! WHAT THE HELL ARE ***YOU*** DOING?!
MAKING SURE YOU DON'T GO AND DO ANYTHING STUPID.
STOP ACTING LIKE YOU'RE SOME GODDAMN GUARDIAN ANGEL. IF I-I--
THE ***KID.*** HE MIGHT BE OUT THERE. HE MIGHT BE ALIVE, NO MATTER HOW SLIM--
I GET IT...
...BUT THERE'S NOT EVEN A ***ROAD*** ANYMORE.
HELL, THE GROUND THE ROAD WAS ***ON*** IS GONE.

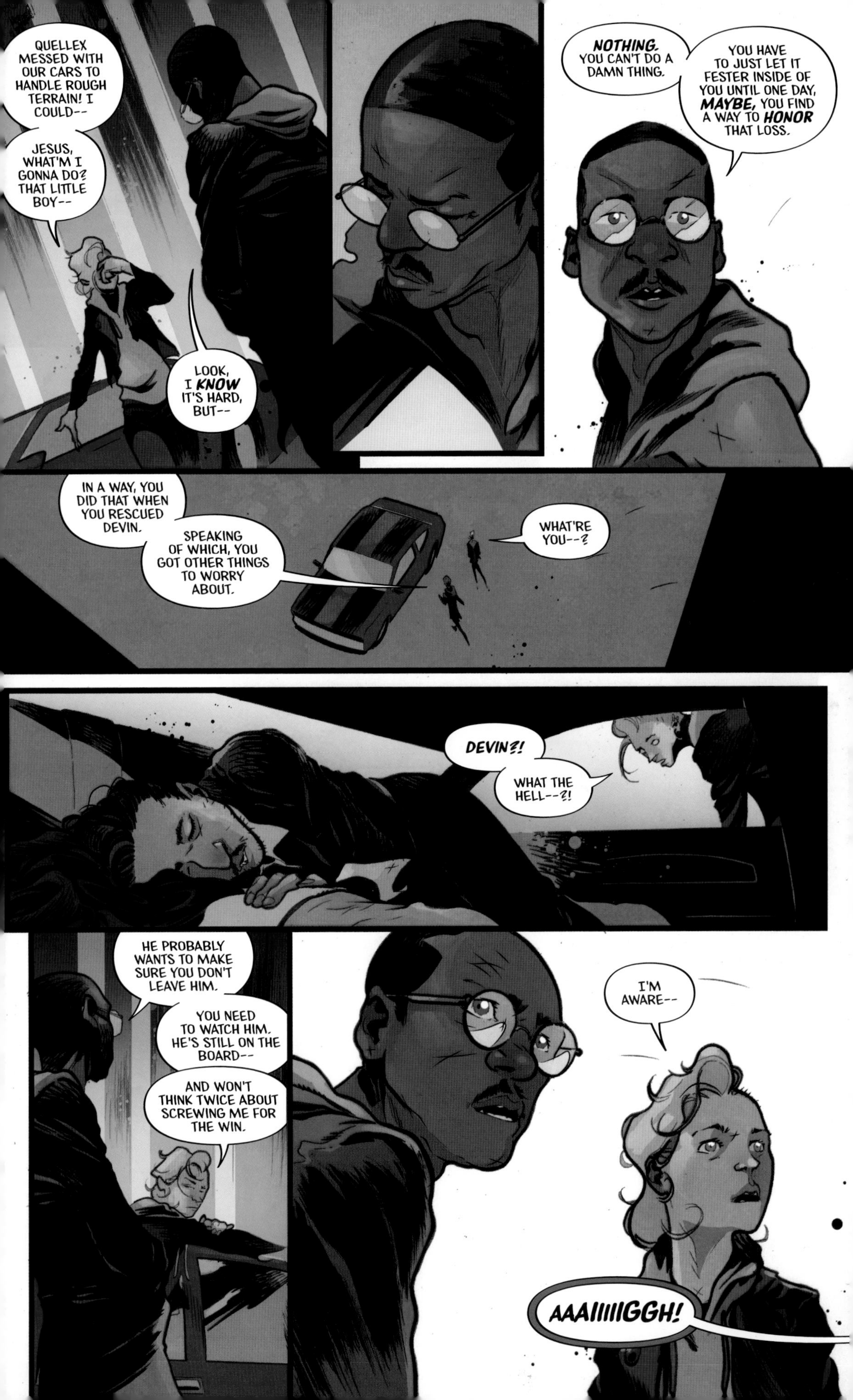
QUELLEX MESSED WITH OUR CARS TO HANDLE ROUGH TERRAIN! I COULD--
JESUS, WHAT'M I GONNA DO? THAT LITTLE BOY--
LOOK, I **KNOW** IT'S HARD, BUT--
NOTHING. YOU CAN'T DO A DAMN THING.
YOU HAVE TO JUST LET IT FESTER INSIDE OF YOU UNTIL ONE DAY, ***MAYBE,*** YOU FIND A WAY TO ***HONOR*** THAT LOSS.
IN A WAY, YOU DID THAT WHEN YOU RESCUED DEVIN.
SPEAKING OF WHICH, YOU GOT OTHER THINGS TO WORRY ABOUT.
WHAT'RE YOU--?
DEVIN?!
WHAT THE HELL--?!
HE PROBABLY WANTS TO MAKE SURE YOU DON'T LEAVE HIM.
YOU NEED TO WATCH HIM. HE'S STILL ON THE BOARD--
AND WON'T THINK TWICE ABOUT SCREWING ME FOR THE WIN.
I'M AWARE--
AAAIIIIIGGH!

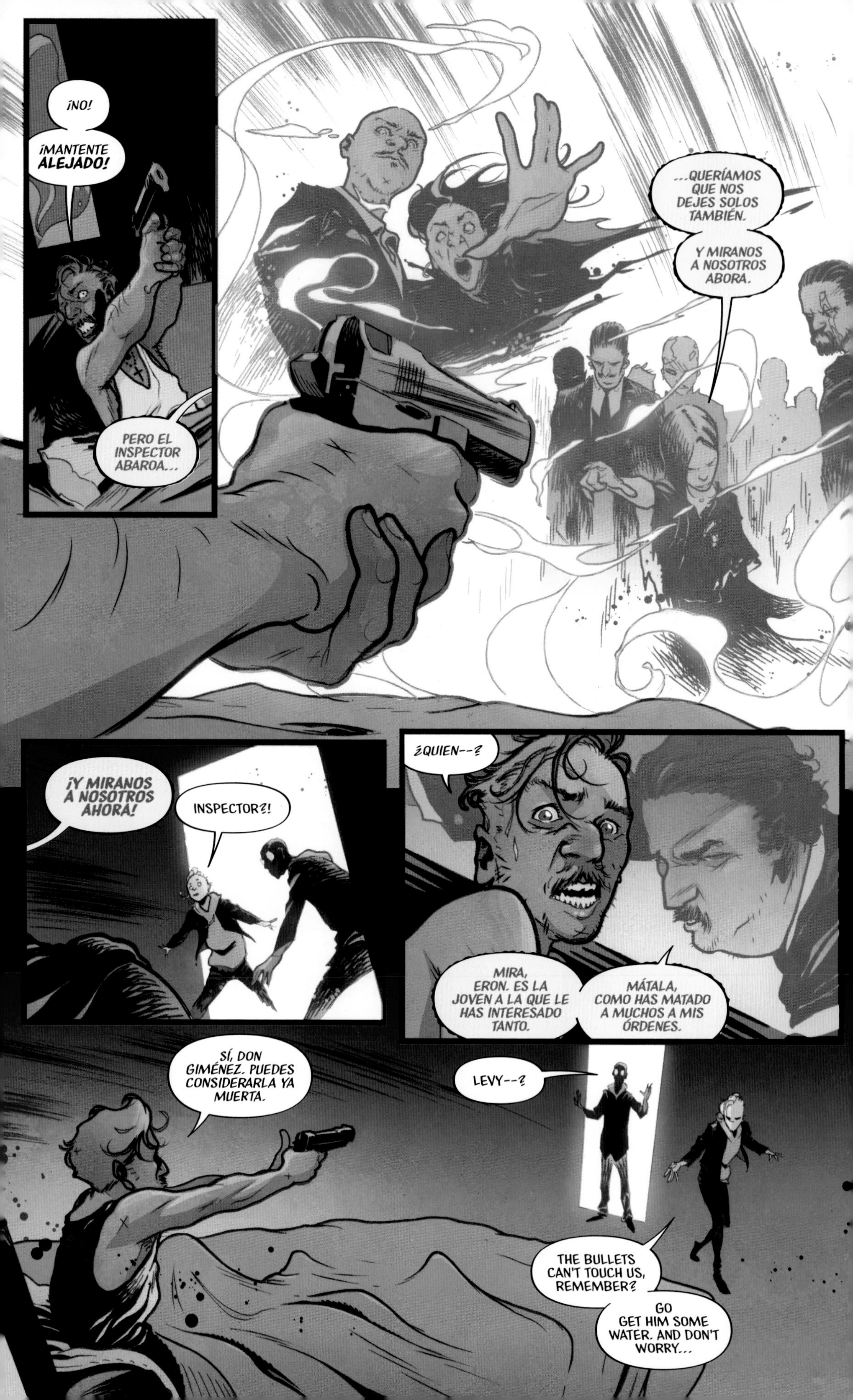

¡NO!
¡MANTENTE ALEJADO!
PERO EL INSPECTOR ABAROA...
...QUERÍAMOS QUE NOS DEJES SOLOS TAMBIÉN.
Y MIRANOS A NOSOTROS ABORA.
¡Y MIRANOS A NOSOTROS AHORA!
INSPECTOR?!
¿QUIEN--?
MIRA, ERON. ES LA JOVEN A LA QUE LE HAS INTERESADO TANTO.
MÁTALA, COMO HAS MATADO A MUCHOS A MIS ÓRDENES.
SÍ, DON GIMÉNEZ. PUEDES CONSIDERARLA YA MUERTA.
LEVY--?
THE BULLETS CAN'T TOUCH US, REMEMBER?
GO GET HIM SOME WATER. AND DON'T WORRY...

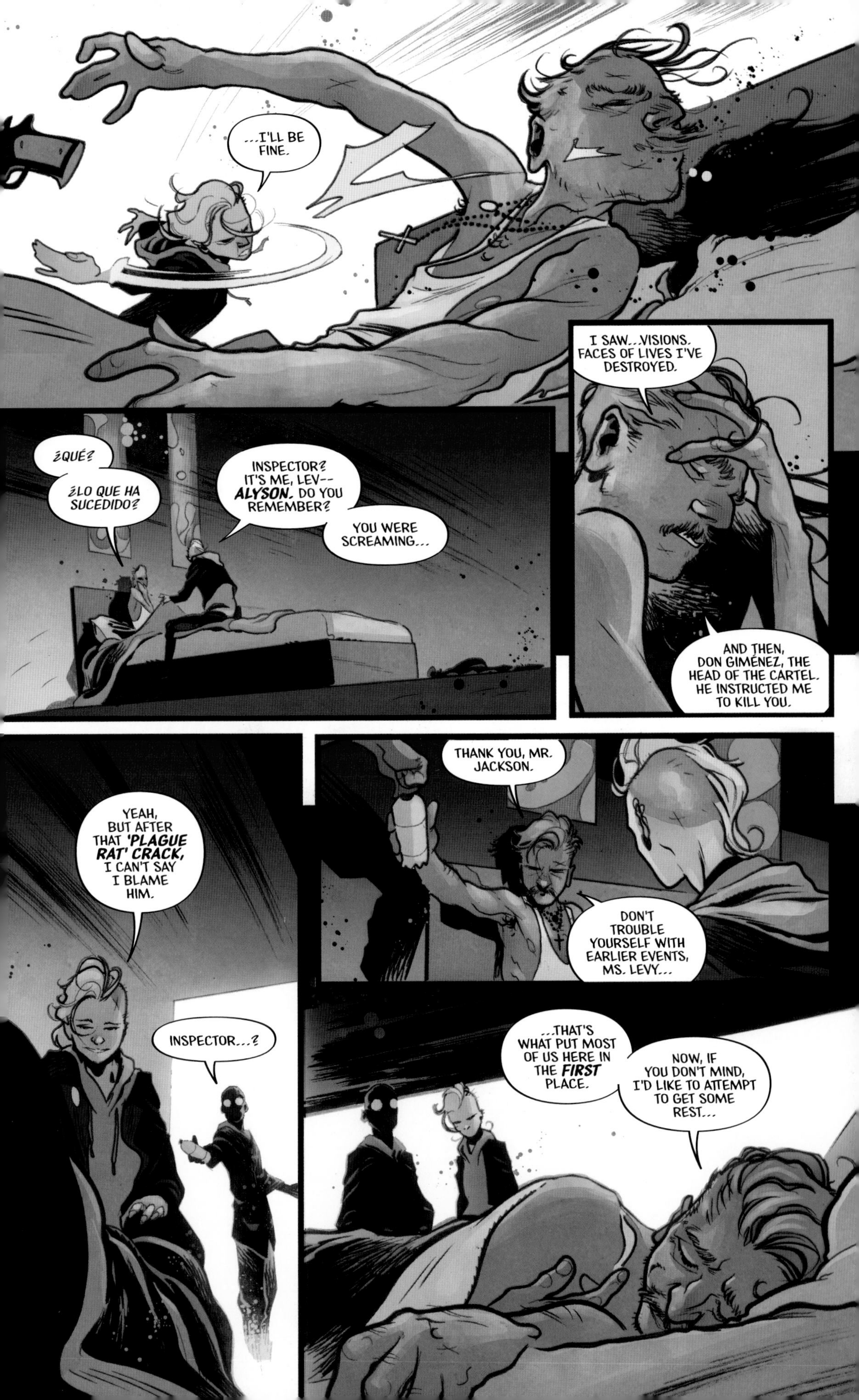
...I'LL BE FINE.
I SAW...VISIONS. FACES OF LIVES I'VE DESTROYED.
¿QUÉ?
¿LO QUE HA SUCEDIDO?
INSPECTOR? IT'S ME, LEV-- ALYSON. DO YOU REMEMBER?
YOU WERE SCREAMING...
AND THEN, DON GIMÉNEZ, THE HEAD OF THE CARTEL. HE INSTRUCTED ME TO KILL YOU.
YEAH, BUT AFTER THAT 'PLAGUE RAT' CRACK, I CAN'T SAY I BLAME HIM.
INSPECTOR...?
THANK YOU, MR. JACKSON.
DON'T TROUBLE YOURSELF WITH EARLIER EVENTS, MS. LEVY...
...THAT'S WHAT PUT MOST OF US HERE IN THE FIRST PLACE.
NOW, IF YOU DON'T MIND, I'D LIKE TO ATTEMPT TO GET SOME REST...

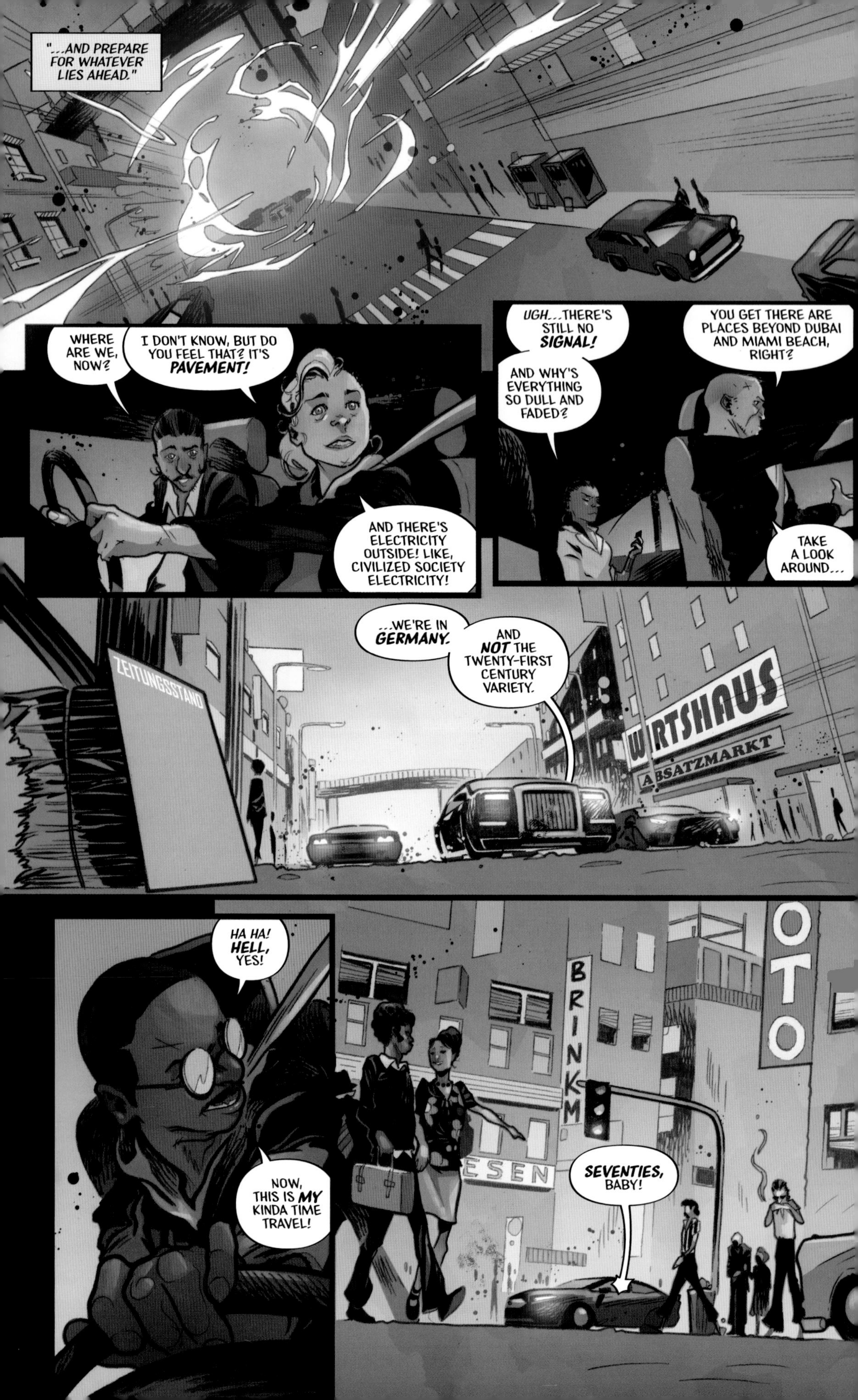
"...AND PREPARE FOR WHATEVER LIES AHEAD."
WHERE ARE WE, NOW?
I DON'T KNOW, BUT DO YOU FEEL THAT? IT'S PAVEMENT!
AND THERE'S ELECTRICITY OUTSIDE! LIKE, CIVILIZED SOCIETY ELECTRICITY!
UGH... THERE'S STILL NO SIGNAL!
AND WHY'S EVERYTHING SO DULL AND FADED?
YOU GET THERE ARE PLACES BEYOND DUBAI AND MIAMI BEACH, RIGHT?
TAKE A LOOK AROUND...
ZEITUNGSSTAND
...WE'RE IN GERMANY.
AND NOT THE TWENTY-FIRST CENTURY VARIETY.
WIRTSHAUS
ABSATZMARKT
HA HA! HELL, YES!
NOW, THIS IS MY KINDA TIME TRAVEL!
BRINKM
ESEN
OTO
SEVENTIES, BABY!

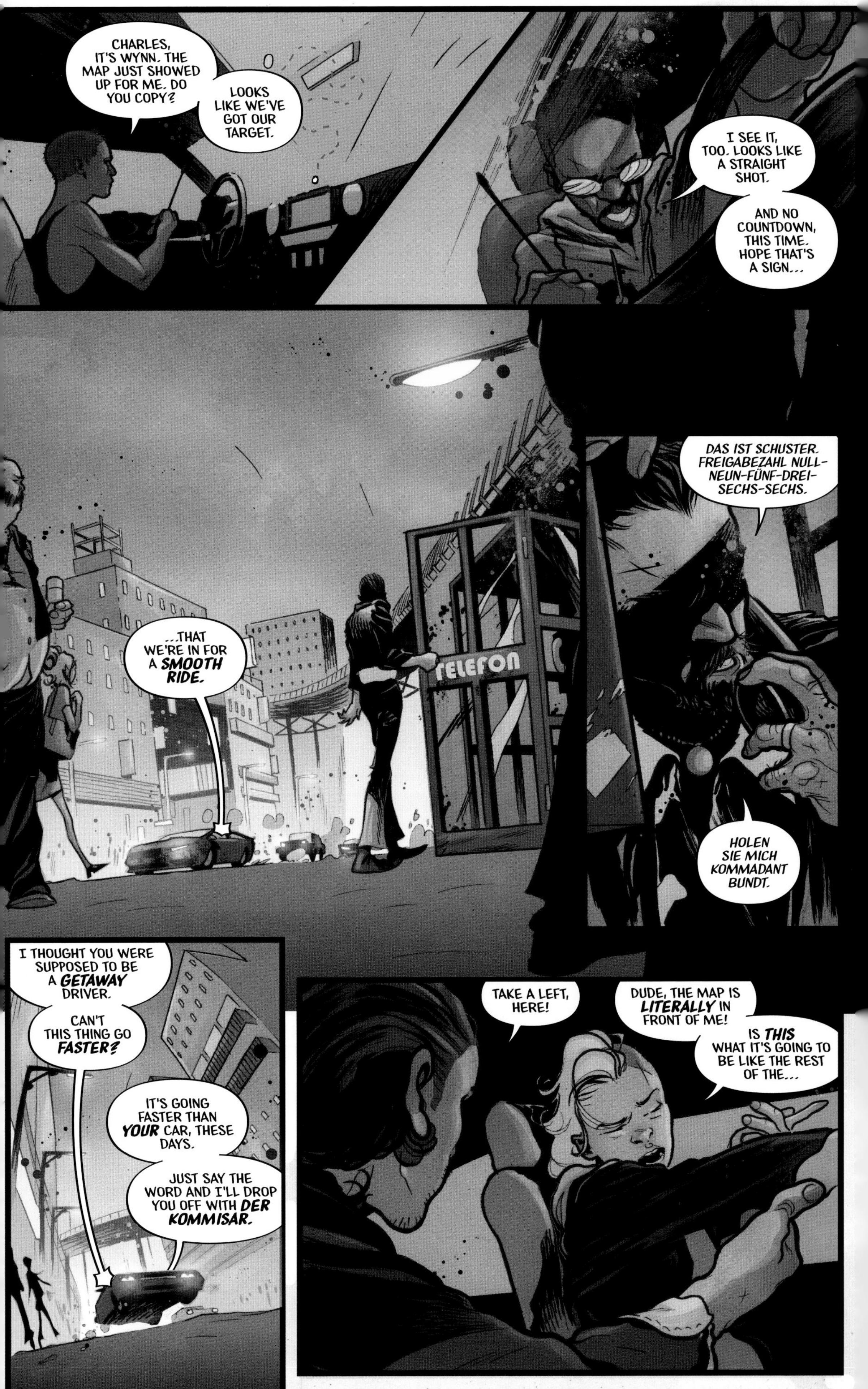
CHARLES, IT'S WYNN. THE MAP JUST SHOWED UP FOR ME. DO YOU COPY?
LOOKS LIKE WE'VE GOT OUR TARGET.
I SEE IT, TOO. LOOKS LIKE A STRAIGHT SHOT.
AND NO COUNTDOWN, THIS TIME. HOPE THAT'S A SIGN...
...THAT WE'RE IN FOR A SMOOTH RIDE.
TELEFON
DAS IST SCHUSTER. FREIGABEZAHL NULL-NEUN-FÜNF-DREI-SECHS-SECHS.
HOLEN SIE MICH KOMMADANT BUNDT.
I THOUGHT YOU WERE SUPPOSED TO BE A GETAWAY DRIVER.
CAN'T THIS THING GO FASTER?
IT'S GOING FASTER THAN YOUR CAR, THESE DAYS.
JUST SAY THE WORD AND I'LL DROP YOU OFF WITH DER KOMMISAR.
TAKE A LEFT, HERE!
DUDE, THE MAP IS LITERALLY IN FRONT OF ME!
IS THIS WHAT IT'S GOING TO BE LIKE THE REST OF THE...

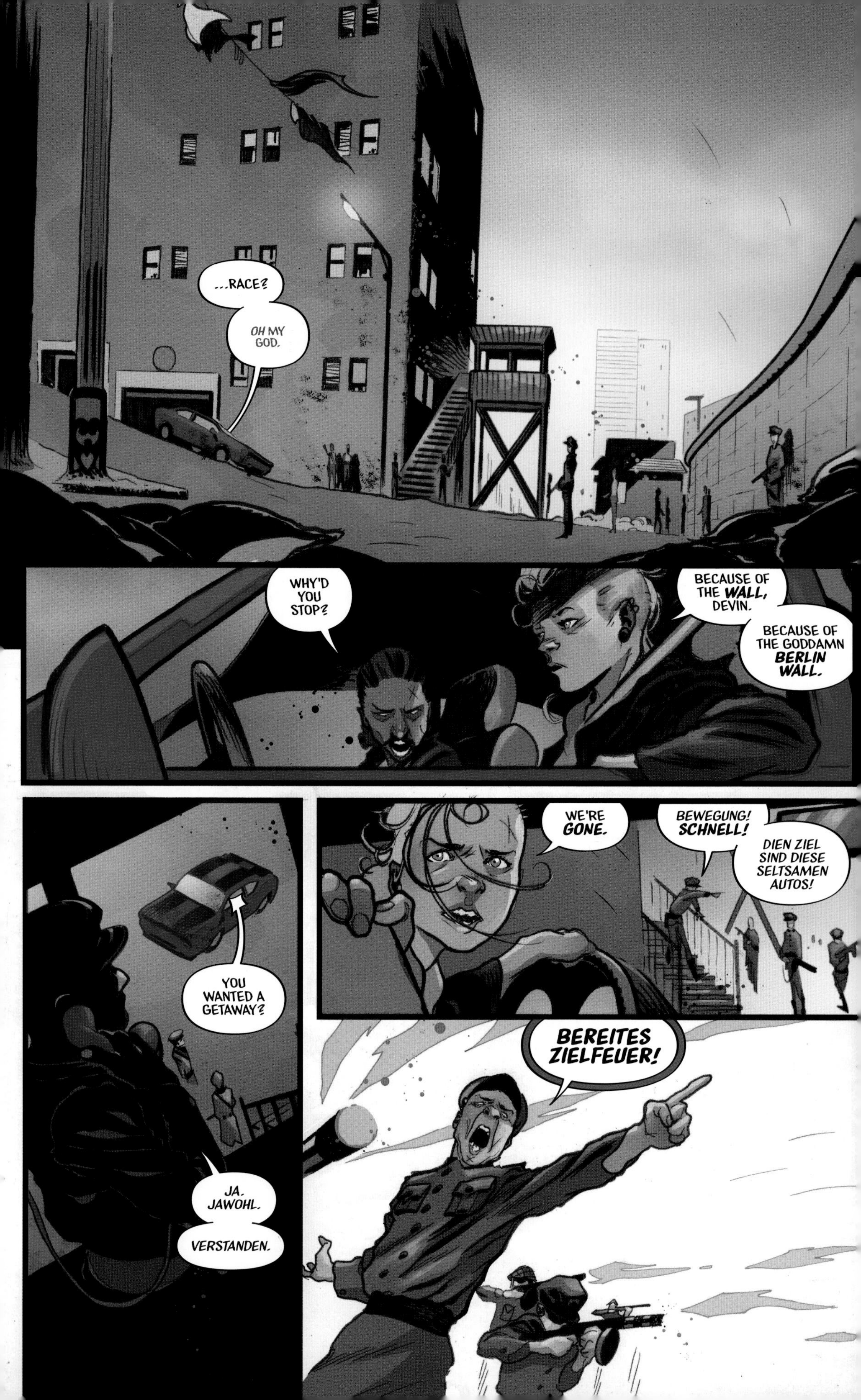
...RACE?
OH MY GOD.
WHY'D YOU STOP?
BECAUSE OF THE WALL, DEVIN.
BECAUSE OF THE GODDAMN BERLIN WALL.
YOU WANTED A GETAWAY?
JA. JAWOHL.
VERSTANDEN.
WE'RE GONE.
BEWEGUNG! SCHNELL!
DIEN ZIEL SIND DIESE SELTSAMEN AUTOS!
BEREITES ZIELFEUER!

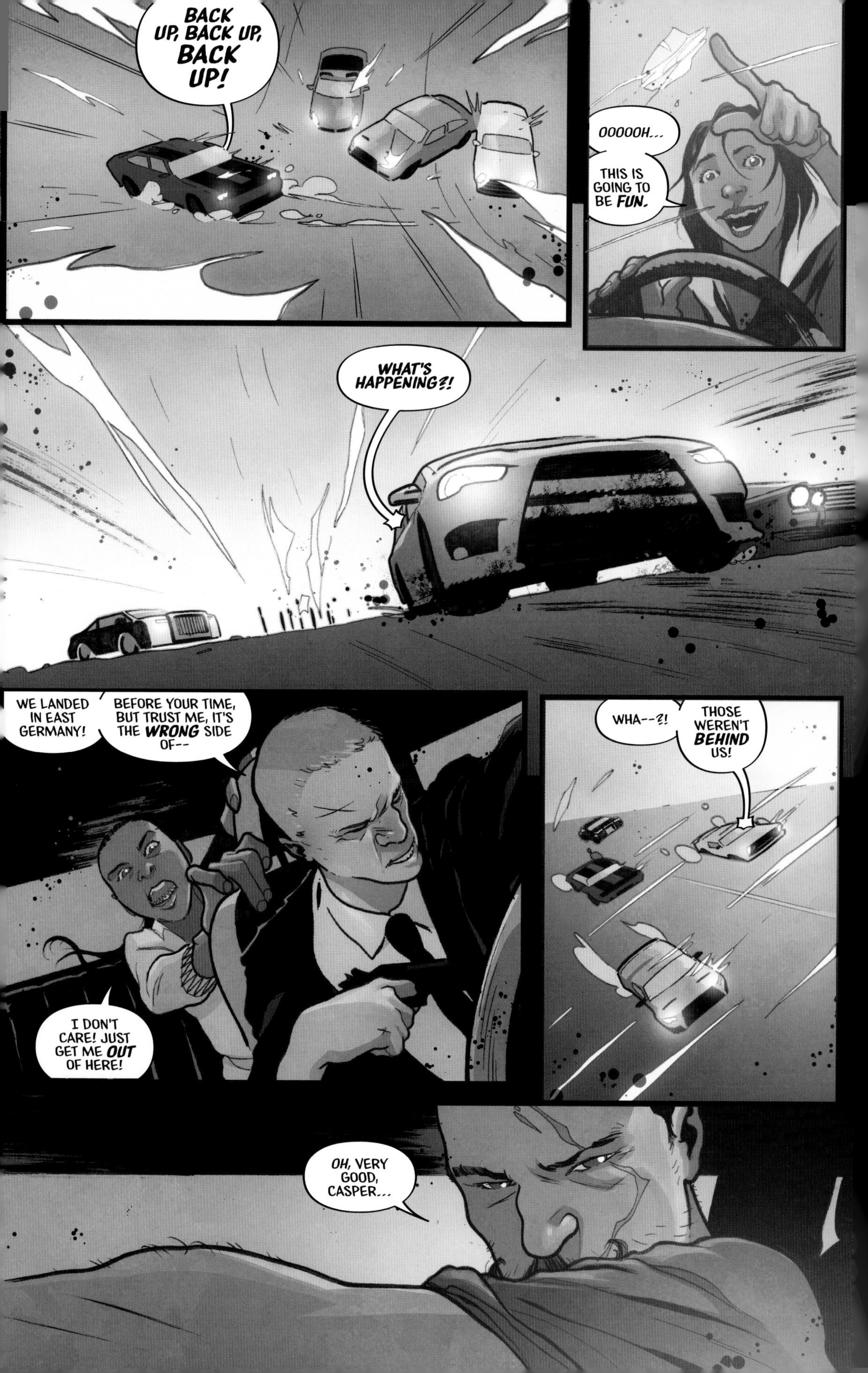
BACK UP, BACK UP, BACK UP!
OOOOOH...
THIS IS GOING TO BE FUN.
WHAT'S HAPPENING?!
WE LANDED IN EAST GERMANY!
BEFORE YOUR TIME, BUT TRUST ME, IT'S THE WRONG SIDE OF--
I DON'T CARE! JUST GET ME OUT OF HERE!
WHA--?!
THOSE WEREN'T BEHIND US!
OH, VERY GOOD, CASPER...

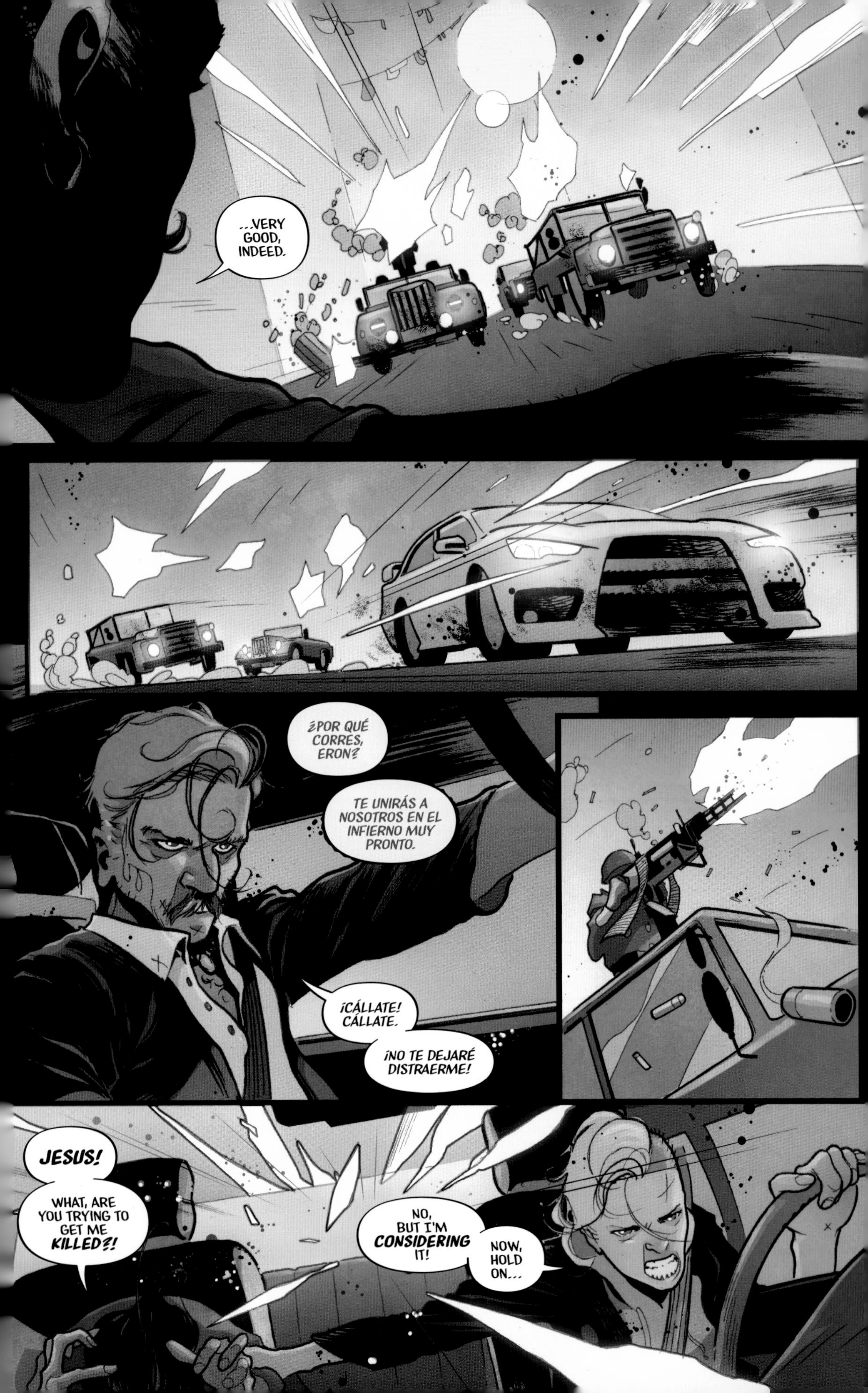
...VERY GOOD, INDEED.
¿POR QUÉ CORRES, ERON?
TE UNIRÁS A NOSOTROS EN EL INFIERNO MUY PRONTO.
¡CÁLLATE! CÁLLATE.
¡NO TE DEJARÉ DISTRAERME!
JESUS!
WHAT, ARE YOU TRYING TO GET ME KILLED?!
NO, BUT I'M CONSIDERING IT!
NOW, HOLD ON...

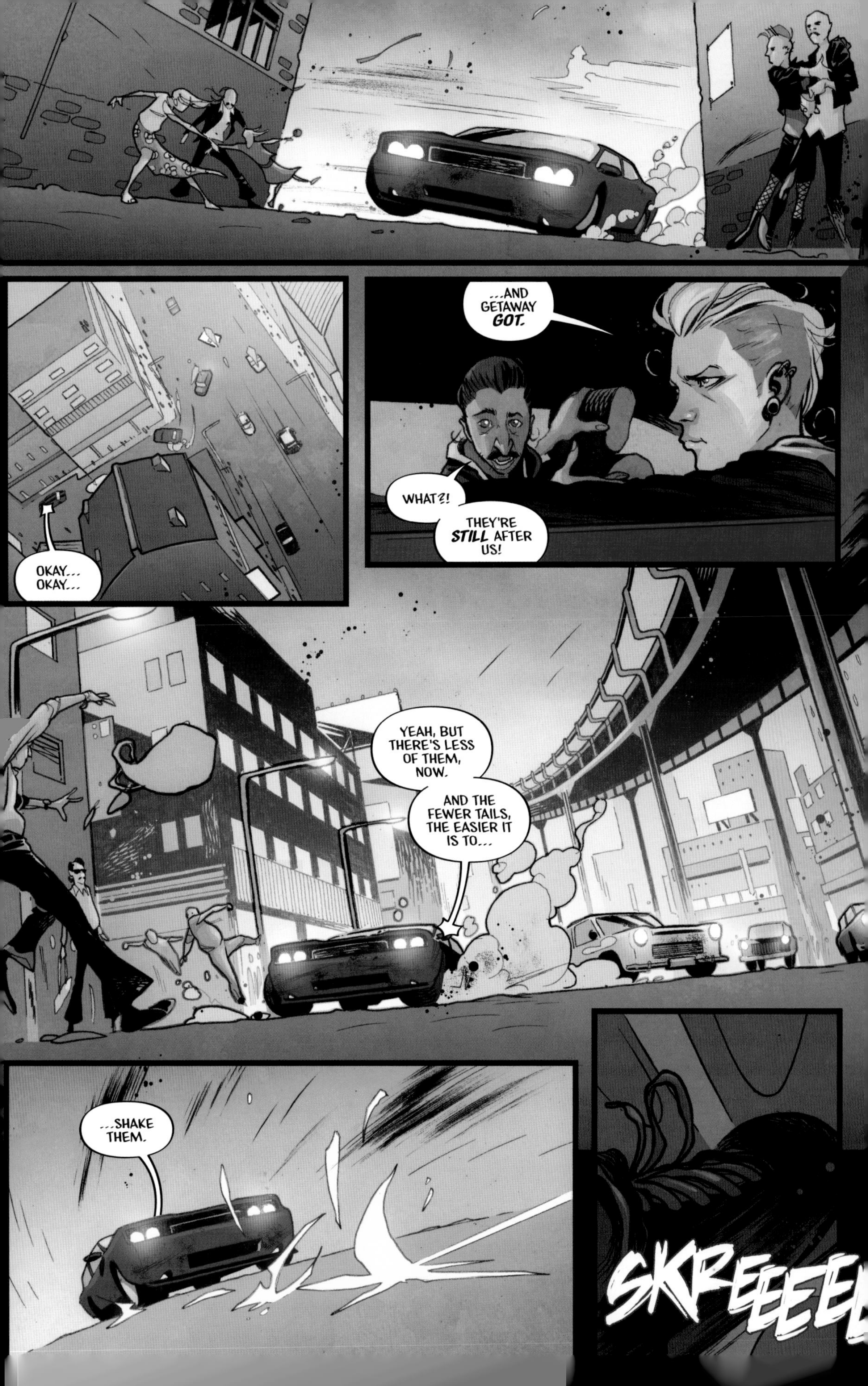
OKAY... OKAY...
...AND GETAWAY GOT.
WHAT?!
THEY'RE STILL AFTER US!
YEAH, BUT THERE'S LESS OF THEM, NOW.
AND THE FEWER TAILS, THE EASIER IT IS TO...
...SHAKE THEM.
SKREEEEE

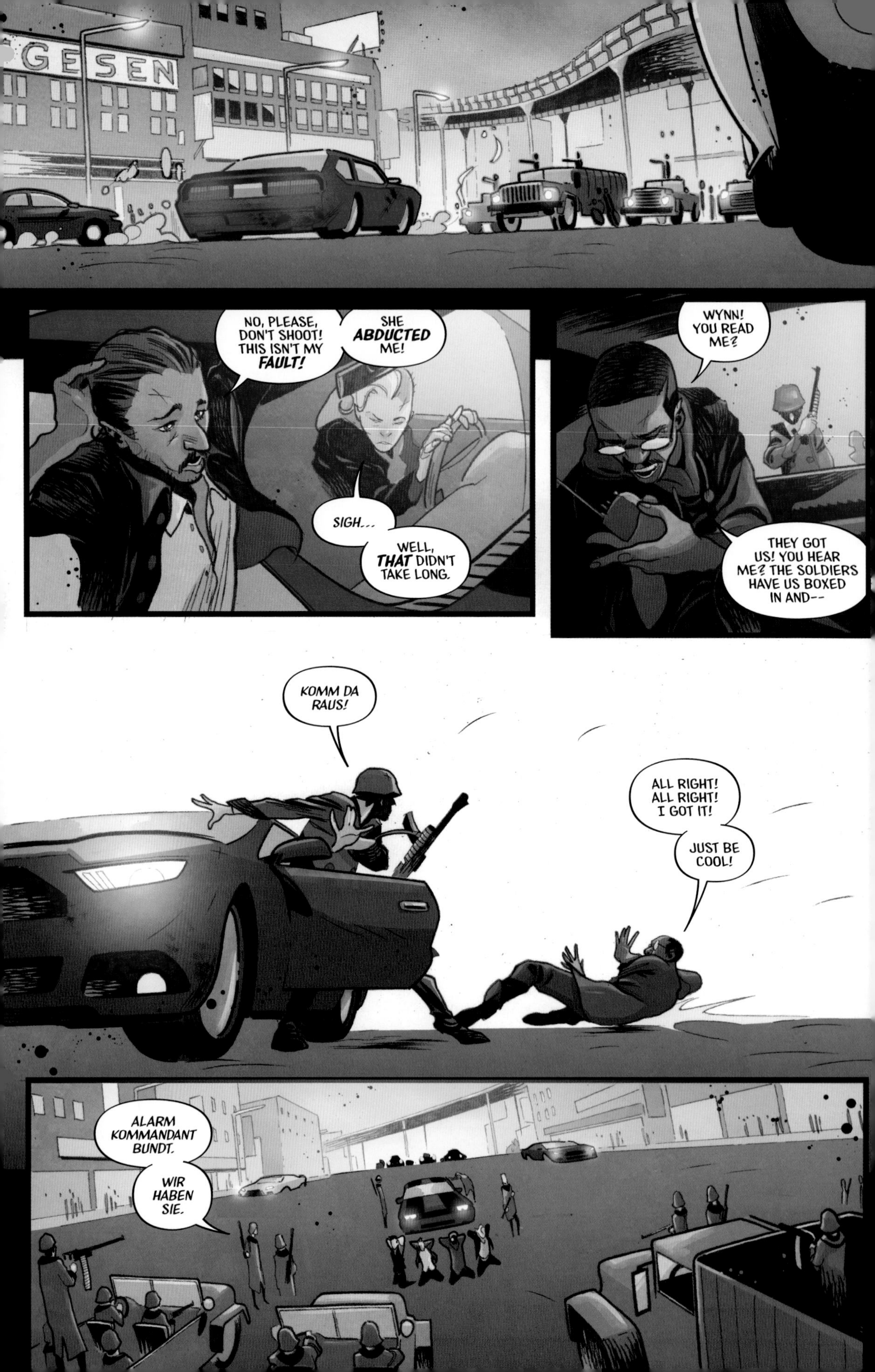
GESEN
NO, PLEASE, DON'T SHOOT! THIS ISN'T MY FAULT!
SHE ABDUCTED ME!
SIGH...
WELL, THAT DIDN'T TAKE LONG.
WYNN! YOU READ ME?
THEY GOT US! YOU HEAR ME? THE SOLDIERS HAVE US BOXED IN AND--
KOMM DA RAUS!
ALL RIGHT! ALL RIGHT! I GOT IT!
JUST BE COOL!
ALARM KOMMANDANT BUNDT.
WIR HABEN SIE.

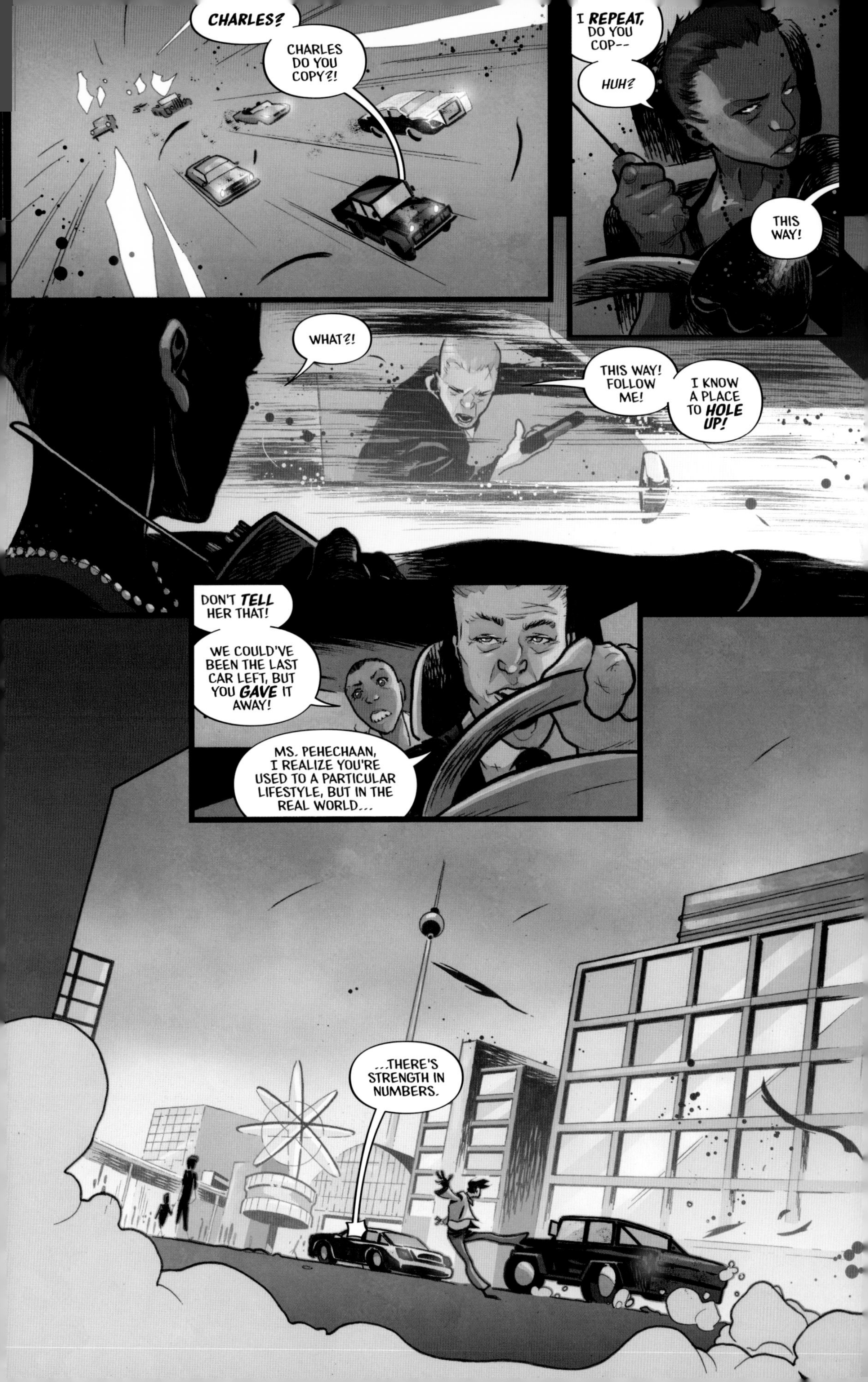
CHARLES?
CHARLES DO YOU COPY?!
I REPEAT, DO YOU COP--
HUH?
THIS WAY!
WHAT?!
THIS WAY! FOLLOW ME!
I KNOW A PLACE TO HOLE UP!
DON'T TELL HER THAT!
WE COULD'VE BEEN THE LAST CAR LEFT, BUT YOU GAVE IT AWAY!
MS. PEHECHAAN, I REALIZE YOU'RE USED TO A PARTICULAR LIFESTYLE, BUT IN THE REAL WORLD...
...THERE'S STRENGTH IN NUMBERS.

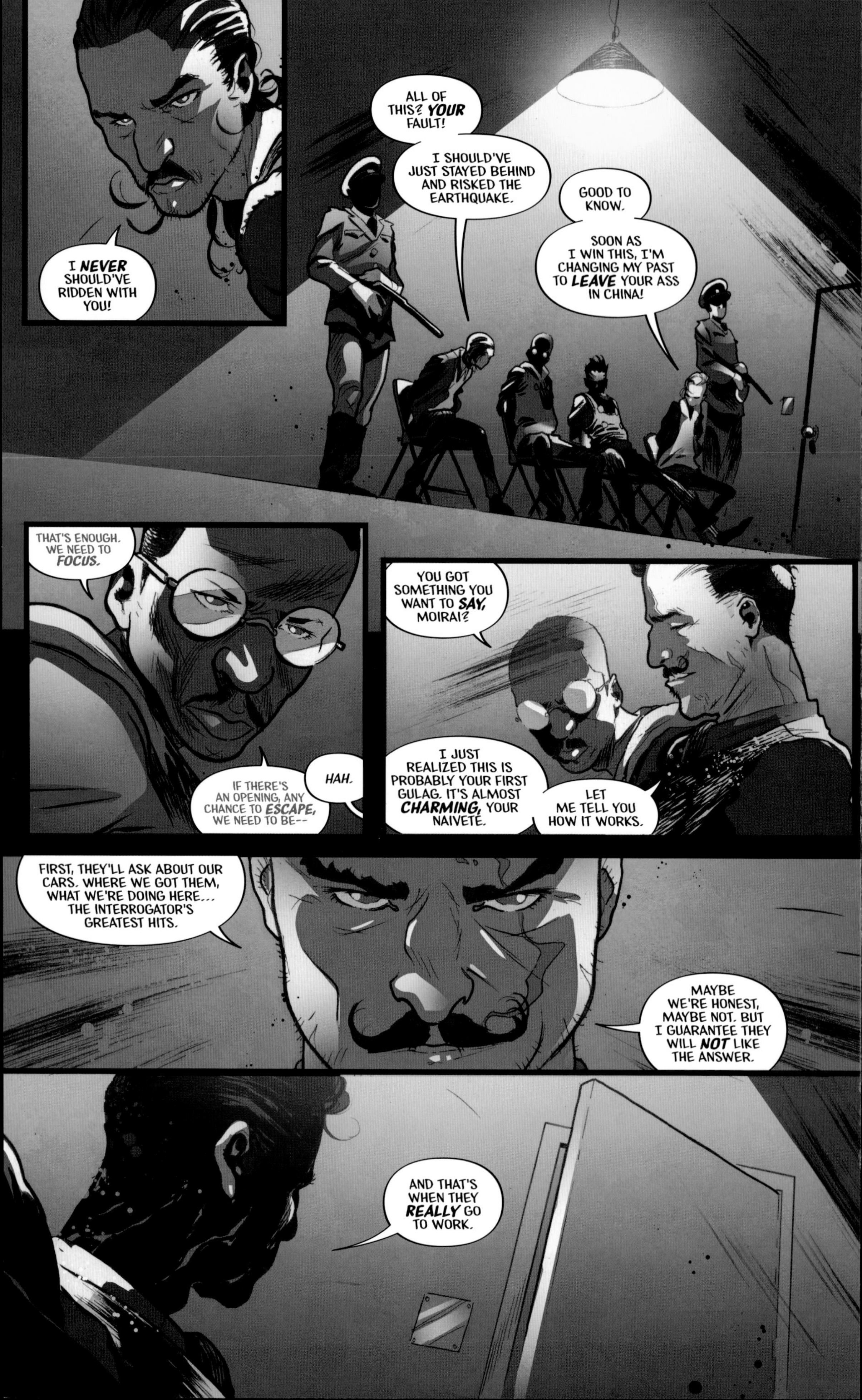
I NEVER SHOULD'VE RIDDEN WITH YOU!
ALL OF THIS? YOUR FAULT!
I SHOULD'VE JUST STAYED BEHIND AND RISKED THE EARTHQUAKE.
GOOD TO KNOW.
SOON AS I WIN THIS, I'M CHANGING MY PAST TO LEAVE YOUR ASS IN CHINA!
THAT'S ENOUGH. WE NEED TO FOCUS.
IF THERE'S AN OPENING, ANY CHANCE TO ESCAPE, WE NEED TO BE--
HAH.
YOU GOT SOMETHING YOU WANT TO SAY, MOIRAI?
I JUST REALIZED THIS IS PROBABLY YOUR FIRST GULAG. IT'S ALMOST CHARMING, YOUR NAIVETE.
LET ME TELL YOU HOW IT WORKS.
FIRST, THEY'LL ASK ABOUT OUR CARS. WHERE WE GOT THEM, WHAT WE'RE DOING HERE... THE INTERROGATOR'S GREATEST HITS.
MAYBE WE'RE HONEST, MAYBE NOT. BUT I GUARANTEE THEY WILL NOT LIKE THE ANSWER.
AND THAT'S WHEN THEY REALLY GO TO WORK.

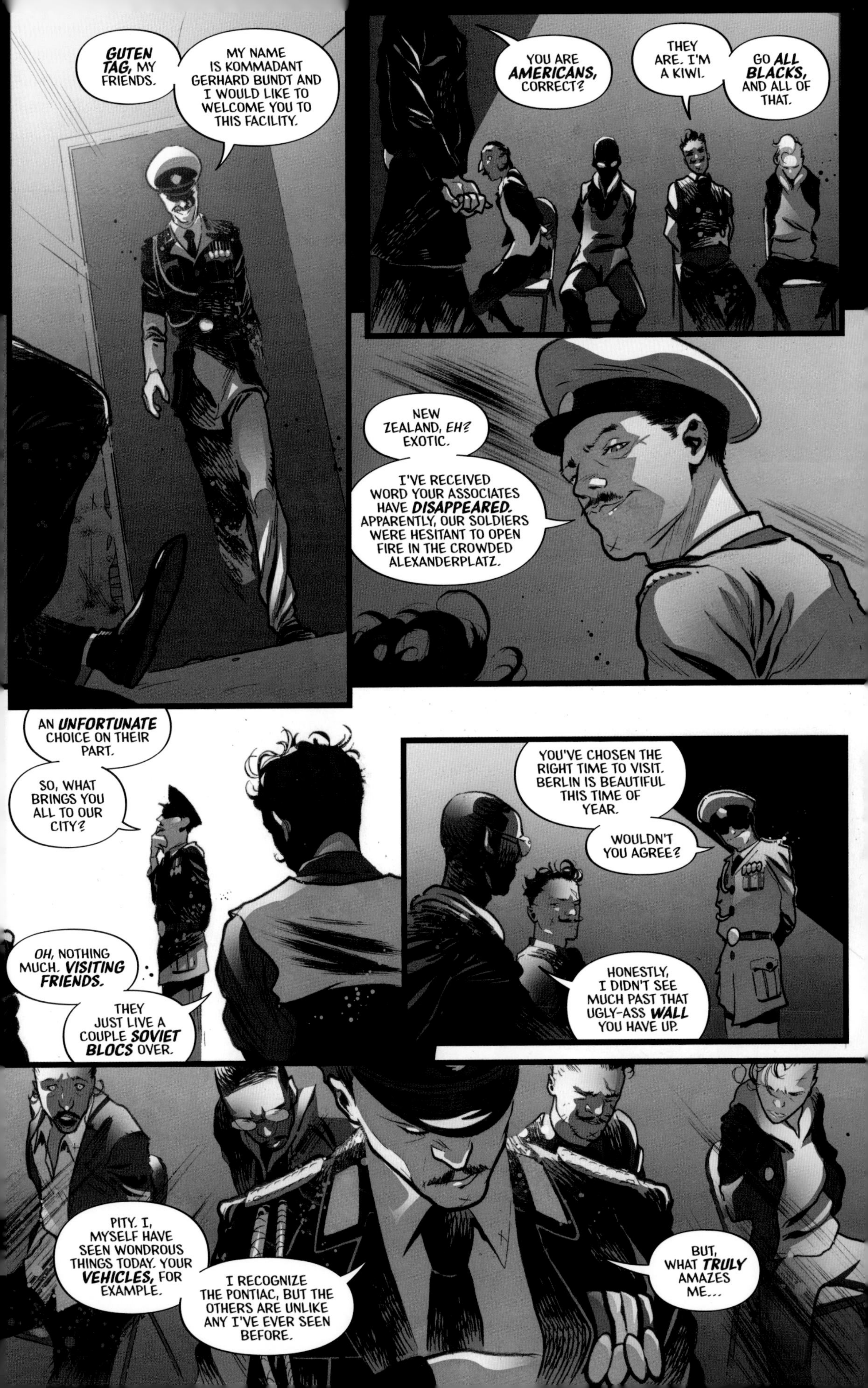
GUTEN TAG, MY FRIENDS.
MY NAME IS KOMMADANT GERHARD BUNDT AND I WOULD LIKE TO WELCOME YOU TO THIS FACILITY.
YOU ARE AMERICANS, CORRECT?
THEY ARE. I'M A KIWI.
GO ALL BLACKS, AND ALL OF THAT.
NEW ZEALAND, EH? EXOTIC.
I'VE RECEIVED WORD YOUR ASSOCIATES HAVE DISAPPEARED. APPARENTLY, OUR SOLDIERS WERE HESITANT TO OPEN FIRE IN THE CROWDED ALEXANDERPLATZ.
AN UNFORTUNATE CHOICE ON THEIR PART.
SO, WHAT BRINGS YOU ALL TO OUR CITY?
OH, NOTHING MUCH. VISITING FRIENDS.
THEY JUST LIVE A COUPLE SOVIET BLOCS OVER.
YOU'VE CHOSEN THE RIGHT TIME TO VISIT. BERLIN IS BEAUTIFUL THIS TIME OF YEAR.
WOULDN'T YOU AGREE?
HONESTLY, I DIDN'T SEE MUCH PAST THAT UGLY-ASS WALL YOU HAVE UP.
PITY. I, MYSELF HAVE SEEN WONDROUS THINGS TODAY. YOUR VEHICLES, FOR EXAMPLE.
I RECOGNIZE THE PONTIAC, BUT THE OTHERS ARE UNLIKE ANY I'VE EVER SEEN BEFORE.
BUT, WHAT TRULY AMAZES ME...

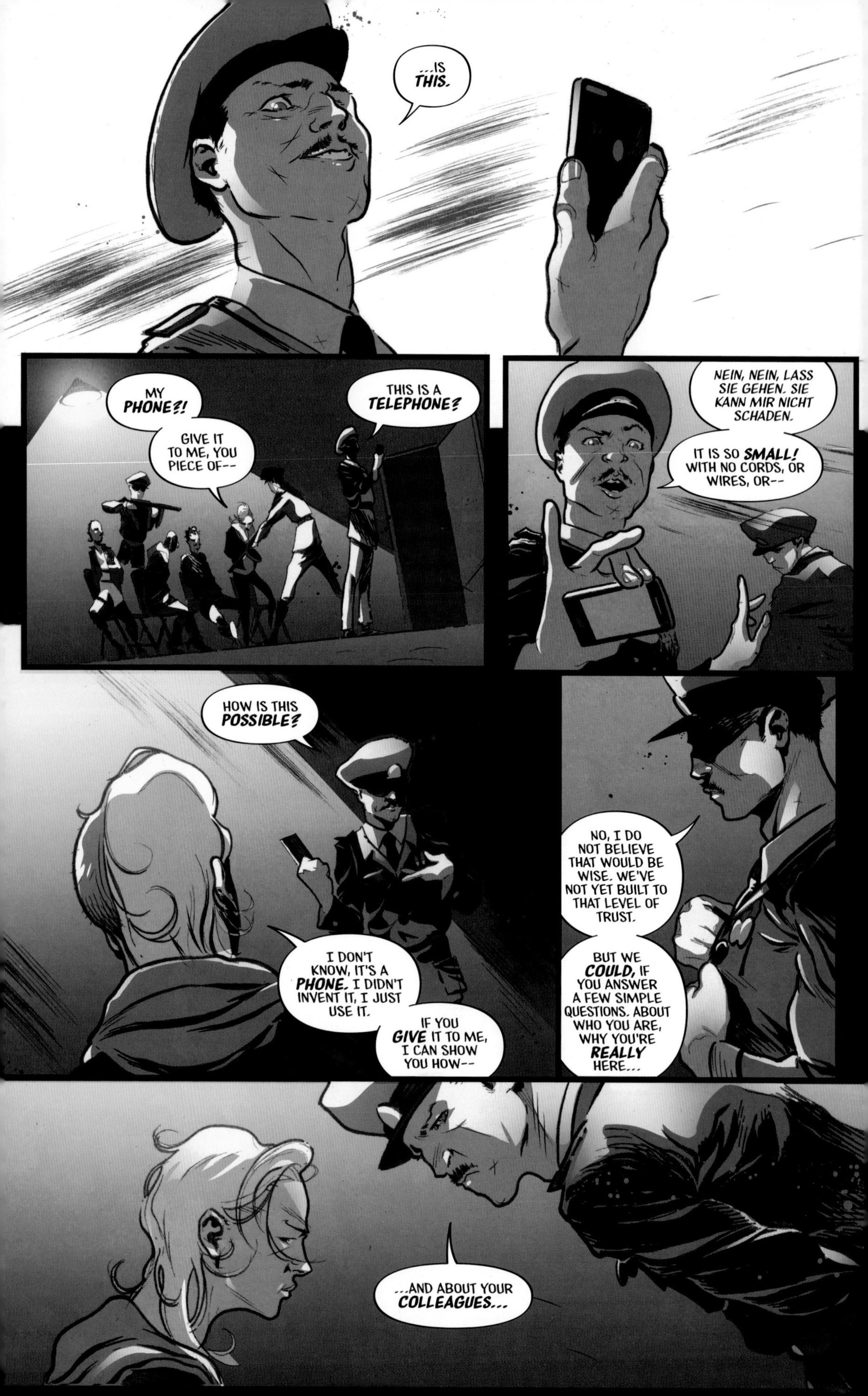
...IS THIS.
MY PHONE?!
GIVE IT TO ME, YOU PIECE OF--
THIS IS A TELEPHONE?
NEIN, NEIN, LASS SIE GEHEN. SIE KANN MIR NICHT SCHADEN.
IT IS SO SMALL! WITH NO CORDS, OR WIRES, OR--
HOW IS THIS POSSIBLE?
I DON'T KNOW, IT'S A PHONE. I DIDN'T INVENT IT, I JUST USE IT.
IF YOU GIVE IT TO ME, I CAN SHOW YOU HOW--
NO, I DO NOT BELIEVE THAT WOULD BE WISE. WE'VE NOT YET BUILT TO THAT LEVEL OF TRUST.
BUT WE COULD, IF YOU ANSWER A FEW SIMPLE QUESTIONS. ABOUT WHO YOU ARE, WHY YOU'RE REALLY HERE...
...AND ABOUT YOUR COLLEAGUES...

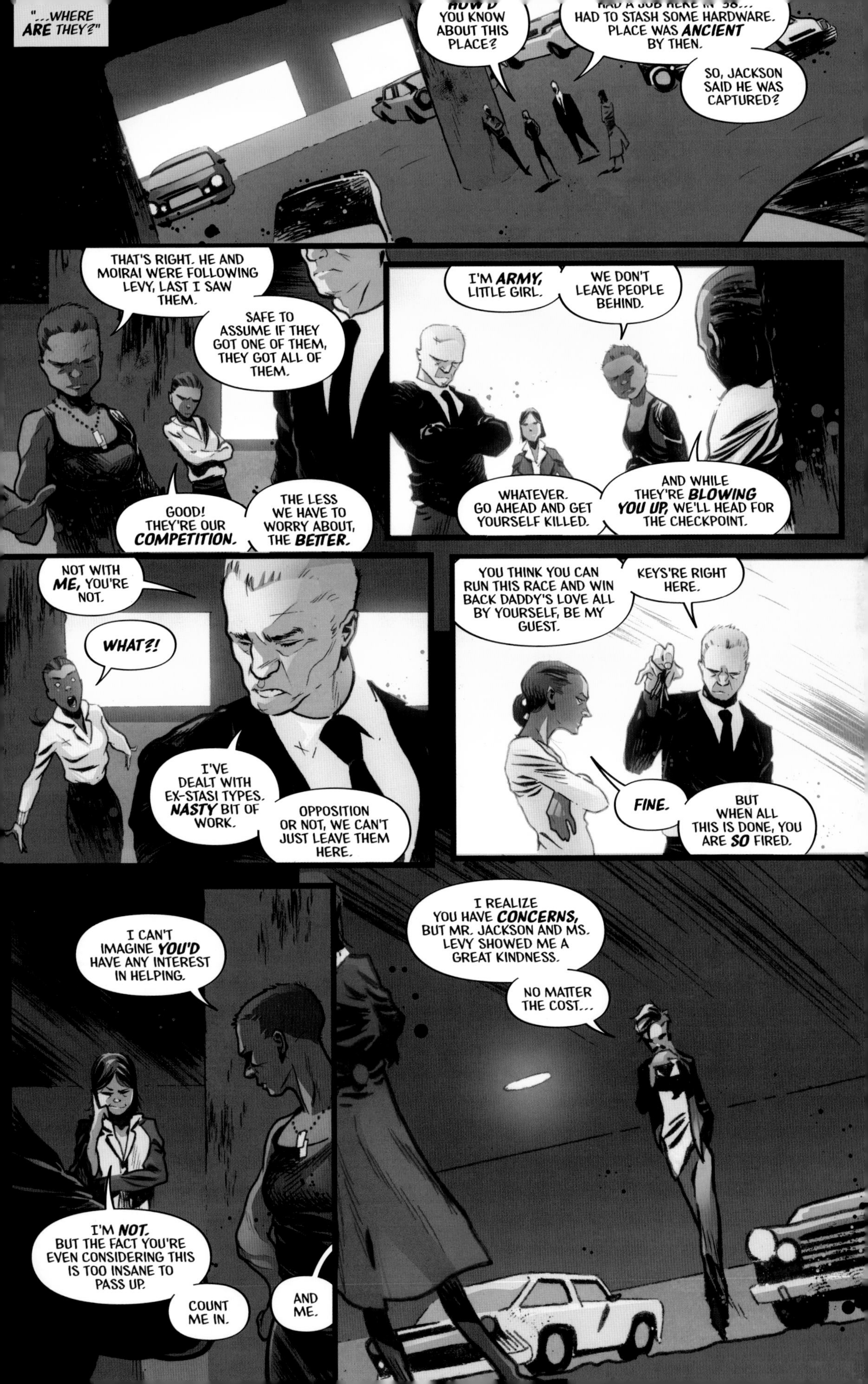
"...WHERE ARE THEY?"
HOW'D YOU KNOW ABOUT THIS PLACE?
HAD A JOB HERE IN '58... HAD TO STASH SOME HARDWARE. PLACE WAS ANCIENT BY THEN.
SO, JACKSON SAID HE WAS CAPTURED?
THAT'S RIGHT. HE AND MOIRAI WERE FOLLOWING LEVY, LAST I SAW THEM.
SAFE TO ASSUME IF THEY GOT ONE OF THEM, THEY GOT ALL OF THEM.
GOOD! THEY'RE OUR COMPETITION.
THE LESS WE HAVE TO WORRY ABOUT, THE BETTER.
I'M ARMY, LITTLE GIRL.
WE DON'T LEAVE PEOPLE BEHIND.
WHATEVER. GO AHEAD AND GET YOURSELF KILLED.
AND WHILE THEY'RE BLOWING YOU UP, WE'LL HEAD FOR THE CHECKPOINT.
NOT WITH ME, YOU'RE NOT.
WHAT?!
I'VE DEALT WITH EX-STASI TYPES. NASTY BIT OF WORK.
OPPOSITION OR NOT, WE CAN'T JUST LEAVE THEM HERE.
YOU THINK YOU CAN RUN THIS RACE AND WIN BACK DADDY'S LOVE ALL BY YOURSELF, BE MY GUEST.
KEYS'RE RIGHT HERE.
FINE.
BUT WHEN ALL THIS IS DONE, YOU ARE SO FIRED.
I CAN'T IMAGINE YOU'D HAVE ANY INTEREST IN HELPING.
I'M NOT. BUT THE FACT YOU'RE EVEN CONSIDERING THIS IS TOO INSANE TO PASS UP.
COUNT ME IN.
AND ME.
I REALIZE YOU HAVE CONCERNS, BUT MR. JACKSON AND MS. LEVY SHOWED ME A GREAT KINDNESS.
NO MATTER THE COST...

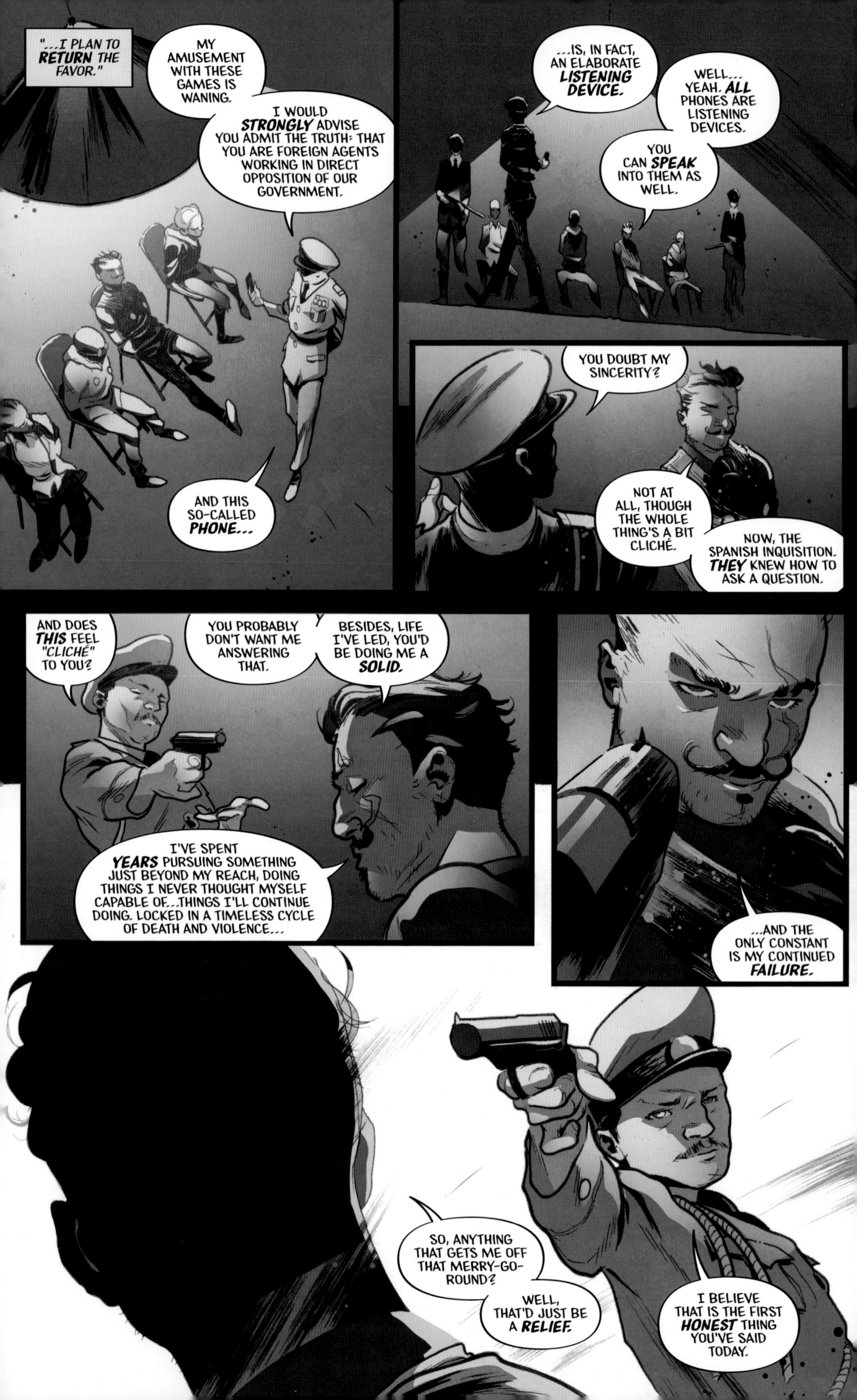
"...I PLAN TO RETURN THE FAVOR."
MY AMUSEMENT WITH THESE GAMES IS WANING.
I WOULD STRONGLY ADVISE YOU ADMIT THE TRUTH: THAT YOU ARE FOREIGN AGENTS WORKING IN DIRECT OPPOSITION OF OUR GOVERNMENT.
AND THIS SO-CALLED PHONE...
...IS, IN FACT, AN ELABORATE LISTENING DEVICE.
WELL... YEAH. ALL PHONES ARE LISTENING DEVICES.
YOU CAN SPEAK INTO THEM AS WELL.
YOU DOUBT MY SINCERITY?
NOT AT ALL, THOUGH THE WHOLE THING'S A BIT CLICHÉ.
NOW, THE SPANISH INQUISITION. THEY KNEW HOW TO ASK A QUESTION.
AND DOES THIS FEEL "CLICHÉ" TO YOU?
YOU PROBABLY DON'T WANT ME ANSWERING THAT.
BESIDES, LIFE I'VE LED, YOU'D BE DOING ME A SOLID.
I'VE SPENT YEARS PURSUING SOMETHING JUST BEYOND MY REACH, DOING THINGS I NEVER THOUGHT MYSELF CAPABLE OF...THINGS I'LL CONTINUE DOING. LOCKED IN A TIMELESS CYCLE OF DEATH AND VIOLENCE...
...AND THE ONLY CONSTANT IS MY CONTINUED FAILURE.
SO, ANYTHING THAT GETS ME OFF THAT MERRY-GO-ROUND?
WELL, THAT'D JUST BE A RELIEF.
I BELIEVE THAT IS THE FIRST HONEST THING YOU'VE SAID TODAY.

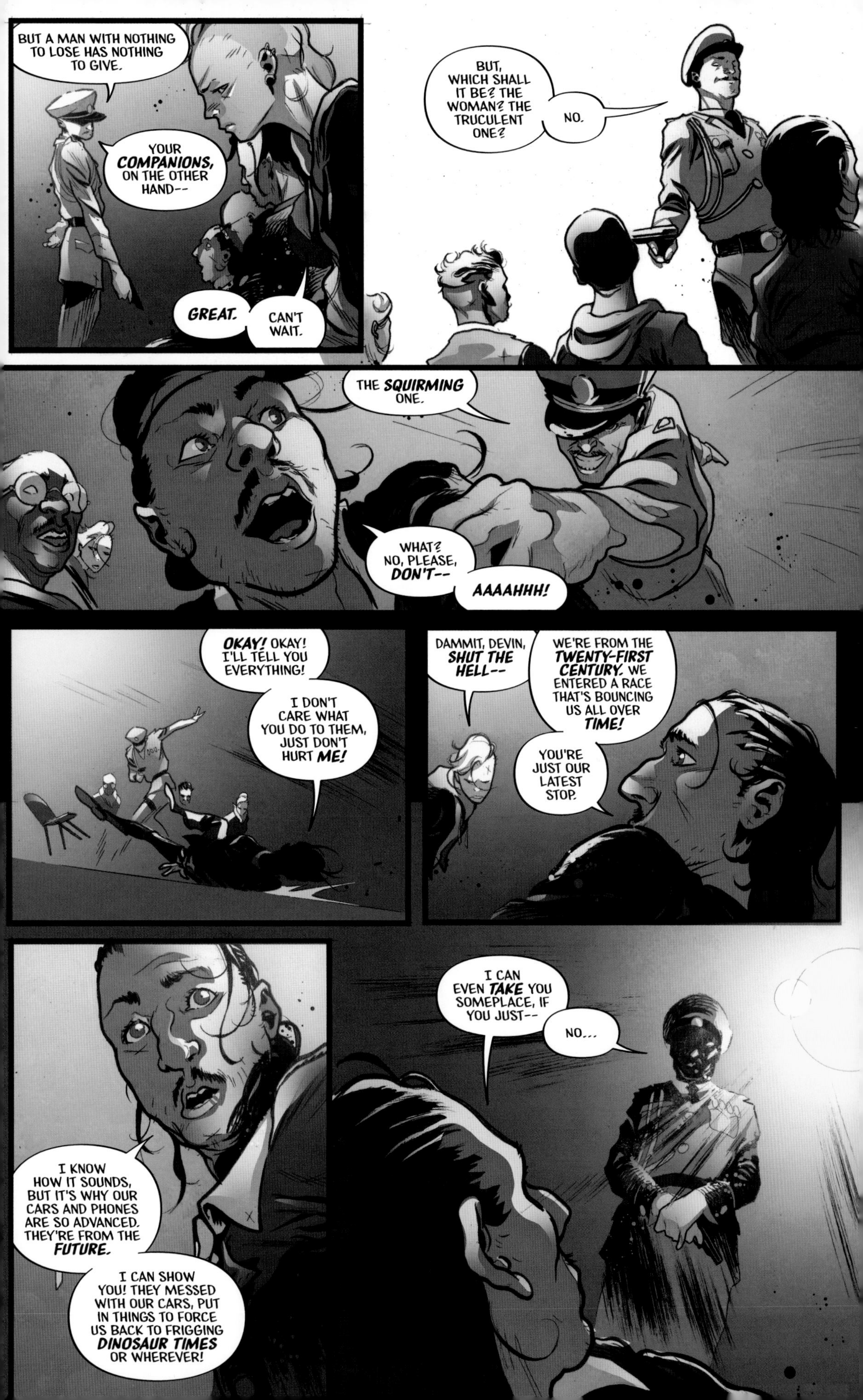
BUT A MAN WITH NOTHING TO LOSE HAS NOTHING TO GIVE.
YOUR COMPANIONS, ON THE OTHER HAND--
GREAT.
CAN'T WAIT.
BUT, WHICH SHALL IT BE? THE WOMAN? THE TRUCULENT ONE?
NO.
THE SQUIRMING ONE.
WHAT? NO, PLEASE, DON'T--
AAAAHHH!
OKAY! OKAY! I'LL TELL YOU EVERYTHING!
I DON'T CARE WHAT YOU DO TO THEM, JUST DON'T HURT ME!
DAMMIT, DEVIN, SHUT THE HELL--
WE'RE FROM THE TWENTY-FIRST CENTURY. WE ENTERED A RACE THAT'S BOUNCING US ALL OVER TIME!
YOU'RE JUST OUR LATEST STOP.
I KNOW HOW IT SOUNDS, BUT IT'S WHY OUR CARS AND PHONES ARE SO ADVANCED. THEY'RE FROM THE FUTURE.
I CAN SHOW YOU! THEY MESSED WITH OUR CARS, PUT IN THINGS TO FORCE US BACK TO FRIGGING DINOSAUR TIMES OR WHEREVER!
I CAN EVEN TAKE YOU SOMEPLACE, IF YOU JUST--
NO...

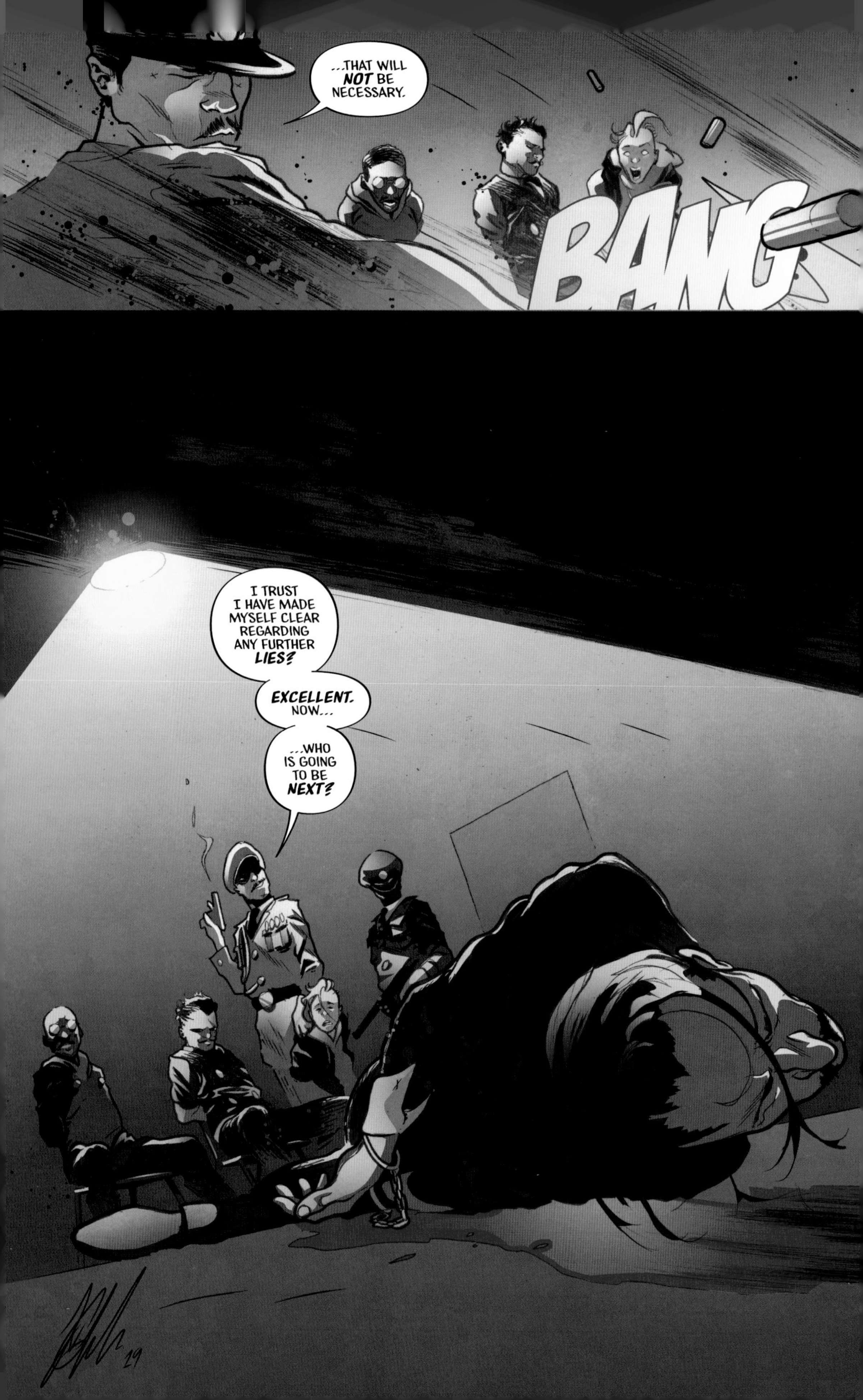
...THAT WILL NOT BE NECESSARY.
BANG
I TRUST I HAVE MADE MYSELF CLEAR REGARDING ANY FURTHER LIES?
EXCELLENT. NOW...
...WHO IS GOING TO BE NEXT?

CHAPTER
5

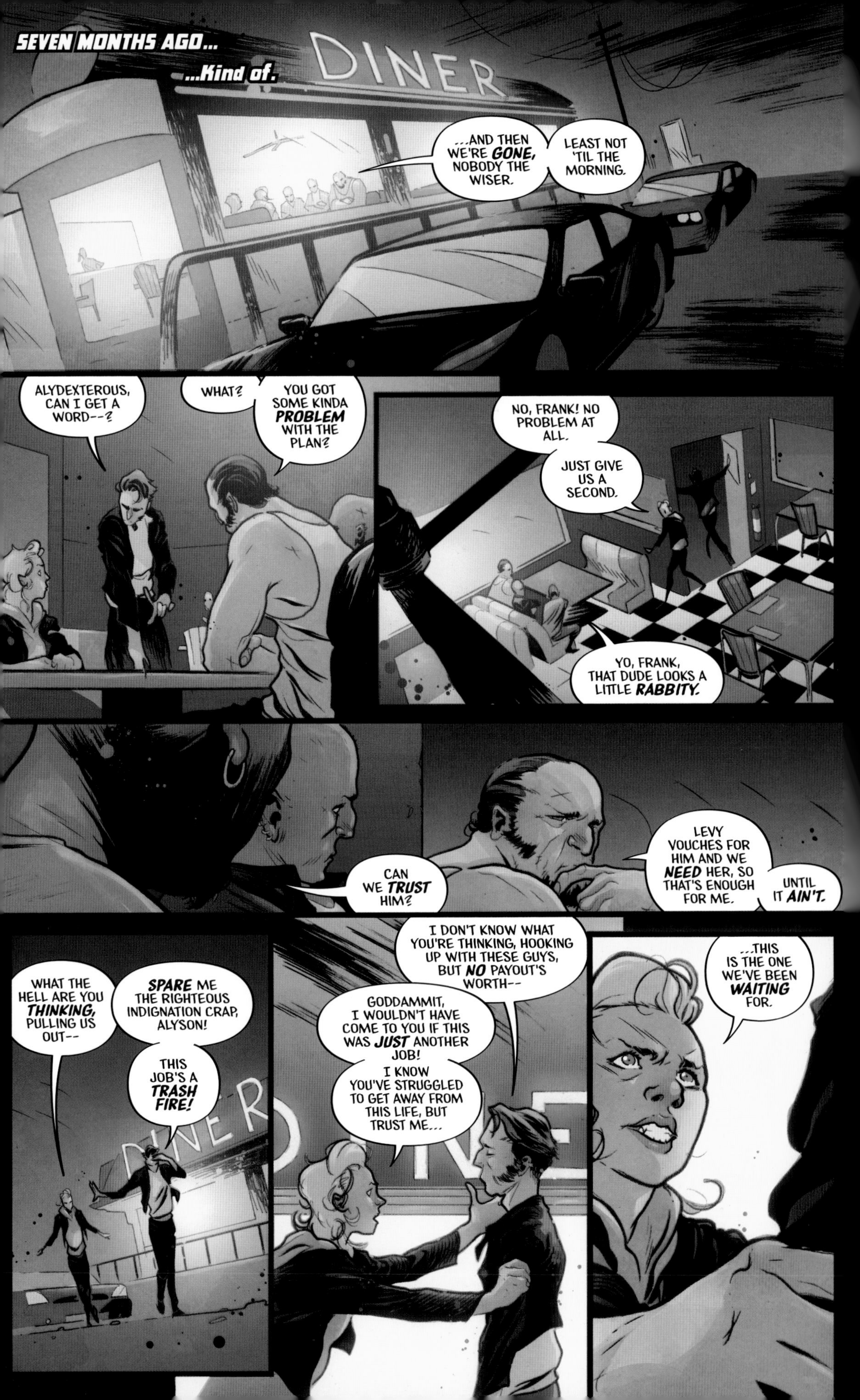
SEVEN MONTHS AGO...
...Kind of.
DINER
...AND THEN WE'RE GONE, NOBODY THE WISER.
LEAST NOT 'TIL THE MORNING.
ALYDEXTEROUS, CAN I GET A WORD--?
WHAT?
YOU GOT SOME KINDA PROBLEM WITH THE PLAN?
NO, FRANK! NO PROBLEM AT ALL.
JUST GIVE US A SECOND.
YO, FRANK, THAT DUDE LOOKS A LITTLE RABBITY.
CAN WE TRUST HIM?
LEVY VOUCHES FOR HIM AND WE NEED HER, SO THAT'S ENOUGH FOR ME.
UNTIL IT AIN'T.
WHAT THE HELL ARE YOU THINKING, PULLING US OUT--
SPARE ME THE RIGHTEOUS INDIGNATION CRAP, ALYSON!
THIS JOB'S A TRASH FIRE!
I DON'T KNOW WHAT YOU'RE THINKING, HOOKING UP WITH THESE GUYS, BUT NO PAYOUT'S WORTH--
GODDAMMIT, I WOULDN'T HAVE COME TO YOU IF THIS WAS JUST ANOTHER JOB!
I KNOW YOU'VE STRUGGLED TO GET AWAY FROM THIS LIFE, BUT TRUST ME...
...THIS IS THE ONE WE'VE BEEN WAITING FOR.

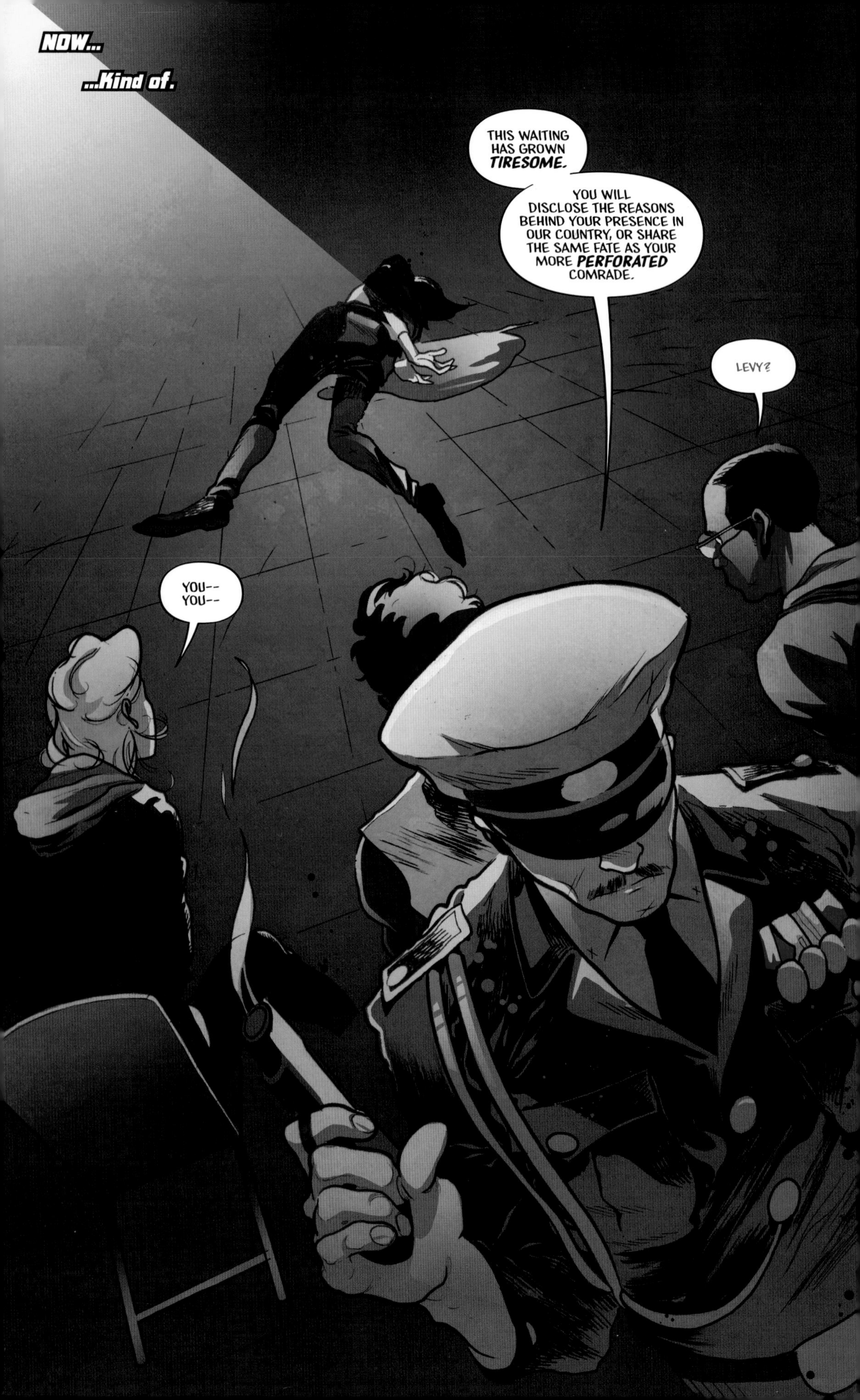
NOW...
...Kind of.
THIS WAITING HAS GROWN TIRESOME.
YOU WILL DISCLOSE THE REASONS BEHIND YOUR PRESENCE IN OUR COUNTRY, OR SHARE THE SAME FATE AS YOUR MORE PERFORATED COMRADE.
LEVY?
YOU--
YOU--

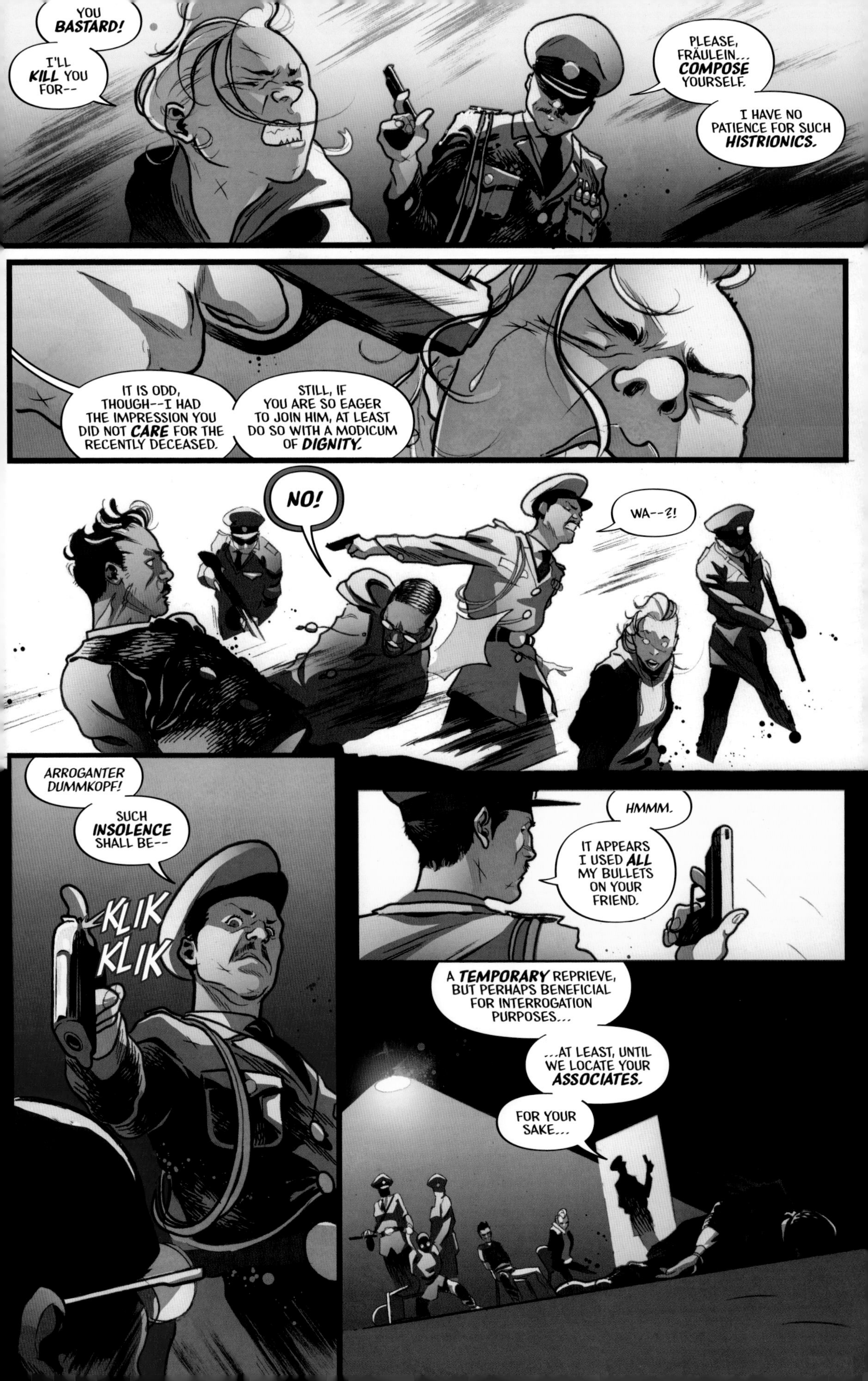
YOU BASTARD!
I'LL KILL YOU FOR--
PLEASE, FRÄULEIN... COMPOSE YOURSELF.
I HAVE NO PATIENCE FOR SUCH HISTRIONICS.
IT IS ODD, THOUGH--I HAD THE IMPRESSION YOU DID NOT CARE FOR THE RECENTLY DECEASED.
STILL, IF YOU ARE SO EAGER TO JOIN HIM, AT LEAST DO SO WITH A MODICUM OF DIGNITY.
NO!
WA--?!
ARROGANTER DUMMKOPF!
SUCH INSOLENCE SHALL BE--
KLIK KLIK
HMMM.
IT APPEARS I USED ALL MY BULLETS ON YOUR FRIEND.
A TEMPORARY REPRIEVE, BUT PERHAPS BENEFICIAL FOR INTERROGATION PURPOSES...
...AT LEAST, UNTIL WE LOCATE YOUR ASSOCIATES.
FOR YOUR SAKE...

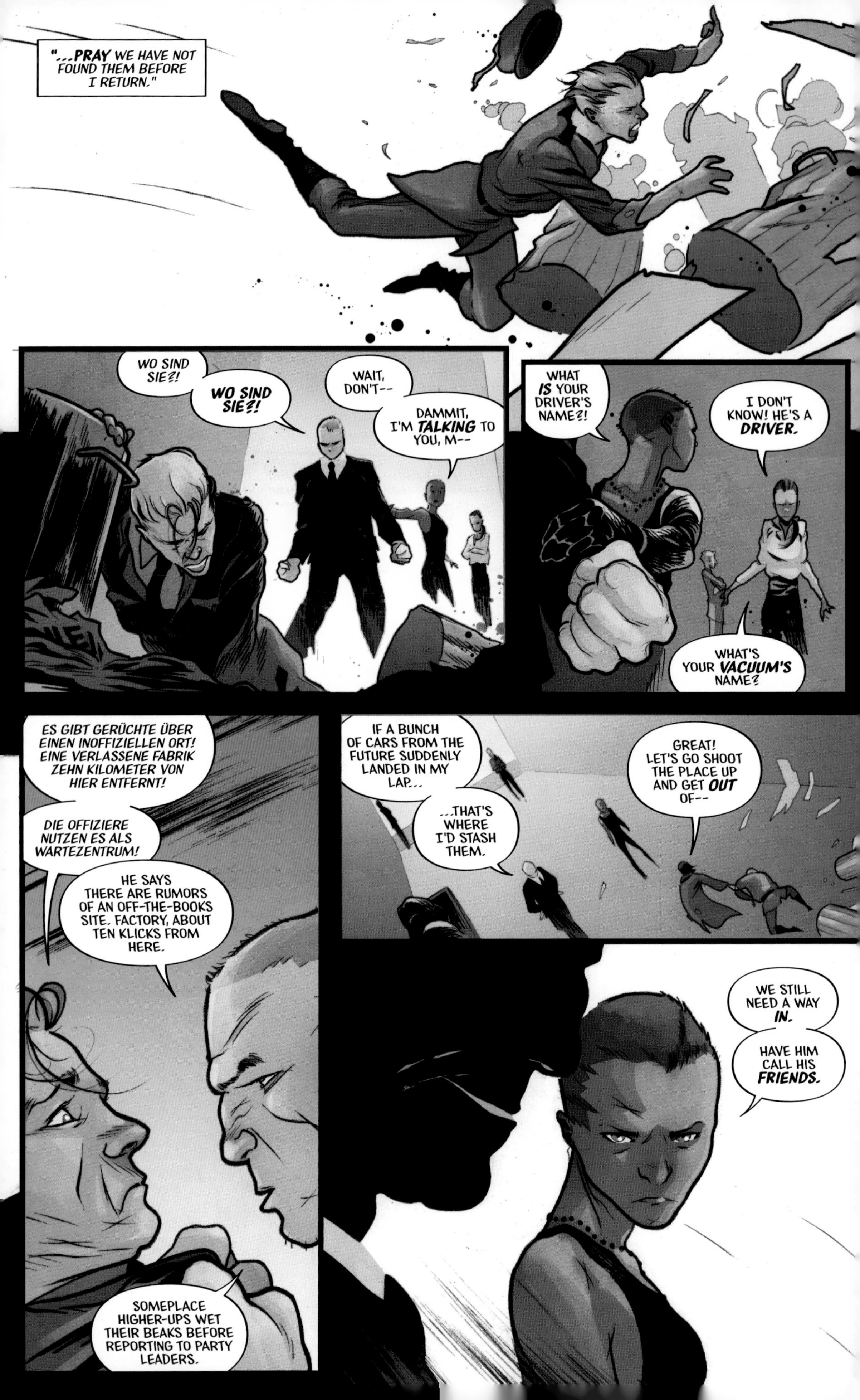
"...PRAY WE HAVE NOT FOUND THEM BEFORE I RETURN."
WO SIND SIE?!
WO SIND SIE?!
WAIT, DON'T--
DAMMIT, I'M TALKING TO YOU, M--
WHAT IS YOUR DRIVER'S NAME?!
I DON'T KNOW! HE'S A DRIVER.
WHAT'S YOUR VACUUM'S NAME?
ES GIBT GERÜCHTE ÜBER EINEN INOFFIZIELLEN ORT! EINE VERLASSENE FABRIK ZEHN KILOMETER VON HIER ENTFERNT!
DIE OFFIZIERE NUTZEN ES ALS WARTEZENTRUM!
HE SAYS THERE ARE RUMORS OF AN OFF-THE-BOOKS SITE. FACTORY, ABOUT TEN KLICKS FROM HERE.
SOMEPLACE HIGHER-UPS WET THEIR BEAKS BEFORE REPORTING TO PARTY LEADERS.
IF A BUNCH OF CARS FROM THE FUTURE SUDDENLY LANDED IN MY LAP...
...THAT'S WHERE I'D STASH THEM.
GREAT! LET'S GO SHOOT THE PLACE UP AND GET OUT OF--
WE STILL NEED A WAY IN.
HAVE HIM CALL HIS FRIENDS.

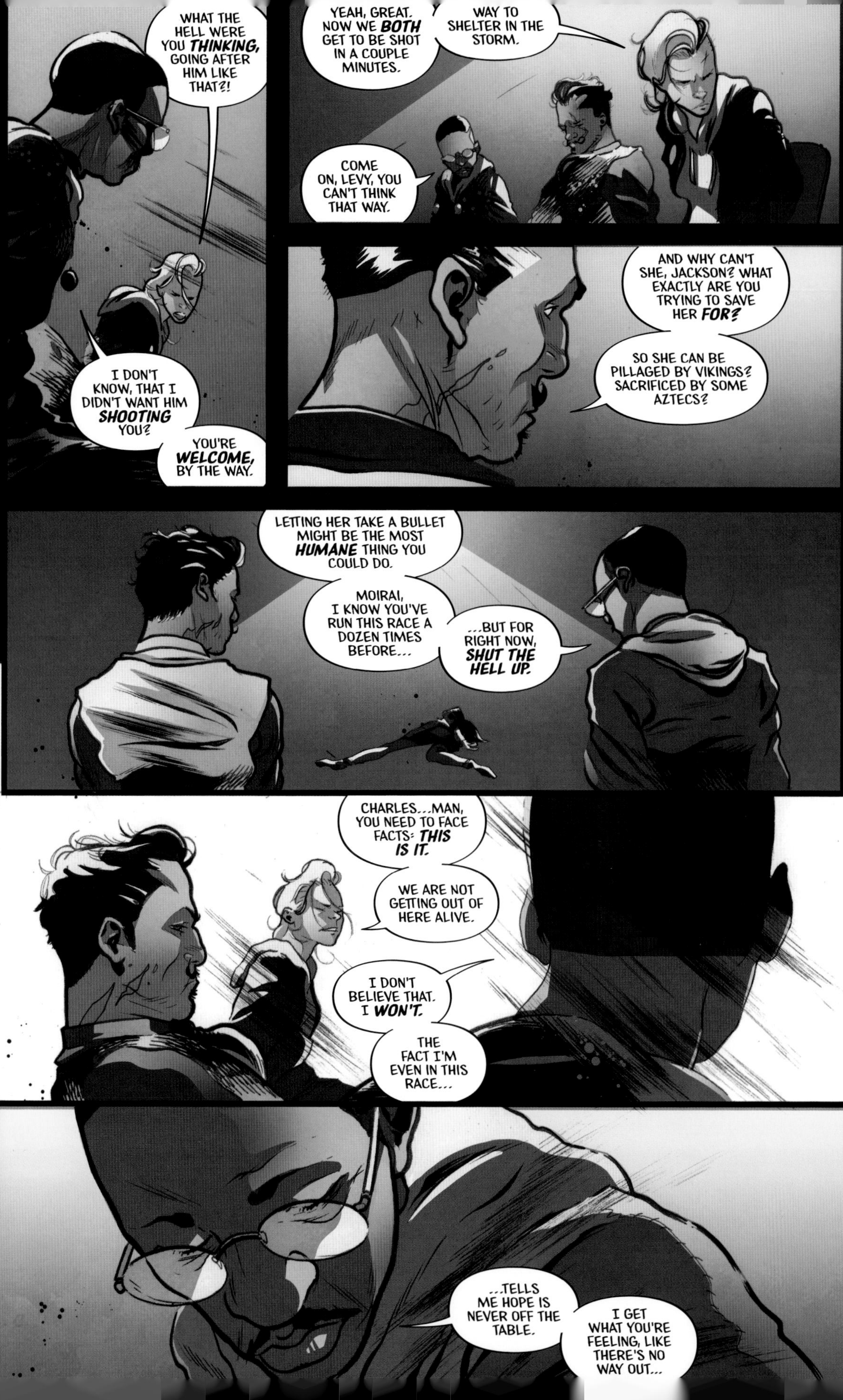
WHAT THE HELL WERE YOU THINKING, GOING AFTER HIM LIKE THAT?!
I DON'T KNOW, THAT I DIDN'T WANT HIM SHOOTING YOU?
YOU'RE WELCOME, BY THE WAY.
YEAH, GREAT. NOW WE BOTH GET TO BE SHOT IN A COUPLE MINUTES.
WAY TO SHELTER IN THE STORM.
COME ON, LEVY, YOU CAN'T THINK THAT WAY.
AND WHY CAN'T SHE, JACKSON? WHAT EXACTLY ARE YOU TRYING TO SAVE HER FOR?
SO SHE CAN BE PILLAGED BY VIKINGS? SACRIFICED BY SOME AZTECS?
LETTING HER TAKE A BULLET MIGHT BE THE MOST HUMANE THING YOU COULD DO.
MOIRAI, I KNOW YOU'VE RUN THIS RACE A DOZEN TIMES BEFORE...
...BUT FOR RIGHT NOW, SHUT THE HELL UP.
CHARLES...MAN, YOU NEED TO FACE FACTS: THIS IS IT.
WE ARE NOT GETTING OUT OF HERE ALIVE.
I DON'T BELIEVE THAT. I WON'T.
THE FACT I'M EVEN IN THIS RACE...
...TELLS ME HOPE IS NEVER OFF THE TABLE.
I GET WHAT YOU'RE FEELING, LIKE THERE'S NO WAY OUT...

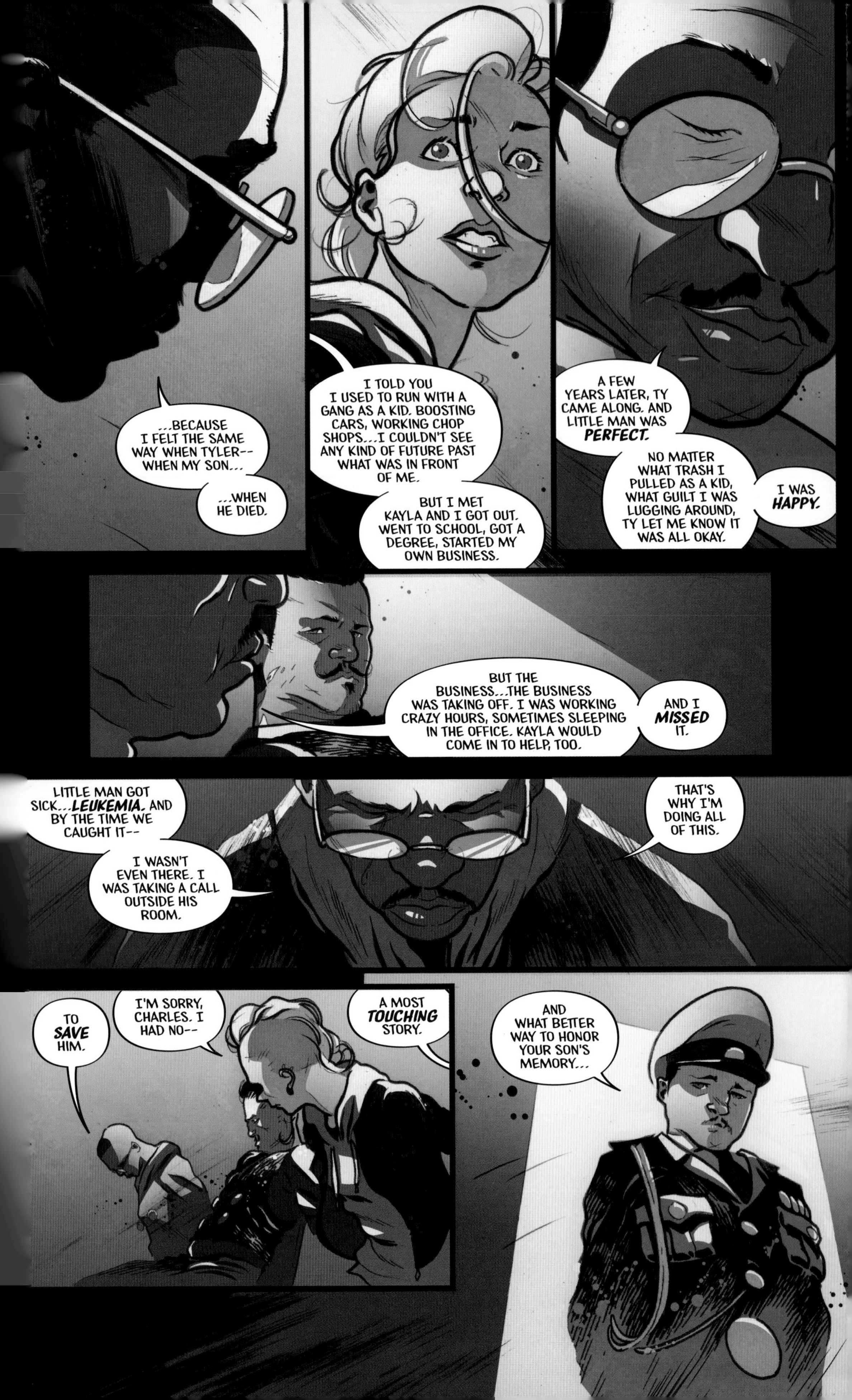
...BECAUSE I FELT THE SAME WAY WHEN TYLER-- WHEN MY SON...
...WHEN HE DIED.
I TOLD YOU I USED TO RUN WITH A GANG AS A KID. BOOSTING CARS, WORKING CHOP SHOPS...I COULDN'T SEE ANY KIND OF FUTURE PAST WHAT WAS IN FRONT OF ME.
BUT I MET KAYLA AND I GOT OUT. WENT TO SCHOOL, GOT A DEGREE, STARTED MY OWN BUSINESS.
A FEW YEARS LATER, TY CAME ALONG. AND LITTLE MAN WAS PERFECT.
NO MATTER WHAT TRASH I PULLED AS A KID, WHAT GUILT I WAS LUGGING AROUND, TY LET ME KNOW IT WAS ALL OKAY.
I WAS HAPPY.
BUT THE BUSINESS...THE BUSINESS WAS TAKING OFF. I WAS WORKING CRAZY HOURS, SOMETIMES SLEEPING IN THE OFFICE. KAYLA WOULD COME IN TO HELP, TOO.
AND I MISSED IT.
LITTLE MAN GOT SICK...LEUKEMIA. AND BY THE TIME WE CAUGHT IT--
I WASN'T EVEN THERE. I WAS TAKING A CALL OUTSIDE HIS ROOM.
THAT'S WHY I'M DOING ALL OF THIS.
TO SAVE HIM.
I'M SORRY, CHARLES. I HAD NO--
A MOST TOUCHING STORY.
AND WHAT BETTER WAY TO HONOR YOUR SON'S MEMORY...

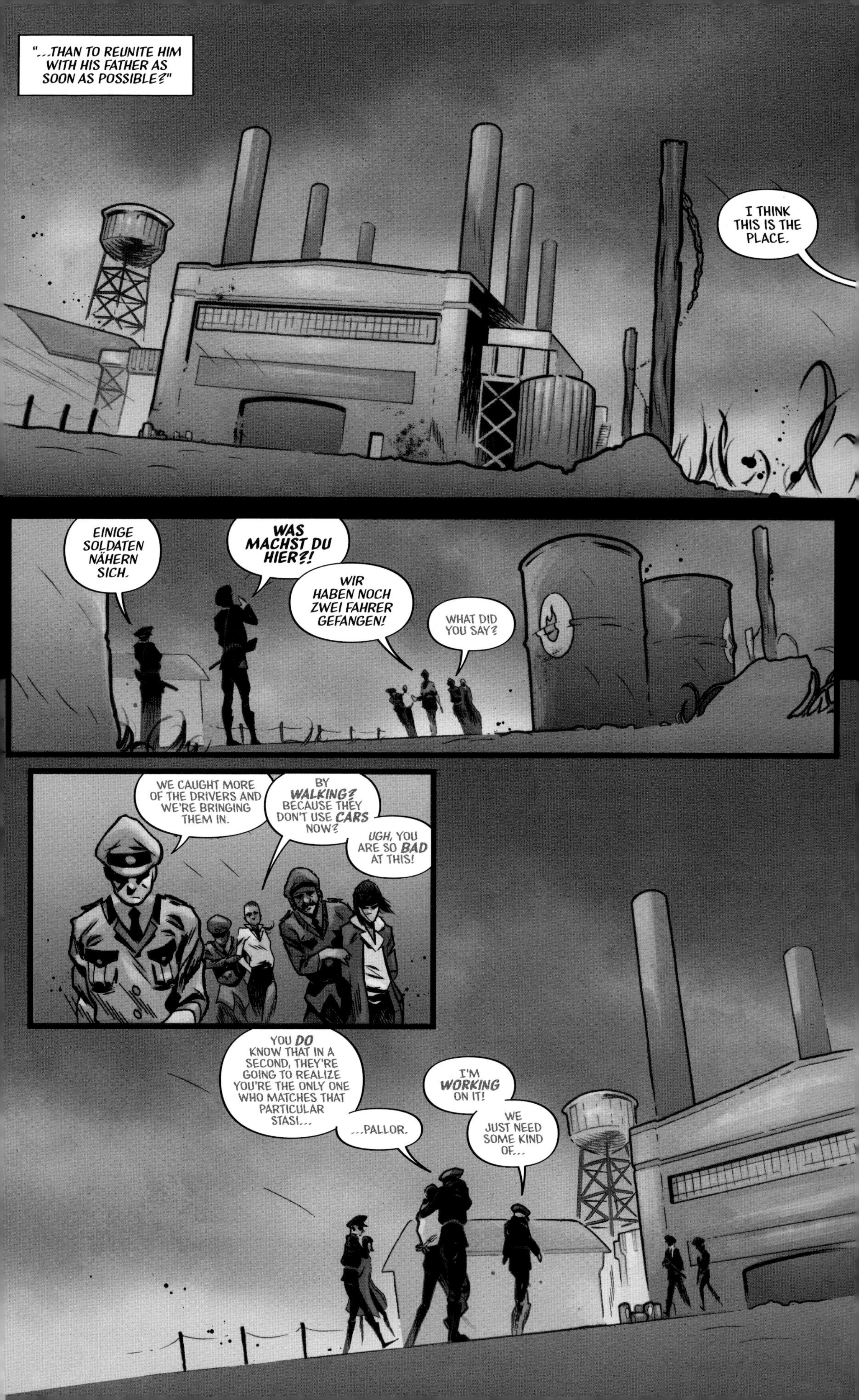
"...THAN TO REUNITE HIM WITH HIS FATHER AS SOON AS POSSIBLE?"
I THINK THIS IS THE PLACE.
EINIGE SOLDATEN NÄHERN SICH.
WAS MACHST DU HIER?!
WIR HABEN NOCH ZWEI FAHRER GEFANGEN!
WHAT DID YOU SAY?
WE CAUGHT MORE OF THE DRIVERS AND WE'RE BRINGING THEM IN.
BY WALKING? BECAUSE THEY DON'T USE CARS NOW?
UGH, YOU ARE SO BAD AT THIS!
YOU DO KNOW THAT IN A SECOND, THEY'RE GOING TO REALIZE YOU'RE THE ONLY ONE WHO MATCHES THAT PARTICULAR STASI...
...PALLOR.
I'M WORKING ON IT!
WE JUST NEED SOME KIND OF...

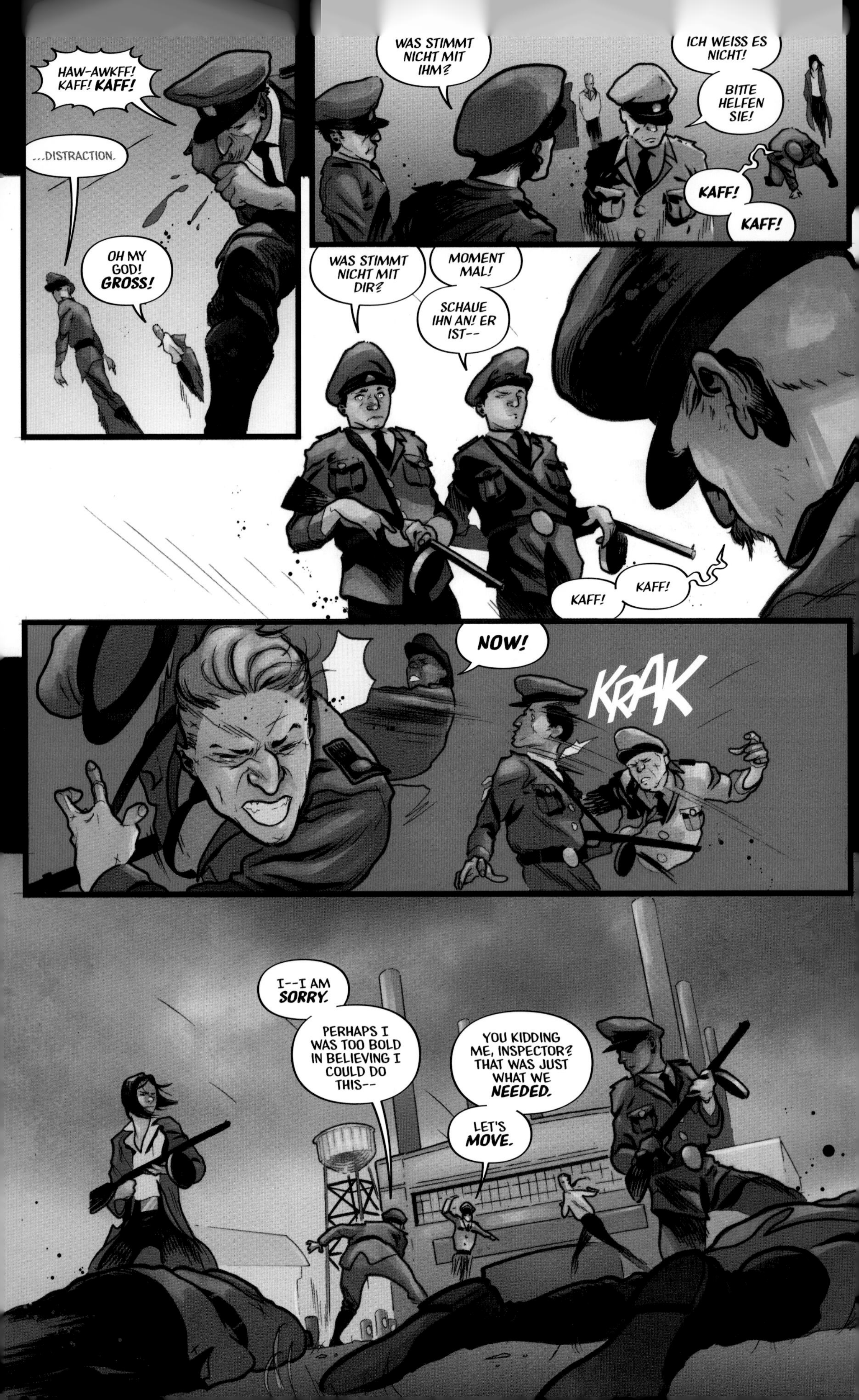

HAW-AWKFF! KAFF! KAFF!
...DISTRACTION.
OH MY GOD! GROSS!
WAS STIMMT NICHT MIT IHM?
ICH WEISS ES NICHT!
BITTE HELFEN SIE!
KAFF!
KAFF!
WAS STIMMT NICHT MIT DIR?
MOMENT MAL!
SCHAUE IHN AN! ER IST--
KAFF!
KAFF!
NOW!
KRAK
I--I AM SORRY.
PERHAPS I WAS TOO BOLD IN BELIEVING I COULD DO THIS--
YOU KIDDING ME, INSPECTOR? THAT WAS JUST WHAT WE NEEDED.
LET'S MOVE.

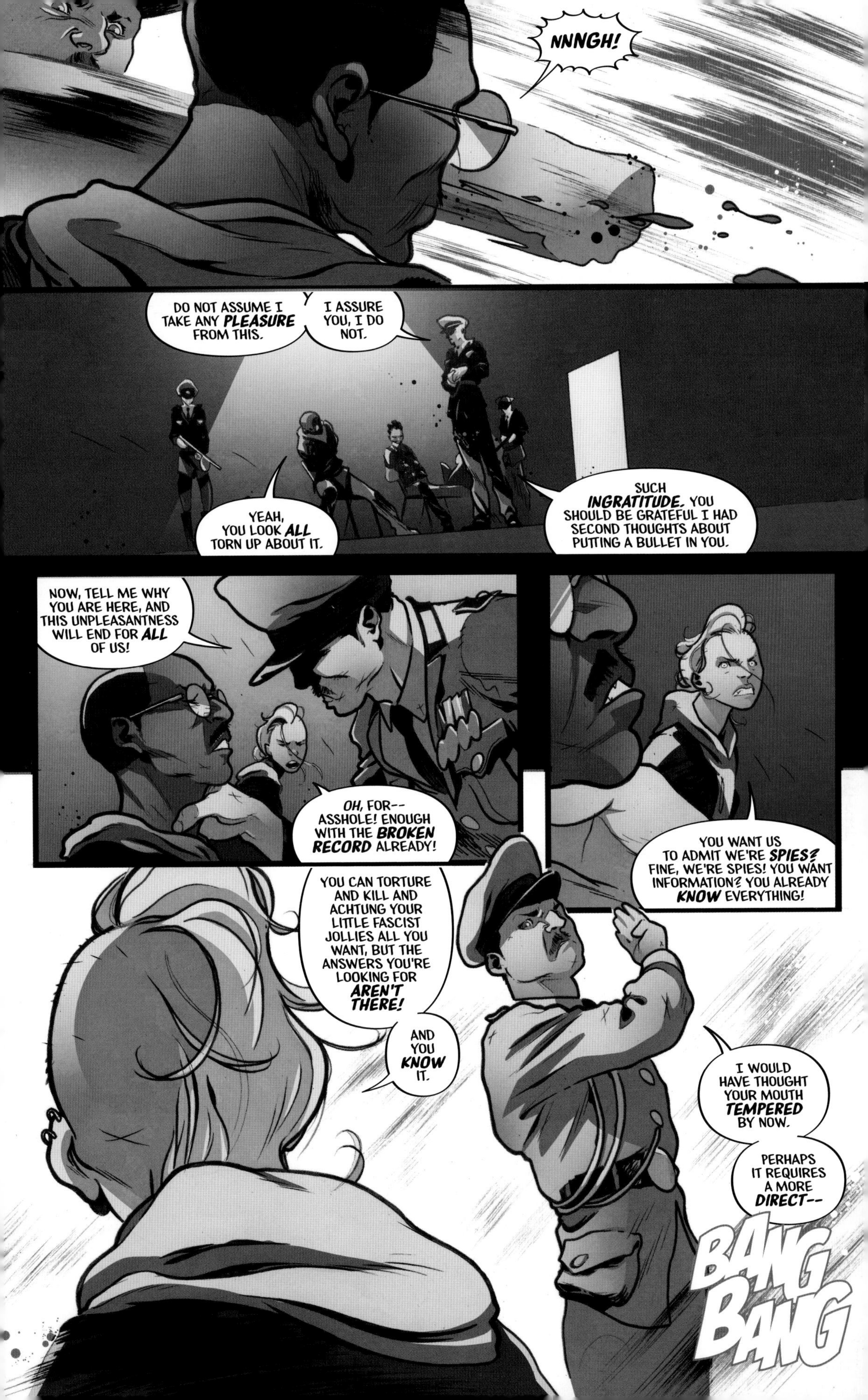
NNNGH!
DO NOT ASSUME I TAKE ANY PLEASURE FROM THIS.
I ASSURE YOU, I DO NOT.
YEAH, YOU LOOK ALL TORN UP ABOUT IT.
SUCH INGRATITUDE. YOU SHOULD BE GRATEFUL I HAD SECOND THOUGHTS ABOUT PUTTING A BULLET IN YOU.
NOW, TELL ME WHY YOU ARE HERE, AND THIS UNPLEASANTNESS WILL END FOR ALL OF US!
OH, FOR-- ASSHOLE! ENOUGH WITH THE BROKEN RECORD ALREADY!
YOU WANT US TO ADMIT WE'RE SPIES? FINE, WE'RE SPIES! YOU WANT INFORMATION? YOU ALREADY KNOW EVERYTHING!
YOU CAN TORTURE AND KILL AND ACHTUNG YOUR LITTLE FASCIST JOLLIES ALL YOU WANT, BUT THE ANSWERS YOU'RE LOOKING FOR AREN'T THERE!
AND YOU KNOW IT.
I WOULD HAVE THOUGHT YOUR MOUTH TEMPERED BY NOW.
PERHAPS IT REQUIRES A MORE DIRECT--
BANG
BANG

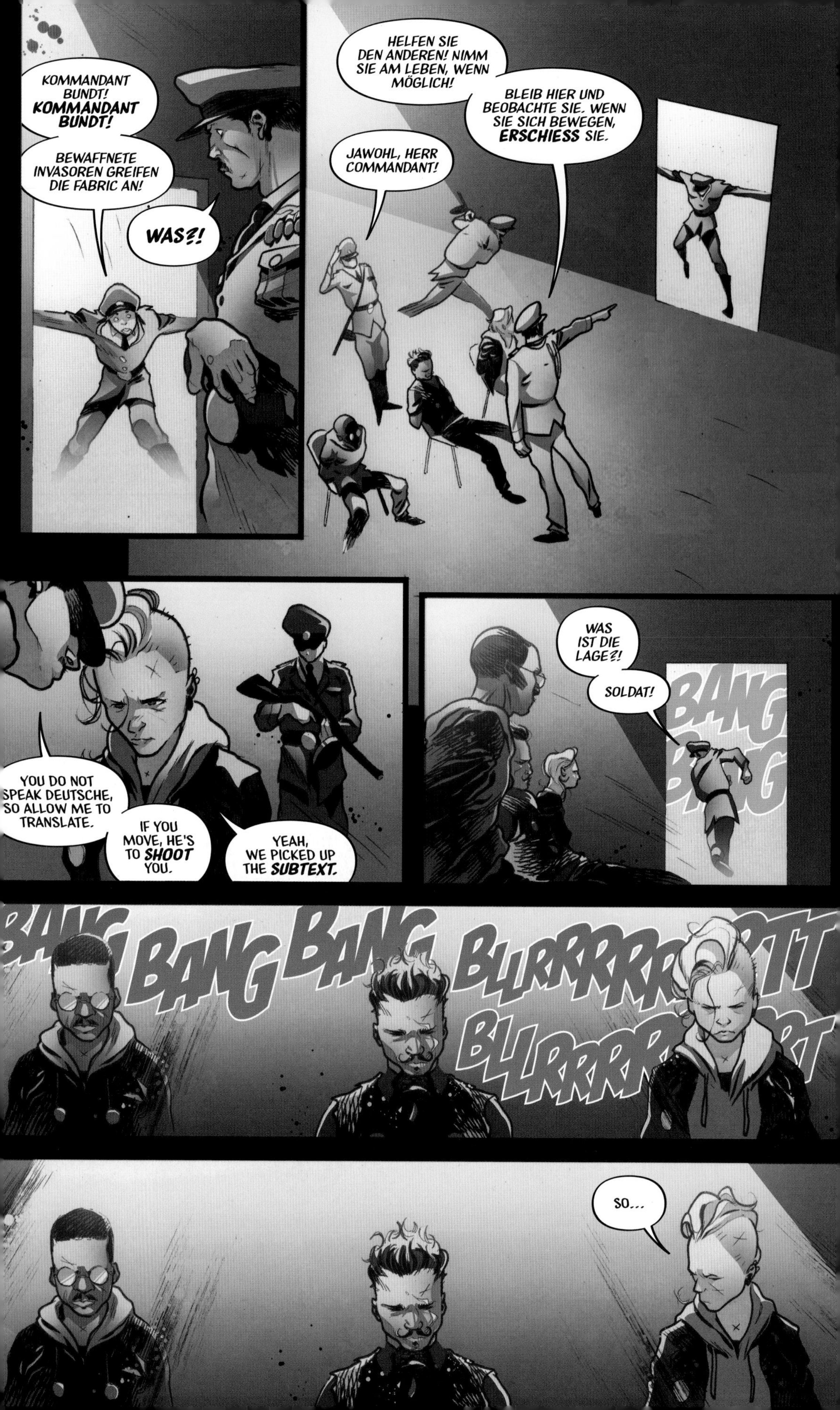
KOMMANDANT BUNDT! **KOMMANDANT BUNDT!**
BEWAFFNETE INVASOREN GREIFEN DIE FABRIC AN!
WAS?!
HELFEN SIE DEN ANDEREN! NIMM SIE AM LEBEN, WENN MÖGLICH!
JAWOHL, HERR COMMANDANT!
BLEIB HIER UND BEOBACHTE SIE. WENN SIE SICH BEWEGEN, **ERSCHIESS** SIE.
YOU DO NOT SPEAK DEUTSCHE, SO ALLOW ME TO TRANSLATE.
IF YOU MOVE, HE'S TO **SHOOT** YOU.
YEAH, WE PICKED UP THE **SUBTEXT.**
WAS IST DIE LAGE?!
SOLDAT!
BANG
BANG
BANG BANG BANG BLRRRRRRRTT
BLRRRRRRRT
SO...

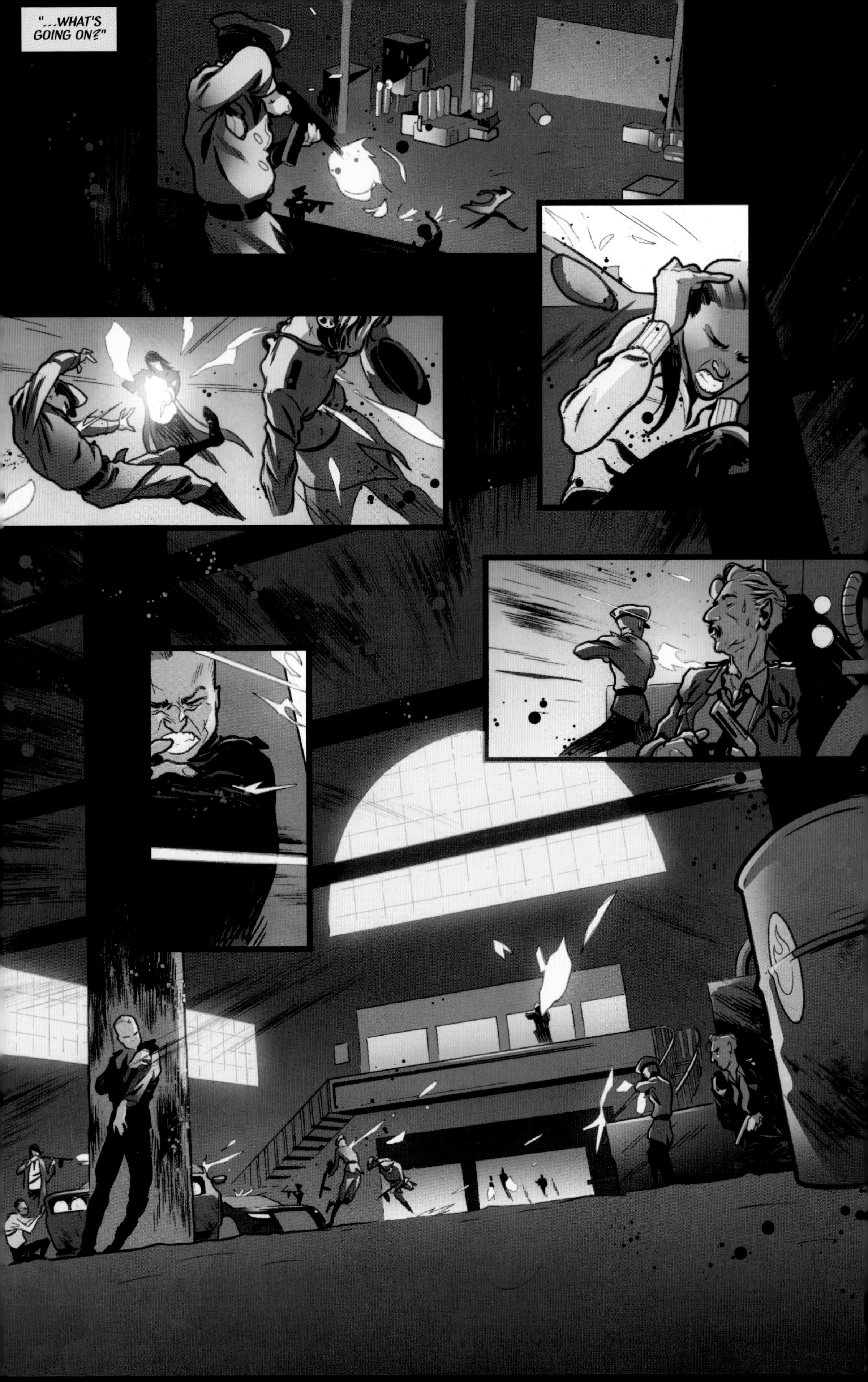
"...WHAT'S GOING ON?"

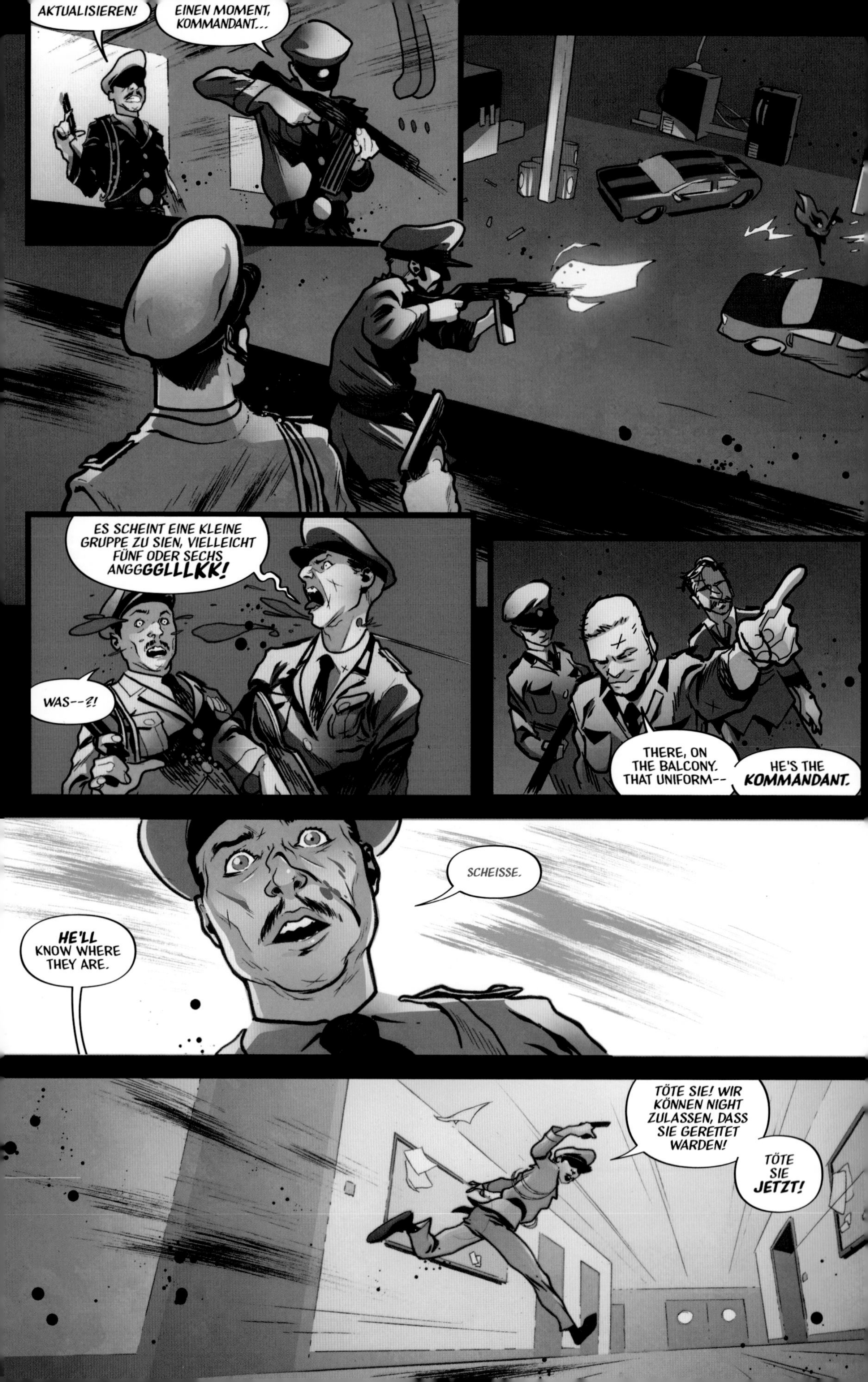
AKTUALISIEREN!
EINEN MOMENT, KOMMANDANT...
ES SCHEINT EINE KLEINE GRUPPE ZU SIEN, VIELLEICHT FÜNF ODER SECHS ANGGGGLLLKK!
WAS--?!
THERE, ON THE BALCONY. THAT UNIFORM--
HE'S THE KOMMANDANT.
SCHEISSE.
HE'LL KNOW WHERE THEY ARE.
TÖTE SIE! WIR KÖNNEN NIGHT ZULASSEN, DASS SIE GERETTET WARDEN!
TÖTE SIE JETZT!

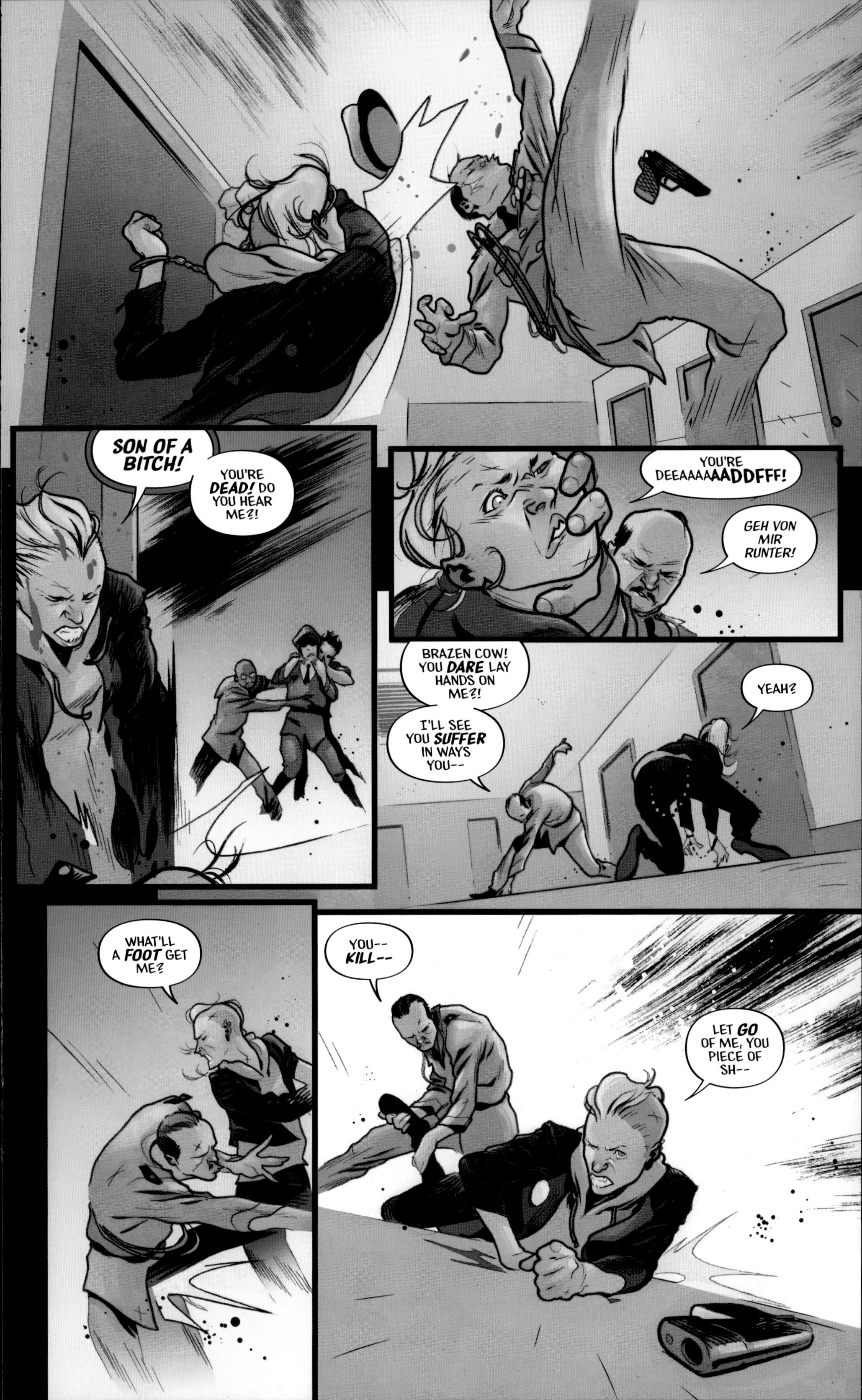
SON OF A BITCH!
YOU'RE DEAD! DO YOU HEAR ME?!
YOU'RE DEEAAAAAADDFFF!
GEH VON MIR RUNTER!
BRAZEN COW! YOU DARE LAY HANDS ON ME?!
I'LL SEE YOU SUFFER IN WAYS YOU--
YEAH?
WHAT'LL A FOOT GET ME?
YOU-- KILL--
LET GO OF ME, YOU PIECE OF SH--

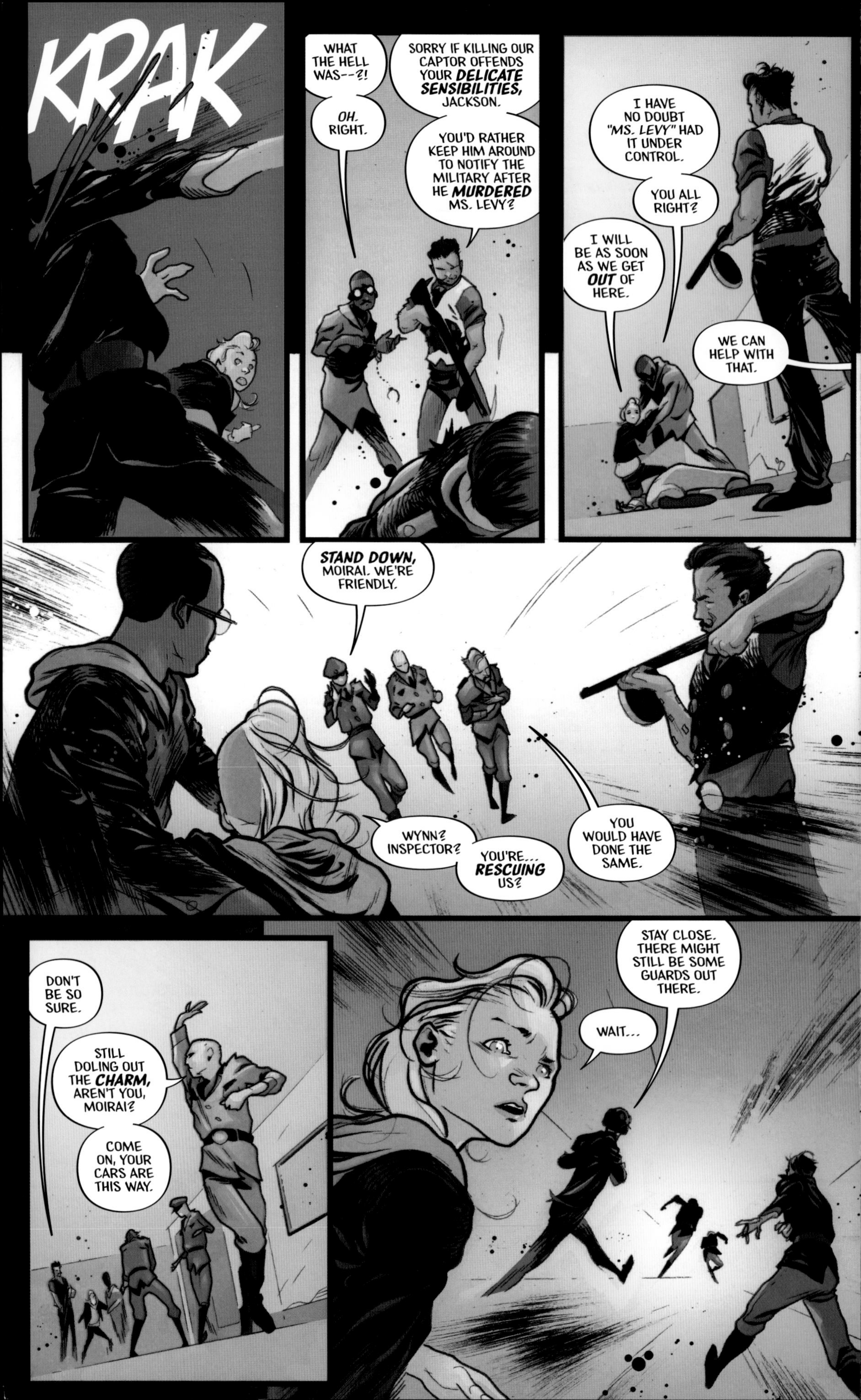
KRAK
WHAT THE HELL WAS--?!
SORRY IF KILLING OUR CAPTOR OFFENDS YOUR DELICATE SENSIBILITIES, JACKSON.
OH. RIGHT.
YOU'D RATHER KEEP HIM AROUND TO NOTIFY THE MILITARY AFTER HE MURDERED MS. LEVY?
I HAVE NO DOUBT "MS. LEVY" HAD IT UNDER CONTROL.
YOU ALL RIGHT?
I WILL BE AS SOON AS WE GET OUT OF HERE.
WE CAN HELP WITH THAT.
STAND DOWN, MOIRAI. WE'RE FRIENDLY.
WYNN? INSPECTOR?
YOU'RE... RESCUING US?
YOU WOULD HAVE DONE THE SAME.
DON'T BE SO SURE.
STILL DOLING OUT THE CHARM, AREN'T YOU, MOIRAI?
COME ON, YOUR CARS ARE THIS WAY.
STAY CLOSE. THERE MIGHT STILL BE SOME GUARDS OUT THERE.
WAIT...

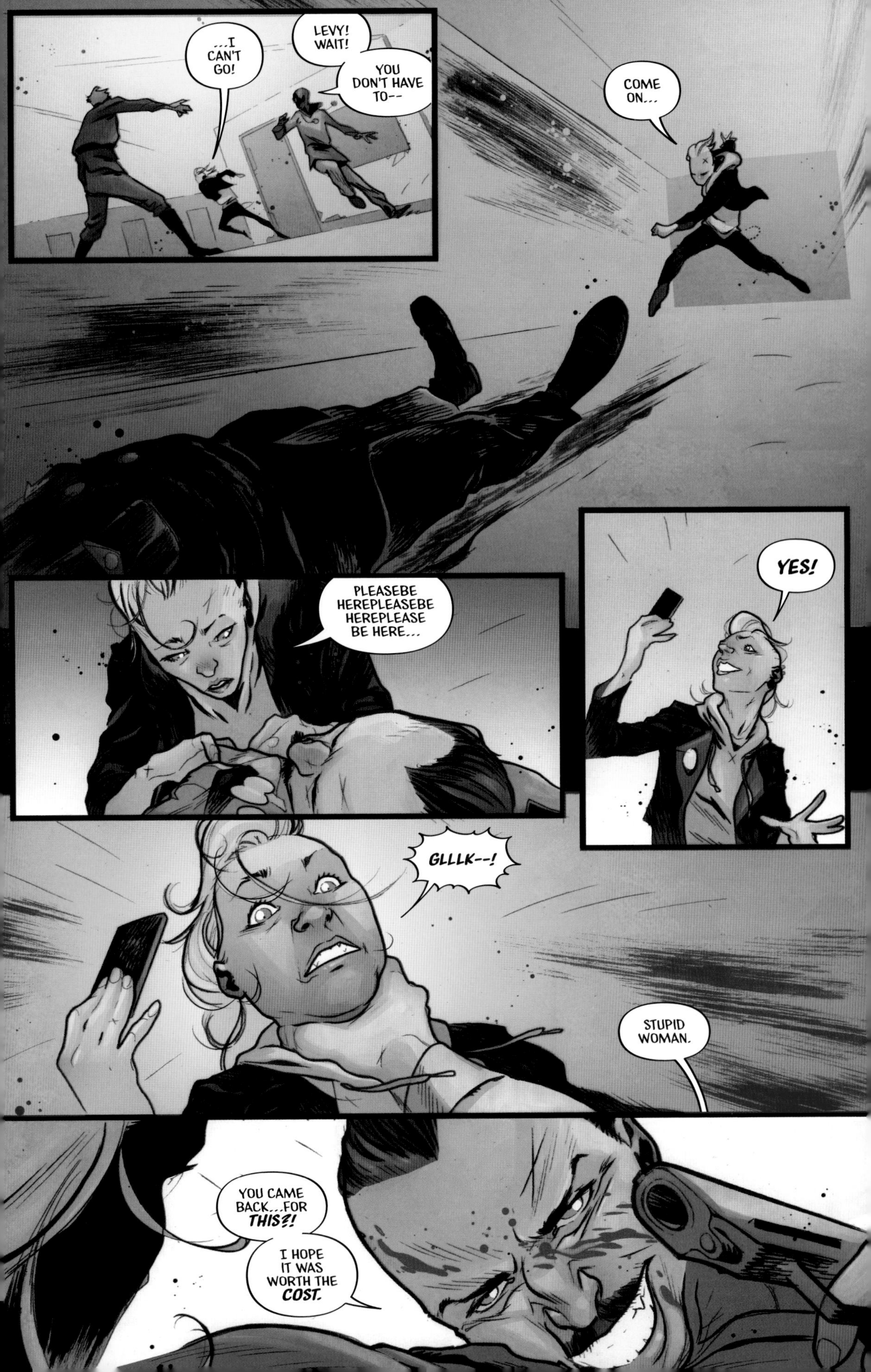

...I CAN'T GO!
LEVY! WAIT!
YOU DON'T HAVE TO--
COME ON...
PLEASEBE HEREPLEASEBE HEREPLEASE BE HERE...
YES!
GLLLK--!
STUPID WOMAN.
YOU CAME BACK...FOR THIS?!
I HOPE IT WAS WORTH THE COST.

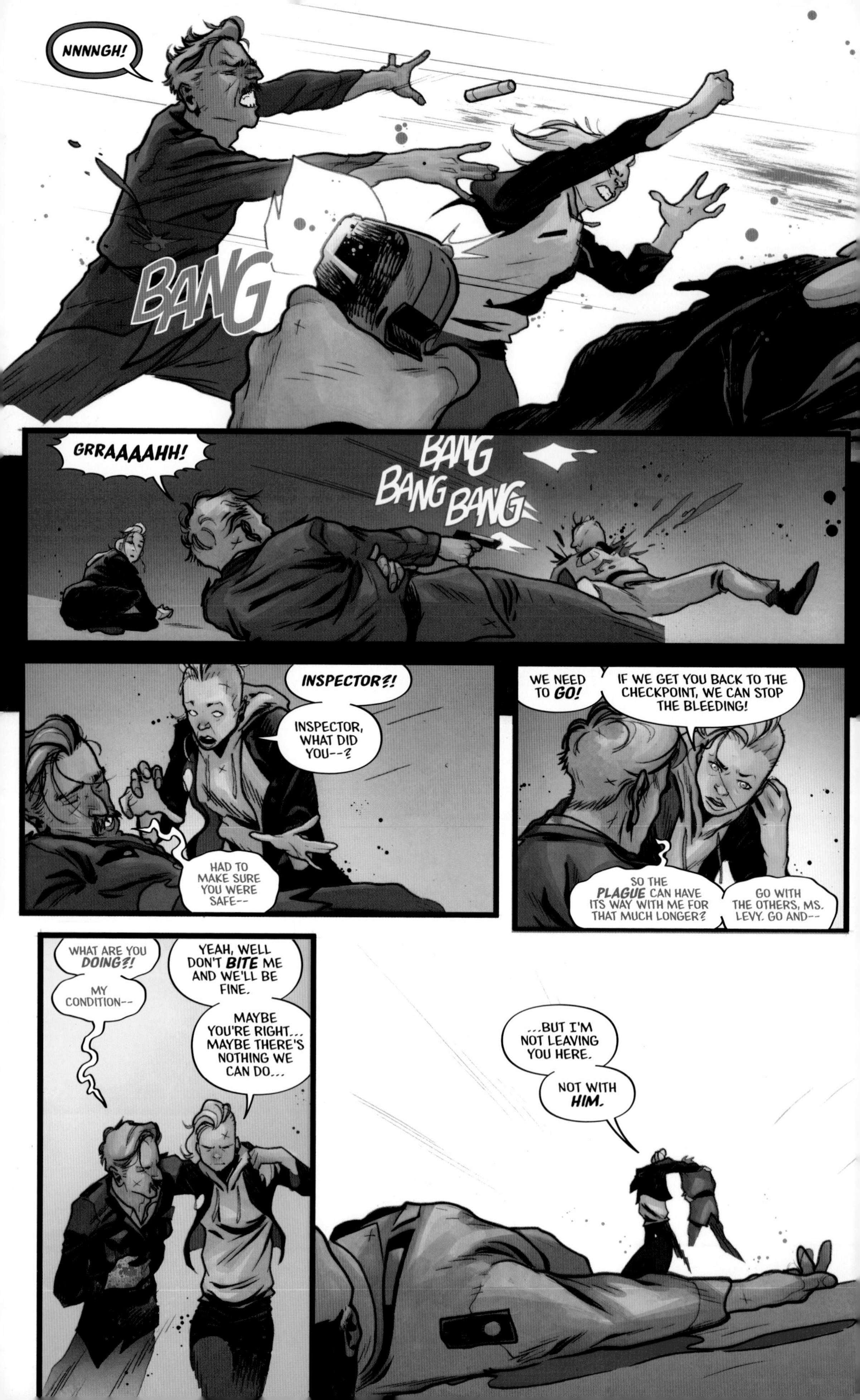
NNNNGH!
BANG
GRRAAAAHH!
BANG
BANG BANG
INSPECTOR?!
INSPECTOR, WHAT DID YOU--?
HAD TO MAKE SURE YOU WERE SAFE--
WE NEED TO GO!
IF WE GET YOU BACK TO THE CHECKPOINT, WE CAN STOP THE BLEEDING!
SO THE PLAGUE CAN HAVE ITS WAY WITH ME FOR THAT MUCH LONGER?
GO WITH THE OTHERS, MS. LEVY. GO AND--
WHAT ARE YOU DOING?!
MY CONDITION--
YEAH, WELL DON'T BITE ME AND WE'LL BE FINE.
MAYBE YOU'RE RIGHT... MAYBE THERE'S NOTHING WE CAN DO...
...BUT I'M NOT LEAVING YOU HERE.
NOT WITH HIM.

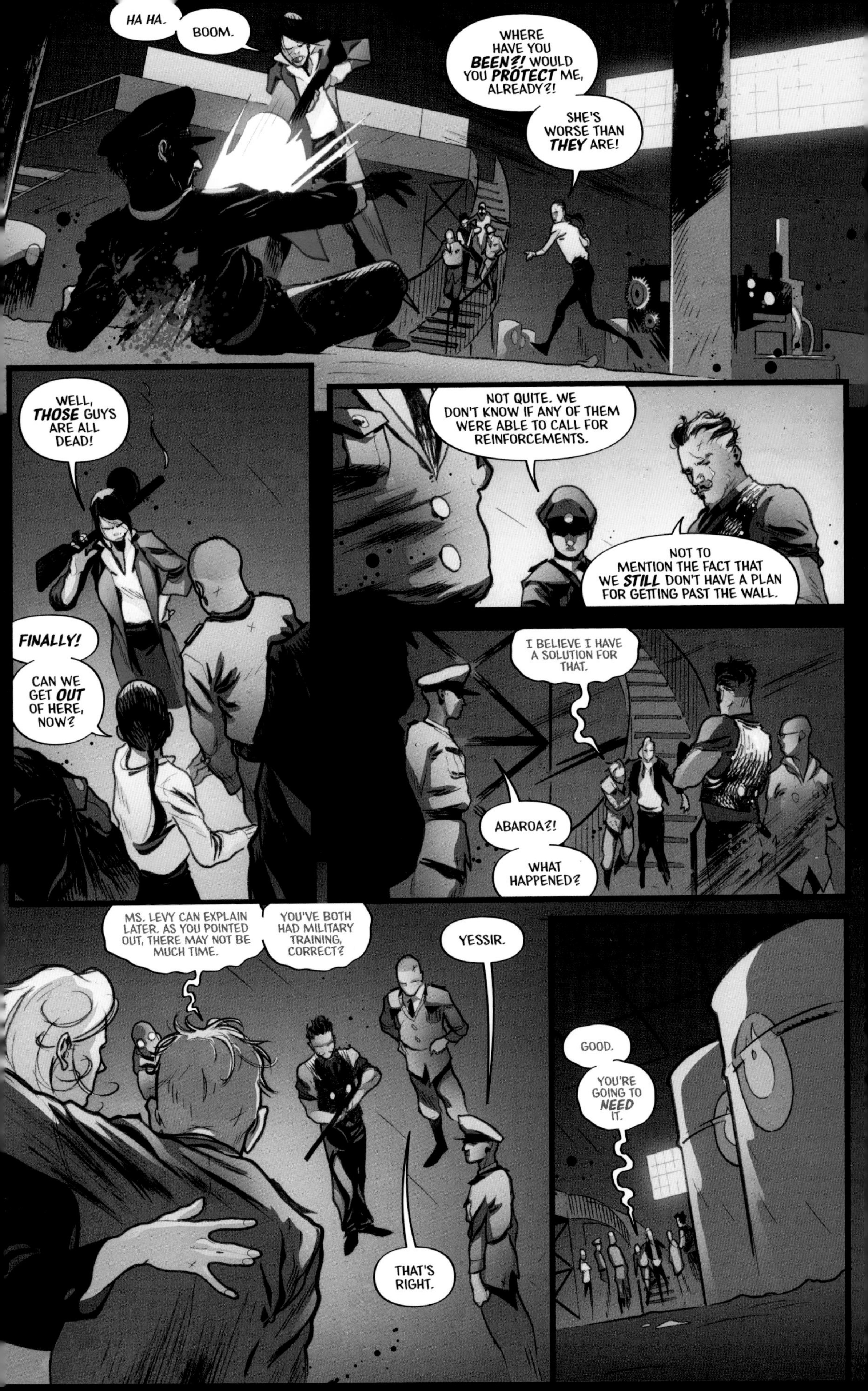
HA HA.
BOOM.
WHERE HAVE YOU BEEN?! WOULD YOU PROTECT ME, ALREADY?!
SHE'S WORSE THAN THEY ARE!
WELL, THOSE GUYS ARE ALL DEAD!
NOT QUITE. WE DON'T KNOW IF ANY OF THEM WERE ABLE TO CALL FOR REINFORCEMENTS.
NOT TO MENTION THE FACT THAT WE STILL DON'T HAVE A PLAN FOR GETTING PAST THE WALL.
FINALLY!
CAN WE GET OUT OF HERE, NOW?
I BELIEVE I HAVE A SOLUTION FOR THAT.
ABAROA?!
WHAT HAPPENED?
MS. LEVY CAN EXPLAIN LATER. AS YOU POINTED OUT, THERE MAY NOT BE MUCH TIME.
YOU'VE BOTH HAD MILITARY TRAINING, CORRECT?
YESSIR.
THAT'S RIGHT.
GOOD.
YOU'RE GOING TO NEED IT.

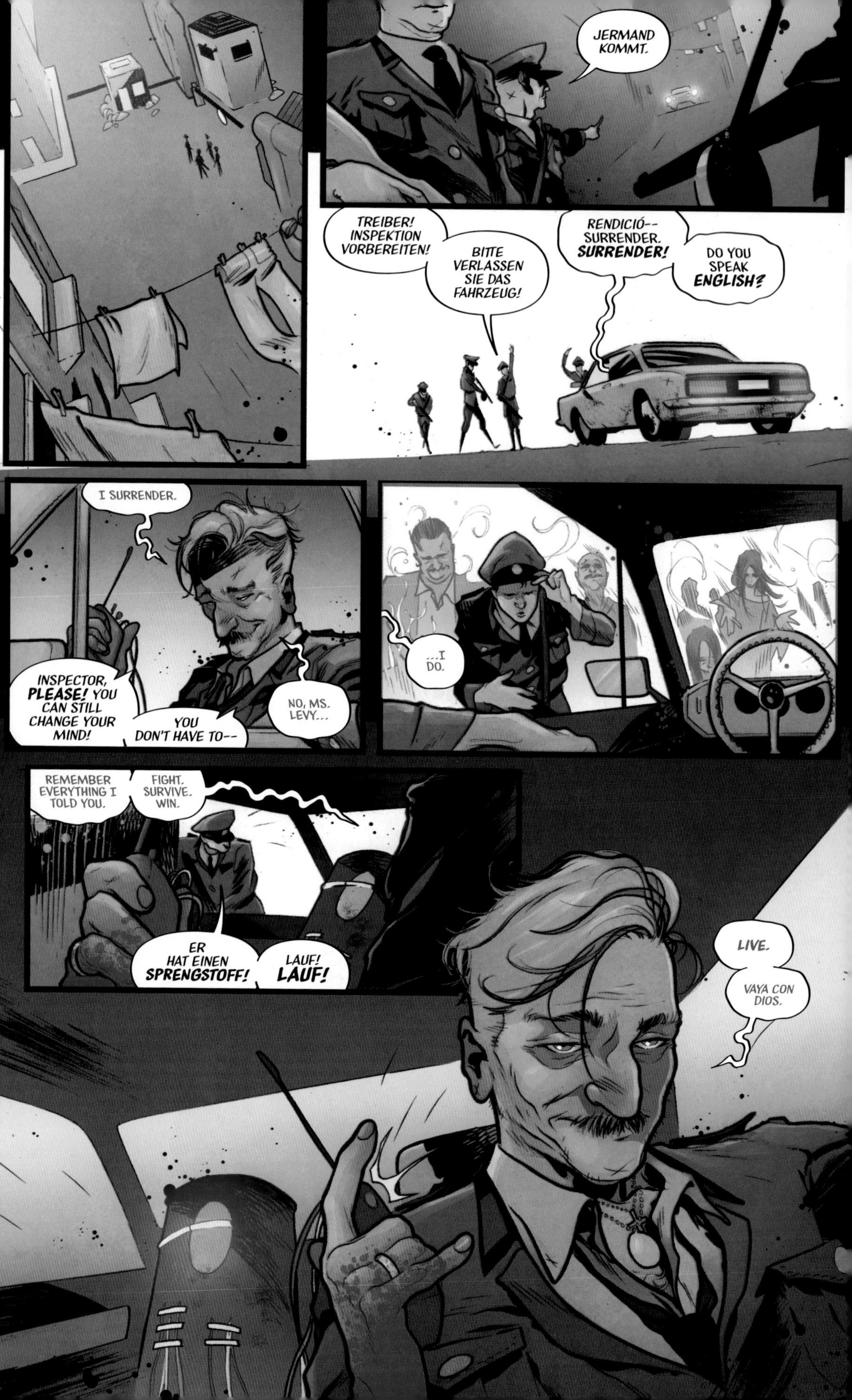
JERMAND KOMMT.
TREIBER! INSPEKTION VORBEREITEN!
BITTE VERLASSEN SIE DAS FAHRZEUG!
RENDICIÓ-- SURRENDER. SURRENDER!
DO YOU SPEAK ENGLISH?
I SURRENDER.
INSPECTOR, PLEASE! YOU CAN STILL CHANGE YOUR MIND!
YOU DON'T HAVE TO--
NO, MS. LEVY...
...I DO.
REMEMBER EVERYTHING I TOLD YOU.
FIGHT. SURVIVE. WIN.
ER HAT EINEN SPRENGSTOFF!
LAUF! LAUF!
LIVE.
VAYA CON DIOS.

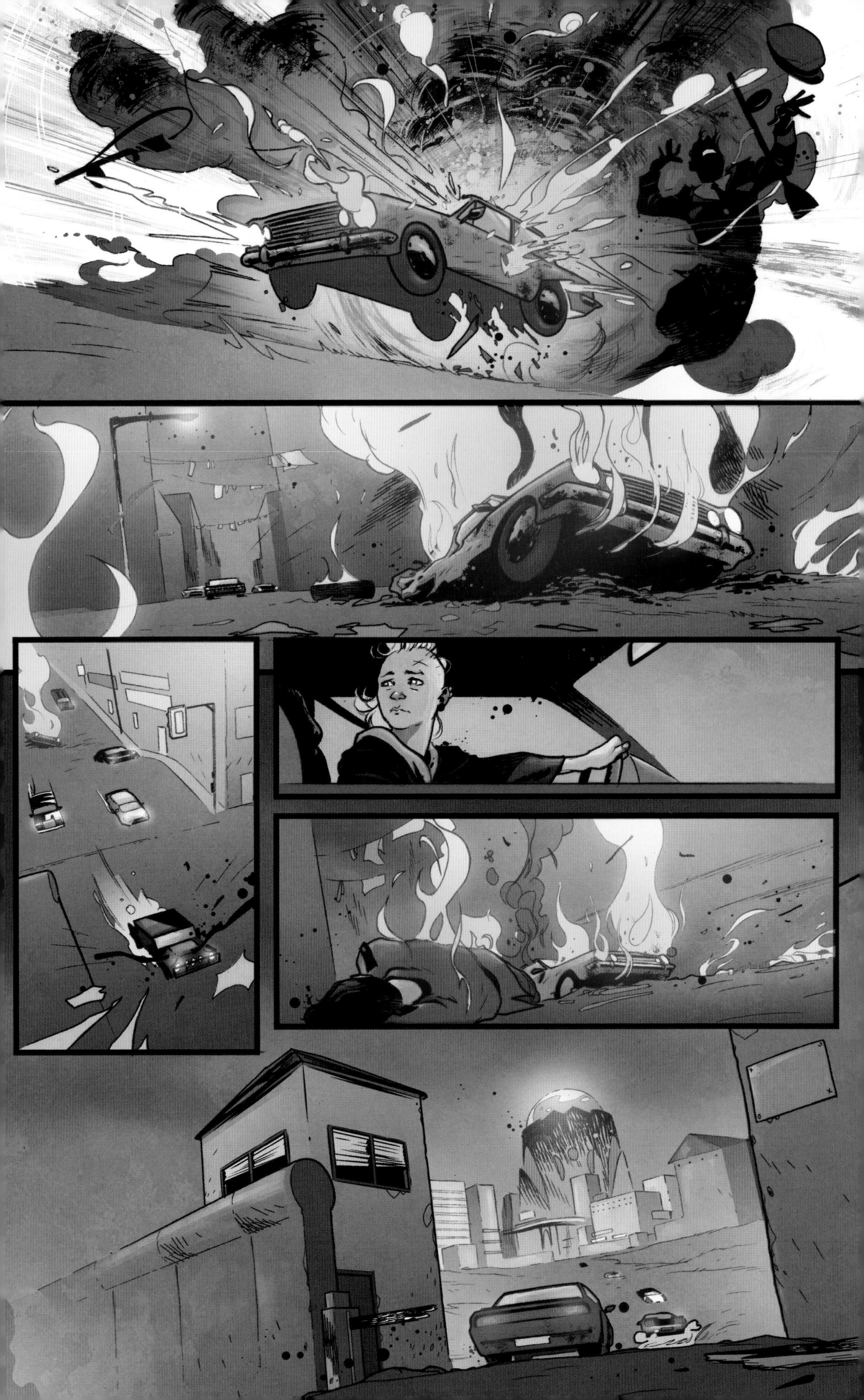

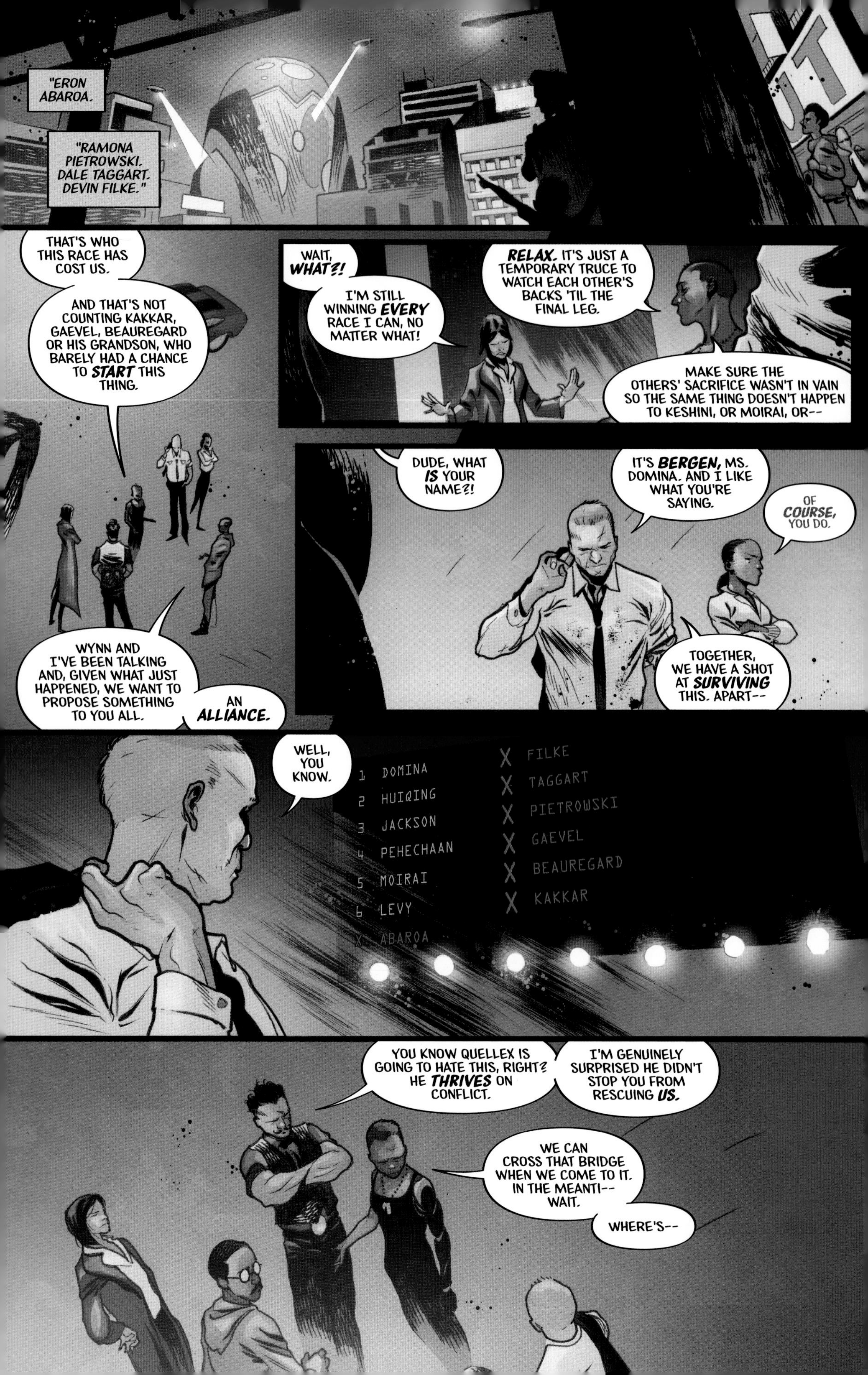
"ERON ABAROA.
"RAMONA PIETROWSKI. DALE TAGGART. DEVIN FILKE."
THAT'S WHO THIS RACE HAS COST US.
AND THAT'S NOT COUNTING KAKKAR, GAEVEL, BEAUREGARD OR HIS GRANDSON, WHO BARELY HAD A CHANCE TO START THIS THING.
WAIT, WHAT?!
I'M STILL WINNING EVERY RACE I CAN, NO MATTER WHAT!
RELAX. IT'S JUST A TEMPORARY TRUCE TO WATCH EACH OTHER'S BACKS 'TIL THE FINAL LEG.
MAKE SURE THE OTHERS' SACRIFICE WASN'T IN VAIN SO THE SAME THING DOESN'T HAPPEN TO KESHINI, OR MOIRAI, OR--
WYNN AND I'VE BEEN TALKING AND, GIVEN WHAT JUST HAPPENED, WE WANT TO PROPOSE SOMETHING TO YOU ALL.
AN ALLIANCE.
DUDE, WHAT IS YOUR NAME?!
IT'S BERGEN, MS. DOMINA. AND I LIKE WHAT YOU'RE SAYING.
OF COURSE, YOU DO.
TOGETHER, WE HAVE A SHOT AT SURVIVING THIS. APART--
WELL, YOU KNOW.
1 DOMINA
2 HUIQING
3 JACKSON
4 PEHECHAAN
5 MOIRAI
6 LEVY
X ABAROA
X FILKE
X TAGGART
X PIETROWSKI
X GAEVEL
X BEAUREGARD
X KAKKAR
YOU KNOW QUELLEX IS GOING TO HATE THIS, RIGHT? HE THRIVES ON CONFLICT.
I'M GENUINELY SURPRISED HE DIDN'T STOP YOU FROM RESCUING US.
WE CAN CROSS THAT BRIDGE WHEN WE COME TO IT. IN THE MEANTI-- WAIT.
WHERE'S--

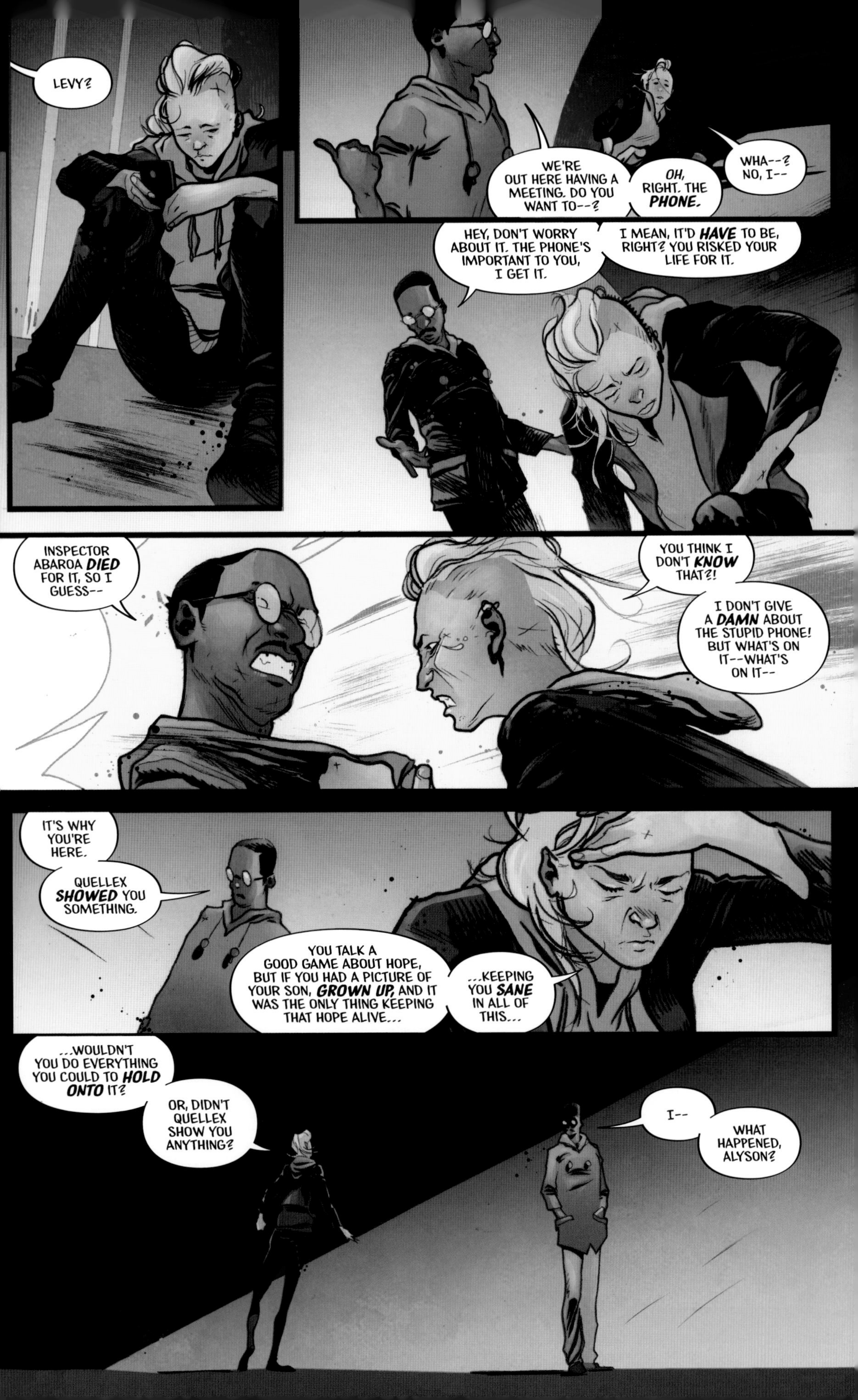
LEVY?
WE'RE OUT HERE HAVING A MEETING. DO YOU WANT TO--?
WHA--? NO, I--
OH, RIGHT. THE PHONE.
HEY, DON'T WORRY ABOUT IT. THE PHONE'S IMPORTANT TO YOU, I GET IT.
I MEAN, IT'D HAVE TO BE, RIGHT? YOU RISKED YOUR LIFE FOR IT.
INSPECTOR ABAROA DIED FOR IT, SO I GUESS--
YOU THINK I DON'T KNOW THAT?!
I DON'T GIVE A DAMN ABOUT THE STUPID PHONE! BUT WHAT'S ON IT--WHAT'S ON IT--
IT'S WHY YOU'RE HERE.
QUELLEX SHOWED YOU SOMETHING.
YOU TALK A GOOD GAME ABOUT HOPE, BUT IF YOU HAD A PICTURE OF YOUR SON, GROWN UP, AND IT WAS THE ONLY THING KEEPING THAT HOPE ALIVE...
...KEEPING YOU SANE IN ALL OF THIS...
...WOULDN'T YOU DO EVERYTHING YOU COULD TO HOLD ONTO IT?
OR, DIDN'T QUELLEX SHOW YOU ANYTHING?
I--
WHAT HAPPENED, ALYSON?

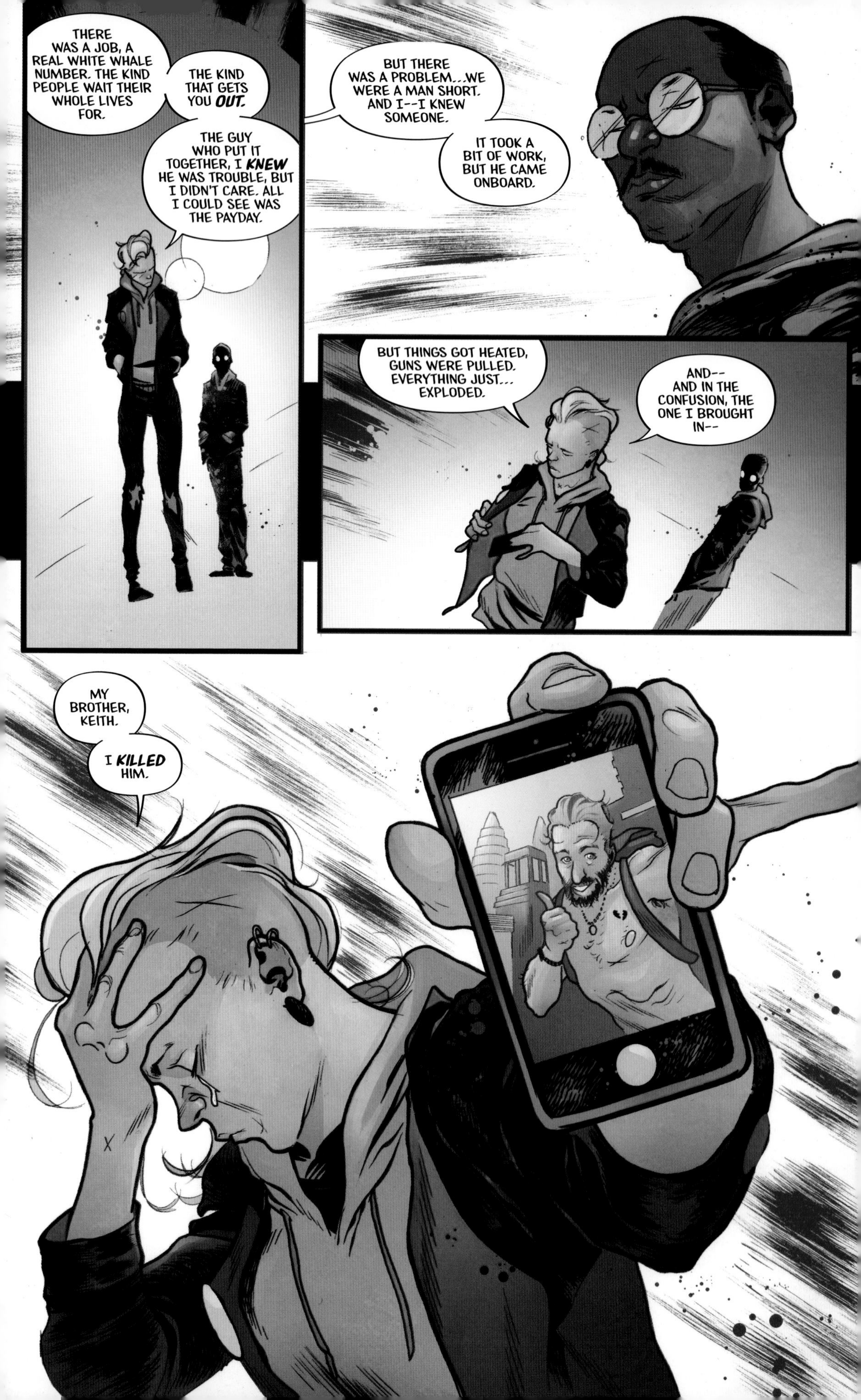
THERE WAS A JOB, A REAL WHITE WHALE NUMBER. THE KIND PEOPLE WAIT THEIR WHOLE LIVES FOR.
THE KIND THAT GETS YOU *OUT.*
THE GUY WHO PUT IT TOGETHER, I *KNEW* HE WAS TROUBLE, BUT I DIDN'T CARE. ALL I COULD SEE WAS THE PAYDAY.
BUT THERE WAS A PROBLEM...WE WERE A MAN SHORT. AND I--I KNEW SOMEONE.
IT TOOK A BIT OF WORK, BUT HE CAME ONBOARD.
BUT THINGS GOT HEATED, GUNS WERE PULLED. EVERYTHING JUST... EXPLODED.
AND-- AND IN THE CONFUSION, THE ONE I BROUGHT IN--
MY BROTHER, KEITH.
I *KILLED* HIM.

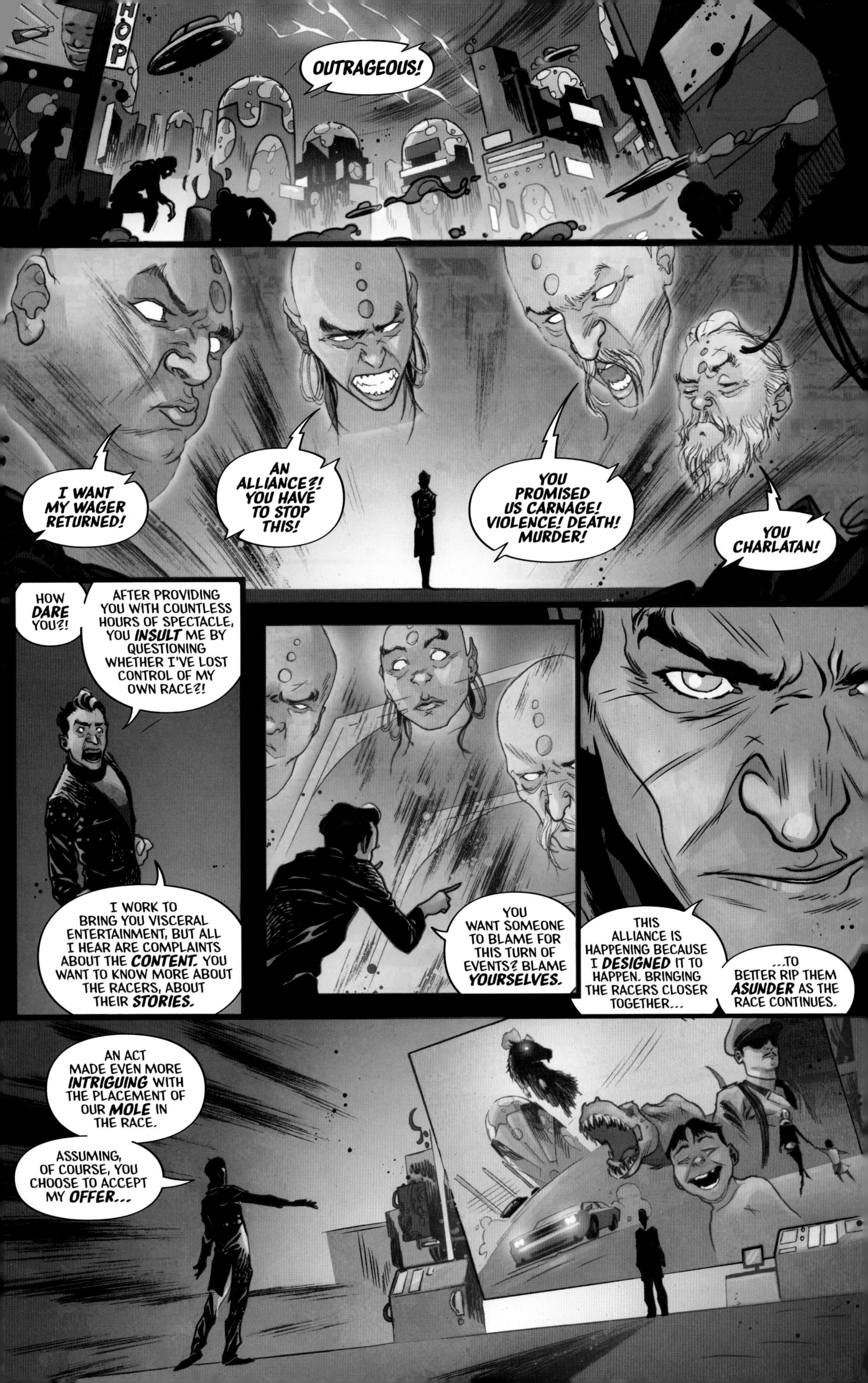

HOP
OUTRAGEOUS!
I WANT MY WAGER RETURNED!
AN ALLIANCE?! YOU HAVE TO STOP THIS!
YOU PROMISED US CARNAGE! VIOLENCE! DEATH! MURDER!
YOU CHARLATAN!
HOW DARE YOU?!
AFTER PROVIDING YOU WITH COUNTLESS HOURS OF SPECTACLE, YOU INSULT ME BY QUESTIONING WHETHER I'VE LOST CONTROL OF MY OWN RACE?!
I WORK TO BRING YOU VISCERAL ENTERTAINMENT, BUT ALL I HEAR ARE COMPLAINTS ABOUT THE CONTENT. YOU WANT TO KNOW MORE ABOUT THE RACERS, ABOUT THEIR STORIES.
YOU WANT SOMEONE TO BLAME FOR THIS TURN OF EVENTS? BLAME YOURSELVES.
THIS ALLIANCE IS HAPPENING BECAUSE I DESIGNED IT TO HAPPEN. BRINGING THE RACERS CLOSER TOGETHER...
...TO BETTER RIP THEM ASUNDER AS THE RACE CONTINUES.
AN ACT MADE EVEN MORE INTRIGUING WITH THE PLACEMENT OF OUR MOLE IN THE RACE.
ASSUMING, OF COURSE, YOU CHOOSE TO ACCEPT MY OFFER...

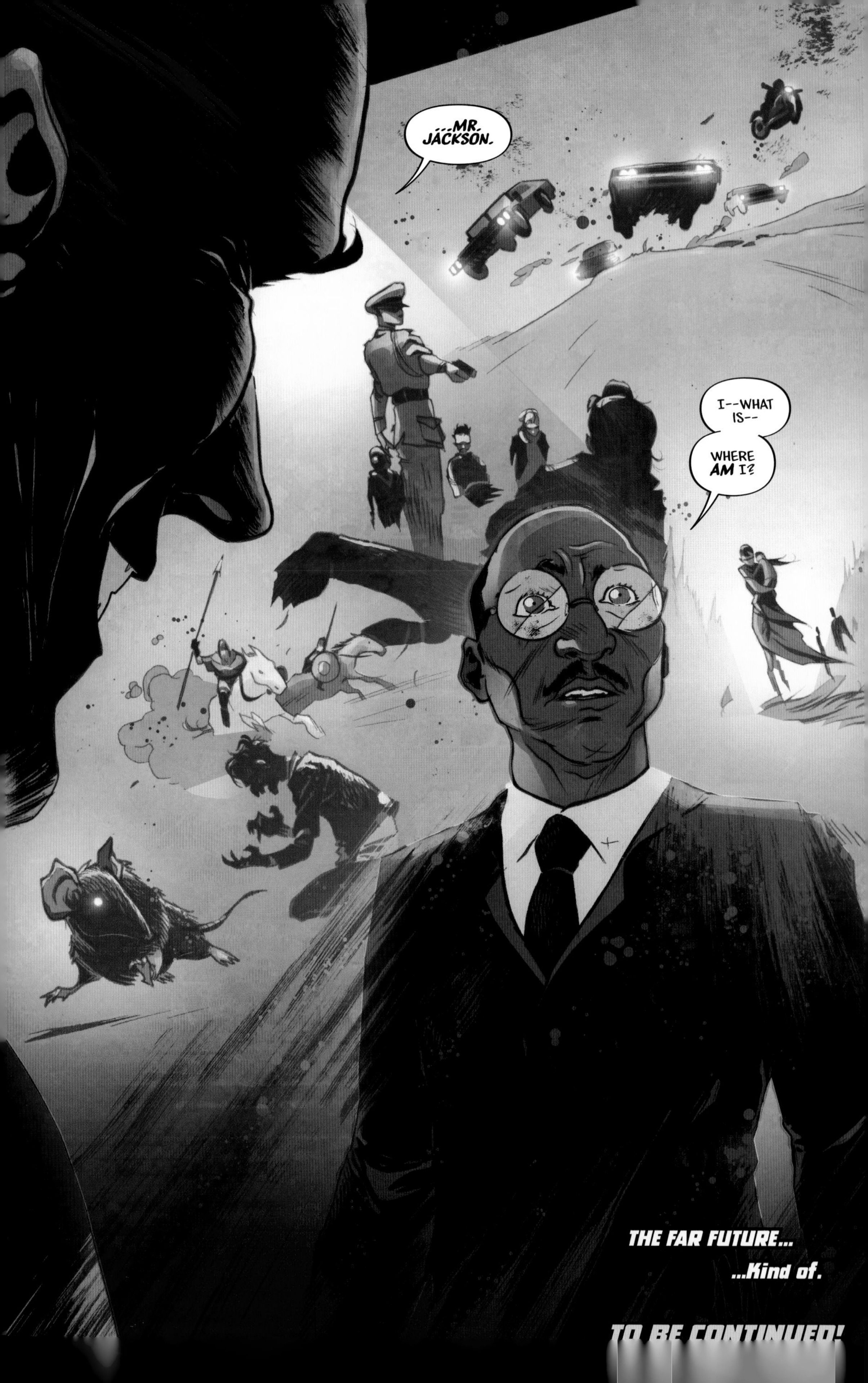
...MR. JACKSON.
I--WHAT IS--
WHERE AM I?
THE FAR FUTURE...
...Kind of.
TO BE CONTINUED!

COVER GALLERY

COVER ARTWORK BY MARCO D'ALFONSO

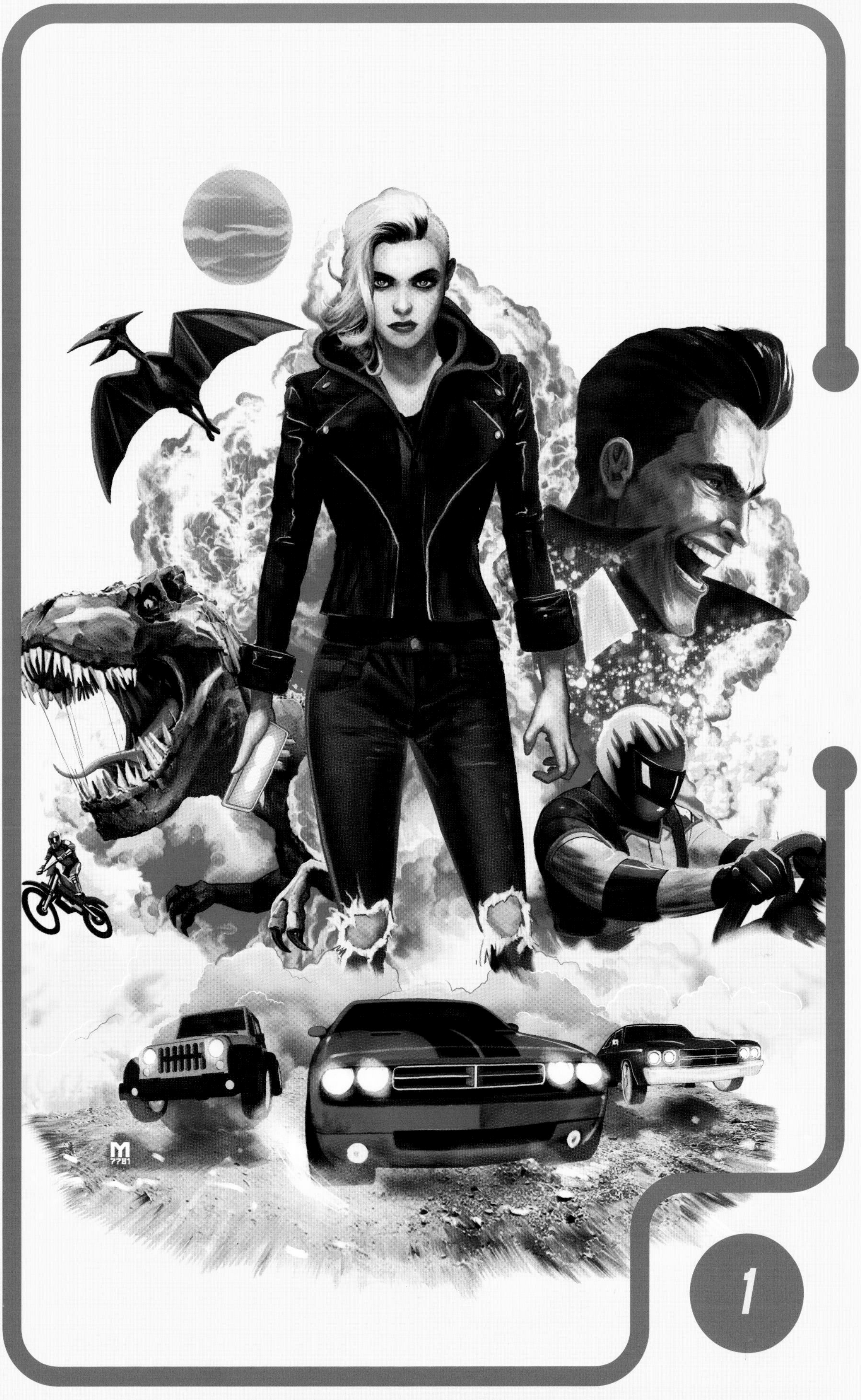
1

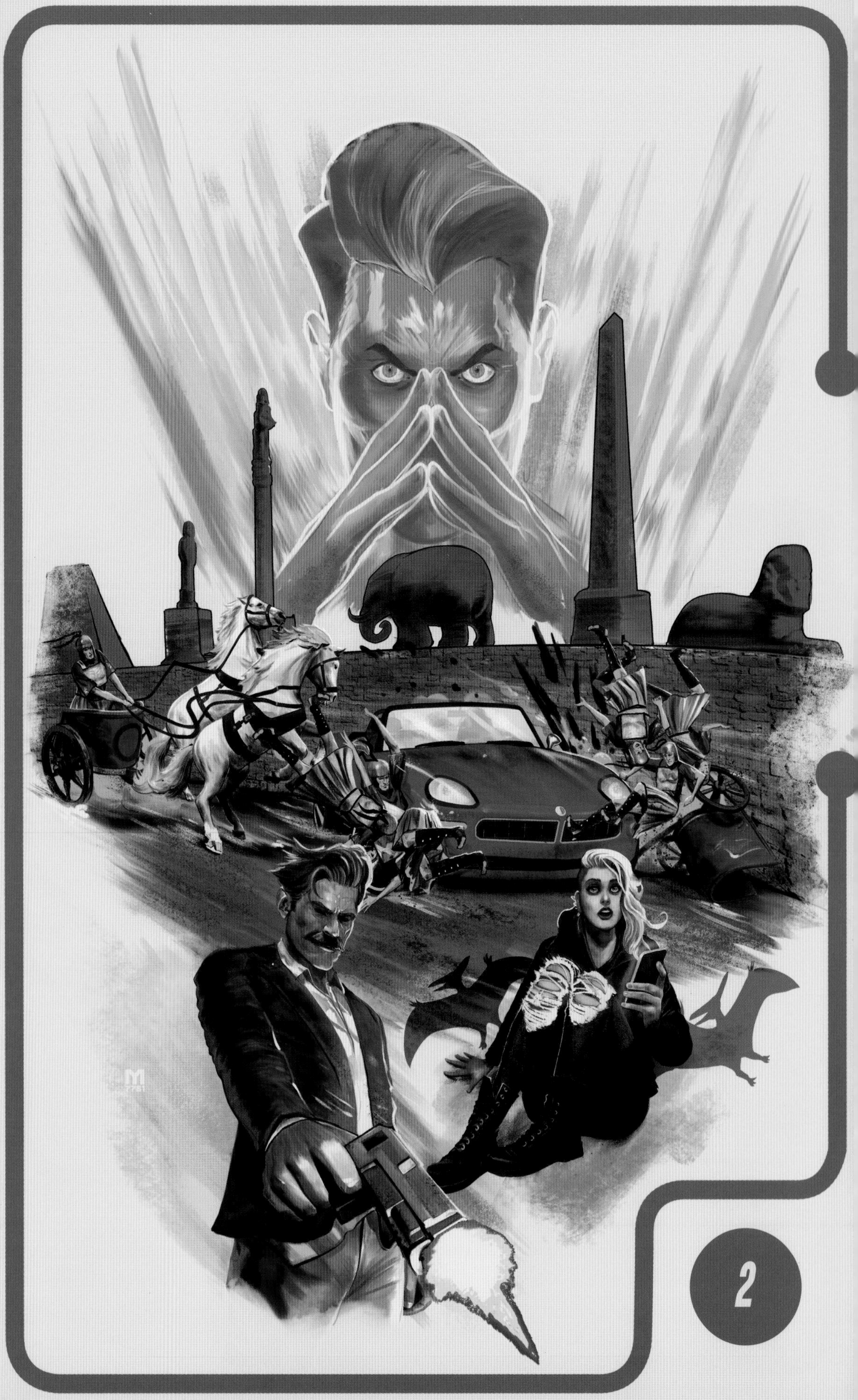
2

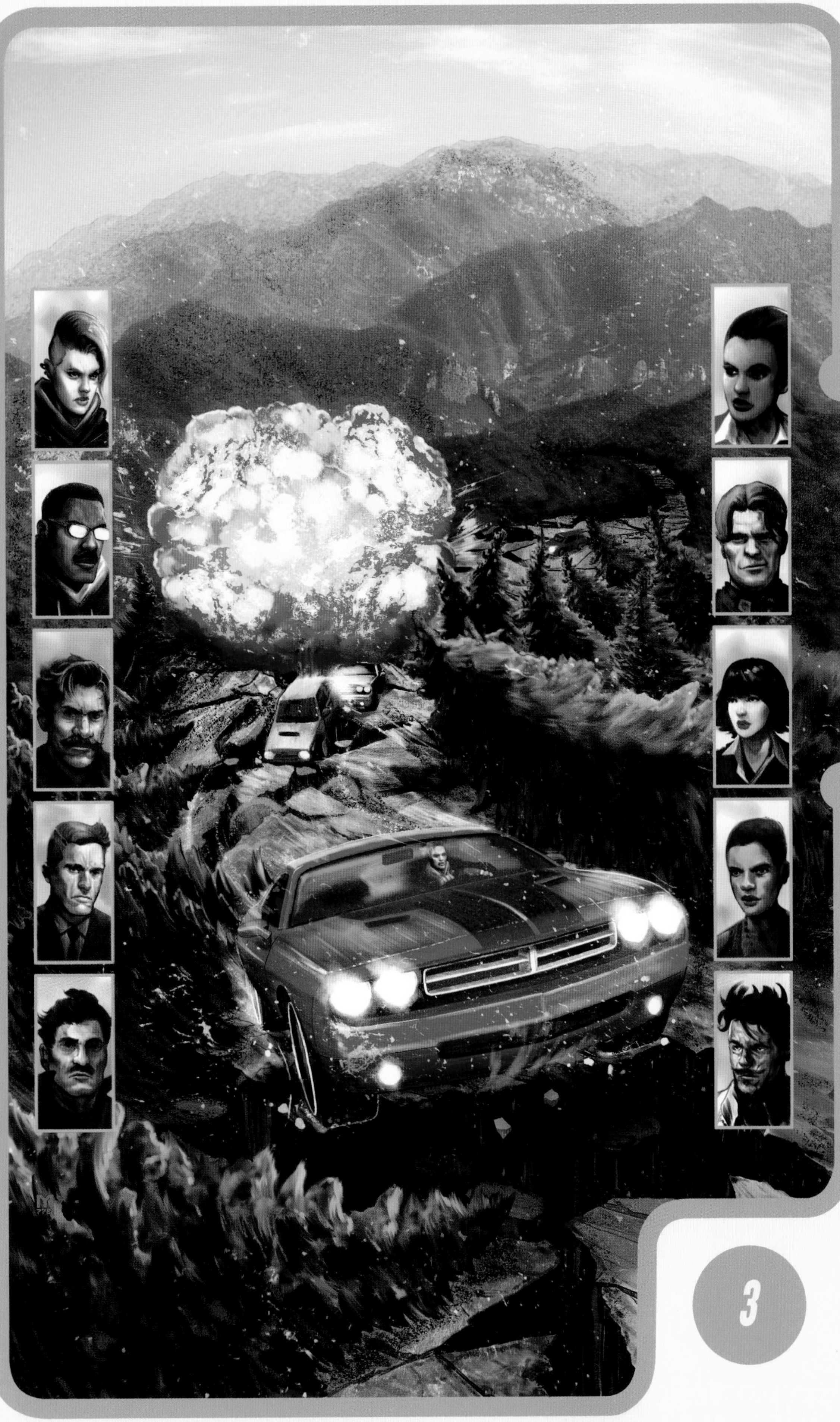

3

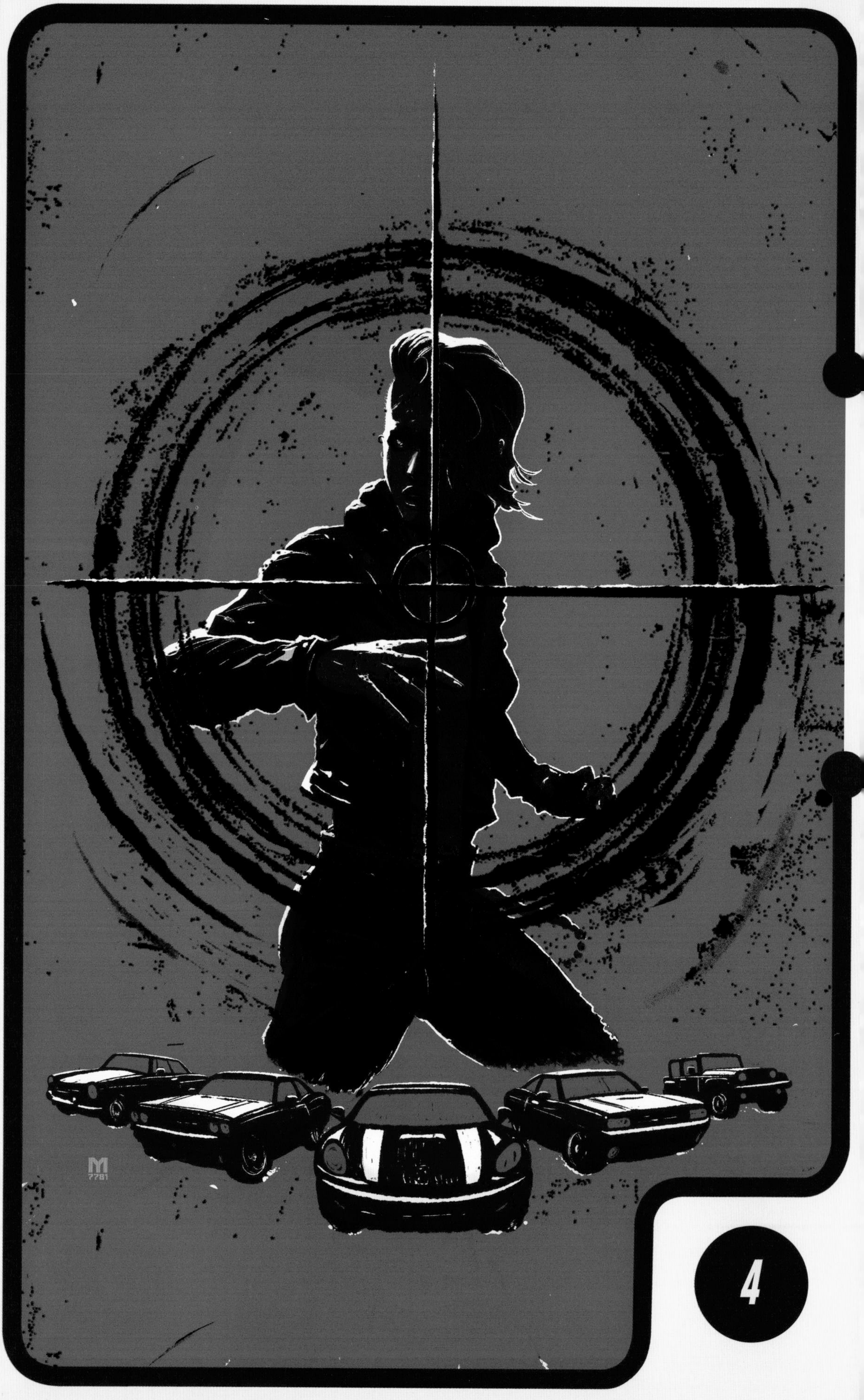
4

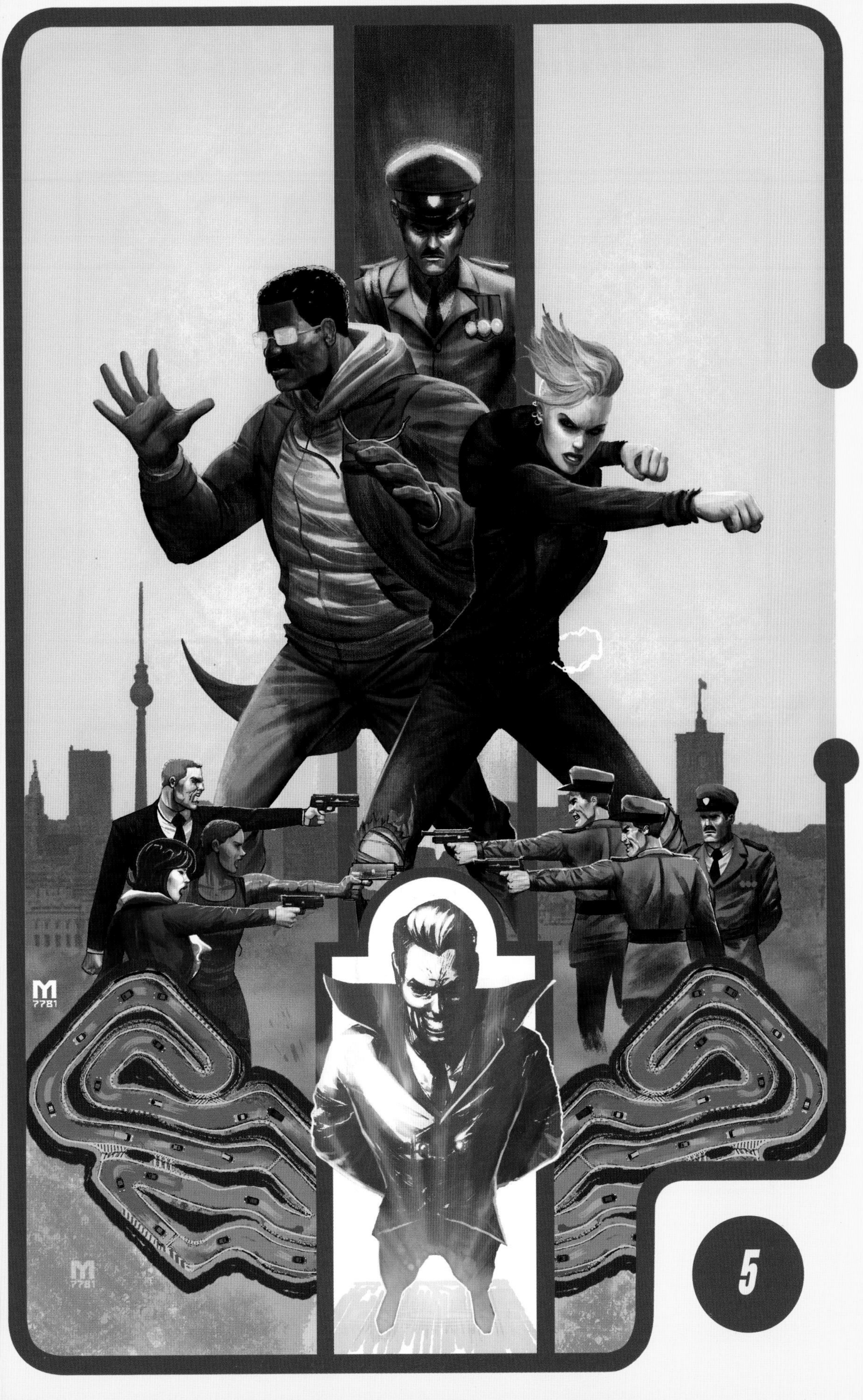
5

CHARACTER SKETCHES

ALYSON LEVY

CASPER QUELLEX

CHARLES JACKSON

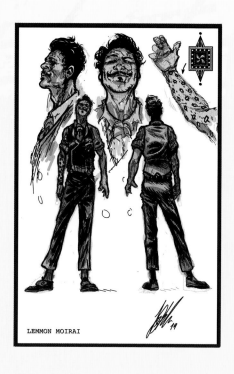

LEMMON MOIRAI

JAKE ELPHICK

BACK-TRACKS

The Unofficial Soundtrack for *BACKTRACK*

VOLUME 1

1. I Rule the Ruins
   WARLOCK

2. Destination Unknown
   MISSING PERSONS

3. Run Thru the Jungle
   CREEDENCE CLEARWATER REVIVAL

4. Ocean Drive
   DUKE DUMONT

5. Don't Speak (I Came to Make a Bang!)
   EAGLES OF DEATH METAL

6. Feet Don't Fail Me
   QUEENS OF THE STONE AGE

7. Tusk
   FLEETWOOD MAC

8. This Ain't a Scene, It's an Arms Race
   FALL OUT BOY

9. Misery Business
   PARAMORE

10. Ride Like the Wind
    SAXON

ALSO BY ONI PRESS

DRYAD

WIEBE
OSTERLING

Kurtis Wiebe & Justin Osterling

AT THE END OF YOUR TETHER

ADAM SMITH · V.V. GLASS · HILARY JENKINS

Adam Smith, V.V. Glass, & Hilary Jenkins

UPGRADE SOUL

A GRAPHIC NOVEL

Ezra Claytan Daniels

"STUMPTOWN IS, FOR MY MONEY, THE PERFECT RUCKA BOOK."

STUMPTOWN

GREG RUCKA · MATTHEW SOUTHWORTH
LEE LOUGHRIDGE · RICO RENZI

NOW A SERIES ON abc

VOLUME 1
THE CASE OF THE GIRL WHO TOOK HER SHAMPOO (BUT LEFT HER MINI)

Greg Rucka & Matthew Southworth

THE SAVAGE BEARD OF SHE DWARF

STORY AND ART BY
KYLE LATINO

Kyle Latino